SPLIT

THE PRICE OF TALENT: BOOK THREE

SPICY DYSTOPIAN SCI FI ROMANCE

AK NEVERMORE

DEDICATION

For D.

CONTENTS

A HEADS UP ON CONTENT

This book explores themes which some readers may find uncomfortable or offensive. If violence, gore, war-time atrocities, difficult pregnancies, smut, various kinks, salty language, references to alcoholism, drug use, abuse, and generally unsavory behavior are triggers for you, please put this novel down and back away slowly.

Still here? Awesome. Just remember, it's a fantasy, people. Don't try this stuff at home.

TERMS

*Talent [***tal**-uhnt *] noun*

1. *An individual denoted by halos surrounding their irises with the ability to manipulate reality, i.e. Breakers, molecular destruction; Binders, molecular cohesion; Shifters, translocation; Fixers, transfixation; Finders, spatial orientation.*

– Excerpt from
A Treatise on Talents,
Third Edition

"Everything that happens, happens as it should, and if you observe carefully, you will find this to be so."

– Marcus Aurelius

ROGAN'S HEART ached as Jane wended her way through the meadow, picking flowers, her hair brilliant spun gold beneath the bright June sun. She smiled to herself, holding the bouquet to her nose. Even from afar, he could make out the clear sky blue of her eyes.

God, she was beautiful.

She turned, retrieving her bike from the tall grass and placed the flowers in its basket before pedaling from sight. He sighed, leaning back against the tree trunk, feet dangling from a branch—

Something sharp struck his arm.

Ow! What the—

He rubbed the spot and frowned down into the bushes.

Cal.

Jackass was below with another rock and a shit-eating grin.

Rogan laughed. "Christ, you're a dick."

"Yeah? Says the stalker," his best friend taunted, flipping the sandy blond hair from his eyes and whipping another rock up at him. Rogan dodged and swung down. The asshole couldn't stop smiling. Figured, in another few hours Elize would be back for the summer. Cal slapped Rogan's shoulder. He was one of the few people tall enough to look him in the eye, though Rogan was three times as broad. Kid looked like a zipper when he stuck out his tongue. "You making your move tonight?"

"Yeah." The thought made him wanna puke.

"About time. She's a hell of a lot finer than Lucy Wells."

She was, but—"It's not like that." Jane was…Jane.

"If you don't bag her, somebody else will," Cal said, shrugging his skinny shoulders and pulling out a pack of Lucky Strikes. "Christ, I might. You get the booze?"

He was full of shit, but Rogan's fists still clenched. "Yeah, it's already at the quarry…you really think she'll come?"

"Karen said she would." Cal patted his pockets. "Shit. Where did I —" Rogan tossed him his Zippo. "Thanks. Want one?"

"Later. I gotta stop back and if he smells it on me, there'll be hell to pay."

Cal frowned, breathing out a long plume. "Two more months until the big one eight."

"Yeah." And enlisting to get out of this shit town was looking better every day. Rogan ran a hand down the side of his head, glancing askance at Cal. It always got weird between them when Rogan leaving came up. Cal got it, but didn't. Shit was different for him.

"Then I'll see you up there," his friend muttered, disappearing through the brush without a sound. Kid had to be part ninja. If it wasn't for the trail of smoke perpetually following him, you'd never know where the hell he was.

Rogan headed in the opposite direction, through the field. His footsteps slowed the closer he got to the trailer. Was the old man off Tuesdays or Wednesdays this week?

"Hey, Red!" his Uncle Blaine yelled, coming up the path from the pond. "You don't wanna do that."

Shit. Must be Tuesdays. Sweat pricked the waistband of Rogan's jeans. "I gotta get something."

His uncle gave him a long look. "He's been at it since mid-morn.

Forget whatever it is and figure on bedding down at the shack tonight. Sean's in no fit temper, today of all days."

Today of—Christ. It was the fifteenth. Fuck. Rogan ran a hand over his mouth, looking toward the trailer. But if his father was hitting it as hard as usual, maybe he'd already be passed out… "I'll be quick."

Blane shook his head. "He's gonna kill you if you don't learn how to stay out of his way. Especially when he's like this."

Rogan shrugged, pushing past his uncle. Good. It'd put them both out of their misery.

He crossed the junk-strewn patch of dirt in front of the trailer, wiping his palms over his jeans. *Springer* blared from the sagging doublewide as he eased open the screen door.

Nothing but buzzing flies. Past the peeling linoleum, the brown recliner was empty and the bathroom's accordion door shut. Place reeked like beer-shits.

Rogan slipped into the squalid kitchen, dodging cans and garbage to his room, just big enough for the bare twin mattress half-covered with paperbacks. Darting a quick look over his shoulder, he scrounged an envelope from beneath the pile—

A hand ripped it from his grip.

"Wha' the fuck's this yer sneakin' around for?"

Shit. Rogan's throat bobbed, eyes raising to the hulking man's as he turned. He was big, but his father? Raven-haired and built like a Sherman tank, Sean McGuire wasn't someone you wanted to piss-off, sober or otherwise. Not that it took much, even on the rare occasion sobriety applied, catching sight of his son was usually enough to set him off.

And on the anniversary of Rogan's mother leaving them?

His throat bobbed. Blaine was right, his father was gonna kill him.

Sean squinted, rocking back on his heels as he tore the envelope open. "Wha's this then?" He dumped it into his palm. "A trinket, ya?" He held the necklace up to the light, its little heart charm twinkling, then flipped it into his fist. "For who?"

Rogan glanced past his father to the door, tensing to make a break for it—

A meaty paw slammed his head into the jamb, a line of dripping fire blooming across his ear.

"Who's it for, boy? Ye deaf? Know ye ain't stupid with all them books." His father grabbed a hank of Rogan's hair and ground his face against the wall. "Yer jest like that ginger whore. Look like her. Talk like her. Think yer fuckin' better too, don't ye?"

Rogan spat a bloodied globule at him, and Sean laughed, the red-tinged spittle dripping across his teeth. He jerked him close, his fetid breath hot.

"Bet it's for that littl' blonde yer always sniffin' around, the doctor's daughter." Rogan stiffened, and his father grinned, his fist coming out of nowhere, sending him reeling down the hall.

He hit the worn linoleum hard and skidded, head ringing, and his eye swelling shut. Dazed, it took a couple minutes before he could push himself up to sit against the kitchen cupboards. He licked the blood at his lip, breathing hard, fury beating in his veins as his head spun. He'd kill the asshole! Soon as his father was passed out, he'd come back and kill him…

Sean crouched down between him and the door. "Ye know wha' happens when a McGuire tries to reach too high, laddie? Everythin' we touch turns to shit. That girl, ye wan' her because she's pure an' yer filth." He backhanded him, pain exploding crimson across Rogan's vision.

His father stood, rasping a hand across stubble thick as iron filings. He grabbed a fifth off the counter, chugged the last of it, then smashed the bottle in the sink. Glass sprayed across the kitchen, peppering the counters and floor. A shard nicked the asshole's arm and he didn't even notice. Rogan wished it'd opened a fucking vein.

"She's everythin' yer not. An' yer there," he scowled, "pathetic. Hoping she'll make ye better, but she won't, and soon as ye touch her, ye'll fuckin' ruin her, and she'll hate ye for it." Sean glared at him and pulled another fifth from a paper bag. He downed a mouthful, then threw the necklace at Rogan. "Give it to that littl' slut yer always fuckin' in the milk shed. Least she earned it."

He lumbered from the room. A moment later, the recliner creaked under his weight.

Rogan picked the necklace from his shirt, hand closing around it. He stumbled to his feet, room swimming, and leaned against the sink, spitting out blood. Anger pounded in his skull. He reached toward the knife block. Fuck waiting until tonight. He'd fucking kill the son of a bitch now. Slit his goddamned—

The charm bit into his fist.

Rogan clenched his aching jaw and pawed the gore coating his face, adrenaline surging.

He grabbed the bag of liquor.

At its crinkle, his father roared, but Rogan was already out the door and down the path. Behind him, a massive crash and the squeal of metal. He laughed. Asshole must've gone through the screen. He hoped he'd broken something other than the door.

Like his goddamned neck.

Cal was already at the quarry, feeding a fire. He shook his head when he saw him. "Got you good."

Rogan shrugged, wiping blood from his lip again. His nose was all fucked up, bubbling when he breathed. He dropped onto a log and rummaged through the bag.

"What's that?"

"Dunno, just grabbed it." He gingerly stretched his jaw. Fuck, that hurt. "S'June fifteenth." He tossed Cal a fifth, and his friend whistled at the label, his green eyes wide.

"Bushmills? He's gonna kill you."

Rogan pinched a clot of blood from his nose and flicked it away. Not if he got the fucker first. He shrugged, chugging one of the beers that'd been in there with it, and ripped a massive burp. It echoed through the quarry, and they both laughed.

"Serves the asshole right. Gimme a smoke." Cal tossed one over and Rogan lit it. He pulled the necklace out, laying the fine gold chain across his knee. Three months of Micky D's, dumpster diving, and odd jobs to pay for it. His rough fingers brushed across the filigreed heart, his dirty, blood-spattered jeans showing through the whorls.

Filth.

What the fuck had he been thinking? In two months he was outta here. Jane deserved someone who would stick around. Someone that wouldn't turn her life to shit.

Someone that wasn't him.

He threw the necklace into the fire.

Cal stared at him through the flames. "That it?" He didn't sound surprised.

"Gimme another smoke." Rogan tucked it behind the ear that didn't feel like cauliflower, trying not to see the necklace caught on a branch, spinning as it blackened. He kicked it into the coals, wishing it would just melt and have done. Fuck, he wished he could burn all of it, the entire fucking town with his asshole father in it.

He cracked the fifth and stalked farther into the quarry, drinking and winging rocks up at the U-shaped wall.

An excited squeal echoed off the stones, and he rolled his eyes, stopping to take a piss. Elize and Enoch were here. Whoop-d fucking do. Rogan took his time going back, sure Cal was already dick-deep in the senator's daughter.

As expected, Enoch was sitting alone by the fire with a bottle of something expensive. He raised a sculpted eyebrow, eyes roaming over Rogan's face. "I see things haven't changed since last summer."

Rogan shrugged, taking a hit off the fifth, his skin crawling. Dude was a fucking perv, and it wasn't that he did guys. It was how he did them. "No. Nothing's changed."

Enoch's lips curved into a smile. "That remains to be seen."

He also didn't take no for an answer. Rogan snorted and rooted round in the paper bag for another beer. Man was barking up the wrong damned tree.

Laughter came from the path. Richard and Karen walked around the bend with Jane between them. Rogan's heart dropped into his stomach. Her brow knit, and she came to sit beside him, laying a hand on his cheek. He pulled away, scuffing the ground with his boot and wiping a hand under his nose. Shit. He was still bleeding.

"You okay?"

He nodded, not looking at her. "Yeah, fine."

Her hand was on his knee and she smelled like she'd been making cookies. Karen sat next to her, and Jane's hip pushed against his. Rogan ran a hand over his jaw, pain dampening the surge of lust she sent through him. Christ, he wanted her.

…Ye wan' her because she's pure…

He got up, stumbling to the overlook, the booze hitting hard. He swayed, staring down the mountainside to the factory far below. In the valley, the town's lights were winking on like little flames. If only. He pulled the cigarette from behind his ear and held it to his lips. All of it, up in fucking smoke. *Poof!* Then he'd never have to think about any of it again.

Or her. Shit, she was all he thought about.

A hand smoothed over his back, and Jane pushed under his arm with a wine cooler. He grinned down at her. Girl was partying hard tonight.

She slid around to face him. "If I could, I would take all this pain from you." She dabbed at his face with the sleeve of her flannel, tracing the edges of the bruise.

The comment put him off balance, and he stumbled, pulling her close to steady himself. God, she felt good. Smelled good. His nose was in her hair, hands sliding to the curve of her hips, lower. Drawing her against him. Jesus, right there… He bit his cheek, semi pressing against her abdomen. She gasped and it went rock hard. Her arms laced around his neck, tits pressed against his chest, eyes so wide and blue… she wet her lips.

Rogan's head dipped toward her upturned face. Maybe his father was wrong. Maybe—

White light seared over the mountainside.

An explosion rent the night, ripping up from the factory below. The ground trembled, then shook. Rogan held Jane to him, falling, the air, stones, everything wavering, a sonic boom tearing through them, leaving his insides raw and aching. He hit the ground hard, cushioning her fall, then pushed onto his hands and knees above her.

What the—

Jane screamed, pointing at the sky.

Holy fuck. It'd peeled back from itself, a void through the heavens like an egg had been cracked then split wide open like they'd been existing in a snow globe. Beyond it, a strange velvet, darker than black, studded with points of shimmering light. They weren't stars...they were alive... Whips of magnetic aura pulsed outward, rippling reality and a keening hum filled the quarry, the stones around them resonating.

Rogan's mind screamed at him to run, but his body was rooted, numb from the mounting vibrations coursing up through the earth.

Ribbons of energy flicked from the void, washing over them. His temper spiked, the world dissolving into crimson. The overwhelming desire to destroy devoured rational thought, his body abruptly free of its paralysis. He shook with rage, pushing from the ground and tearing into the quarry, flinging his anger out ahead of him. Boulders exploded, debris bursting into flame, rock becoming ash. Time fragmenting along with the quarry, the mountain blasted to bits beneath his fury. Nothing. There would be nothing fucking left. He laughed manically, sending out torrents of destruction—

"Rogan!"

Cal. His voice was raw, like he'd been screaming for hours.

Rogan spun.

No one was there.

But the rising sun was. He stumbled backwards, rubbing his eyes. Had he been up here all night? Shit, the last thing he clearly remembered was Jane pressed against him. Christ, if he'd fucked her—

He shook his head, fisting his hair. No, that hadn't happened. There'd been an explosion, and then...

His mouth went dry at the piles of smoldering scree surrounding him. Jesus, half the fucking mountain was missing or on fire. That wasn't...how—he stared at his fingers. Crimson tongues of flame flickered between them, disappearing and reappearing. Laughter burbled from his lips. No. This shit wasn't happening. Christ, he'd lost it, he—

Invisible hands grabbed his shirt, shaking him. "Calm the fuck down!"

What the—

The flames around him flickered, dying back. "Cal?"

"Yeah." A sigh and the sound of a cigarette lighting. Smell of smoke.

Where the fuck—

"Come on, the others are waiting."

Invisible boots scuffed through the sand on the path, leaving a trail leading away. Rogan followed them. No more fucking Bushmills. Not after this. He'd lost his goddamned mind…

All of them save Cal sat around the smoldering campfire, stone sober.

Fuck that. Rogan took the fifth from his back pocket and chugged it. Their eyes… Christ, they were all off…changed. Weird rings of color surrounded their irises. Silver, bronze. Elize and Enoch both had purple.

"Yours are red," Jane said.

He turned to her. Wide golden bands hugged the blue of her eyes. "Jesus, you're an angel with those halos." He raised his hand to cup her cheek and his thumb left a smear of filth in its wake.

His father was right.

Uncontrollable rage boiled up inside him, a seething blackness searing his core. Jane stepped back. Rogan's stomach clenched at the fear in her eyes.

If he touched her, he would ruin her.

Then she'd hate him, and he'd break.

He couldn't do that to either of them. He loved her too much.

Rogan turned away from her, a howling wrongness gnawing at his bones as he screamed his fury into the dawn and fled the quarry, trailing flames.

CHAPTER ONE

Commons [kŏm'ənz] noun

> 1. *The lowest caste of Glynfyls society, comprised of those least affected by the Surge.*

— Excerpt from Glynfyls: A History

"In exchange for our protection, the commons have acted as the engine of Glynfyls's economy, providing the menial labor and skilled craftsmen to bring the economic endeavors of the Original Houses into fruition. However, long periods of relative peace have given birth to dissatisfaction among the lower rungs, most recently resulting in the Dock Uprising only a decade ago…"

— Lord Talos, Preceptor of History,
Academy of Glynfyls

GLYNFYLS WAS BURNING.

Flynn stared out the window of the Assembly Hall, overlooking the eastern spokes of the city. Beyond the wavy glass, the rising sun was a crimson smear across the smoke-streaked horizon. Below, the clamor of an angry mob rioted through the streets.

How the hell a cluster fuck of this magnitude had gotten kicked off last night—he scrubbed at his face. Shit. He knew exactly how.

His hand rose and talent the color of old blood flickered between his fingers, sparking off and singeing the carpet. He scuffed it out with his boot, jaw clenching. After the past few weeks of trying to play the goddamned part, he'd fucking split when he put Riegel down and, caught in a catch twenty-fucking-two, the entire city had seen him do it.

But if he hadn't, the boost the Breaker was rigged with would've blown Glynfyls to shit. Flynn sighed. Instead of the city, everything he'd worked for had gone with Riegel into the hereafter. Christ, Julia and Lord Morris must be having a fucking field day with this. Both of them would be in chambers now, smug as shit, lambasting the room with big fat I-told-you-so's...

God, he was gonna puke. Dual-Talents couldn't hold office, and he'd used both a Shade's talent to phaze away the blast, and a shit ton of Breaker ability, publicly. He'd saved the city only to hand it over to Julia, and she'd pass it right on to Titus.

His eyes closed, seeing it all play out. Legally, he was screwed. The Shades were gonna abjure him from his seat on the Assembly. Lords Klein and Ketsing, the Fixer and Binder Firsts that'd pledged their line's fealty to him, would pull their support. Then Crandall would bury him. He'd gleefully drive the last nail into Flynn's coffin by tying him to the Sons that'd been slaughtered out on the plateau.

And as for Phyllis and Markham? Neither one of them was gonna do a fucking thing. No, check that. Markham would mop the sweat from his brow when they came at Flynn with a rope to hang him. Couple of minutes swinging, then done deal, Flynn'd be in a box and they'd be back to business as usual.

Until Titus sent in his troops and Peacekeepers harvested the lot of them.

"I wish I was a fucking twist, then I wouldn't have to pretend..."

Of all the wishes he'd ever made, it figured that would be the one granted. God had to love fucking with him.

Kara pushed up under his arm. "We can tell them it was me—"

"No. I won't lie about it." They'd gone over this. If Merchant couldn't get him off, he'd cloak them at Meddleton until the baby was born, then head west. Disappear. He'd done it before, he could do it again. He kissed the top of Kara's head, wrapping his arms around her.

"You should try and sleep."

She laughed, the strain of the past twenty-four hours etched across her brow. Once the adrenaline from the bout last night at the Pony had faded, Riegel's death had triggered a cascade of memories. Each one left her more brittle than the last, and that damned talent debilitation plaguing her pregnancy was back. Add to it being locked up in this goddamned conference room without any idea of what was going on other than one hell of a shit show…

Christ. What a fucking mess.

The door opened and Merchant hustled in, looking grim. His suit was rumpled and his grey-streaked hair awry. A servant came in after him and set a coffee service and two plates of eggs on the conference table. Flynn's stomach growled. Damn, he could go for—Kara turned to his chest, pale with nausea. Goddamn it, he needed to get her home.

"Take it away, please."

The woman looked at him in surprise, then wet her lips, glancing at Merchant. She pulled a scrap of paper from the napkin, holding it out with trembling fingers, and flashed her colors. Thin rings of fuchsia pulsed around her irises. It was the signal Flynn and Dorian had agreed upon for when the Finder had turned something up on Crandall.

Flynn took it from her, and she bobbed a curtsy, fist to heart. Vassal to Overlord. He snorted, like that was gonna fucking happen—his temper spiked at the contents of the note, and it smoldered where he gripped it. Damn it—His anger was too close. Too easy to pull from. All this time, is that what that constant simmering rage had been? Talent just waiting to come out?

"I suggest you cloak this conversation." Merchant frowned, tossing a newspaper onto the table. "They're attempting to charge you with inciting the commons."

Flynn's jaw dropped, note forgotten. *That's not*—His halos flared verdigris, cloaking them. "But they all saw—"

"A great deal of talent being used. As evidenced by that front page still and multiple reels. You haven't developed concentric halos. By definition, a twist evidences a dual-halo, and without a second ring around your irises, you cannot be considered as such. Additionally, without confirmation from the Breaker line as to whom was doing what, any and all charges are unsubstantiated, and will be treated as libel and or slander. Now, I suggest we focus on the matter at hand." He snapped open his briefcase.

"The matter at—are you serious?" He—there was no way—how was this not about him splitting? Was Merchant seriously getting him off on semantics? Shit, Cal had said he was good, but no one could be that good.

The little barrister tapped a folio of papers square. "The Assembly's charges are predicated upon legislation enacted in response to the Dock Uprising, however, the reels clearly establish that it was your arrest, not the fight, nor your actions afterwards, that sparked tensions."

Flynn's mind struggled to shift gears. The Dock Uprising? Those riots had gone on for months, and half the city had burnt down. That's what was going on outside? Jesus Christ, what the fuck had he done?

Aside from saving all their asses. A manic laugh burbled from his lips.

Merchant wasn't amused. "Breakers called conclave, the city's up in arms over your detainment, and Assembly's been in session since you were brought here. If you didn't have half their oaths, your head would already be on a pike."

Flynn dropped into a chair. Out of the frying pan and into the fire. Either way, he was toast. Kara sat beside him, picking up the paper as Merchant continued.

"To further complicate matters, the international press has been running with the story and the Sons of the Messiah have officially declared jihad. There are riots all over the Deep South. Anti-Talent sentiment is at an all-time high."

Kara slid the front page over. *THE MAN WHO WOULD BE KING*

was printed in bold block letters over a still of him, halos blazing, holding up Riegel's heart. The inset was of her, mouth painted crimson with the Breaker's blood. She took his hand, as pale as he felt. They looked like fucking psychopaths.

"It gets worse. The Source has filed paperwork to enact the Harvest Clause, citing your threats of retaliation last night as provocation through aggression."

Flynn laughed—shit, Merchant was serious.

"We've filed a counter suit," the barrister continued, "and given the precedence set by Banoi and Tombago—"

"What did Cal say?"

Merchant pursed his lips. "I've been unable to get in touch with Master Scot."

Flynn stared at him. Where the f—"You got a cigar?"

"I—no."

He grunted, running a hand over his beard. If they were gonna try to screw him with this…shit. Borrowed or not, it gave him time. He needed to play this out. "Fine. I fucked up. I'll stay as long as I need to, but none of it has to do with Kara—"

"What? No. I'm staying with you."

"You're past due for your shot." He ran a hand down her cheek, neither one of them able to pretend that creeping exhaustion wasn't edging in again. She wouldn't look at him.

"The lady has medical needs?" Merchant glanced between them and sighed. "I'm not going to lie. Legally, they can't hold you with what they've presented, but this isn't going to play out in court. The next one will. I haven't raised objection because we're fighting an uphill battle against public opinion. You need to be seen as cooperative. If you have something to disclose…please. Help me, help you." His eyes flicked to the note.

Flynn bit the scar on his lip. Christ, he had to trust someone, and Cal was putting Merchant's kids through school. There were worse reasons to be loyal.

"Three days ago, they had Riegel in police custody. He was released under the recognizance of a Master Eid. I can't prove it, but I damned well know Crandall let him walk. He let that fight happen, all this fallout is on him." Flynn's temper jumped again, his fingertips sparking. He snuffed them in his fist. Asshole had probably hoped the Breaker would kill him.

"I'd encourage you to keep the fact you know the Breaker's name to yourself." The little barrister took off his glasses, rubbing a cloth over the lenses. "As far as Master Eid is concerned, I'm assuming he doesn't exist, and no one knows anything about the alleged incarceration."

"You would be correct."

"God, I hate politics." Merchant could say that shit again. He replaced his glasses, looking even more dour than when he'd come into the room. "And the lady?"

Flynn frowned. "We haven't announced, but she's pregnant, and is suffering from a talent deficiency. There's a regimen she's got to follow."

Kara chewed her thumb, and he could feel her annoyance through their bond. Too damned bad. She was gonna end up on bedrest otherwise.

Merchant took a seat. "You do realize how ludicrous that sounds, given her performance in the ring last night?"

Flynn's temper spiked, and she put a hand on his leg. He gritted his teeth, that weird burst of strength he'd felt during the bout coursing through him with his anger. Christ, he had to keep it together…

"I don't give a shit how it sounds. The ladies will confirm she's carrying my heir, and Jon's got her fucking labs if you need to enter an exhibit—"

Feet pelted down the hall. Shouting. Glass shattered somewhere in the building, and the sounds of the angry mob grew louder. The door flung open. Markham stood there panting. It wasn't a good look on the First Fetch.

"Quickly, the commons have breached the main doors!"

Flynn grabbed Kara and bolted to the big man, Merchant already at his side—

Colors ran.

Markham shifted them to the center of chambers. The massive doors were barricaded, and a contingent of Fixers stood by them, halos blazing bronze, holding them shut with their talent. Others held the gallery entrances, the white marble awash in the metallic glow. Pounding and rabid cries came from beyond them. What the hell—

Riggs cleared his throat. The speaker sat at his lectern in lavender striped pajamas and a robe. Was he wearing bunny slip—

"Lord Scot. If you'd take your seat so we can begin?"

Something big hit the doors, the boom reverberating through the hall. The light from the Fixer's halos flared brighter. Flynn swallowed, directing Kara to his box. Nothing about this was gonna end well. Merchant took the chair Lot usually occupied. His father was in the seats above, scowling.

Dawn bled through the tall windows, spiking across the chamber and highlighting the empty Breaker section. Kara's anxiety was on overdrive, bleeding through their bond to fuel Flynn's. She stumbled, and he caught her elbow, moving the chair from beside Merchant next to his, its legs scraping too loudly against the marble. Flynn's heart thudded in his ears. He took his seat and her hand again, kissing her trembling knuckles. She wasn't doing well, jumping as Riggs banged his gavel. The call to order echoed over the booms coming from outside the room, the swelling clamor from the mob ratcheting up everyone's tension.

"I call this special session to order. Well, then, Laughlin. Would you care to explain yourself?" the elderly man asked.

He bit back a no, running a hand over his beard. "For what?"

"Everything last night!"

Right. That. Flynn took a deep breath and stood, shoving his hands into his pockets. Christ, he needed to calm down…"When I returned to Glynfyls, certain individuals refused to let me settle a debt I'd incurred before leaving. The bout last night was how they insisted payment be made. Given the prohibition against Firsts entering into any form of competition, Lady Scot graciously stepped up in my place."

A wrenching squeal and another boom came from the doors. Were there Breakers out there? Phyllis's pinched face glaring at him from the crowd last night flashed before his eyes. Damn, there might be—

Lord Klein's halos flared, his talent bolstering the other Fixers. "Goddamn it, Markham! Can't you control your line?"

"My line—" The big man mopped at his brow. "The Fetches, ah, I— I'm afraid things are a bit strained at the moment, and keeping the public from these proceedings—"

"Then we should expedite them," Crandall said, stroking his greasy little goatee far too calmly. Flynn grit his teeth. Yep. Asshole was about to bury him. "If you would continue, Lord Riggs?"

The speaker scanned the page in front of him. "Laughlin's brought up a point Lord Ketsing requested clarification on."

"Yes." The Binder First said, wringing his hands. "We were led to believe that Lady Scot was a Binder. After last night—" He licked his lips, about to make an accusation he wouldn't be able to take back.

Flynn's temper surged with Kara's dread. If her called her a fucking twist... Why couldn't they leave her out of this? "Her halos were witnessed by the entirety of my line during her Introduction, what other proof—"

"Can I speak?"

She'd come up beside him. His surprise cut through his barely contained rage.

"Yeah." Flynn glared around the room, daring someone to say otherwise. She was terrified, but had raised that elfin chin... Goddamn, he loved her. Her fingers tightened on his sleeve, keeping him at her side.

"My genetics are both Binder and Breaker, my progenitors First of their lines at the Source." She held out her wrist, baring the barcode tattoo from beneath her sleeve. "I'm more than happy to provide the metrics proving my Binder genes ascendent. Though registered as a duality, I was slated to replace my d—my mother as First Binder when she aged out."

The room broke into scandalized outcry at the public disclosure of her duality. Since she only presented Binder talent, it wasn't the same as being a twist, but all these assholes would consider her bloodline tainted. Didn't matter that she had more talent in her pinky than all of them put together. God, he hated this fucking city.

The Binder section erupted into fervent discussion. Between her declaration and him splitting, the odds any of their children being a pureblooded talent were slim to none. He didn't give a shit, but they would. Their line's pledge of fealty had been predicated on the possibility of a Jester heir ascending to hold the position of First Binder one day.

So much for that. House Scot was probably shit out of luck, too. Flynn knew he was, but what the hell else was new?

Riggs banged his gavel. "If we can hold discussion to the end? Lady Scot is not here to defend her pedigree, although the clarification is appreciated." He smiled, motioning for her to sit and turned back to Flynn. "If you would finish with your version of events?"

He gritted his teeth. His version of events. Like they hadn't all seen it. "What's there to tell? I contained the blast and severed the Breaker's channel. Look, the Source is coming. Last night proves that they have people here, preparing the way for a harvest—"

Lord Ines stood, and Flynn broke off, surprised Julia wasn't at the man's side...or anywhere else in the room. Why wasn't she here? You'd think she would've been first in line to tear out his throat.

"And you've done that for them, haven't you? They've entered a lawsuit—"

"And in doing so, admitted their guilt. I didn't name names, and if I hadn't acted, Glynfyls would be a smoking pit!"

"It's not far off now," Crandall said dryly.

"Maybe you should've thought of that before you had me detained."

"I wouldn't have had to detain you, if you hadn't usurped the prerogatives of the individual lines by taking the oaths of the commons."

Flynn's brows knit. The oaths of the commons...he hadn't done that. Though, he could see how it'd be assumed he had, given the way with those Breakers last night and the Finder earlier had saluted him as Overlord... Fucking hell. His knuckles popped, wanting to put his fist through that weaselly little Finder's—"Why shouldn't I? Original Houses were given authority over those less talented in exchange for our protection—"

"Which is the purview of their duly elected Firsts!"

Flynn riffled his hair, jaw clenched. That was the pretense they were trying to hang him with? Of all the patronizing fucking—"So let me get this straight, Original Houses are free to pledge as they see fit, but the commons need permission." Crandall tried to backpedal and Flynn wasn't gonna let him. "As per the codes, commons enjoy the same liberties we do, less the ability to vote. If this was such a damning issue on principle, why wasn't it brought up when lines other than Shades began pledging?"

Crandall's lips pursed, and Flynn laughed, wanting to pummel the pompous prick. The rest of the room fidgeted, the noise from the mob calling them on their bullshit. Something hit one of the windows, and several woman shrieked, moving closer to the floor.

Flynn laughed. "Fine, I'll play along with your elitist hypocrisy. You wanna split hairs, Crandall? None of the Breakers swore, and I wasn't approached by any Finders last night. I hold the oaths of the Fixer and Binder Firsts, which gives me carte blanche over their lines in addition to my own. All that out there? Your doing, not mine."

There was another outcry over that, and Flynn didn't give a shit. It was fact, and they'd all lined up willingly to pledge. He dropped into his seat. Jesus fucking Christ—

"Point of law," Merchant chimed in. "Lord Scot is correct that there is nothing legally preventing him from taking the oath of any citizen of the Northern Territories, regardless of their affinity."

"Nothing other than him being a goddamned twist!" Morris's irate voice boomed from behind them.

Fuck. A growl rumbled through Flynn's chest at Kara's flinch, not surprised that odious prick was gonna try to whip up even more of a shit storm.

The room went still.

"Any speculation as to my client's talent—"

"Speculation? Bah! I've said it before and I'll say it again, man's a mongrel! We all saw what happened, why he's not in chains—"

"Yes. We all saw what happened, and today's front page." Markham stood, mopping at his chins. He glanced at Crandall and then at Lord Klein. His head was bowed, dark hair falling across his face. The rest of the Fixers weren't doing so hot either. How much talent outside those doors were they trying to mitigate? "I see no evidence of Laughlin being a twist, and given the current situation, the Fetches would like to pledge—"

The fuck?!

"Are you serious, Markham?!" Morris frothed into the room's stunned silence.

"I shouldn't have to remind you of the last time the lower spokes revolted. Whether you realize it or not, that whole sordid affair only served to further engrain the commons's dissatisfaction with the status quo. Tonight was just the spark that lit the tinder. Listen to them out there! We can't afford another strike, especially not now, and swearing fealty to a man capable of what I saw last night seems prudent."

The uproar was immediate.

"Let them strike!"

"How dare they threaten—"

"Prudent! What we saw was murder!" Morris blustered above it all. "Scot admitted to severing the man's channel! That Breaker should've been held for questioning instead of being silenced with the same savagery evidenced on the plateau! Crandall couldn't rule out a Shade's involvement, and I'd bet Scot killed him to stop from being fingered as an accomplice!"

The room erupted again, and Kara's head whipped around, her bloodlust churning black through their bond. Flynn's own rose up to meet it. Shit, that was gonna be a problem—

"That's a lie! Riegel was fitted with a boost. The tech negates a Finder's talent—"

The clamor died, everyone staring at her. Behind them, Merchant made a pained sound, and Kara's hand rose to her throat.

"Riegel," Crandall drawled, standing and straightening his lapels. "You knew him personally, Lady Scot?" he asked the question staring at Flynn.

Fucker already knew. Kara slumped against him, and Flynn tamped down the urge to blast the man to hell. "That's a House Matter. You should be more concerned that he was a common Source Breaker, not a Peacekeeper. Twelve thousand of which are gonna be storming our walls, and all of you are playing into their goddamned hands. The chaos out there? Shit, you don't think they know about it? Forget about spies kicking around, that Breaker was implanted with tech I'm convinced was streaming holo back to the Source. If we're lucky, putting him down like that bought us some more damned time."

And what was going on out in the streets was pissing it away. Motherf—

"Tech?" Riggs asked.

"I'm sure Crandall can confirm." Shithead had to be good for something.

"There is evidence of plaz contamination, though given the condition of the corpse, we're unable to ascertain its purpose."

The room didn't chew on that for nearly long enough.

"And your use of talent, Lord Scot?" Riggs pressed.

"I told you, I contained the blast and severed his channel."

"I'd say you did a bit more than that," someone snorted.

Riggs kept looking at Flynn. He rocked back in his seat, trying to pull up that blanket of calm… The noise from outside crested again, more projectiles striking the windows.

The Assembly waited.

Fuck them. He dropped the legs of his chair, disgusted. Kara leaned against him and he put his arm around her. She needed to go home. He tamped down his rage, done with all of their bullshit. They wanted to indict him, have fucking at it, and send him a memo when they'd figured it out.

Riggs adjusted his glasses, looking around the chamber. "Well, then, anything else?"

Crandall smirked and Flynn wanted to pummel the fucker.

"Yeah," he spat, standing. "Instead of raking us over the coals, you should be asking how that Breaker was released from the constabulary's drunk tank three days ago, despite his description being posted throughout the city. If Crandall had been doing his job, none of this would've happened. I won't apologize for cleaning up his mess. Any further questions can be directed to my lawyer."

Flynn picked Kara up, pulled talent, and phazed them through the mob.

The surprised indignation on the Intelligencer's face as the room turned its attention to him was almost worth being hauled in for.

TITUS CHUCKLED at the events playing out in the North. The discord his operatives had spread throughout the lower rungs had been more effective than he could have possibly hoped. The fallout from sending Riegel up had been exactly what they needed to spiral the city into absolute chaos. He smirked, sipping his bourbon and watching the mayhem from a thousand different vantages as his bots streamed holo from the rabble storming the Assembly hall.

A communications orb pulsed. That would be the board.

Titus flicked the feeds away and answered it. Nine frames materialized in front of him. Of the original sixteen chairs, ten remained. Only seven had shares in the Source. The rest had been bought out, suffered questionable deaths, and in one case, a very public execution.

His gaze went to Albanach, the ancient, hairless albino in one of the central squares. They were due another one of those.

"Good, we're all here," Orin wheezed. The chemical burns that had scarred the tech chair's bloated visage were gone. Pity. He must've finally struck a deal with Albanach for one of his Binders. Curious. The old dragon had to have wanted something very badly to offer that up.

"Yes. How fortuitous."

Yin. Titus's eyes snapped to the hag in the upper left hand corner, the rest of them content to lurk. From her tone, she'd caught the twitch of his lip.

"Why doesn't Titus start, since he's so chipper," she snipped. "Tell me, what is it about that rabid dog of yours escaping and causing world-wide rioting and international censure that puts you in such a jolly mood?"

"I don't know why you're asking me. Albanach is the one who can't seem to keep track of his Talents. Perhaps if he spent less time napping—"

"Kara Jester's escape is the least of our concerns," the old man snapped. "Between the North's sanctions and this lawsuit stemming from your sloppy grabs of wild Talents, we're already on the back foot. Add to it a goddamned Breaker outfitted with a boost landing in the middle of Glynfyls—Christ, Titus, how far was your head up your ass when you filed that suit for breach of clause? You're all but admitting you sent the man to Glynfyls, and if the international courts prove it, they'll bankrupt us!"

Mmm. Yes. If. Good luck doing that before all was said and done.

Yin narrowed her dark eyes, financials always her first concern. "How did that Breaker end up with a boost? Wasn't the program scrapped?"

"It was, and I couldn't tell you," Titus lied. "The man was being held in stasis until the paperwork to cull him was complete. My people are reviewing holo and should have something soon."

Rache paled, feeling the ax, no doubt. Titus restrained himself from smirking. As she should, after being stupid enough to be manipulated into moving against him and securing the Breaker's freedom. Remorseless, Titus sipped at his bourbon, already adding her shares to his.

"The list of people who can perform the boost implantation procedure with access to the tech is short," Orin said, inspecting his enameled nails. The French tips protruded from his fleshy fingertips like gravestones.

"And you're one of them."

The man fluttered his feathered lashes. "As are you."

"To what advantage?" Titus snorted. "I've stated repeatedly that I believe a harvest is necessary. Wiping out the city with a suicide bomber is rather counterintuitive, don't you think?" It was also accidental after someone had tampered with the man's kill switch.

Orin's smirk grew.

"We have a larger problem." Kasham broke in. The Source's whore-mistress was flustered enough to be wearing clothes, her usual bevy of bed-fellows absent. "Lord Scot. The talent he exhibited is completely undocumented. That he was able to mitigate a boost detonating…not even a nullifier can do that, and regardless of who was responsible for setting that Breaker loose, Scot's threats of retribution were directed at the Source. I, for one, am not willing to get caught in the crosshairs."

Titus tsked. "Please. He's one man, and I still maintain we're within our rights to a harvest after that speech. If it's your lily-white neck you're worried about, I've recalled several companies of Breakers to patrol Outside. Quite frankly, the Sons concern me more than a single Northern blowhard a thousand miles away."

"And your troops situated at the border?" Orin asked, the rest of them tensing.

Titus shrugged it off. "A deterrent. Insurance. Call it what you will, and should the North move against us, well then. That would satisfy our need for new genetics, now wouldn't it?" And that was all but guaranteed once Barton, the assassin he'd dispatched to acquire Kara Jester, succeeded. Scot would retaliate; of that, Titus had no doubt.

"I call it provocation." Albanach blew out a plume of smoke and tapped his cigar into the ugly crystal ashtray at his elbow. "Why does this remind me of your assurances before that whole mess in Diytan?"

"Because his arrogance is the same," Yin frowned, "and *that* debacle cost us billions. We should cut our losses, I've no interest in being held responsible for another's hubris."

Titus went cold. "What are you suggesting?"

"Liquidation." Yin threw up several charts too quickly for them not to be prepared ahead of time, outlining the Source's declining profitability. As of two weeks ago, the slow slide had fallen off a cliff. "I took the liberty of extrapolating the financials through year-end close based on the budget requests for next year, and it's not sustainable. I can't think of one good reason to sink anymore capital into that sucking pit."

Titus sat back as Yin pursed her wrinkled lips. Sucking pit indeed. Too many of the others were nodding like the hag was making sense. He snorted. "A single quarter in the red—"

"Compare last year to every year before it. Better yet, compare the genetic division as a whole to our other holdings. How much capital are we going to throw into the void?"

Another graph sprang up of where the Source stood in relation to the Corporation's other concerns. It was damming. Titus grit his teeth, a sharp pain behind his eyes as he mined his own numbers.

"Without the new genetics you've been teasing us with—"

"And are on the cusp of acquiring!"

"At what cost?" Kasham snapped. "This new talent must be taken into account—"

"The time frame has become proscriptive," Yin continued over her. "Even if you're correct, we're looking at a decade of significant loss before having a salable product—"

"And whose fault is that?" Titus snapped. "I warned you of this a century ago, and you all turned a blind eye. In your forensic analysis did you bother to correlate those dips in profitability with policy? Eighty-seven percent of sustained downturn can be directly attributed to practices promoted by Albanach. One would think that he's been trying to sink the division!"

The old man gave a wheezing laughed that dribbled into a cough. He pulled out a handkerchief and spat something noisome into it, wiping at his bloodless lips. His amusement didn't extend to his eyes.

"And here I thought you lacked a sense of humor. I have a considerable amount of capital tied up in the Source. Why on God's green earth would I have been working to bankrupt myself?" He rolled the ash off his cigar, narrowing his oyster-grey gaze as Titus opened his mouth. "But, I can understand your frustration, and Yin's concerns…not that I share them."

Words died on Titus's tongue. What was this?

"He's right in that we're on the cusp, and after last night, something's gonna give. We've two months till year-end close. Plenty of time for Titus to deliver on his promises. Bringing a Shade to market could very well erase a decade of deficit in the first year, and as far as funding up until that point…" The man shrugged. "We could work something out."

Was he seriously offering to fund the Source for the next decade? What kind of resources did the old dragon have? The board stared at him with varying degrees of incredulity and out-right hostility. Yin was one of the latter.

"And if he's unable to deliver?"

Albanach inspected the tip of his cigar. "We shut it down."

"You're still ignoring the threat Scot poses," Kasham said.

"I'm sure it's nothing that the Commandant can't deal with while this plays out, and like Titus said, Scot's just one man."

Titus's grip tightened on his bourbon, positive Albanach's flippant mention of the Commandant was meant to rile him, but to what end? Both of them would be censured if the board found out that Marcos and Nora Jester had escaped…

But damn the man, Albanach was far too smug not to be working an angle.

"Yes, the Commandant has the situation well in hand, and while I have you, we need to set a meeting to discuss contracting your Binders on the off-chance military intervention is required. Include that Jester woman, won't you?"

Albanach's grin grew around his cigar. "Have your secretary contact mine. Wouldn't want it to conflict with a nap."

MARCOS PEERED through a slice in the blinds at the chaos on the street below. His hand drifted to his sidearm, the rabble sending up another cry. Just what they needed, to be stuck smack dab in the middle of a civil uprising. He frowned, crossing the sparse room to Nora's bedside. She was sleeping soundly, her color and breathing back to normal since Pithy had healed her. Marcos pulled the rough wool blanket closer to her chin. When she'd wake was anybody's guess.

The door pushed open and Trick, Pithy's assistant, came in carrying a tray set with breakfast for two. "Good Morning, good morning. Big doing's afoot. Some coffee and eggs for ye, on the house. Paper t'pass the time."

Marcos didn't argue, sitting at the table and tucking right in. When you got food in the field, you ate it.

The little Fetch rubbed his hands together. "And how's the lady? Still sleeping, I see. Not to worry there. Pithy said she'd be right as—" The crowd outside sent up a mighty roar, and he chuckled.

Pithy. Marcos wanted answers about that Binder, but now wasn't the time. "What's all that about?"

"That? Commons is rising, friend. Them hillies has gone too far again, need a reminder whose city this is, bless their black hearts. S'all in there." He motioned towards the paper, and Marcos flipped it open; his jaw stopped mid-chew.

Kara. Meal forgotten, he scanned the article, eyes lingering on the corpse, then focusing on the man beneath the headline.

He recognized both.

Trick sat down across from him, his head cocked to one side. "Somewhat of interest?"

"What can you tell me about Lord Scot?"

The little Fetch pursed his lips. "He's Original House, but ain't much like them other hillies. A right carouser before he quit Glynfyls, mess of scandal there. Come back recently with a lady of some intrigue. Done well for hisself since, but that spell of years he'd been gone, a bit of a mystery, that…good coin to be made if it's solved for the right ears…"

Marcos snorted. "Breaker?" The color of his halos was wrong, but the rest of it—

"Shade, though rumor's rife on the point, 'specially after last night. Pithy says ye can stay as long as ye need. Fitz…" Trick tapped his knuckles on the table, frowning. "Well, then, there ain't no rush. Sleep's the best thing for the lady."

"He reliable?" The kid that had shifted them up here hadn't seemed all on the up and up, but that was to be expected with Fetches. They were as shifty as their talent, and him disappearing before Nora was stable didn't give Marcos a lot of confidence in his dependability.

"Who, Fitz?" Trick laughed, standing. "Not in the slightest, but he's a good lad. S'money to be made, he'll turn up. Try not to be too hard on him when he do. Dealing with them hillies is more painful for him than most. 'Specially with all thems goings on out there. Now, I'll leave ye t'it. Busy day, busy day…"

Marcos grunted as the Fetch left, pulling the paper back over.

Riegel was dead.

Little emotion other than a fleeting sense of relief accompanied the fact. He ran a finger over the gory still of his son and Nora's, then over the inset of Kara, spattered with her half-sib's blood. The second page was peppered with close-ups of the corpse. Marcos pushed his eggs away. Gah, didn't these people have scruples?

His eyes drifted back to the man beneath the headline. Why was he so familiar? Marcos prided himself in the fact that he could call most of the troops that'd served beneath him by name…but Scot wasn't a Breaker.

Marcos snorted, tossing the paper away. Like hell he wasn't.

There was a crash in the hall, and someone swore, fumbling at the knob. The reek of alcohol proceeded a curly blond head into the room, followed by a lanky body, its owner none too steady. Fitz propped himself against the doorframe and tipped back a bottle, more than a little intoxicated.

No. Not reliable in the slightest.

"Eh…ye ready then?" He rubbed a hickey on his neck, studying his worn boots.

"Not until you've sobered up." Marcos growled, pouring him some coffee. Last thing they needed was to shift into the middle of a wall.

The young man laughed and took another swig from his bottle, smacking his wide lips. "Then ye prefer t'stay. Fine by me—"

"Sit your ass down, son."

Fitz blinked at him from behind a curtain of tangled curls. His hand went to his pocket, fiddling with something. "Eh…right then." He staggered over and flopped into the chair Trick had vacated, abandoning the bottle for the other plate of eggs. He shoveled up forkfuls like he hadn't had a meal in days.

"You're welcome to what's left on this one, too," Marcos said, pushing over his plate. "When's the last time you ate?"

"Eh…pizza last night. Dove's special this morn'. Eggs ain't as good as this, but them kippers…" He poked his fork at him. "Them is delightful."

Despite the list, he could've fooled Marcos. He'd never seen food disappear so fast, and having frequented a Breaker mess-hall, that was saying something. The crowd outside roared again. "You know anything about that?"

"S'right fuckin' mess."

"You don't say." Marcos watched Fitz inhale what was on the plate and start in on the other. Low booms sounded in the distance. The boy's eyes flicked to the window, then to the door as Trick came back in.

"There ye is. Sisters has put out word, wanting ye."

Fitz looked ill. It was little wonder after bolting all that down. He pulled at the scrap of beard under his lip, other hand back in his pocket. "Eh…know what for?"

The little man gave him a look that said he damned well knew what for. Boy grabbed his bottle, upending it. Marcos had the uncomfortable feeling of swimming in an unknown sea, and the undercurrents were decidedly dangerous. What had they fallen in with? "Somebody want to tell me what the hell's going on?"

"House Matter," Fitz mumbled.

"I don't know what that means."

The boy's blood-shot eyes snapped to his. "Means ye drop the fuckin' subject. Ain't nothing t'concern ye."

"What we're walking into is my concern," Marcos growled, looming across the table at him.

Fitz surprised him, glaring back. "And that ain't none of mine."

His halos flared, and he was gone.

"Shite, he's in the wind now…" Trick muttered, coming over to collect the plates. "I told ye t'go easy—"

"What did I say?"

The little Fetch sighed, his face weary. "All that out there ain't the first of this. Ten years back, Fitz's da…he were a good man—a fuckin' saint as far as them hillies go. Bastards killed him for it, along with them two angels of his. Boy's about t'make his majority, and when he do…well, some would see him take up the torch. Rest would hang him before he gets the chance. Them Prydee sisters…" Trick shook his head and looked like he was going to spit.

"But that ain't nothing for ye t'worry about, now is it, friend? Question is, what t'do with ye? Lad were tight-lipped on where ye was bound…" He cocked his head expectantly, and Marcos glanced at the bed.

"I'm afraid I don't have an answer for you until Nora—" A booming screech of metal came from outside, setting his teeth on edge and the crowd roared again.

The little Fetch's gaze narrowed, but didn't waver. "Fair enough. I've got t'pop out for a spell, loo's down the hall, first door. Imagine it goes without saying, but it's best ye keep t'these four walls." Trick flashed a broad smile and shifted from the room.

Marcos's eyes fell on the bottle Fitz had abandoned and poured himself a jot. He threw it back, lips puckering, and pulled his sidearm. Placing it on the table, he settled in, listening to a revolution.

ROGAN SCRATCHED his back against the roughly hewn stone of the conclave chamber's wall, wondering again why the hell he'd let Cal talk him into this shit. The longer he was in Glynfyls, the more fucked up the situation got. He sighed. Some things never changed. Especially when that asshole was involved. Even when they were kids he'd been all, *"it'll be fun,"* or, *"think of the great story it'll make..."*

More often than not, it ended up with the both of them blotto and covered in pig shit.

A goddamned millennium later, only thing that'd changed was the severity of said shit, and all Rogan was thinking of now was how loud the crack was gonna be when he bitchslapped the prick the next time he saw him. No, no catch, just pick up where you left off...

Several thousand pissed off Breakers was definitely not where Rogan'd left anything. A fraction of them packed the stone tiers below, ringing a wide circle of sand. Phyllis Breakspear stood in the center of it, the air was dank with 'lust. He had zero sympathy for the position the First Breaker had gotten herself into, but no real interest in seeing her go down in flames, either. Too bad the latter was still gonna happen. Rogan blew out a breath, buzzing his lips, and tried to pay attention to the debate.

Debate. Shit show. Six of one, half dozen of another. Commons were tearing her a new one, and the woman didn't have a leg to stand on as far as he was concerned.

"Ye ain't got no fuckin' right—"

"I've every right! As your elected—"

"Elections is for civs! Breaker's right is might!"

The walls boomed with the crowd's agreement, and Phyllis drew herself up taller, sending out a cloud of 'lust. The pheromone didn't do much to mollify the room. Especially not after what Flynn had dumped on them a few hours earlier.

Any doubt he was an Alpha was gone. Fucking kid had no idea what the hell he'd set off. Breakers didn't give a shit if he was dual-talented or not, but the rest of the lines…

Flynn was more than a goddamned problem, he was a liability.

"In trine." Phyllis shrilled back. "As you were reminded at the moot two days ago, bloodlust is only one of the three necessary criteria to be considered a Breaker."

"With me own eyes, I seen plenty o' talent last night," a common spat back.

"An' far as might, he beat half of us bloody 'fore he left. Them's three in me book."

Phyllis's fists clenched at her sides. "None of which were proper challenges—"

"Were closer t'one than we've gotten from your lad!"

The statement was met with vehement agreement.

Rogan eyes went to the auburn-haired pretty boy in the bottom row, staring at his shoes. The few times he'd glanced up, the resemblance between him and Phyllis was undeniable. So was the fact that he was way too comfortable letting mommy hold the reins. Little Billy, the presumed heir to her throne, hadn't made a peep, and them calling him out on it hadn't changed that. Rogan spat to the side. Pathetic. Fucking nepotism had no goddamned place in the hierarchy.

"A proper exhibition?" Phyllis laughed. "You've all seen him bout, he's taken the Academy title—"

"Nah. Not none of your hillie shite. Here on the sands—"

"Scot ain't never been afeared t'trade sweat with us—"

A gray-robed Menot gripped his staff and rose from amidst the line of elders making up the council. The conclave went still, and Rogan's eyebrow quirked. This should be interesting. As a rule, the Breaker priesthood didn't get involved with mundane matters.

Phyllis's jaw clenched as she bowed her head and ceded the floor to him. She sat beside her son, the old man taking her place on the sands.

He pushed back a wide sleeve and grazed his scarred forearm with a blade, letting the blood fall. A low hum began from the seated Breakers, resonating throughout the stone chamber.

The Menot pounded the butt of his staff into the sand. Once, twice, three times.

Silence.

"I speak the Way."

"We listen," the room intoned, touching between their brows.

"Grimmight, greatest of Menots, warned of a seeping corruption, and it has come to pass. The rot is here. In me. In you—" Phyllis opened her mouth to protest, and he raised his staff, a warrior still. Rogan grunted his approval.

"Would you challenge me, daughter of Herrik? Then face me upon the sands! I fought with your grandfather at Bridgemas. Was there when your father fell holding the wall in Kryton. Held vigil for your mate. Breakers all! Swords of Glynfyls! I look at you and see only the shadow of wings across your vest."

Shamed, she gritted her teeth at the murmurations of the crowd. They'd all know Rogan had bested her and sliced them off, deeming her unfit to call herself a Valkyrie. He didn't care, she wasn't. His attention was on her boy. He sat as if receiving a death sentence. At least the kid wasn't stupid.

"The Way of Honor is the hierarchy, and the hierarchy is the Way!" the Menot cried.

The crowd responded. "It draws us from the darkness, and keeps the rage at bay."

He lowered his staff, grinding its butt into the sand. His eyes met Rogan's. "Will you take up what is yours by right and lead us?"

"No." They could get themselves out of this mess. He wasn't a goddamned babysitter.

"So be it. The Alpha Prime has passed judgement. He returns, but not to House Breakspear, Fellshaft, or Brightarrow. We are unworthy, and will remain so, until we revert to the Way as it was intended; each Breaker's rung ascribed by merit, not accident of birth!"

"So sayeth the Way."

"Hear the council's will! Trials are to commence."

The room exploded into excited whispers, and Rogan chuckled. Nice. They'd just knocked everyone off their rung and were starting from scratch. It was about fucking time.

"But you can't!" Phyllis cried, rising to her feet. "The border—"

"Has been abandoned." A grizzled lord strode into the chamber, a handful of troops behind him, fresh from battle. He came to stand at the edge of the sands, blood on his uniform. "Our biggest threat right now is the goddamned Sons camping out in the Northern Territories. They've hit all of the bigger settlements and outlying towns in the past few hours. Hamlin, Turnbury, they've been razed. We've pulled out of the South and are hunting them down as we return."

Her face was white. "But—"

"I'm tired, Phyllis, and don't like repeating myself. It'll wait for Assembly." He turned from her, touching between his brows and bowing to the Menot. The old man grunted, thumb rubbing against his staff. He struck the sands again, and the room quieted.

"Hear our will! On the matter of Laughlin Scot, the Way is clear, our Alpha determines the pack. The council abstains from ruling until the hierarchy is decided." There was an uneasy murmuring, but the council's will was final.

"And her?"

The Menot turned to a pretty, dark-haired woman near the floor. "If you're referring to Lady Scot, the same applies."

"Then you should strip her of those leathers!"

"As tempting as that suggestion may be," the Menot smirked, "in this the Way is also clear. If you want them, Natalia, you'll have to strip them from her yourself."

There were chuckles, and Rogan grinned. That he'd pay to see, and by the crowd's reaction, he wasn't the only one.

The Menot raised his staff again. "Hear our final will: though not of our line, neither were any of the other Overlords, save the first, yet our forebearers pledged to them all. Shade, Finder, Fetch, Fixer, and Binder alike. Roughly half the council has decided to offer fealty. There are no proscriptions against any of you doing the same." He directed the last at Phyllis, and she bowed her head in acceptance.

But her veiled expression said she sure as hell didn't like it.

CHAPTER TWO

Council [ˈkaŭn(t)-səl] noun

1. *An assembly comprised of the eldest Banes and Menots. Reclusive
   in mundane matters, their collective will trumps that of the Alpha.*

– Excerpt from The Way of Honor

---

*"Throughout our entire history as a people, a single dyad has been recorded.
Its veracity is admittedly difficult to credit, but its role in the founding of
Glynfyls cannot be discounted. The amount of talent required to shift and fix a
single building is prohibitive, never mind the conglomeration we find
ourselves inhabiting today. Interestingly, other bonded dualities have not been
able to achieve the same echelon of ability, begging the question as to if this is
a repeatable phenomenon, or something that was unique to the original Fixer
and Fetch..."*

– Lord Talos, Preceptor of History,
Academy of Glynfyls

KARA LAY in bed with Flynn curled around her back, and Hiss snuggled up to her front. Her fingers idled through the cat's fur. As much as she wanted to, she couldn't sleep, even after that stupid shot. Jon had left muttering to himself about absorption rates and partition coefficients. She had no idea what the geneticist meant, but the drain on her talent was miserable, and what was clamoring around in her head wouldn't let her rest.

"Stop thinking so loud, it's keeping me awake," Flynn murmured behind her ear.

"I can't help it. He's really…" Riegel was dead. Her eyes welled up, and she blinked away tears. It wasn't that she regretted her half-sib's death, not by a long shot, even before he'd succumbed to the bloodlust, he'd been a monster. It was just…ugh! Without being able to use her talent to bind the memories of abuse associated with him, they'd assailed her. Bile rose in her throat—

Glory, she didn't want to think about them.

Couldn't help but think about them.

Flynn's arms tightened around her. "It's over, Kara. He's never gonna hurt you again."

She nodded, he was right, but she was still stuck processing her past trauma until it integrated into her psyche. It was miserable, but kind of status quo since she'd left the Source.

Everything that'd gone down yesterday wasn't. She waffled between which was worse. What had already happened, or what could.

"What are they going to do to us?"

Flynn snorted, rolling onto his back and dragging a hand over his face. "The Assembly? Not a fucking thing. We didn't do anything wrong. The commons have been pissed off forever because the Original Houses treat them like shit. Hell, I'd be ripped if I was in their position, and it's not the first time they've flipped out. When I left, there were massive riots over a bunch of tariffs down at the docks. It got ugly."

She could feel the there was more to it and propped herself up on her elbows to look at him. Hiss stood up and stretched, leaving them to it. Smart cat. "Ugly how?"

"There was a lord…" He bit his lip, bothered by whatever he was about to say. "His House wasn't very powerful, but he was popular with the commons. He tried to advocate for them. I don't remember a lot of the details aside from him ending up dead and this big custody battle over his heir. The commons rioted. Miriam's House was hip deep in that—"

"That's awful. What happened to the heir?"

"I dunno. That's about when I left, but it wasn't anything good. He was the one that Crandall dragged in to Assembly to finger Riegel for all those abducted Talents and the murders. Kid could've been straight outta the Pinch." Flynn face softened at her confusion. "That's Glynfyls's ghetto. No one lives there that doesn't have to, and the people that do sure as hell don't want to."

Kara went to chew her thumb, and he pulled it away from her mouth.

"Hey, I'm not worried about it."

"How can you not be?"

"Look, House Scot has got a hell of a lot more political pull than House McCreedy ever did, and half of the hill has given me their oaths. If I wanted to be a complete dick, I could call my banners and make life really difficult for them."

"Are you going to?"

"Not unless I have no other choice. The timing of this is for shit, but if the Fetches pledge, I'll have the majority vote in Quorum."

Her brow furrowed. "What do you mean, if? They said they wanted to—"

"Fetches are notoriously shifty, and Markham's about as spineless as they come. The commons have him over a barrel now, but until I see something in writing, I dunno. It'll be what it'll be. I'm more concerned about what the Breakers are gonna come back with. If they confirm I split… Christ." He scrubbed his face again.

"Like you said, it'll be what it's going to be, but Phyllis was really mad." More like livid. If looks could kill, they would've been on the floor next to Riegel. Kara put her head on his shoulder, and he kissed her brow. "Although, she protected you after the train attack on the plateau—"

Flynn snorted. "No, she blackmailed me, and I'm ninety-nine percent certain that's because Crandall has something on her." Anger spiked red through their bond, along with a creeping regret. "I shouldn't have thrown that shit about letting Riegel go in his face. My temper—"

"It feels different since the fight."

He raised his hand, flickers of talent playing about his fingers and condensing into a ball of scintillating force. "I sucked at cloaking when my talent came in. It's like, I dunno. Wrapping yourself in mist. This… this is the sun burning it away." The ball dispersed into flickers, sparking onto the fur coverlet. Acrid smoke wafted up. He grimaced and dropped talent, running a hand over the singed spots. "It's like I barely have to pull, and it's just there."

He was a mass of churning emotions, dominated by old hurt. "Tell me."

Flynn sighed. "You've met my line, Kara. I stick out like a sore thumb. Big as a Breaker. Kids are shitty to people who are different. Some of it got really nasty." He chewed his lip. "And now I find out they were right and that bastard Cal knew I was a fucking split all along."

Kara looked into his eyes. The ring of color around his irises churned hypnotically, the rust specks flowing into the copper verdigris seamlessly, belonging there. "No one would know to look at your halos."

"I know," he said miserably.

"Is it really that awful? After all of this, I'm still me, and you're still you."

"Tell that to Glynfyls. Dual-Talents can't hold public office."

"That's stupid."

"There's a lot of that going on up here." He rolled, gazing down at her, and smoothed her hair from her brow. His knuckles dusted over her cheek and he kissed her softly. "Now, what do I have to do to get you to go to sleep?"

Kara quirked an eyebrow, running her fingers through his hair. "I dunno. What are you suggesting?"

He scratched his jaw and shrugged, mischief flickering in his hazel-green eyes. "I hear sex is great for releasing tension."

"Are you serious?" She laughed. "After all that earlier?"

"Mmm. Especially after all that earlier." He kissed the edge of her smile, working from her jaw to the hollow beneath her ear.

She shivered as he tongued the oblong scar his teeth had left at the base of her neck, feeling his satisfaction with it through their bond. Her hand smoothed over his broad shoulders, fingers tracing the subtle network her nails had left over him in turn. Claiming each other. Leaving their marks. His hand cupped her breast, thumb brushing over her nipple. Kara sighed, arching into his touch with a little gasp as he rolled the pebbled peak between his fingers.

"I ever tell you I think it's sexy as fuck when you wear my clothes?" he rumbled, lips trailing down her throat.

"What?" She laughed. The tee she had on was one of the ratty ones he worked out in that French kept trying to throw away. It hung on her like a sack.

"Mmm. It's like I'm all over you." Flynn flipped the covers back. His hand dropped, sliding the tee's hem up her legs, the tip of his tongue darting out to trace the scar on his lip as he exposed her bit by tortuous bit.

Kara's thighs pressed together. Her breath sped then hitched at his arousal coloring their bond. Wanting the same thing he wanted. Needing it. "Please, Flynn…"

"Shhh…this is my favorite part," he rumbled, scooting farther down the mattress, teasing the shirt up over her sensitized flesh until it just grazed her mons. "Open for me, baby…that's it." His head dipped to kiss her inner thigh, nose sweeping the length of her slit. He inhaled with a low groan. "So fucking pretty." His tongue retraced his path, then delved into her honey-sweetened folds, thumbs spreading her wide.

She gasped, fisting his hair as she undulated against him. "Oh Glory, yes…"

"Get naked, baby," he murmured against her heat. "I wanna see you play with your tits while I eat your pussy."

She pulled the tee up over her head and tossed it to the side, hands sliding from her ribcage inward to cup and squeeze, tugging her nipples to tight peaks. Flynn groaned, his lust searing through their bond and stoking hers. The softness of his mouth enveloping her. The rasp of his beard chasing it, then the tug of his lips at her clit. His fingers circled her opening, teasing. Withholding. Passion building, denied, then cresting again—

He pulled his fingers away, and she whimpered. Flynn chucked, the vibration sweet agony. "You want something, baby?" His gaze held hers, the lower half of his face hidden as he lapped along her dripping seam. "Ask me for it."

"Oh, please, Flynn…let me c-come…"

"How?" His tongue flicked out, circling her swollen nub, then sucking it into his mouth.

She moaned, writhing against his face. "On your cock. Oh Glory, please. Stop teasing and give it to me…"

Flynn gave a satisfied growl and shucked off his sweats, the long, hard length of him bobbing. He sat back on his haunches and ran a hand over his girth, thumb sweeping away the beading moisture at its tip to slick over himself. His gaze roamed her body as he slowly worked a hand up and down his cock. "Goddamn, you're beautiful. You want my dick? Come over here and take it."

Kara bit back a smile, her teeth dimpling her bottom lip. She leaned forward to crawl across the bed. Hands on his thighs, she flicked out her tongue, licking over his dewy slit and around his crown as he held his cock for her.

His free hand fisted her hair, pressing his tip to her lips. She opened, and he gave a low moan, his hips pistoning forward, the length of him dragging against her tongue, salt and musk and him suffusing her senses. Talent prickled her skin, gathering in the room. The pleasure he was feeling surging through their bond, her core a throbbing mess, weeping with desire. Her fingers found his sac, caressing and tugging gently. He gave up control as her hand wrapped around his base. He leaned back on his elbows, abs rippling with the rock of his hips.

Kara took him deeper, eyes watering as her throat opened to accept him, reveling in the slide of his cock between her lips. The sporadic bursts of salt flavoring its path. His breath speeding, then hitching as he held it.

His fingers tangled in her hair as her nose met her fingers stroking from his root. "Fuck, that's good…so fucking good…" he murmured, his sac drawing up—

Kara pulled back, smirking at his growl of dismay. "If I can take it so can you…" She licked down his dripping length to tongue his balls.

He groaned again, his cock jumping. "Fuck, Kara, get on my dick."

"Like this?" She climbed his body to straddle his thighs. Her nails teased up the back of his neck, bringing her lips to his. Toothpaste, tobacco, and the taste of her own desire. She licked it from his mouth, and he groaned, grabbing her hips and slicking himself against her core. Tongues dueling, mouths devouring. Talent swept over their skin, thickening.

He reached between them to sweep his crown through her folds. "Yeah, like that. So wet," he murmured, notching himself at her entrance. "Mine."

"Yours."

His face dipped, claiming her lips again as he pressed into her. Her fingers tightened on the back of his neck, gasping at the delicious stretch of him filling her, swallowing his moan as her velvet tightness enveloped him. Feeling complete as he bottomed out deep inside her.

Her, feeling him, feeling her.

She rocked forward, eyes rolling back and closing at the blissful drag of his flesh through hers. Her core tightened around him, fluttering, breath coming fast. His hands caged her hips, fingers dimpling her rear, his movements mirroring hers. Her breasts swayed, glossed with sweat, nipples tender from the rub of his chest. Her halos cast the room in gilded shadows, his tinting them verdigris. Talent pricking at them. Pulling. Wanting…

"Please, Flynn," she whimpered.

"Come for me, baby. Come with me," he panted. His hands skated up her back, settling firmly between her shoulder blades, his mouth on her throat. He thrust into her, hitting that spot so deep inside…

White light burst across Kara's vision, passion tipping, Flynn's bellow twining with her cries. Talent surged around them, filling them to replete. His cock growing impossibly hard as she spasmed around him, pleasure radiating through her, to him, and back again. Feeling their echo. The heat of his release lashing against her inner walls, filing her with his seed. The violent tremors of her abandon slowly subsiding around him.

And reversing. The sensation of satiation fleeting. All that talent that had filled her ebbing like a drain had been pulled...then sucked away as if it'd never been.

Kara's mouth went dry. That wasn't...wasn't right.

Flynn didn't seem to notice. Heartbeat racing, breath still coming fast, he pulled the covers around them and wrapped her in his arms, his lips brushing her temple.

What had just happened?

She lay there, afraid to move. Listening to his breathing even out and deepen. Wishing she could fall asleep as easily. This time it wasn't thinking about the angry mobs or the Assembly. It wasn't the stupid memories of Riegel plaguing her, either.

Kara's stomach twisted and her hand drifted to her abdomen. It was this pregnancy. Channeling all of that talent at the Pony had done something, and whatever it was, terrified her.

She pressed closer to Flynn. His arms tightened around her, and she chewed her thumb, unable to shake an awful sense of foreboding.

WELL, that had been edifying on a multitude of levels.

Otto tucked his softening cock away and wiped a sticky hand down the side of Julia's chair, bookmarking that bit of holo to watch again later. The bots Riegel had infected Kara with before his well-deserved demise were proving more entertaining than he'd anticipated. Unfortunately, as delightful as that interlude was, the rest of what Scot had just revealed was not.

The man was a split.

Otto flicked past the realtime metrics from her and Scot, powering down the plaz tablet's parasitic feed. Titus would interpret the data.

Otto had no patience for the research the man delighted in, and he'd already gotten ever so much more than he'd bargained for.

Laughlin Scot was more than they'd bargained for.

A fucking split, able to pull Breaker and Shade talent equally. That had to be the "other" Barton had sensed from Scot's carnage of slaughtered Sons out on plateau. Otto grimaced, completely disconcerted that Mother hadn't foreseen that wrinkle amongst the possible outcomes.

Unless she was playing a deeper game than even he knew.

It was the more likely of the possibilities. Her plans thus far were flawless. The Sons were busy achieving her goal of expunging every Talent in the Southern Hemisphere, driving the rest north, into the city, and Glynfyls was in chaos. It should guarantee limited resistance when Titus's troops converged to harvest.

But then, Kara should've been on her way to Halja right now, either with Scot in pursuit, or broken and ineffectual. She also should've been the Unmaker to Otto's Maker. Not the Binder to Scot's Breaker.

… She's beyond you, Otto…

He ground his teeth together. Yes, Mother had to have known Scot was a split, but what did she stand to gain from it? The manifestation of his latent talent had the potential to become problematic. If Titus was right and that damned Jester extra already allowed them to share talent, how much easier would it be for them to become a dyad?

Otto snorted, calming himself. No need to chase that unicorn. If that were the case, Marcos and Nora would be equally susceptible, and considering their dual use of talent during their escape from the Source, they'd had ample opportunity to present as such.

Otto tapped his teeth. Still…there was an angle he was missing.

He reached down to fondle the gating stone in his pocket, loathe to use it. A quick meeting of minds should suffice. On the off-chance Mother hadn't foreseen this outcome, he'd be putting himself at enough risk psychically. Giving her access to his person would be suicidal.

He made his way through the dilapidated estate, upstairs to Julia's room. Never strong to begin with, her mind, fractured by years of his less-than-delicate tampering had been shattered by Scot's coup of the

Assembly, and Titus's subsequent threats against her son. Otto supposed that was on him, but it was pathetic, really. Especially considering their little hostage couldn't give a pig's fart about her.

Julia's limp form was as he'd left it, sprawled atop the faded silk coverlet of her sagging bed. All the woman needed was a tattered wedding gown to complete the Dickensian vibe of the manor. He flicked a blanket over her. Wouldn't want the sweet dear to catch cold. The draft from the cracked window pane was several degrees below frigid. The North was such a miserable locale.

His gaze roamed over her insensate form, pausing to appreciate Mother's skill. The last of her directives would be busy taking root. She cultivated minds much like her garden, training them into fantastic shapes against the trellis of her will. Otto preferred to use a hedge trimmer. It was ever so much faster, though admittedly the results had the tendency to be a bit coarse…

No matter. The bloom had faded from this particular rose and it was only a matter of time before it became compost. But then, Mother wasn't going for a bouquet, she was after fertile soil.

Of that there would be plenty.

He put a hand to Julia's forehead and pulled talent, sending out his consciousness along the bind linking her back to Halja, and to Mother.

She was waiting. Or rather, Jane was.

Blue-eyed, blonde, buxom, and beautiful. Otto often wondered if the semblance of her psyche was what she'd looked like pre-Surge, or if it were a construct designed to manipulate. Either way, it was effective.

"Did you miss me? Bit soon for a visit, and you've much to do." She perched upon a garden bench, weaving a garland of flowers. Her cheek dimpled, peeking up at him from beneath a thick fringe of bangs teased by the warm sea breeze.

He sat at her feet, because it was expected, not because he was fooled by her affable demeanor. "He's a split."

Her rosebud lips pursed. "He is."

"You knew."

"I suspected." She laughed. "Cal's always had such a flare for showmanship. When he counters, he does so with panache, and that boy's a peacock of a piece."

Otto was less sanguine. "You sound as if you approve."

"Oh, but I do. Games are never any fun without a worthy opponent. Nor are they enjoyable without ever-increasing stakes."

"And what happens should that peacock prove to have talons?"

Pearly white teeth dented her lip, fingers twisting the garland into a coronet. She smiled at him, holding it up for his inspection. He smiled back despite himself, an odd ache in his chest. Was this what she'd been like before? Jane, as opposed to Mother? The disparity between her personas had always intrigued him. What had incited it?

She set the crown of flowers upon his head, laughing as it dipped to cover an eye. He pushed it up, not caring that he must look a fool. She sighed, gazing out into the distance, her palms sliding together. "Do you believe in unicorns?"

He started, that word usage wasn't a coincidence. Neither was the coronet's abrupt tightening, sharp thorns springing from the greenery to pierce his skull. Tendrils invaded his mind, flipping through it. He juddered against the bench, eyes rolling. Jane smiled beatifically, her thumb brushing a rivulet of blood from his temple.

"I used to, a long, long time ago. Read every book written, heard every tale, and you know what I find fascinating? Almost without exception, that mythical creature skewers every man that approaches." Her lips grazed his brow.

Blackness.

Otto awoke on the floor of Julia's room, her maid, Charlotte, shaking his shoulders.

"Master Otto! Laud! You gave me a fright!"

He sat up, his hands going to his head, the greasy feel of Mother's psyche lingering on his. What had she... He ripped the coverlet off Julia, trembling with the overwhelming urge to bathe. Charlotte wrung her hands, fetching another blanket from the closet to settle over the woman.

"Is there anything—"

"Run a bath. Hot as you can make it."

Eyes wide, her heels clicked down the hall at a run.

Otto turned his attention inward. His Breaker blood guaranteed Mother couldn't make any lasting changes to his mind, but she could influence him short term…ah. There. A blurb of thought, rather like she'd posted a sticky note in his brain.

… Use the feed to muddy the waters in Glynfyls. Then after you've cleaned up, I expect you to attend to your duties with the Sons and facilitate the girl's delivery. Dress warm. XXOO…

Otto snorted, hugs and kisses indeed.

NORA'S EYES FLUTTERED OPEN, wool scratching her chin and a lumpy mattress beneath her. Low voices spoke, Marcos's rumble one of them. Where…?

Across the stark room, he sat at a table with a large man dressed in finery. Marcos's eyes met hers, and he broke off in the middle of what he was saying. He hurried to sit at her bedside, his brow furrowed. She ran her fingers over the ridges to the silvering at his temples, trying to convince herself that this was all real.

He captured her hand in his and brought it to his lips. "There you are. How do you feel?"

"Much better." She shuddered at the memory of their combined talent frying her insides along with the nanobots Titus had infected them with. The effort had almost killed her. Hopefully, this time they'd been expunged. She doubted that she'd survive a second attempt to eradicate them. Her eyes fell on the man at the table. "Where are we?"

"Glynfyls." Marcos glanced over his shoulder. The big man hefted himself from the chair, mopping his brow with a very white cloth as he bowed. "Lord Markham is here to take us to Meddleton."

Nora pushed up to sit, light-headed.

He held out a puffy hand, fingers studded with rings. "No, no rush. I'll give you two a moment."

Her gaze followed him out, then returned to Marcos, feeling his upset through their restored bond. "What is it?"

He stood, retrieving a newspaper and handed it to her. Nora

scanned the front page, her stomach cramping. Kara… She flipped to the next page, a soft cry escaping her lips.

And Riegel.

Marcos put an arm around her. Their son had needed to be put down, but that it had happened this way—

"She'll be infected." Nora twisted her ring, her eyes on the blood at Kara's mouth. Both her and Laughlin if the bots were indeed transmitted sexually…along with God knew how many others. There was no other plausible explanation for Riegel being up here. The last of her intel had him in stasis awaiting culling, and that massive influx of talent the paper described…he'd been fitted with a boost.

She pushed from Marcos's embrace. "We need to get to Meddleton, now."

He grunted, and she smiled, the feel of his upset morphing to action. Glory, to have him back—his lips brushed hers, and he helped her sit at the edge of the bed. She smoothed her grubby sweatshirt, swallowing her nerves as he left her to get the Fetch.

Meddleton. Going back to the palatial estate after all this time… It felt wrong. Nora twisted her ring. No. It felt wrong going there when she was responsible for Deirdre's death, and now that she was bonded to Marcos again… Damn. She'd never thought he'd be part of this, but Albanach—no, Cal, would understand.

Marcos came back with Lord Markham. He was sweating prodigiously. "Very good. Shall we?" His halos flared before they could answer, and colors ran.

They stood in Meddleton's foyer. A wave of sorrow crested over her; the last time she'd been here, Kara was still in diapers, and Deirdre… Nora looked up at the sweeping staircase, remembering how the vivacious woman would skip down, two steps at a time, a wide smile on her face, holding the hand of a little boy—

"Lord Markham, Lady Jester, sir."

A dignified older man with an impossible mustache approached. French. He'd become so dour… She blinked back the burn of guilt at her eyes. "French. Is Cal in his study?"

The butler's lips pursed. "Indeed. I believe you know the way." He turned his back on them, and left.

Lord Markham's jaw dropped at the breach of protocol. Nora swept past him. It was no more than she deserved. She tried to calm her breathing, to measure out her steps. Marcos's confused concern streamed through their bond... Glory, she didn't want to do this...

The door was before her. She raised her hand and knocked.

"Yeah?" Albanach's—*Cal's* voice.

Marcos and Lord Markham were waiting on her. Another deep breath. *Be the ice queen they think you are.* She opened the door and stepped inside.

The room was stuffy, the air striated with smoke, and the tinge of scotch riding beneath it. Cal stood when he saw her. So very handsome in his true guise. Marcos put his hand on her shoulder, and what had been on Cal's face melted away as if it'd never been.

Couldn't be anymore.

He knew, and her heart ached.

Marcos's fingers tightened on her shoulder.

"Master Scot." Lord Markham made his way forward with a rolling gait to shake Cal's hand. "I must apologize for the delay. I'm afraid Fitzpatrick isn't at his best with all the to do."

Cal's gaze slid from Nora to the lord. "No harm done. Important thing is she's here. Appreciate you stepping in to take up the slack."

"It was my pleasure. Ah, I'll leave you to it, then." He bowed and shifted out.

The crackling of the fire in the hearth was very loud. Nora went to stand in front of it, warming her hands. Marcos followed, taking a seat in one of the plush leather chairs. Everything was exactly like she'd remembered it, even Cal, frozen in time. Deirdre's voice and a little boy's laughing reply ghosted past the doorway. Laughlin. What was she going to say to him?

The silence stretched.

"Well, since she's not going to, I suspect I'll introduce myself. Caliban Scot." He came over and extended a hand to Marcos.

"Com—ah, Marcos."

Nora watched him stand from the corner of her eye. They shook, looking to be of an age with maybe half a head difference between them, but Marcos was twice as broad.

He was also wary. "You want to tell me how you know Nora?"

"I brokered a marriage contract with her between Kara and my grandson, Flynn," Cal said smoothly. Man had a gift for telling you everything and nothing at all. He was going to leave that to her. Nora's fingers swept across her damp cheek, not knowing whether to bless or curse him for that.

She turned to them. "I'm sorry, I'm not at my best. That healing took quite a bit out of me. Could I trouble you for something to eat?"

"Healing—of course. I'm surprised French isn't in here with something already." Cal went to his desk, and Nora leaned against Marcos, not surprised in the least.

"What aren't you telling me?" he murmured into her hair.

She shook her head. "Later, please."

He frowned as she settled onto the settee, her mind shying away from doing far more upon it. The look Cal gave her when he came back over said he wasn't shying away from anything. Damn the man. He flopped down into the other chair with a grin.

"French'll be up with something in a few. What the hell took you so long?"

The two of them took turns recounting their flight from the Source. The tunnels, discovering the bots, then being hunted by Peacekeepers. Nora had a dim recollection of being ill in the garage safe-house, but not of being shifted north, or of the Binder.

"He had a barcode?"

"He did," Marcos said taking a sip of the coffee that'd been delivered. "You know anything about that?"

Cal shrugged. "Most of the Source Talents up here are culls, and even that's not easy to do. They run a tight ship down there." Nora watched him from beneath her lashes. He knew exactly who that Binder was. Why didn't he want to disclose? Man was infuriating with his secrets.

"When can I see Kara?" she asked.

He exhaled a long stream of smoke, rolling the cigar in his fingers. "She's upstairs with Flynn. You certain they've been exposed to this tech?"

"If you knew Titus, there wouldn't be any question." Marcos growled.

Cal glanced at her. "Boy's not gonna be in the most receptive mood."

Nora felt ill. Of course he wouldn't be. Not after what she'd done—

"Pardon the interruption, Master Scot," French stood in the doorway, eyes alight. "A runner has just arrived from the Assembly. The commons breached chambers and ah, presented their concerns. As a result, they've been cleared to pledge, and the charges of incitement have been dropped."

Cal fell back in his chair. "I'll be damned…"

"Indeed, sir. A flurry of related paperwork has been arriving. Shall I have it brought here?" Cal grunted a yes, raking back his thick white hair.

"I'm assuming that's a good thing?" Marcos asked when the butler had left.

"It's six of one, now we need a half-dozen of the other." Cal got up and poured himself a glass of scotch. "Those bots need to be dealt with, but Flynn…if I cloak the two of you, can you scan him for the damned things?"

"Yes." Nora worried her ring. "That would also allow us to study them a bit more and adjust the weave. The one we used almost killed me. I wouldn't dare use it on Kara, especially if she's bred."

Cal threw back his scotch and grimaced. "She is at that. Give me ten. When you've got it figured out, turn the handle on your teacup to the fireplace." His halos flared a vibrant green, cloaking them, and he left the room.

"It's later, Nora."

She winced. Of course it was. "Cal and I meant something to each other once. His daughter-in-law's death changed that…changed a lot of things. I—I'd rather not talk about it. We need to figure out this weave."

Marcos's lips pursed. He'd give her a reprieve, but that's all it would be, and it wasn't going to last long. It'd be so much easier if she could just—no. Cal's secrets weren't hers to tell. She'd have to figure a way to skirt around him influencing the Northern Territories and the Corporation between his two personas, and in the meantime…

She had to face Laughlin.

Nora's mouth went dry. She'd played this out a thousand times, and even in her imagination, it'd never gone well. Marcos moved to the couch and took her hand.

"You all right?"

She forced a smile, and he could feel the lie.

Both her loves and a man who'd want her dead all under the same roof. How was she going to do this?

SOMEONE WAS POUNDING on the bedroom door.

Flynn tightened his arms around Kara, groaning. Christ, they'd just gotten to sleep.

"Who—" She went to lift her head, and he held her closer.

"Ignore it."

The pounding became more insistent, then Cal swore and flung the door open. The lights flipped on. Flynn pulled a pillow over his head. Motherf—

"Jesus H. Christ! Do you have any idea what just happened?"

His temper spiked, and he pushed up on an elbow to glare at the old man. "No, but I've got a pretty good idea what's gonna if you don't get the—"

"They dropped the charges and commons are free to pledge."

"What?" Flynn laughed. "Are you kidding me?"

"Not in the goddamned slightest. They managed to break down the damned doors and more or less held a knife to the Assembly's throat. Stacks of oaths are coming in. People have started giving them by proxy."

"How the hell does that work?"

Cal shrugged. "On the hill, the theory is that the head takes the pledge of everyone in his House, then he pledges them to the First of his line, who passes all of them on to you. Works the same way in the commons, but think the chain is more building, street, neighborhood, spoke before it gets to whoever's handing them off to you. Regardless, all of them are tributaries feeding into the main line."

Flynn stared at him. The city had lost its collective mind. "But I split—"

"Hearsay and supposition. You're gonna ride this horse until it drops. Both of you get dressed, it ain't all sunshine. I want you in my office in twenty." The old man left, and Flynn sat there in shock. Kara ran a hand down his back, and he kissed her temple, brow furrowing as he increased the talent he was pushing her.

That damn debilitation was back in spades. He didn't understand how it was getting worse after they'd been together and Jon had given her a shot. Both usually supercharged her. Instead, he could feel it gnawing at her through their bond, her cheeks sunken and dark circles shadowing her eyes.

"Whatever he wants, I'll take care of it. Get some more rest." Flynn frowned at her nod, her lack of argument more troubling than all the rest of it.

He didn't want to, but he made it to Cal's office in thirty and grabbed a coffee from the spread French had set out. Flynn eyed the assortment of appetizers. "You expecting people?"

"That I am. I suggest you mind your manners when they show up. They're my guests, and you'll treat them accordingly."

Flynn's eyebrow cocked. Cal's voice had that same timbre to it as when Lot was involved. Great. He didn't bother waiting for the old man to disclose who the hell it was. By the set of his jaw, he wasn't talking. Flynn sighed and pulled a stack of oaths onto his lap. Cal hadn't been joking, there were piles of the damned things. He needed to get a stamp.

"Fetches will be here in a few hours to bleed on you. Kara coming?"

"No. She's—Jon's shot isn't keeping up with what she needs. You need to get him back here." Flynn bit the scar on his lip. "There wasn't anything in those—"

"I'll look again, but I don't think so. Might be one more place I can try."

"You need to do it sooner than not. Last night took a lot out of her." Too much, but if she hadn't pulled like that, they'd all be dead. Christ, he couldn't wrap his head around how she'd—they'd—channeled so much. They both should've burned out.

"You don't say. I thought I told you to be circumspect."

Flynn scowled at him. "You also told me to use whatever it was on the plateau to get this shit done."

Cal exhaled a long stream of smoke, raking back his hair. "Yeah, but I didn't mean for you to piss off the planet in the process."

"Then you should've been more specific."

"Duly noted." His eyes flicked to the sitting area. "Do me a favor and keep your pants on for this."

"Keep—what?"

A Binder's weave settled over him, followed by a burst of Breaker talent that doubled him over. "What the fuck?!" he panted up at Cal. Felt like he'd stuck a fork in a light socket.

"Titus infected Riegel with some kind of tech, and he passed it on to you. We think it's for surveillance, but I doubt that's all. That should get you clear of it."

Flynn pushed himself upright, not surprised about the tech, but—"We?"

"Mind yourself, boy." Cal's halo's flared, and Nora fucking Jester was sitting on the couch next to the Commandant.

Flynn's hand went to where his sidearm used to ride before he could stop himself, and the man's eyes narrowed. Fuck! Flynn gripped the arm of his chair, wood crackling beneath his fingers, feeling Kara's alarm, anger suffusing him with strength—

"Laughlin," Cal's voice warned. "They're my guests."

He growled. Guests. That fucking bitch had murdered his mother.

A whisper of 'lust hit his nose, and his eyes shot to the Commandant, something in him rising up to meet it. Man's nostrils flared and his lip curled as he put himself between Flynn and that woman.

The whisper tinged to an "I'm going to put you in the ground" flavor.

Flynn stood, slamming his chair backwards. *Bring it, asshole.*

"Well, if it isn't Kendall's right hand," the Commandant drawled. "The one he jerks off with, if I'm not mistaken."

"It was a short-lived romance."

"Not as short as I'd assumed."

"How do you two know each other?" Cal asked, way too interested.

"Diytan. Banoi Crater, to be exact," the Commandant growled. "Always wondered how Kendall managed to get his unit out when three companies of Breakers couldn't. You want to shed some light on that?"

Flynn shrugged. "I wasn't with them."

"That's not what I asked."

"That's still my answer." They'd squared up toe-to-toe, the air thick with 'lust. Flynn cracked his neck and grinned, hoping this time the fuck would hit him. "God, this is just like déjà vu all over again. How'd it go next? Oh, yeah."

He blew him a kiss.

The Commandant's fist came at him, and Flynn shouldered under it—

"Marcos!"

Golden light flared at them, and Flynn threw up a shield, deflecting it. He slammed into the Breaker. The Commandant staggered, Flynn's uppercut snapping his head back and sending him reeling. He caught his balance on a side table and grabbed it, swinging it like a bludgeon.

Talent crackled across Flynn's skin, flicking off him and pock-marking where it hit. The table splintered into a cloud before it finished its arc. The Commandant returned a blast, and Flynn phazed it into nothingness.

His right fist crunched into the Breaker's nose, the left driving the air from his gut. The Commandant clipped him in the side of the head, and Flynn's rage redoubled, strength pouring into him, talent sparking. He hauled back and hit the man with a wicked cross, laying him out on the carpet—

Shit! What was he—that influx of power drained away, leaving Flynn light-headed. He wavered. Chest heaving, he stepped back.

Dropped his shield. Nora waded through the cloud of settling debris to the Commandant sprawled across the carpet.

Fuck.

The place was trashed. Furniture blasted apart like it'd been hit with bird-shot. Black smoke curled up from the carpet, a wide, charred circle beneath Flynn's feet. He laughed, running a hand over his beard. Jesus fucking…

The Commandant dragged himself to sit, slumping against the wall. He shook his head as if to clear it. Nora pulled talent, setting his nose, but it was a half-assed job. The man was bruised up like a raccoon. "Well, that was unexpected," he muttered.

"Nora?"

Kara stood in the doorway, looking like hell, eyes wide as she took in the destruction. Cal swore and halos flared. She crumpled to the ground, retching violently.

Flynn was at her side, pulling her into his arms when her vomiting subsided. "The fuck did you do to her?!"

"We could ask you the same thing, she looks half dead," the Commandant growled.

Flynn's lip curled as he fought the urge to lunge at the man.

Nora ignored his glower. She put a hand on Kara and pulled talent, her furrowed brow breaking through Flynn's anger. He swallowed past the lump in his throat, his fingers tightening. God, Kara—the baby—

Nora glanced up. "They're fine, Laughlin, but she shouldn't be out of bed."

Kara's hand caressed his cheek and a choked sob burst past his lips, followed by anger. God, it was too fucking close…

Nora turned to Cal. "What protocol do you have her on?"

"Something Jon cooked up, but I'm sure he'd appreciate your input." He raised an eyebrow at Flynn.

Fucking Cal. This bitch was who he'd been talking about? Goddamn it.

Kara nestled closer. Jesus, she seemed even frailer than when he'd left her… What had that been, not even an hour ago?

"What was that?" she asked.

"A weave of my talent and Marcos's…" Nora started blabbering. Flynn tuned out, his temper spiking at her dissertation. Fuck, he wanted to hit something.

Someone.

The Commandant met his eye, but there wasn't a challenge there. Whatever it was, Flynn liked it a hell of a lot less. He riffled his hair and cleared a spot on the couch to get Kara settled, then snagged one of Cal's big black cigars, not wanting to listen to whatever the poisonous bitch was spewing.

"Mind yourself, boy," his grandfather said, grabbing one for himself.

"I don't want that fucking woman in my house," he said, not giving a shit if she heard him. This building anger… Christ, he hadn't felt this pent up since he was fifteen.

Cal pursed his lips, looking at the smoking ruin in the middle of his office. "Give me some time to sort them."

"Tomorrow, they're gone." Just knowing she was here set his teeth on edge, and she kept fucking talking—

"…We think Titus has your biometrics and holo of anything you experienced between that fight and a minute ago.…"

Kara went pale, and Flynn's knuckles cracked. "Biometrics?"

Titus knew about the baby.

"I'm afraid so."

"Did you say holo?" Kara rasped, her face too pale to be healthy.

"Yes," her mother confirmed with a look of distaste.

The floor around Flynn's boots started smoking. That motherfucker had a holo of them in bed. Of Kara—"Are they gone?" he growled, fighting not to incinerate Cal's study.

Nora twisted her ring. "Tentatively, yes. Before, the bots always came back within minutes. We've been clear for days, but we don't know enough about them to be certain."

Flynn picked Kara up and she buried her face against his neck, weeping. Christ, she was a mess. He wasn't much better. "Then go see Jesse and get certain," he spat, leaving.

They met French in the hall. "Take all those goddamned pledges upstairs, and let me know when that bitch is gone. I don't wanna see her again."

The butler nodded, and Flynn stormed past, Kara's hurt flooding their bond. Goddamn it.

"I can't, Kara. Not here." The words choked him, and he tried to hang onto his anger.

What was beneath it scared the shit out of him.

CHAPTER THREE

redress [ri-ˈdres] verb

1. *Equitable restitution required after a board member's actions are deemed damaging to another, most commonly taken as a monetary payment.*

– Ethics Clause 18c., Concerning Conduct, Corporation Charter

---

"The Sons see themselves as the Mother's chosen. Differing from other cults, she is not revered as a divinity, though she does inspire a similar zealotry amongst her followers. Instead of worship, their fervor is focused on eradicating Talents in the hopes of reversing the Surge. The culmination of this delusional ideology espouses a Judgement Day and the coming of a Messiah who will lead them in the final battle. Interestingly, they refer to this as Isenben, an event also prevalent in Breaker lore..."

– Lord Talos, Preceptor of History,
Academy of Glynfyls

"WELL, THAT COULD'VE GONE BETTER," Cal said, lighting his cigar. He pulled the good scotch from his bottom drawer and poured himself a glass, then offered one to Marcos and Nora.

They looked at him like he was crazy. He shrugged and took a seat. The two of them started in with that hushed discord thing couples did when they were fighting in public. Couldn't say he missed that. French came in with a small army of servants and began cleaning up the mess. Cal chewed his cigar, watching them shift away ruined furniture. He was pissed about the carpet, they didn't make them like that anymore—

Nora huffed and sat on the couch with a cup of tea. Well, that'd be the end of whatever they'd been snarling about. He looked at Marcos. "So…tell me about Banoi."

The Commandant glanced at her, then came over to pull out the chair Flynn hadn't turned to kindling. Cal offered him the scotch, and this time, he took a glass.

"He was at negotiations for Khi-gon's withdrawal as Kendall's second," the Commandant said staring into his glass. "That mercenary outfit specializes in antagonizing the Source, and are damned good at it."

Cal knew exactly who they were. For the past several years, half the legal shit the Corporation was embroiled in stemmed from ops Kendall been involved with. That span Flynn was so mum about fit the beginning of the trend a bit too neatly.

"I thought we had them dead to rights in that crater. Kendall looked like he was going to fold, then he hit our line. I sent in three companies to put them down, and the damned volcano erupted. Should've been the end of them, but then they turned up in Hexspar. Kendall's second was a woman that time. Figured the man I'd met in Diytan was dead."

Cal grinned around his cigar, what a story that had to be…

"Something amusing?" Marcos glowered.

"Hmm, no. Flynn's just got a penchant for being difficult. Nice to see I'm not the only one it frustrates the hell out of."

"If he hadn't just bested me, I'd say he's flat-out insubordinate."

Cal grinned again. Boy definitely had his moments, and that'd been one of the finer ones.

"He was also more on edge than the situation warranted. Talent cracking like that, man's a loaded gun. Either of you want to clue me in?"

Nora tensed. How much had she told him? Cal didn't think his alternate ego or their relationship had been part of it, but the rest... "Between you, me, and the lamppost, the boy split last night. Doesn't have a handle on it yet."

"That actually happens?" Marcos snorted. "Well, he better get a handle on it, and fast. Forget about Banoi, just now he was holding enough talent to blow a sizable crater here. Breakers can't pull like that without a hell of a lot of emotion behind it."

"I'm responsible for his mother's death," Nora said, her eyes downcast.

Cal winced. God, how many times did they have to hash this out? "Nora—"

"I took Deirdre from the tower, and she died because of it." Her breath hitched before regaining control of herself.

Marcos's brow wrinkled, probably trying to wrap his head around the significance of that. Cal doubted he could. The way they'd partitioned families and relationships down there—

"I'm assuming they were close," the Commandant asked.

"Boy thought the sun rose with that woman's smile." Christ, they all had. Deirdre was something special.

The Commandant grunted, his eyes finding Nora's. Something passed between them, and she shook her head. He frowned again and threw back what was in his glass.

Deirdre's name had cast a pall over the room. The servants had mourned her passing as much as any Scot. Couldn't imagine Nora's admission was gonna win her any favors there. Cal raised his scotch along with his gaze and met French's.

Case in point. The chill in the butler's voice proved out that assumption. "Mistress Glass has some availability tomorrow evening to assess your guests' wardrobe needs, sir. Shall I instruct her to meet them at the flat in the city, whilst I see to other arrangements?"

"That would probably be best, and I need Jon back here pronto." Marcos was right, Kara had looked like shit. Sooner they sussed that out the better, preferably without getting the Breakers any more involved in this than they already were. Calling a Bane for help… Cal was about as eager to do that as he was to make another call to Orin.

The last one had cost him a hell of a lot more than three month's salary, but it was time to make the tech director an offer he couldn't refuse. Those bots stank of Source engineering which meant that bedazzled shit was in bed with Titus. Cal needed to nip that unlikely romance in the bud, fast.

French bowed and the servants exited the room. It was as clean as it was gonna get until a carpenter could be called in. Boy had fried the damned floorboards. God help him if this went anything like Rogan's talent coming in. Half the estate would be in flames by breakfast. Cal pursed his lips, turning back to Nora and Marcos.

"Flynn's suggestion you meet with the Engineering Guild's proctor was a good one. I'm sure Jesse would love to grill you on any number of things, and if those bots are as infectious as I suspect, we're gonna need a way to mitigate them, fast."

Nora fiddled with her signet. "I may have an idea. When I was here last, that gate we used to get into the city. If a weave could be bound to the entrance…"

Cal nodded, not for the first time appreciating how her mind worked. It was gonna be good to make use of it again, even if the rest of her was off limits. That ship had sailed. Wouldn't be the first, or the last, but it had been a damned fine ride. He chewed his cigar, trying not to glower at Marcos.

"Suggest you hop to it then. I'll set up a meeting with Jesse for tomorrow."

Nora forced a smile, and they left the room. Cal drummed his fingers on his desk, his mind going back to Kara. What the hell had Titus bred into his females? Cal pulled a plaz tablet from his desk, reviewing the records on the Source's server. There wasn't anything that didn't look standard, but he supposed that didn't mean much. Nora'd know more. She'd had rounds at the Laborium where the females were sequestered while they gestated.

Cal refilled his scotch and took a long drag of his cigar. He went to throw the tablet back in the drawer, and that chip Flynn had found in the plaz converter Leo had been so hot to get his hands on caught his eye. Probably dirt on somebody. Cal pulled it out. He could use the distraction.

He popped it into the port, and a stream of data populated the screen. What the hell…?

He wasn't even a quarter of the way through it when Rogan came in. Cal slid the tablet back in the drawer, willing his hands not to shake.

The Breaker cocked an eyebrow at the singed floor and lack of furniture, and snagged the scotch. "Glad whoever tried to kill you missed the minibar."

"I was just a bystander this time."

"I'm guessing you left 'innocent' out of that intentionally."

Cal snorted. "More of an oversight. Flynn and the Commandant got into it."

"That the sour prick out in the foyer?"

"That'd be him. Boy kicked his ass."

"Upper cut?"

"Cross."

Rogan pulled over a mildly singed chair and grunted at the floor. "We got bigger problems than the kid freebasing testosterone. Breakers are holding trials."

Cal choked on his scotch. "Starting when?"

"About an hour ago. Good news is, until they have an Alpha, they're keeping mum about last night. Bad news is, until they're done establishing the hierarchy, not one of them is gonna be manning those walls, and they've pulled out from the border. Sons razed Hamlin and every other town big enough to have a postal code. They're mopping them up on the way back, but you better pray to God the Source stays put in the meantime."

"Damn it." Cal's stomach clenched, the rest of the bullshit that'd been going on falling into perspective. That chip had enough on it to keep Titus leashed, but Jane and those damned Sons of hers were an entirely different story.

This Dual-Talent shit needed to be dealt with so Flynn could be invested as Overlord, ASAP. If the Sons were hitting them that hard, she was making her move.

"Interesting weave they put on the gate," Rogan said, clueless as to the implications. Cal schooled his face. It needed to stay that way. "Haven't seen anything like it for quite some time."

He grunted around his cigar. "Titus managed to infiltrate the city with some nasty tech they were on the receiving end of. Need you to escort them to the Engineering Guild tomorrow. Proctor there's about a dozen shades past brilliant. If anyone can figure out what we're dealing with, it's her."

Rogan took a sip of his scotch and sucked air in through his teeth. "When I agreed to this—"

"Yeah, yeah. Drink your drink. Pretty sure the pig shit's on its way."

OTTO STOOD amidst the smoking ruins of what had once been a prosperous town, the air tinged with the piquant tang of charred flesh. It did little to rouse his appetite, but went a long way towards sating his darker predilections.

His gaze tripped over the abundance of blackened corpses smoldering where a church had once stood. So much for their faith. No longer discernible as male or female, the crisped mass of each form was the only rough indication of age. Sons hooted and yelled throughout the frost-blasted landscape. The icy drifts at the edges of town bled pink toward the trees, trunks slapped red as they passed. Hunting those that had escaped. They'd live long enough to regret that. The madness of the attack passed, the ones caught now would be toyed with. A smile jagged across his lips. As Mother's messenger, he'd have first pick of those.

Victor approached. A squat man with an impressive mohawk, he spat a stream of chew to the side and sucked on his lower lip, the bulge tucked behind it distorting his already unappealing visage.

"Them freaks is comin' up from the south. Nixed the men we left a couple of towns back."

Otto frowned, but Mother had been firm with her instructions. "Then we need to move. Assemble everyone." The man sent out a piercing whistle, and Sons began to congregate on what was left of the town's green, trampled black by the thick soles of their ash-stained boots.

They encircled Otto, packing in tight. He activated the stone in his pocket, gating them dozens of miles south, behind Glynfyls's advancing troops. The other chapters had similar means for the short term.

He separated himself from the scrum to inspect the little device as they dispersed, setting up camp. Its pearlescent exterior had dulled to a chalky grey. The pebbles were sad copies of the great gates studding Glynfyls. Although inconvenient, it gave him a certain satisfaction that even after being bound for a millennium, Mother was unable to harness the full extent of the original Fixer's talent. Without it, the weaves eroded and the stones disintegrated into nothingness. At most, he could expect the one in his palm to gate him elsewhere once, perhaps twice more. It taking him all the way back to Halja? That was out of the question.

He chuckled. How unfortunate that he'd be unable to attend to Mother in person. Returning to the Source held no savor for him either. He had little patience for troop placement and legalities, and until Barton delivered Kara, the refresher Titus had been given last night was more than adequate for him to maintain status quo.

Which left Glynfyls, and Otto, to his own devices.

His lips pursed to whistle, looking over the assembled men. Business before pleasure. More chapters had arrived. Plenty of options to choose from…

He'd previously fiddled with several of the captains' psyches, but Victor's vendetta against Scot, the man he knew as Wolf, lent itself to the mindset Mother required. Otto chuckled to himself. If nothing else, Scot's past was rife with things to exploit. And, after he'd massacred a handful of Victor's chapter and humiliated the rest at the Cross and Pinion, the captain's ire was fresh. His squalid little form wasn't exactly a deterrent either. Otto grinned. Mother was just going to delight in tempting that. He rubbed his icy hands together, eager to be done.

Victor was issuing orders to his rabble around a campfire they'd set up, this one devoid of bodies. For the moment, at least. By the screams from the bracken, it wouldn't remain that way for long. He lured the man away from the others and placed a hand upon his leather-clad shoulder, lacing tendrils of talent through his psyche. Like every Son, a small thread bound the man back to Halja. Otto expanded it, strengthening Victor's zealotry. She would do the rest.

"You are the Mother's chosen. She comes, be prepared."

Victor's eyes took on a fevered light. He grunted, pulling his knife to finger the blade, its ricasso caked with gore. "How long?"

"Soon."

"And Wolf and his woman?"

"All yours when we breach the city." Otto stepped back at the man's satisfaction, caressing the stone in his pocket, and gating away.

He appeared in the shadowed foyer of Julia's estate, the scritching sound of her pen clawing from the study. She'd be writing up a rather incriminating dossier. Otto ghosted to the doors.

His appearance elicited no response, not that he expected it to. The damage to her psyche had left her little more than a shell, functioning solely on directives. Her pen stilled, having completed the first of them. She stared blankly ahead as he slid the pages from her blotter.

Marvelous.

An accusation from an Original House that Scot knew of his dual-status guaranteed his incarceration. That in turn would force Kara into the open, allowing Barton to grab her without dealing with the damnable man.

Otto brushed his thick fingers over Julia's temple, shivering at the crystalline structures of thought Mother had erected. They bound the few remaining fragments of the woman's persona to her will. He modified one of the directives, and Julia went rigid. Perhaps he should have spent more time, but patience had never been one of his virtues.

"Easy, my darling. You've already been through so much keeping such a damning secret. That's it. Off to the constabulary with you. Pity it had to come to this…"

He stood back, watching her bustle about the room, gathering everything into a folio, and taking the cube he'd loaded with a snippet of the feed he'd watched earlier. She called for Charlotte, and the maid met her in the foyer, glancing at him. Otto nodded in response. She knew what he required of her.

Charlotte bobbed a curtsey and led her mistress through the gate.

Otto took Julia's seat at the desk and put his feet up, claiming the untouched bowl of stew at its corner. Shame to waste it. Intrigue always gave him an appetite.

FITZ CRACKED A GUMMY EYE, then slammed it shut.

Too bright.

He ran his felty tongue over his teeth and threw out an arm, searching for a bottle. His fingers found a glass beaded with moisture and two small round tabs at its side.

Shite.

He blew out a breath foul enough to melt paint, squinting through slitted lids. Sunlight glinted off a chandelier, throwing rainbows across orange, silk-papered walls. Christ, the fuckin' auras in this place… He battened down his sight quick, head throbbing with the effort, and cracked an eye again.

Markham sat at his big oak desk on the other side of his study, watching him over the top of his paper.

Double shite.

"Ah, Fitzpatrick, you're awake."

"S'Fitz," he muttered, pushing up to sit on the brocade couch. He steadied hisself, elbows on his knees, and hung his head, the room spinning. Design on the Persian carpet always made it worse. Aside from the smell, if he puked on it, nobody'd notice. He swept up the aspirin and chewed them, eyeing the water. "Ain't ye got naught stronger?"

Markham snapped his paper closed.

That hurt.

"Finish what's in that glass, and I'll see what I can do."

Fitz picked it up, water sloshing. Blighting shakes. He put it back down. "Rather not."

His uncle frowned at him, then looked to the study door as it opened. A servant came in with a tray and set it on the low table in front of Fitz. He dug in. They had a routine. Food, and as soon as the servant left, Markham would start harping on the error of his ways. Fitz didn't rush eating. That usually took a while.

The door clicked shut.

"I was hoping that you'd be an adult about this. To get yourself into such a state, and with all that's going on! You can't just disappear like that, people worry about you—"

Fitz snorted. That were a new one. "Eh…job come up."

"So I heard. Your cousin, Grantham, asked for my assistance. I delivered the Jesters to Meddleton earlier, since you were unavailable to finish it."

Nark. Fitz shrugged and kept eating. Were good. Pasta with cheese.

Markham blotted his brow. "Now the sisters want a word with you about it."

A full body shiver went through him, and he belched bile.

"For God's sake, what were you thinking, crossing the border to pick up Talents for Caliban Scot, and then just leaving them with Pithy?"

"Were thinking that me rent's due, and now I'm thinking I'll take that drink."

"Water first."

"Ain't boiled."

Markham made an exasperated squeak. "You know very well that up here it doesn't need to be—"

The door flung open, and Bernice strode in. "Do you have him?"

Fitz shifted.

The chill of his tenement struck him hard after the warmth of his uncle's study. Someone had been there. He relaxed his sight, energy popping back into view as he slid down the rough plaster wall, slapping the door to the hall shut. Goddamned Prydees. They'd gone through his things. His maps was in disarray and a bottle of ink tipped over, ruining what'd been on his board and dripping to the floor. More were splattered across the walls.

Why couldn't they leave him be?

A loud roar went up outside; the crowd's cries for blood changed to a merrier sort. He scrubbed at his curls. Goddamn 'em all.

"...*if I don't speak up for them, lad, who will?*"

Fat lot of good that'd done, and now his da weren't speaking, period.

"Fitz?"

He wiped an arm across his face. "Ya."

Adelaide came into the room, long blonde hair swishing across her backside. His sight showed a rosy glow surrounding her lithe form. Too fuckin' rosy. She pulled a fifth from her market basket and handed it to him, then started righting the mess. "Were hoping to have this tidied before ye turned up."

He rolled the bottle of rum between his hands. "Ye here for it?"

"Nah." She glanced over her shoulder at him, the bruise around her eye faded to green. "Ye okay? Missed ye last night. Were cold."

Were always cold. He leaned his head against the wall. "Right as rain."

"Rent's due."

"Tis." He cracked the bottle and took a pull, watching her bustle around.

"Pony's looking for girls again, but I don't fancy giving half me wages t'that shite Gerrard. Though hear tell he took a bath with the fight. Think that lord, Patton's taking over. Ain't nobody thought that chit would win."

Fitz fingered the coin in his pocket. That weren't entirely true. Too bad it were already spent. "Ye'd get a room, and he'd feed ye. S'better than what the 'Tail were offering. Either'd have a man at the door."

She capped what was left of his ink. "I thought...maybe..."

Blight it. He didn't want to do this right now. Again. At all. "I told ye, love—"

"Ye did." She smiled and came to sit beside him. He offered her the pint, and she took a swallow, then passed it back. Her fingers teased the curls from his face, tracing a sideburn to its tapered point, mid-cheek. Her lips followed, flickers of red and gold spinning through her aura. He closed his eyes, head against the wall. Shite.

"Just been nice, havin' only one man for a spell."

Fitz moved her hand from his crotch. "Ain't in neither of us to keep it that way. I'm spent, love, leave it."

"That where ye was last night?" Her eyes was at the love bite on his neck.

He stood, going over to his board and unpinning the ruined paper. Fuckers. He balled it up, feeling her glare. "Part of it. Markham picked me up."

"Were it Kendra?"

"Do it matter?"

"Way she lords it over me every time ye spread her fat thighs, it do."

"Weren't Kendra." His stomach knotted, and he ran a hand over his mouth.

"What did Markham want?"

"Ain't important. Ye get anything t'eat?" He went to root around in her basket and pulled out a roll just shy of concrete. Fitz tapped it on the table, thinking of the bowl of pasta he'd left. Goddamn Bernice and every other Prydee to ever darken the earth.

More cheers went up outside. He crossed to the grimy window and pushed aside the shade. Looked like a party down there. "What's this about?"

Adelaide came to stand at his side. "Them's on the hill is letting us pledge." She held up a slim hand, a shallow cut grazed across her palm. It shimmered, the faintest line of energy streaming from it into the distance. "Council cleared us Breakers early this morn. They been setting up proxies by spoke. Ye gonna do it?"

Fitz pulled at the patch of beard beneath his lip. "Hadn't thought about it."

"Marl'll tan yer hide if ye don't."

He grunted. And the Prydees would skin it from him if he did. Her aura pulsed around him, arms twining about his neck. She'd gone gaunt since she'd been out of work, eyes enormous, and the way she looked at him—

"I'm cold. Ye want t'go t'bed?"

He pushed away from her, his voice rough. "Told ye I'm spent. Were at the Dove."

"Ye saw Sarah! But ye said—"

"I lied. Now I gotta see about rent." He grabbed his heavy jacket, not shifting out quick enough to miss the angry hurt on her face.

But it were better than seeing it blue after she'd been floating in the bay.

KARA TREMBLED in Flynn's arms. The thought of the Source watching her again, watching them, made her physically ill. Her stomach clenched, but there was nothing to come up. Ugh, she felt so dirty knowing those things had been inside her, that people had been leering over her and Flynn's most intimate moments…

He hugged her to him, his rage battering through their bond in waves. She bathed herself in it, letting his anger scour away everything in its path. His temper had been so raw since the fight…

"I'm gonna kill them, Kara. I'm gonna wipe the entire fucking Corporation off the face of the earth." His cold certainty sent an icy prickle through her. "As long as they exist, us, our kids, we're all in danger, and I'll be damned if it stays that way."

"Is that why you and the Commandant were fighting?"

He sighed, nose in her hair. "No. That's—I don't know what that is. I mean, I ran into him down south on my last op with Kendall. Him being here…it complicates things."

Kara frowned. Flynn had told her a little bit about his time in the Deep South, but like most of his past, he didn't like to talk about it. His anger fading to dread gave her the feeling that Marcos "complicating things" translated to him knowing something that would get Flynn in trouble.

"What did you do?"

He tensed. "What makes you think I did anything?"

"Call it feminine intuition."

"I—" He gave a frustrated growl. "Long story short, I dumped a shit ton of plaz into an active fissure. It went downhill from there."

Wait—"You're talking about Banoi." Kara laughed. The fervor that failed military operation had caused at the Source, all the international delegations, the meetings Albanach had been subjected to... "The volcano. You did that?"

"It—It was gonna happen anyways, I just kind of helped it along. Look, I didn't have a whole lot of options. If they'd gotten control of that mine full of iridium—whatever, it's not important. What is, is that the Commandant can finger me as being there. Shit, Kara, anyone makes that connection, there's no question the Source'll win that provocation suit, and it won't just be them coming after us. The Diytanese government's no joke."

"Oh, I don't know, maybe they'd give a pass to the Hand of God."

Flynn rolled his eyes. "Don't bet on it, and there's nothing divine about plaz. Shit's nasty." He frowned, stretching out his shoulders like they hurt. "I dreamt of you when I was down there."

"Really? You did?"

"Yeah...it was weird. I had the worst feeling I needed to come back north. It had to have been the pull...then all that shit happened and I had to leave."

"So what was the dream?"

He grinned, kissing behind her ear. "It didn't involve clothes."

"Why am I not surprised?" Ugh, she wished she felt better. His hand grazed over her abdomen, fingers splaying across her belly. "Channeling all that talent...it did something to me, Flynn. Something to the baby, and now...it's like it's eating me. What Nora did helped, but that feeling's still there."

A mishmash of Flynn's emotions streamed through their bond, clashing with hers.

"Jon will be here later. I don't want her in this house, Kara. I know she's your mother, and I'm glad you feel better, but I can't. Not here."

It hurt to nod, but she did. He was hurting worse. "What happened?"

He sighed, his breath hot on the top of her head. "My mom went down to the Source to finalize the contract between our Houses. She wanted to see you…probably to verify halos." His voice cracked. "We fought before she left. I wasn't—shit, you were a kid and—I wasn't interested in any of it. I dunno all the details. Nora, took her somewhere, one of the patrons…she died."

Kara chewed her thumb, events clicking. "Albanach killed him."

"Cal—what? He did?" Flynn's shock colored their bond.

"Yes. He claimed redress. Absorbed all Dionis's assets, his heir suicided…there's an unspoken rule that patrons don't touch another's property, but no one could understand why Albanach'd been so upset over a su—unaffected person." She bit her lip and turned, smoothing his furrowed brow. "I'm sorry."

"Cal killed him? Really?"

"I wasn't there…but I heard he walked up to him in the middle of a fête and slit his throat." Kara shook her head at the disbelief in his eyes. "Albanach is feared, Flynn. Even by the Talents he owns. We had more autonomy than most, but…he's ruthless, and you don't cross him. They call him the Dragon."

"He never told me—I didn't think he had it in him. He's a dick, but Jesus…" His shock was morphing into a simmering anger. Had she made a mistake telling him? Why wouldn't Cal?

"They were different after. He wasn't around very much, and Nora…" Kara bit at her thumb. Her mother had become distant, and there was a tension between her and Albanach that hadn't been there before.

A tension Kara felt with Flynn now. "It had to have been an accident—"

"I don't give a shit. She's still dead. Get some rest. I gotta shower before I take these fucking pledges." He got up and stormed into the bathroom, the door slamming behind him. Kara stared at its panels, the grain of the wood blurry behind her tears.

CHAPTER FOUR

gating stone [gat·ing stōn] *noun*

1. *A construct of talent resulting in an iridescent concretion capable of instantaneous transportation to any envisioned local. Completely indestructible, the material is unique to Glynfyls and its surrounding estates.*

– Excerpt from Glynfyls: A History

"…the entire situation is distasteful, and the most recent developments have left us without recourse. I see no other way to mitigate the fallout. At minimum, this will afford us the opportunity to regroup. Capitulate to whatever he demands. If we can keep the other divisions clear of this, it'll be worth every penny…"

*– Encrypted Private Transmission,
Origin, The Source*

TITUS STROLLED DOWN the Triam's sterile white hallway for his monthly inspection, observing Breakers through the mirrored panels of plex running its length. Enough of his Talents were kept at the Source to allay suspicion, but this blacksite of Elites and females was where his real treasure lay.

He paused to appreciate two bitches sparring. They were magnificent creatures. As fierce as their male counterparts, they had the same inbred need for physical release. It was a shame he was unable to integrate them into the military, but they were far too valuable to lose in the field.

The bout ended, and he moved on, through the keyed portlocks and into the Triam's Laborium. Techs checked the vitals on females in various stages of gestation. They lined the room on metal gurneys, the hiss and click of the ventilators keeping them in stasis loud in the bleak room.

Titus pursed his lips, flipping through a gravid bitch's chart. She was slated to welp the average litter of three, bringing his numbers to thirty-two offspring for the month. He made a slight adjustment to her nutritionals, the last metrics from the Jester girl preying on his mind.

Barton needed to make haste.

Titus caressed the milky stone set into his pinky ring and appeared back in his offices. The holo of her bout still played on loop above his desk. He sat, running a finger over his lips, and slowing down the segment where she spat out a piece of Riegel's tongue.

Spectacular. She was an Alpha bitch beyond compare, and the implications of her breeding with Scot were staggering. The talent he'd negated was on par with an incident during the boost trials that had created a crater some three miles wide, necessitating the addition of kill-switches to subjects.

The failure of Riegel's to detonate still irked.

A sub delivered Titus's bourbon, and he swirled a mouthful, pulling up the metrics of the bots' final transmission from Scot and the girl. They'd both recorded a talent signature too similar to Nora and Marcos's before their bots winked out to be coincidental. That stood to reason; the last visual he'd received from the girl's feed was of the two of them.

Interesting, but what Titus had seen on Scot's feed had been more so, and he wasn't referring to that delightful interlude the two of them had shared. Though a bit too soft-core to suit his tastes, he imagined there would be plenty of buyers champing for the footage. Pity that at this juncture it would give the game away…but it did keep his back pocket warm.

He turned back to the data, fingers itching to—

A communications orb pulsed into existence. Salist. Perhaps his coconspirator had dug something up on the board. This notion of liquidation was troubling. Titus sighed, flicking away Scot's metrics to answer.

"There you are. Have you finished sulking?" Salist lounged somewhere in the Deep South. Palm trees and very blue water made up the background, the bright sunlight eaten by the ebony of his skin. He idly stroked the tiger pelt thrown over his chaise, the other hand raising a flute of something carbonated to his lips.

"Why would I have cause to sulk? I'm about to win a great deal of money from you."

Salist's sculpted brow quirked. "That's quite optimistic, considering the North has abandoned the border."

"Mmm, yes, and yet, I'm positively shitting rainbows."

The dark man spat out his drink.

"The tech sent back an interesting bit of footage." Titus forwarded a clip of Marcos and Nora in the same room as Scot.

Salist broke off mopping at his robes. "So, your hunch about Northern collusion played out…but I don't see how that brings you any closer to your goal, and Yin's threat of liquidation—"

"Has the board chosen a side?"

The other man frowned. "All of them would welcome the old Dragon's demise, and none of them are willing to stick their necks out to get it done. That offer of his to fund the Source for the next decade just served to remind them of his resources."

"Time isn't one of them."

Salist snorted. "Neither is it one of yours. Unlike the rest of them, I'm well aware that if the girl isn't put into stasis and pumped full of whatever fertilizer you've concocted, she'll be dead within the next few weeks and her genetics lost. Quite frankly, I was shocked that bout didn't send her over the edge."

How astute of him. Titus pursed his lips, looking into his glass. "I'm assuming her Binder genes are playing a factor, but you are correct; she's begun to slide." And that burst of talent she'd channeled had stimulated the litter's development, increasing their needs exponentially. Never mind weeks, plural, if she lasted one Titus would be surprised. He scowled. Though that had been happening with alarming frequency of late.

Salist templed his long fingers, appraising him. "What of your little byplay with Albanach? Don't think I didn't notice, and Yin's too clever by half. You're taking her threats of liquidation far too lightly. In the event the Source becomes insolvent, so do you."

"None of it is of any concern. I intend to take out an insurance policy before that happens." Titus smirked from behind his bourbon. He downed the last of it, his fingers lingering upon the leaded crystal as he slid the empty glass onto his desk. The light from the communications orb glimmering upon its facets and throwing rainbows.

———

FLYNN STALKED the halls to Cal's study, feeling like an asshole and pissed about it. When he'd gotten out of the shower, Kara had been asleep, but her hurt clashing with his own mess of emotion had him on the hairy edge. He wasn't in the mood to deal with Markham or the rest of the Fetches coming to pledge.

Fuck, he was having trouble dealing, period. That goddamned gnawing in his guts…

Serenity now. Because that always worked.

He rifled his hair, needing to hit someone. Goddamn it, why the hell did that bitch have to show up? He swore, knowing how much Kara wanted her here. Shit, needed her, but Jesus fucking Christ—

He couldn't. Meddleton had been his mom's place, and it was all he had left of her.

Flynn stumbled, gripping the wall at the grief crushing down on him. Too fresh with that bitch here. He pinched a hand over his eyes, the bridge of his nose. Scrubbed at his face, needing to pull it together.

His throat bobbed, and he looked at the ceiling. Five. Ten...sixteen scrolls looped down the cornice. Right. Deep breath.

He pushed off the wall and made himself keep walking.

Cal was in his office with Rogan, kibitzing over cocktails. Flynn grabbed a coffee from the service and pulled over one of the arm chairs.

"Rough day?"

He ignored the Breaker, swiping a cigar and book of matches from Cal. "Surprised you wanted to see me. Figured you'd be dick deep in that bitch by now."

His grandfather didn't bat an eye. "That'd be my preference, but she's bonded the Commandant. French has 'em settled at the flat until he finds something else. City's a goddamned mess."

Flynn snorted, sure that was gonna go over like a fart in church with Lot. Good. The three of them deserved each other. He waved out the match, his level of anxiety dropping with the likelihood of running into either of them next time he turned a corner. Tomorrow he'd take Kara over, and then she could visit whenever she wanted—

"I was just telling Cal the Breakers've pulled from the border..."

And his anxiety was back. His temples throbbed as Rogan laid out the situation. Christ, the fucking Sons, the Commandant, and a busted hierarchy. Sounded like the setup to a bad joke. Flynn ran a hand over his mouth, looking at the scotch and feeling like the punchline.

... God grant me the serenity to accept the things that I cannot change...

Shit. He had enough to deal with without adding a bender to the mix.

His head said that, but his mouth was still watering.

"So...what do you plan on doing now, kid?" Rogan asked, putting his feet up on the desk. "Secret's out."

They were both staring at him. "I—" Didn't want to talk about it. Shit, he didn't want to think about it. He started counting ceiling tiles.

"Showing up at Assembly might be a good start," Cal said from around his cigar.

"Yeah. I'd planned on it." Flynn's gaze dropped to his empty cup. Christ, that was gonna suck. It'd been hard enough showing his face when people hated him for the shit he'd done. Now they'd hate him for what he was. He needed another coffee.

The two of them exchanged a glance as he got up.

"You okay, kid?"

He laughed, refilling his cup and coming back to sit. "Not in the fucking slightest."

"Anything in particular weighing on you?"

Flynn looked at the Breaker. Was he serious? "Kara's a mess, the city that has no army, there are hordes of fanatics terrorizing the countryside, and this asshole just invited the fucking Commandant and the woman that murdered my mother to move in. Oh, and the entire planet knows I'm a split."

"That all?"

"I may have glossed over the whole Source situation."

"Well, at least you got a jump on the one with the Breakers. Heard you laid out the Commandant." Rogan grinned, and Flynn wanted to put a fist through his teeth. That anger rose up—Asshole ran a finger under his nose and smirked like he'd just proven a point. Goddamn it.

"You feel like working off more steam, there's plenty of Breakers at the conclave…"

Flynn's temper jumped again. "I'm not a fucking Breaker."

Rogan snorted. "That reel says otherwise, and besting the Source's Beta proves it out. I suggest you be prepared for challenges to your rung."

The stab of rage that shot through Flynn was visceral. His teeth gritted down on his cigar. Screw the Breakers and their hierarchy. His fucking rung. He was gonna take it and jam it straight—

Man looked fucking tickled. "Anyone ever tell you you're cute when you're mad?"

"Fuck you."

"You're not my type. Look, I'll get a read on the Breakers. Trials will screw things up for a while, but they're not gonna stand aside if shit starts going down."

Flynn blew out a thick cloud of smoke, pulling zero. Asshole was trying to set him off, and Kara needed sleep. "Random squads are as much of a liability as none at all," he muttered into his coffee, then grimaced at the looks they were giving him.

Cal tapped off his ash. "So…The Commandant tells me you were acting as Kendall's second."

Damn it. "The Commandant should keep his fucking mouth shut."

"Why, there something you need to tell me?"

"No."

"Bullshit. I'm guessing you pulled talent to get them out of that crater." He didn't say anything and his grandfather grunted. "What else?"

Flynn ran a hand over his mouth. Fuck it. He was tired and didn't give a shit anymore. "I blew it up. The mine. Crater, whatever. All of it."

They stared at him, and he shrugged.

"How?" Rogan asked, eyebrow cocked behind his glass of scotch.

Damn, that looked good. "Plaz."

Cal choked up a burst of smoke. "Where the hell did you get plaz? The radiation that shit puts out—Christ, how in God's name did you transport it?"

Flynn squirmed against the chair, the memory of burns searing his back. The smell of his flesh melting… "Downed craft, fifty-five gallon drum. I carried it."

His grandfather just about dropped his cigarette. "How the hell are you still breathing?"

"Double dose of p-funk and a Binder. It was close."

"Jesus."

"Nice." Rogan grinned, finishing his scotch.

"Not if they finger me for it."

The two assholes looked at each other and laughed.

"You think anyone'd actually believe it if they did?"

Goddamn, he wanted to smack the smirk off Cal's face. "Yeah. Kendall had a Northern connection feeding him intel. For a while I thought it was Crandall or you, but neither makes sense. Somebody up here put those Talents in my path, and I'll be damned if I know who."

Cal pinched the cigar from his teeth. "That's worrisome, but I still don't think—"

"Forgive the interruption, sir," French said from the doorway, "Lord Markham has arrived."

Christ, he was early, but couldn't be any more irritating than these two. Might as well get it over with. Flynn stood, glowering at them as he left.

French had put Markham in the East Drawing Room. The big man was sitting on the edge of the gold brocade settee, mopping his chins. How the hell anyone could sweat that much was a goddamned mystery. He hefted himself up and extended a hand.

"Laughlin."

"Kyle." They shook and Flynn helped himself to more coffee. Markham wasn't a bad guy, for a Fetch, but that entire line was sketchy. If he was here now, he wanted something, and whatever that was, he wanted to keep it quiet. "You're here early."

"I hope you don't mind, I wanted to speak to you before the individual heads arrived."

"Go for it, but I'll warn you, I'm in a shitty mood." Flynn dropped into one of the wingback chairs, too spun up to bandy words. Markham settled himself again, worrying his handkerchief.

"Ah, yes, that's understandable. I'll start by apologizing for this morning. Crandall… well. It was never my intent to prevent any of the Fetches from pledging, common or no. The perceived reluctance of my line thus far has been more of a, ah, strategic move."

"Even with the rumors about my status?"

"Are they true?"

Flynn chewed his cigar. Shit was gonna come out sooner or later, and he'd rather they walk away now. "I can't say they're unfounded."

Markham pursed his lips. "My line's prosperity, and my role in particular, are heavily dependent upon maintaining a good relationship with Glynfyls's common element. The hill's attitude towards those of a dual nature has never been shared by the lower rungs, and quite frankly, I'm more concerned with getting shivved by one of them than the Assembly's censure."

Plausible, but bullshit.

"Not even Crandall's? I swear to Christ, you keep sucking his ass after pledging, and I'll bury you. There's no way I'm gonna smooth out shit with your line just to have you stab me in the back."

Markham's eyes glittered. "I've always respected your forthrightness, so I'll do you the same courtesy. To be brief, I'm no more in Crandall's thrall than you. Do you recall the role his House played in the Dock Uprising?"

"Vaguely." And couldn't give two shits about any of it.

"Mmm. They sided with the Prydees in trying to subjugate House McCreedy. Aside from the shear audacity of involving themselves with my line's politics to influence an unsanctioned House War, I'm rather fond of Fitzpatrick, and dead or not, I owe his father a heavy debt. Consequently, I owe you one as well for your involvement."

"My involvement…" Snippets of a very blurry memory following an edict forbidding the Shades from aiding or abetting during that clusterfuck surfaced. "I hate to break it to you, Kyle, but getting that kid from point A to point B was solely to piss Lot off, not from any sense of altruism."

"Regardless, if you hadn't, things would've ended badly for the boy."

He snorted. "Seems like that happened anyways."

"You're not wrong, but it's…complicated. Much of my role as First is, especially given Bernice's familial connections. Being married to one of the Prydee sisters can be, ah, trying." Markham sighed, still playing with his handkerchief. "But be that as it may, after Crandall had you detained, I used my influence to, ah, stir the pot."

"*You* incited the commons?"

Markham wet his lips. "I did."

"Un-fucking believable." Flynn took a slow drag of his cigar, trying to rein in his temper. If there was one more man standing behind the fucking curtain—God, he hated Glynfyls.

"I'm in a difficult position that I'm unable to elaborate upon. Ah, a House Matter, I'm afraid. However, I want you to be assured of my support…in what capacity I'm able to provide it."

Flynn gave a wry laugh. "So what you're telling me is that although you'd love to be pals, the Prydees and Crandall are in bed together, and they've got your nuts in a vice."

"Essentially. Do you mind if I get a glass of something a bit stronger?"

Flynn raked back his hair, waving at the sideboard. Goddamn, he hated this shit. "So what happened to the kid?"

"Who, Fitzpatrick?" Markham asked over his shoulder. "He gets by. Has no interest in becoming a lord, and very few prospects. The sisters aren't kind to him, but I do what I can. He's as stubborn as Denis ever was. House McCreedy's pride rivals any upon the hill. I regret that everything of late has been quite difficult for him."

"The sisters? Miriam and all of them are still making the kid's life miserable?" Not counting her two brothers, there were like eighteen of them or something, and Markham's nuts weren't the only ones they had in a vice. Half the city squeaked when they twisted.

"Yes. Denis bonding Rebecca was a massive scandal, and Fitzpatrick had the audacity to be born male. Can you believe they've only had five boys between them in the last three generations, and none since him? I've fifty-six nieces."

"Must make Christmas easier."

"Hah. You'd be wrong. Why the interest in the lad?"

"He never picked up what Cal owes him."

Markham snorted. "The commons don't typically pay for a job half done."

"As much as I wish he hadn't done it at all, I'm not the commons. Next time you see him, send him my way to collect."

"Generous of you. I will at that." He settled himself back on the settee. "Forgive me if I'm prying, but I couldn't help but note the resemblance between your lady and the one I delivered earlier…your mother-in-law, by chance?"

Flynn grunted, not wanting to get into it.

"Well, that explains your foul mood." Markham chuckled and took a sip of his drink. "I find the best way to deal with problematic relations is to develop a hobby that calls one away at opportune times. I have a schooner that requires a great deal of my attention."

"I'm thinking between this war and the whole split thing, I've got that covered."

"True. I'm assuming you'll be at Assembly?"

Flynn riffled his hair, eyes traveling the pattern on the silk moire walls. "Yeah, if they'll let me in."

"Oh, they've no choice but to, and the commons are still demanding you be made Overlord. With my line's support, you could very well force the issue and take it."

He wasn't wrong, but it felt like that would be. "You have any idea what Crandall's up to?"

"Short of world domination?"

Flynn snorted. "You're not the first to say that."

"He's made no secret of it." Markham rolled a mouthful of scotch around. "You may find this difficult to believe, but he's not as bad as his mother was." He chuckled again at Flynn's expression. "Granted, that's not saying much, but I think Bart might care about the Northern Territories more than his ambition. He sees you as a threat to the latter, but I don't believe you're in any personal danger until our safety as a nation is secured…of course that doesn't mean he won't try to leash your influence."

"Is that what he was doing the other night?"

"I couldn't tell you, but I do find it odd he so grossly misjudged the consequences."

Flynn chewed his cigar. He'd been thinking the same thing. What the hell had Crandall's left hand been doing while they'd all been watching the right?

***

ROGAN SAT at the top tier of the conclave, cursing himself for not getting up and leaving.

Damn it, he'd sworn he wasn't getting involved again, but here he fucking was, witnessing the trials below by default, his mouth a thin white line. Witnessing. He snorted. More like reminiscing. Ghosts saluted him and squared up beside the Breakers sparring. His goddamned past was too close in this city, but if the corporeal men on the sands were any indication, it wouldn't be standing for much longer.

Stonefist's men could hold their own, but the rest of them…Christ.

Did he give a shit? Interfering would mean taking responsibility, and the last time he'd done that…

He missed his beach.

Rogan sighed, glancing up as the Menot who'd spoken earlier came over, touching between his brows in greeting. "Alpha Prime."

"Not anymore. Trials knock everyone from their rung. I'm no exception."

The old man smiled, gathering his long gray robes to sit. He reminded Rogan of Obi Wan what's-his-name, not that anyone but Cal would get that reference.

"So sayeth the Way. Lead by example, or not at all."

"I'm not leading anything."

The Menot chuckled, pulling a flask from the folds of his robe. "Perhaps not directly, but those on the sands strive harder beneath your eyes. You honor them with your attention. Their grandchildren will hear of the time they fought before Rogan Firestorm."

"If they last that long."

"Well, there is that. Your reputation proceeds you, but mine is much more fleeting. Voss Mangleshield." The old man offered him his hand and then the flask. Rogan took both. One of the bouts below ended with one of the men in the sand, his arm at an unnatural angle. He groaned, picking himself up, and another pair squared off in the space they'd occupied.

"I don't see the Breakspears."

Voss frowned. "No. Phyllis has enough pride for ten men, and I'm afraid it's been ill-used of late, especially with most of the line pledging to Scot. She'll come around, but it's best to leave her be until she does."

"And her boy?" One of the pairs fighting were Stonefist's men. It was mildly engaging, but they were both making stupid mistakes.

"Billy's a good lad, one hell of a cellist. Has zero desire to become Alpha. Since his father died, it's been strained between them. Woman was born a Steadfast and once she makes up her mind…"

"Could he take it?"

"No. Not with what he puts out for 'lust. His heart isn't there."

Rogan grunted. The larger of the pair sparring botched a block and took a nasty jab. "So who's the most likely candidate?"

"Think you know the answer to that. Taking down the Source's Beta's no small feat." Shit. That hadn't taken long to get out. Rogan glanced over at the Menot, and the man shrugged. "My cousin's in the furniture repair business. I also gather Scot's not particularly enamored with the idea."

"You'd be correct." And good fucking luck changing the kid's mind. "So humor me, who's your second pick?"

Voss pursed his lips. "The Groundfire boy, if I had to put money on it." Voss took back the flask, running a thumb over its monogram. "Shame he's as dumb as a rock."

"Never claimed the Way was perfect."

"No." A smile flitted across his lips. "Nor are any who walk it. Tell me, why did you return?"

The smaller man sparring slipped past the larger's guard and knocked him on his ass.

"I've been asking myself that very question."

"Then this time is different." Rogan raised an eyebrow, and Voss smirked. "You're a bit late to be a harbinger of a coming harvest, and Phyllis already asked you about a mate."

"*… I fuck, Phyllis, I don't mate…*"

Rogan snorted. "Word travels fast."

"When it's that eloquently spoken, yes." They both chuckled. "I can't imagine you weren't tempted, though. Last time I saw a woman fight like Lady Scot—"

"Was a long time ago," Rogan interrupted, hoping that was the end of it. Another pair had squared up. Wasn't worth watching after the first punch was thrown.

"Aye, that it was…but I seem to recall she bonded a Scot as well."

Rogan caught himself scowling. How that could still be a sore subject…water under the bridge like all the rest of it, and for once, Cal hadn't been the guilty party. Shane… Rogan shook his head and looked at his hands, buffing his knuckles.

Didn't matter. She was dead, like the rest of them, and that was on him.

"It may be stricken from the records, but I'm not the only one who remembers. Nor the only one who feels Isenben approaching. House Carmody has dreamt of the sword and shield of a Battle Shade above the city, its blade trailing flame, and last night, a Valkyrie of old stepped forth, drawing on the strength of a man who should be Alpha, and a scion of your House."

"He's also an asshole."

Voss laughed. "Certain traits run strong in families."

And Flynn got it from both sides. Rogan ran a hand over his jaw. "He doesn't know."

"Your daughter would have wanted it that way."

He grunted. And Lord knows Shane had gotten every other damned thing she'd ever wanted, and to hell with the rest of it. So had her mother. Rogan bowed his head, staring at the worn stone beneath his boots, trying not to see their ghosts out on the sand. Why the hell was he here?

"How long do you anticipate the trials taking?"

Voss shrugged. "Most are eager, many settling outside the conclave. Every venue with a ring is booked solid. Lower rungs won't change much, but the middle will be messy. The lesser Original Houses are doing what they can to drag their feet. None of them relish the prospect of a common holding a rung above theirs. A week, perhaps two."

"And if we don't have that?"

"For any that'd pledged, I'd imagine in lieu of the hierarchy, the onus of leadership will fall upon whomever they've given their oaths to." He took another sip from the flask, his face a bit too bland.

Rogan laughed, drawing stares from around the stone chamber. Phyllis must be having a bird.

Voss's lips quirked. "The council is under no illusions as to what's coming for us. Richard Breakspear's death and the others we've lost over the past few years have created an untenable situation, no doubt by design. The Way teaches that when one cannot change a circumstance, one adapts to persevere. It is the council's duty to speak our will and facilitate."

He turned his palm over to show a weeping line of red. "Today, I hold the oaths of those who would give their fealty to Lord Scot. Tomorrow, I kneel in proxy for them. That, out there on the sands, will play out as it will. Regardless, Glynfyls's swords will be ready."

Rogan grunted. They might be, but he wasn't as certain about its shield.

VICTOR SPAT out a steaming stream of chew, his lips twisting into a lopsided grin. The Talent they'd hustled up from the bushes had stopped twitching, but it'd taken the better part of the day. Freak'd been peeled like a cow's tongue then roasted up crisp. One of the Sons cut what was left of it down and dragged the corpse to the edge of camp. A chorus of baying went up. Dogs been eatin' right fine.

"Last one," he told the men around the fire. "Pass it on. I want 'em hungry. Be plenty of freaks soon enough." A murmur of agreement spread through the group. Their numbers had swollen into the hundreds, more arriving with every hour.

"Ain't nobody seen a uniform south of Hamlin," Sam said shuffling over, hands jammed into his pockets and shoulders up around his ears. Not that it was much of a stretch with those dangling plugs in his lobes. Still, was cold and gettin' colder.

"Then we rise with 'em. Start callin' up the rest. Figure we got two, three days till we hit the plateau. They ain't dumb, an' playin' wack-a-mole's gonna get old fast. They'll try to hold us there."

Sam grunted. "Right. I'll get us loaded. Picked up a chapter with a couple plaz-cannons, but they're short on charges. One of 'em said there's a batch comin', but way I hear that city's laid out, nullifier in a sling shot'll be enough to knock it flat."

"Well, we got plenty of them." Victor chuckled as his second left to see it done. Squashin' them roaches sounded a treat. He spat out another stream of chew, watching the dark hole it made spread outwards, tingeing the snow brown. His eyes went funny, and he blinked, a surge of pride filling his chest—

She was with him.

His pleasure centers ignited, flooding him with dopamine. Victor fell to a knee, trembling, a ghostly apparition forming above the fire.

A pixie of a gal with long blonde hair and the bluest eyes he ever done seen smiled at him, teeth white and pearly. He choked on his chew, and the wad rolled from his lip, anger coiling in his belly. Them freaks were gonna pay for spoilin' such a picture.

"Victor."

He shivered at the way her voice caressed his name, little prickles tripping down his spine to his groin. "Mother…"

The vision stepped from the flames and came to stand before him. Beyond her slight form men gathered, removing their hats, standing with bowed heads, silent at the fringe of light. Bearing witness to him experiencing the visitation.

A smile tipped up her blushed pink lips, a slim white hand rising to hover above his head. "It is for you to prepare the way. Continue to strike at the towns, then take the estates. Await me there." Her lips descended, and a whisper pressed to his brow.

Victor's eyes rolled up into his head, and it all went black.

"MOLLY, ME LOVE! ANOTHER ROUND!" Fitz called across the clamor of the 'Pipe, raising his tankard. The barmaid rolled her eyes and started pouring from the tap. Fresh from the farm, she were.

The pub were packed tonight, every Fetch in the commons stopping in to celebrate sticking it to the hill. Fitz were more pragmatic. They'd make 'em pay for it. Bastards always did, and there weren't a fuckin' thing any of 'em could do about it.

"Ye really bet Marl ye'd be able to bed her?" Craig asked, jerking his head toward the winsome girl behind the bar. He flicked somewhat from his nose. S'long as he weren't marking the cards with it, Fitz didn't care. He grinned at his pimply friend.

"Aye. She's a tough nut t'crack, but I'm close."

Craig snorted. "She hates ye."

"S'best part." Fitz threw a unit into the pot and tipped back in his chair.

"Oh ho, that why ye pissed off Adelaide?" Marl asked, matching his bet from across the table. The old man's liver-spotted lips pursed. "Hear tell she's cleared out of yer room and hired on at the Pony."

Fitz's chair clunked down. "That were just a temporary arrangement, and a differing of opinions." The boys around the table raised their eyebrows at each other, knowing exactly what it'd been. He pulled at the patch of beard beneath his lip. Adelaide'd had it bad for him since they was kids, but he didn't—it weren't like that. "S'better that way. Christ, she'll eat a sight finer."

"You ain't gonna." Scotty snickered from behind his cards.

"Bet me." Fitz grinned at the sway of Molly's hips as she worked through the crowd.

She held out her palm. "I'll see yer coin, first."

He clutched his breast. "Think I'd order a round without being able t'pay for it?"

"Think ye'd get away with anything ye can."

She weren't wrong, and her knickers was on the list. Fitz stood, rummaging around in his pocket. He placed the coins on her palm, fingertips lingering. She snatched her hand back and blushed, cheeks the same rose as the edges of her aura as she passed out tankards. Now that were encouraging…

Her tray came up between them like a shield, and she narrowed her eyes. Fitz grinned, stepping aside. She sniffed, tossing her auburn curls behind her shoulder and headed back to the bar.

"What d'ye know, she didn't slap ye that time," Marl said, taking another card.

Fitz sat, retrieving his hand. It were as middling as the rest of 'em had been tonight. "Told ye, the blessed Saint'll answer me prayers, boys." Weren't doing nothing for his card game though.

"Ain't no Saint Cajetan, and ain't none of the real ones granting a lay." Craig snorted.

Fitz took a long pull from his tankard and smacked his lips. "S'where you're wrong. Didn't God hisself say t'be fruitful and multiply? I'm just trying t'practice so I can do right by the good book —" He frowned at a blood-smeared two. "Which one of ye's bleeding on the deck?"

Scotty choked on his ale. "Father Benson catches wind of yer blaspheming, he'll have ye stripped down and whipped against the pulpit." He glanced at the bandage across his palm. "Shite, sorry. Them fuckers cut me deep. Ain't gonna be able t'haul in me damned nets for a week." The others at the table grunted, in the same state. "Ye gonna do it?"

"Course he's gonna," Marl snapped.

"Ain't decided." Fitz took another card.

The old man glowered at him and called, slapping down two pair. That did in Fitz's half straight. So much for rent. His hand went to his pocket, fondling a nine-sided coin. Markham had sent word he had somewhat for him. Were it worth the possibility of getting nabbed by the sisters?

The coin grew warm. That'd be a yes.

Fitz threw back his ale and pushed from the table with a sigh. "I'm out. See ye boys."

He shifted to his uncle's study.

Markham were sitting in one of the big leather chairs by the fire.

"Eh…ye wanted t'see me?"

"I did." The man waved a hand, inviting him to sit. He was surrounded by a nimbus of orange and browns. Shite. Fitz's hand went back to the coin in his pocket. Still warm.

If ye say so, Cajetan.

He crossed the plush Persian carpet, back of his neck itching at the quiet. Firelight glinted off the crystal decanters on a carved table of dark wood. He stopped to pour himself a glass of whatever were in one of them before settling himself on the edge of the other squeaky brown chair. A tray of pasties was on a low table before the fire, and he helped himself to one.

"I pledged our entire line to Lord Scot tonight," Markham said, his fingers worrying at the leather stitching of the chair's arm. "Less Houses Prydee and McCreedy." He glanced at Fitz's hands meaningfully. "You know you're only making it worse for yourself not going. If they have to send someone to collect you—"

"I ain't done a damned thing," he protested around his mouthful.

"It's enough that you're making them wait." His uncle waved a weary hand. "Be that as it may, it's not why I wanted to see you. Lord Scot mentioned you'd never collected what he owes you, and asked me to send you along."

Shite. That'd make rent and then some. Fitz grabbed another pasty. "Ye serious?"

"I am, and would appreciate it if you did so sober."

And if wishes was horses, beggars would ride.

"Fitzpatrick."

He looked up at the man, chewing.

"Laughlin's not like the rest of them, and you owe him a debt. If not for yourself, for your gran."

"S'dirty fuckin' pool right there." Fitz scowled, finishing a mouthful. "He say when?"

A smile flitted across his uncle's lips. "No…but I believe he spends his evenings at Meddleton. You have the imprint."

"Aye." Fitz downed what were in his glass, hissing at the burn, and snatched the last pasty. "Aught else?"

Markham's face was grim. "Just be careful. The sisters…well. Suffice to say they're not pleased with recent developments, no matter how necessary. Bernice mentioned she was meeting them for tea tomorrow at Kristine's." He raised an eyebrow, and Fitz's scowl deepened. He gave a begrudging nod. Fine.

Bugger 'em all, but he'd be there.

CHAPTER FIVE

"The Talent's city of Glynfyls is a nasty little conglomeration of buildings shifted in from several abandoned cities farther south. Set up in a roughly circular pattern, everything has a list to it, the buildings literally shifted into the ground and fixed in place. The surrounding wall is of a similar construction. Without talent to hold it together, the sad excuse for a metropolis would collapse under its own weight…"

— Br873, "Kyles", Source Military Adjunct,
Transmitted Field Report

CAL SAT at his desk disguised as Albanach, all the hair and pigment cloaked from his body. He chewed on his cigar, staring at the swirling blue mist of the communication orb hovering above his desk, listening to the same damned elevator music he'd subjected Titus to looping for the umpteenth time.

Asshole was playing with him.

A pretty brunette woman flickered into view. "I'm so sorry sir, Patron Titus's massage ran over. I'll put you right through—"

The orb blipped, and Titus filled the space. He sat at his desk looking smug, the buttons undone at the throat of his white button-down, far more relaxed than he had any right to be. Cal pursed his lips. Hoped he enjoyed it while he could.

"Ah, Albanach! My apologies, I didn't expect you to be punctual. At your age it's so easy to oversleep." He took a glass of something from a sub and grinned over its rim.

Cal wasn't in the mood to trade barbs, and with what was on that chip, he didn't have to. How Leo had gotten ahold of it—"Let's cut to the chase. What d'you think you have on me?"

"You do like to suck the fun out of everything don't you?" Titus took a sip and hissed air through his teeth. "But if you insist; I've proof that you've been colluding with the North and are actively assisting Talents across the border."

Shit. "That so? I'm assuming you don't plan on divulging specifics."

"I was going to let my lawyers have the pleasure when they filed for an injunction."

Cal exhaled, sending a cloud of smoke over the orb. "You might want to reconsider."

"Why on earth would I want to do that?"

"Oh, I don't know. Maybe to keep the Triam's breeding records from going public." Titus went very still, and Cal grinned around his cigar. "The metrics on your Elites are impressive, as are the number of human rights violations necessary to get them to that point. Pretty sure more than the board's gonna be interested in those…unless we can work something out."

Titus's mouth curdled, but the man knew he'd been trumped. After his military overreach in Tombago and epic failure to secure the iridium mine in Diytan, the international community had a firing squad on stand-by, just waiting for a fuck up like this.

"What would you suggest?" Titus gritted out, rubbing a temple.

"You can start by telling me about your breeding program."

The man's expression became cunning. "Worried about Kara, are you? You should be. If the litter she's carrying doesn't kill her within the next week or so, bloodlust will. The only way to salvage her genetics is by delivering her to me." Titus couldn't keep the grin off his face. "But I'm not unreasonable. Sign her over, and you can have your pick of the litter. The rest I'll take in payment for ensuring their survival."

Pompous prick. "What makes you so certain I have her?" Cal asked, carefully keeping expression bland.

Titus sipped his drink. "And here I thought we were cutting to the chase. I've holo from Talent Jester of the room you're sitting in. I'll admit, it's a great deal more stripped down, but that birdbath you use for an ashtray is quite distinctive. Edinburgh Crystal, isn't it? I'm assuming it's sentimental. It doesn't have much value, even for a pre-Surge piece."

"Is it? Picked it up at a yard sale, there were a dozen of the damned things."

Titus chuckled. "Touché. I'll leave the offer on the table. Sadly, it's only available for a limited time. Until then, it appears we're at a stalemate. Sweet dreams, Albanach."

The orb winked out.

Cal swore, dropping his cloak. If Jon and Nora couldn't figure out what Titus was supplementing those women with pronto... He chewed his cigar. That left getting a Bane involved. Christ, he'd given his word—

He raked back his hair. No. This wasn't about Flynn, it was about Kara, and if he didn't, everything was gonna fall to shit.

Might do that anyway.

Cal scribbled out a note, wanting to throttle Leo. Why was it, whenever he needed that boy, he was nowhere to be found? His spate of temper after he and Flynn had gone at it during the wedding reception wasn't new, but Cal would've thought he'd have shown up by now.

His eyes fell on the drawer the chip was in. And if he knew where the Triam was... Damn it. What was on there that he'd been so hot to get? The lion's share of the data was genealogies. Cal had already grilled Graham. He didn't know anything about what his brother was up to, other than Leo was frantic to get his hands on it.

Cal could relate. He grabbed the bottle of good scotch and twisted off the cap, pretending it was the little shit's neck.

MARCOS SAT on one of the low couches in the entry room of the Scots' flat. It was nothing like the palatial monstrosity he and Nora had been evicted from. Here the rooms were squat and utilitarian, with flickering fluorescent lights and thin, recessed windows. Furniture was spartan and the space could easily be converted to billet troops.

It was a basically a bunker, and Marcos wholeheartedly approved.

Nora was of a different mind. She sat stiffly beside him, her eyes on a massive hole punched into the far wall.

"It's a roof over our heads, and more importantly, it's secure."

Her cheeks flushed. "Of course, you're right. I was just thinking about how angry someone would have to be to do that."

"Having met the most likely suspect, I'd hazard it'd take less than you think."

She twisted her ring, her expression fraught; it had been since they'd gotten up here. "He seemed like such a gentle boy—"

"That was close to thirty years ago, Nora. Time changes everything."

"No, not quite everything…" She smiled at him, and he laughed, a wide grin splitting his face. Last night had been as exceptional as he'd remembered. He pulled her into his arms and sighed, the sapphire of her eyes somehow lacking with her wide golden halos cloaked.

He must've made a face because her brow twitched. "I miss yours, too, but up here, it's the equivalent of running around naked. I wish you would let me do more than just set this." She ran a figure down the bridge of his nose.

"Breaker Business." She gave him a look but left it. He'd wear his shame. Binding it felt like a lie, just like hiding their halos. Not knowing who was who made him nervous. She snuggled against him, this time her gaze falling on the gate across the room. That made him nervous, too. Only Fetches should be able to move around like that. Anyone being able to translocate was unnatural.

He glanced at a spartan clock hanging crooked on the far wall. Someone was supposed to escort them to the Engineering Guild, and whoever it was, was late. Not that they had anything else to do.

"What do you think Titus does to his females?"

Damn it. That conversation with Jon last night about Kara's pregnancy had been weighing on both of them.

"I don't know." Marcos hugged her close so she wouldn't see his face, but their bond laid his self-loathing bare.

She pushed back to look at him. "What is it?"

His thumb worried against his forefinger. Gah, this was the last thing she wanted to hear, but—"My bonds with Breaker females were different than ours. When you went into the Laborium, I could still feel your emotions. With them, I couldn't. They were there, but weren't. And then they were gone."

Nora paled, putting a hand on his arm. "All of them?"

He nodded. "Maybe three, four months in. I don't know what happened to them. Titus sequesters the females in his tower. I'd never seen any of them before, or after. And when I tried to pull files on my offspring, I couldn't find any dates that made sense. Pax's birth was recorded only a few months after I bred Greta."

Nora chewed her lip. "Kara being nine weeks pregnant doesn't make any sense either—"

The Breaker that had passed them in Meddleton's foyer yesterday stepped out of the gate. He looked around and snorted. "Nice to see this is still a shithole. Rogan Firestorm. I'd advise you to stay close until you pull your dick out of the dirt. Every Breaker up here's trying to settle their rung, and with what you're putting off, you're gonna be challenged before you get half-way down the block."

"Your hierarchy's not set?" Marcos stood, his horror visceral.

"It's temporarily in flux." Rogan shrugged. "Line was taking birth into account and it's become a problem. A reset was past due."

Marcos grunted, this concept of family pervasive. How did people live with their autonomy stripped away, completely at the mercy of each other? He dug into his pocket for an antacid that wasn't there. "Hell of a time for it."

"I'd agree. Almost like it'd been planned." Rogan turned to Nora. "Cal said you've been here before. You bind yourselves with heat?"

Marcos stiffened at the man's name. He hadn't gotten the full story about that, and it gnawed at him. Nora looked away, her halos flaring.

A weave settled over them, and Rogan grunted, holding out a hand to her. "Shall we?"

"Yes."

She took it, and Marcos's before he had time to react, pulling him through the plane of swirling mist. There was a moment of disorientation, and then they were standing on a crowded city street, the wind whipping through sharply angled buildings. Marcos gaped. How in the hell—

"Welcome to the fifth rung. Keep your eyes to yourself. Things are tense."

That was an understatement. That spot between Marcos's shoulder blades itched, and he pulled a trickle of 'lust, moving Nora in front of him. Rogan gave an approving nod and started walking. Who was he?

They followed, the frigid wind assaulting them with a foul stench of low-tide and diesel. Nora hunkered down into the collar of her jacket, coughing. *Gah!* Grit stuck to the back of Marcos's throat, his eyes watering. He blinked it away, scanning the buildings crazing the skyline. Never mind an army, anyone ever got near this place with a nullifier they'd be able to hold the entire city hostage.

Abandoned cars and garbage lined the street, graffiti covering the tenements and concrete barriers. Dour people milled about, the press of bodies—someone jostled him, and he growled.

Rogan paused at a cross street, waiting for the traffic to clear. Pre-Surge vehicles rumbled past, spewing toxic fumes into the air, their tires splashing up the grey muck, coating everything like spackle. Nora burrowed beneath Marcos's arm.

"The Source was a lot of things, but this wasn't one of them. Where Cal took me before, it wasn't, I didn't think places like this really existed."

"There's worse out there. With luck you'll never have to see them." With luck, they'd never have to see this again. Her halos shimmered into existence, and he felt her tense. "Bots?"

She nodded. "More than I'd like…maybe one in ten?"

Damn it. He'd been afraid of that and now Titus would have a bead on them. That itching between his shoulder blades increased.

Traffic cleared, and Rogan led them across the street to an ugly, low building. They walked up the steps, and the Breaker held the door for them.

The building's interior reflected its exterior. They followed a trail of tracked-in slush and grime, down a long sloping hall to a pair of double doors. Rogan pushed through into the low hum of a cavernous industrial area, the tang of hydraulic fluid and electronics singeing the air. Marcos took Nora's hand, crossing between islands of antiquated machinery. A painfully thin woman with a grey bob and a lab coat hurried over when she saw them.

"Ah! You must be the group Master Scot was talking about. Jesse Mayfield." She shook their hands with a surprisingly firm grip for one so slight. After introductions, she led them over to a windowed test cube. A hunk of bored-out stone sat in the middle of it.

"I know you're here for a different reason, but I can't resist picking your brains—"

"That one of the cups from the wall?"

"It is." She beamed at Rogan like he was an especially bright recruit. "We've recreated the original weaves to a close approximation of what Lady Scot sketched out, and have been sending micro currents through it to simulate a Breaker's talent. Earlier, we were able to create a kind of dampening mist. I wish I knew if there were any visual effects when it originally operated—"

"There was a faint shimmer. I wouldn't call it a mist though," Rogan said, pushing past her and flaring his halos. "Your approximation isn't close enough." He turned to Nora. "Double check their work."

It wasn't a request. Marcos's jaw tightened at the man's demeanor, tamping down his temper. Who the hell was he? Rogan smirked at him, and Nora put a hand on Marcos's arm before stepping closer to the glass, pulling talent. Her brow furrowed for a long moment.

"Sorry, I'm not familiar with this kind of weave, and it's so faint..."

Her halos pulsed, and the air around the block snapped into an opalescent veil—

And fizzled out with a puff of smoke. The engineers stood in shock, and a tech with deep pockmarks swore. Nora's trepidation colored their bond, and Marcos put an arm around her.

"Oh my, I hope I didn't..."

Rogan let himself into the cube and started poking at the block. "Well, here's part of your problem. The cups need to be filled with mercury. I forget how much."

The assembled techs looked at Jesse. Her fingers were white on her clipboard and her face pinched. "Care to enlighten us with the rest before we waste the next few decades trying to reverse engineer the damned things? Not that I don't appreciate you completing my life's work in the five minutes you've been here."

Rogan looked up, and Marcos's knees buckled at what the man was leaking. Whoever Rogan was, Alpha didn't even come close. He stalked out of the cube and stood in front of the woman with his arms crossed.

"You feel like getting pissy with someone, take it up with Cal. Asshole could've clued you in about this shit just as easily, and it would've served him right." His jaw clenched, attention flicking to Marcos and Nora as he stormed past. "Find your own way home. I'm done babysitting."

"The Alpha Prime has spoken," one of the bigger techs muttered.

Marcos's head jerked around. "Who?"

"Rogan Firestorm is rumored to be—"

"It's not a rumor," the man corrected Jesse. "He *is* the original Breaker, the forger of the Way." He touched between his brows.

"It draws us from the darkness, and keeps the rage at bay," another with a massive black eye intoned, making the same motion.

Marcos's throat tightened. That phrase...

Jesse shook her head, casting them a sidelong glance. "You'll have to forgive them, and me. Breakers have a certain...religious zeal around their line's history. Especially of late, and I've been under quite a bit of pressure to solve this riddle. To have it done so causally, well. Why don't you tell me about these bots? Do you think it would be possible to procure a sample? I realized they're currently problematic, however I'd like to run some tests. I can assure you I'll use the utmost caution."

The question took Marcos aback, breaking him from his thoughts.

He felt Nora's trepidation, and shared it, but desperate times… "Worst case we can fry them."

She gave a halting nod. "Yes, I think I can isolate them."

Jesse handed Nora a vial, and they began discussing the tech. Marcos's eyes went back to the Breakers. That last thing they'd said had struck a chord.

It'd been carved into the back of his desk drawer at the Source.

TITUS TEMPLED his fingers in front of his lips, his eyes on Scot's metrics. He'd run them through every algorithm the Source had access to, and several they didn't. Twice. The results were the same.

And he had no idea what he was looking at.

Breaker and Shade in equal parts, yes, that Scot was a split was indisputable, but they only made up half the man's genetic soup. The rest defied classification.

What the hell was Laughlin Scot?

Titus pulled up several archived news reels from Glynfyls. The answer had to lie in his maternal line, but save for a few grainy stills, the woman was a mystery. Rumored to be unaffected, the first mention of her was in a wedding announcement three years prior to Scot's birth.

That in itself was an impossibility. The triplex that made up a Talent's DNA was immiscible with any other, their chromosomes rendering them an entirely different species. Scot's conception had roughly the same odds of success as a fish and a meteorite procreating, yet not only had it happened, it had resulted in a fecund male.

Gah. Titus swept the holos away and called for a bourbon. The bots were adept at sending raw data, but what he really needed were tissue samples and for Otto to flip through Scot's mind. Titus rubbed a temple, that distinct pinching behind his optic nerve signaling another spate of migraines on the horizon. He snatched his bottle of pills and chewed one preemptively.

Raking back his hair, he pulled up a communications orb. It was time for his meeting. Unlike Albanach, Orin answered right away.

Eagerly, in fact. That was troubling. They stared at each other for a long moment, each taking stock.

Looking for weaknesses.

The bloated man's smile was unpleasant. He wasn't large, but some ailment caused him to look like he'd been partially inflated, then developed a slow leak. "Titus, what can I do for you today?"

"I'm calling to put in a warranty claim on those bots of yours."

"Oh?"

Was his nonchalance due to arrogance or information? The first was more likely, and the second would be costly. "Oh. Talent wasn't supposed to be able to eradicate them, and yet, that very thing has occurred."

"Yes. I've been receiving error messages, along with everything else they've been streaming."

Titus's gut dropped straight to his wallet.

Orin splayed his fingers, inspecting his vivid sky blue manicure. Diamonds winked at the center of each nail. "And before you ask, the disabling of your Breaker's kill-switch wasn't me."

But that was—"Who was it?"

The man smiled, his jowls wrinkling against his ears like an accordion. He waggled a finger at him and then rubbed it against his thumb. "Teaser's free, but you've got to pay to see the show."

Bastard. "I already have, several million units if I remember correctly."

Orin moued at him. "Pity that's not enough for me to disclose and, quite honestly, it should be more to keep my silence. I mean, really, Titus, what would the board say if I were to corroborate Albanach's charge of provocation? This whole Northern kerfuffle has got them in a tizzy. You'd be censured quicker than you can spit, and offered up to an international tribunal on a silver platter."

Titus's temples throbbed at how positively gleeful Orin was at the proposition. "What do you want?"

"That's the question, now isn't it? What do you get for the man who has everything?" He grinned and cut the feed.

Titus slung his glass across the room and ripped at his hair. Goddamn it! The last thing he needed was another fucking boot on his throat, and that it was Orin's high-heeled size eleven only added insult to injury. Titus fumed, his breath coming in sharp bursts—

No. If he hadn't already, Orin wouldn't out him. Despite his parting jab, there had to be something he wanted…something he was waiting for, else he would have already disclosed. Both Yin and Albanach had given him ample opportunity at the last meeting.

Titus had the sinking suspicion it had nothing to do with the procurement of Talents. Though Orin had been copied on the data, the implications of it would be lost on him. The man had zero interest in genetics, his focus purely on tech. His only stake in the Source was exploring where the two met, and without a plaz alternative, the boost remained unmarket—

The iridium mine in the North.

Titus fell back in his chair. Albanach must have promised him access, but how? Glynfyls had completely pulled the mineral from the market after Banoi and shuttered operations. His promises had to be predicated upon harvesting that foul city…which would explain his stance at the last board meeting.

And still, detente.

Damn the man. Titus pulled up Brix's last report, hoping for better news and receiving it. The Elite Breaker that'd replaced the Commandant was nothing if not well-informed. The Sons were very busy depopulating the countryside. Bit of Darwinism there, but Titus had no objections to them culling the herd. Those Talents fleet of feet were heading directly to the city.

Titus's lips twitched up. All the better to harvest them.

NORA SLIPPED OUT of the lift and made her way down the dingy hall of the flat to an equally unappealing sitting room on the first floor. Marcos was deep asleep in their rooms above, and the bind she'd placed on him should keep him slumbering until she returned to his side.

She twisted her ring. He wouldn't understand, and Cal's secrets weren't hers to tell. What they'd shared had been born of connivence, a misplaced passion stemming from their shared belief in the reunification. She was here to facilitate the joining of their people; her role to bind together the Talents of Glynfyls and those from the Source...

Glory, the only thing she was doing was skulking down the hallway like a pre-pube.

Nora glanced at the ceiling, biting her lip, never having imagined Marcos would be here with her, and Cal—Damn them both for putting her in this position.

Damn herself.

He was waiting for her in one of the armchairs by the cold hearth, furniture shrouded beneath ivory sheets. A single lamp burnt beside him, the smoke from his cigar wreathing up around its shade. His green eyes glimmered in the half-light, the dragon assessing his horde.

"Wasn't sure you'd come."

Nora willed herself to be stone, icing her voice. "I had to. We need to talk." She perched on the chair beside his, the cloth puckering beneath her weight. Motes of dust lifted into the haze, then disappeared into shadow. There, but gone. "I didn't tell him."

"Will you?"

The layers two words could evoke... "No. It would complicate things needlessly." The fingers twisting her ring trembled beneath the heat in his gaze, melting her resolve. *Glory, don't do this...*

Cal grunted with that damned smirk of his, and took another drag. Man was impossible. "How was the guild?"

And ever practical. She exhaled, the moment gone.

"I collected a sample of bots for Jesse. She thinks she can modify the tech, though I wasn't clear how. You weren't understating her intellect."

"Good. Things are a damned problem. And our people at the Source?"

"They'll be ready when the time comes. The wards are active, and they have their instructions. I don't know that Serra and her cabal will follow them, but if they're left behind, I can't say I'll be disappointed."

"Woman's a pain in the ass, but we'll need everyone's talent."

"Does that include Pithy's?"

His lips pursed, hiding a smile. "Didn't think you were gonna let that go. When Veronica lost control of her talent, I had an opportunity to move Talents north."

"They're all here?" Nora's pulse raced. Maybe she wasn't the last of her House—

"The dozen or so that survived the explosion are. I'd hoped to integrate them with the line up here, but failed to take Glynfyls's elitism into account. There was a big dust-up…long story short, neither were having any of it. They've got an enclave in the city. Pithy runs an off-book clinic in the Pinch, others run the commons infirmary on the fifth rung. Typically, none of them will treat Original Houses. Based on what Marcos told me, that Fitz kid saved your life vouching for you. The Binders on the hill wouldn't have been able to do a damned thing."

Nora ran her thumb over the tattoo on the inside of her wrist. What had she signed up for? "If the Original Houses won't accept me as one of their own…"

"Didn't say that. House Jester has a vote, and the line's pledged to Flynn based on Kara's strength of talent. Some convoluted Binder's logic I'm sure, but marrying Flynn seems to have granted her a legitimacy the others lacked. I'm assuming that'll transfer to you."

"That was before he split, and if I understand things correctly, the Jester vote was created for an heir. Kara's pregnancy isn't going well. If this was the Source, I would terminate and pull her from the breeding roster."

"Not an option, and I'd keep that to yourself." The dragon was back. Was it concern or avarice he had for the child? The lack of either for Kara stiffened Nora's spine.

"The chances this child will be a pure Binder—"

"Are slim to none, but they've committed." Cal shrugged the dragon away. "This is gonna come to a head a hell of a lot sooner than her pregnancy. You know how to play the game, Nora. Charm the pants off them and do what you gotta do to get this done. I've got enough on Titus to kick things off, but with the Sons coming up in force, he needs to stay put until Flynn gets a handle on things. You have to do the same with your line."

Nora's fingers were at her ring again. "The Breakers up here...do you think their Alpha will be able to best Beritram?" The name took the heat from her body as it left her lips. She should've killed him after he'd gotten her with Kara and damned the consequences. The damage she'd done to his channel had left him even more of a monster.

"Nope. I don't." He patted her knee and stood. "But I wouldn't worry about that too much. I've got one waiting in the wings."

FLYNN POUNDED THE HEAVY BAG, sweat stinging his eyes, running down his torso in rivulets and soaking his shorts. His consciousness fuzzed in and out, maintaining zero impossible with the constant burn through his channel. It was raw with what he'd been pushing Kara, and it still wasn't enough.

What'd the fuck had he done to her?

His eyes stung, feeling her up there, out cold, in the same position as when he'd left her to take those pledges last night. Jon had shot her full of something around two a.m. and her color had improved, but that wasn't saying much. Flynn hadn't slept for shit, checking on her every few minutes to reassure himself she was still breathing. Christ, he prayed to God his uncle could come up with something—

He rested his head against the bag, panting. She hadn't wanted his kid. Maybe it was more than some bullshit Source indoctrination. Had she known on some level what it would do to her? His eyes raised up, past the beams of the vaulted ceiling.

Please, don't take them away...

He dashed an arm across his eyes. It was his own goddamned fault. Christ, he knew he should've kept his fucking mouth shut—shouldn't have told her he loved her, said those fucking words—nothing he'd ever given a shit about lasted. And if this didn't... He grimaced, pulling more talent, feeling his channel fray—

"Is now a bad time?"

An old man in a gray robe stood by the door. Flynn licked the sweat from his lip. How the hell did he get in? "No, but I can't think of one that's gonna be any better. Can I help you?"

"In time. Right now, I'm here for you." He walked over and extended a hand. "Voss Mangleshield. Cal was kind enough to point me in your direction."

Flynn snorted, shaking it. Besides Rogan, he didn't think his grandfather had much use for Breakers. But then again, what did he really know about the asshole, other than what served his fucking agenda? Flynn grabbed a towel and scrubbed his head. "Assembly's in an hour."

"I won't take much of your time. I'm here acting as proxy for the Breaker line."

You gotta be fucking—"Yeah? How's that work?"

"Same way as the others, I'd imagine. You slice your palm, I slice mine…"

Great, another wiseass. Flynn flipped the towel over his shoulder and grabbed a water. "Figured that'd fall under Phyllis's purview." Last thing he needed was to piss her off any more than she already was.

"The council has the ultimate authority over our line, especially now. Trials have knocked everyone from their rung, from the meanest grunt to the Alpha Prime."

"Sure that's been working out well for you." He flicked the bottle's cap away and chugged half of it.

"Better than you'd think. You know, you've been quite the topic of debate within the conclave."

"Wouldn't that fall under Breaker Business?"

"Perhaps." Voss shrugged. "There's some that would argue you qualify as such, but only an Alpha can decide who belongs in the pack." He began to unwind the bandage around his palm. "Until then, you're not a Breaker, but with these pledges, you're accepting control of our line and army, until the hierarchy has been determined."

Flynn stared at him. The fuck? "Why?"

The old man chuckled, making a fist. "Do you know what a Menot is?"

What the hell did that have to do—"Some kind of Breaker priest."

"At times. Our duty is to mentor the young. Teach them the Way of Honor. None can deny that you walk the path, nor that your children will follow you upon it. I had meant to speak with you later today, but since Cal asked to see my mate…" He shrugged again. "I tagged along. Two birds, one stone, and hell freezing over. It's shaping up to be quite a day. We've been waiting for him to contact us since your father was born, but Shane wouldn't allow it."

Flynn stiffened at his grandmother's name. "You knew her?"

"I did, and until two nights ago, had never thought to see another woman fight like that. Their technique is markedly similar, but that stands to reason since the same man taught them."

Flynn grabbed another bottle of water, playing with the cap and not about to follow that trail of breadcrumbs. "What did Cal want?"

"A recipe. Wyn makes exceptional banana bread." Asshole. Voss grinned at his expression, slapping his thighs as he stood. "Now, I've taken up enough of your time. Will you accept our pledges?"

Flynn chewed his lip, eyeing the weeping slash across the man's outstretched hand. Christ, they knew, how could they not, but—"Sure you wanna give them to a split?"

The Menot's hand didn't waver. Neither did his gaze, boring into Flynn's. "Might makes right, and no Breaker throws away a weapon. We know what's coming for us, and have seen what you can do, though I'd imagine it would be even more impressive if you knew how to use it. Sand's open when you're ready." The corners of his eyes crinkled. "But in either event, wielding the swords of Glynfyls can't be too much different than a knife."

Flynn tossed the towel from his shoulder, stomach wrenching. Voss meant the plateau. What he'd done to those Sons. If that's what they wanted…that blackness inside him licked up, seductive.

No. He wasn't gonna be that animal—

Christ, who the hell was he kidding? He'd do whatever it took to keep Kara safe, and Glynfyls couldn't afford for him to say no. The Breakers knew exactly what he was, what he was capable of, and were handing him a fucking army to do more of it. He gave a dry laugh, scrubbing at his head. A squad maybe, but an army? Wasn't happening, neither was trotting his ass down there to spar. Weapons cut both ways, and knocked off her rung or no, Phyllis must be having kittens. How the hell…

When in doubt, delegate.

"Fine, but Lady Breakspear continues speaking as First, and Stonefist retains control of the army. You feel like you need to justify it, have them report to me."

Voss's grin grew. "He will win who has military capacity and is not interfered with by the sovereign. So sayeth the Way."

"No, so sayeth Sun Tzu." Flynn snorted, unwrapping his own palm. After pounding on that bag, it had re-split and the bandage was soaked. "That's a direct quote from *The Art of War*."

The old man laughed, a gleam in his eye. "I look forward to getting to know you better, Lord Scot." They clasped hands, exchanging blood and talent. Flynn grabbed his shirt and walked the old man to the gate, wondering what the hell Cal had really wanted.

He poked his head into his grandfather's office. It did smell like banana bread. An untouched loaf sat on the desk between Cal and Merchant, and they looked grim. Christ, what now? The little barrister stood, gathering papers.

"Laughlin. You have good timing, though the circumstances aren't. The constabulary will be here shortly. You'll let me do the talking."

"The constabulary?" Flynn looked between them. "About what?"

"A reel of you pulling Breaker talent was leaked to the press."

Pulling—

Titus's fucking bots.

"And the only place that could've come from is the Source," he growled, hoping that was the only thing people had a reel of.

"Julia Cree has come forward to corroborate it. Her statement claims you've known your status for well over a decade, and that is why she's been in such opposition to your political involvement. The constabulary has made it clear that they intend to charge you." Merchant's briefcase snapped closed. "I suggest you get cleaned up. I'm anticipating plenty of press."

The barrister's footsteps faded from the room. A manic laugh burbled up Flynn's throat. He dropped into the armchair in front of Cal's desk, pulling at his beard. Fuck. He'd known this was coming, and Julia jumping on it to bury him wasn't a surprise. Christ, she was a snake…

"Merchant says the case is gonna come down to semantics, and I can't remember if a definition was ever established legally differentiating a split from a twist. Damn Incursion wiped out half the records hall, and the copies here…"

Flynn snorted. Cal filed like a squirrel. "Have French get ahold of Dorian Blaise, he owes me. Keep the other Finders and Miriam out of it."

"Any reason, other than the fact that I'm sure this is already giving her a coronary? Woman's a mess between having to leave the farm and Leo missing."

"Prydees are tight with Crandall, and Miriam can't keep her mouth shut. He's been trying to blackmail me with that shit that went down on the plateau, and I threw him under the bus during Assembly. Asshole had Riegel and let him out of lockup three days before the fight."

His grandfather grunted, pulling a folio out from under the loaf of banana bread. "That's a Finder for you. Sure you can trust this Blaise character?"

A vision of that little doll popped into Flynn's mind, along with the scarring beneath Dorian's gloves. "Yeah. Why did you want to see Mangleshield's wife?"

Cal flipped through the folio like he hadn't heard him. "I finally took a look at that chip you gave me. It contains genealogies from a blacksite. Whatever troops you thought Titus had, double it, along with their metrics. I wanna know why your cousin was so hot to get it, let alone how—"

"Who the hell knows why Leo does anything. Answer the fucking question, Cal."

His grandfather ran a hand over his mustache, muttering to himself.

"Mangleshield already spilled that Gran wouldn't let you call him after Lot was born."

Cal glared at him from beneath his brows. "Did he now?"

Christ, this motherf—"Damn it Cal, she's dead! Why the hell wouldn't you tell me—"

"Fine. You wanna know the dirt? When she bonded me, her House disowned her. They didn't speak after that. Couldn't even get them into the same room. She swore she'd never use talent again. Damn woman kept that vow till the day she died, and made me swear if you presented as a Breaker, I'd keep them out of it."

"Keep them—" Flynn ran a shaking hand through his hair. Jesus, he had more family somewhere in Glynfyls? Was that why Cal had threatened to disown him after he'd started banging Breakers? His stomach cramped. He didn't wanna know and yet he did. "Which House is it?"

His grandfather's eyes turned to hard jade chips. Flynn's throat bobbed. Shit. This had been what Kara was talking about, the dragon—

"You'd best wash up."

Dismissed, Flynn scrubbed at his face, going upstairs. Why the fuck did everything have to be a goddamned state secret? Cal had bonded a Breaker. That had to have been a shit show. Everyone had probably declared it a House Matter and buried their heads in the sand like they did with everything else. Shit, he had too, for his entire fucking life. His feet dragged through the bower, stopping to watch the carp flicker beneath the patches of duckweed, rubbing his knuckles.

Feeling hollow.

...arms wrapped around his head, curled on the ground. Boots hard against his spine. "You got nothin', Scot, just a big, dumb loser like your old man! What the hell even are you..."

Exactly what everyone had thought he was. He ran a hand over his mouth, that goddamned gnawing in his guts...

"Flynn?"

Shit.

He went into the bedroom, footsteps echoing across the burled floor, his wavery reflection slinking along with him. Kara was in the big canopy bed at the end of the room, a fire burning beside it in the onyx and obsidian hearth. Sharp points of light flickered from the stone like eyes. Seeing him for what he was.

She was propped against the pillows with the cat in her lap. An IV was set up at the bedside. Whatever they were pumping into her was a weird bruise-color, and a funky iridescence writhed through it like it was alive. He was surprised Hiss wasn't all over that, though the stupid cat left the fish alone, too.

"Gross, huh?" Her smile was fragile, cheekbones too sharp beneath the dark circles rimming her eyes. His heart lurched, reminded of the last time he'd seen Bea, her pregnancy stripping the flesh from her bones at an alarming rate. "A Breaker came. She wouldn't tell me what it was, but I'm feeling a lot better…do I look that bad?"

Why the hell wouldn't Cal—Christ, fuck him. "You're beautiful." He kissed her forehead, sitting at the edge of the fur coverlet.

Her eyebrow quirked. "Liar."

"The Source leaked holo of me pulling talent, I have to go down to the constabulary to give a statement."

Kara went white. "What are they going to do?"

"Merchant says they're gonna charge me."

"They can't—"

"They can. Julia corroborated it with a statement. Cal's trying to track down the legalese to get me clear, but if he can't—"

"What can I do?"

He kissed her softly. "Take care of yourself. I need you here, safe. I don't want you worrying, I'll know."

Her anxiety churned through their bond. "Was that all that they leaked?"

"For now, but we both know the rest of it is only a matter of time."

She gave him a dirty look, and he forced a smile for her. Her expression went hard with the blackness of her 'lust, the hair on the nape of his neck rising at the metallic sharpness of it.

"Shh… I need you better. This isn't gonna play out overnight." His eyes flicked to the IV. What the hell was that stuff? He fingered the tubing running across the coverlet, then kissed her forehead again. "I gotta get cleaned up. Rest."

REST. That wasn't going to happen.

Kara watched Flynn slump into the bathroom. She seethed, her heart breaking. Julia. That bitch was long overdue a beat down. Kara dislodged the cat to adjust the drip on her IV bag, jaw clenching at the accompanying burn. She didn't care. She was going to kill—

"Not planning on getting out of bed, I hope?" Audrey asked, coming in with a tray. She settled it across Kara's lap. Broth and toast. Her temper flared. She wasn't an invalid!

"That's exactly what I plan on doing," she snapped.

"I don't think that's advisable—"

"I don't care what you think!"

Audrey's eyes went wide, glancing at the IV bag. "I don't—"

Kara whipped the tray across the room, slinging soup over the woman. A stab of guilt cut through the blackness. What was she doing? She gripped her temples, trying to pull zero. The burn from the IV surged up her arm to the side of her neck, her head buzzing like she was on some kind of upper…

Audrey was frozen, holding her wet dress away from herself.

Tears pricked Kara's eyes. "I'm so sorry…I didn't mean—" She broke into sobs.

"What the hell's going on out here?" Flynn stood in the doorway, a towel wrapped around his waist and soap in his hair.

Kara sobbed harder.

Audrey smiled. "Nothing, just hormones…"

He grunted, shooting them both a look before going back into the bathroom.

"You were told not to touch this." She readjusted the drip on the IV, then went to smooth her sodden skirts and swore.

Kara laughed. She didn't think the secretary knew that word.

Audrey scowled back at her. "Look, I'm just as angry as you over that…creature smearing Laughlin. I don't know what you thought you were going to do, but you need to beat her at her own game. As much as I'd love to see you kick the shit out of her, that's not going to help him."

Another laugh burbled up. This was Audrey? Her secretary rolled her eyes, bending to pick up the dishes scattered across the floor. "I am sorry."

"The Bane mentioned something like this could happen. You're in a delicate state, and we're all aware that this doesn't help." She returned to the bedside, pushing her glasses up. "It may surprise you, but there was a point in my life I was very angry. As you've experienced, Glynfyls's society isn't easy for anyone who differs from certain expectations."

"Is that when your hair was green?" Hiss jumped back up on the bed, and Kara rubbed under his chin.

Audrey smirked. "Among other colors. I tell you this because my angst led me down the hill. It's a different city than the one you've been exposed to thus far. After Deirdre died, Lot totally cut Laughlin off. He lived down there for a few years and gained himself a reputation, albeit unwittingly, and what he's done since he's been back has only reinforced their good opinion of him. He's a better man than he thinks, and few, if any, below the hill care if he's a split or whatever they're calling it. It's those upon it that have no quibbles about punishing him for it, but they won't risk another uprising."

"But so many of them have pledged…"

"Yes, and this provides a loophole should any of them have buyer's remorse. You need to remain calm and let this…" She gestured at the IV. "Whatever it is, do its magic. Master Scot has instructed me to make the necessary arrangements to transport you to Assembly tomorrow. I'm sure you would prefer to walk instead of being shifted in on a litter."

Kara's stomach dropped, thinking of the last time she'd been in that room. There'd been so many people… Her fingers tensed in Hiss's fur, and he nipped at her.

"By myself?"

"No, Lot will escort you." That didn't do anything to settle Kara's stomach. Audrey hefted the tray against her soggy dress. Her eyes flicked to the bathroom. "I'll be in with some suggested reading after he leaves. I'd advise keeping this discussion to yourself. Laughlin has enough to worry about."

Kara nodded, biting her thumb. That burn in her arm had subsided along with the weird rush. What was that stuff? She was watching it churn through the tubing when Flynn came out of the shower to dress.

"Better?" he asked, pulling on his trousers.

"Yes. It was just a lot to take in. I feel so helpless…"

"You're anything but. I'm hoping this won't take too long. Merchant is gonna try and get me released, but if he can't—" Flynn's face crumpled at the knock at the door, and his dread made Kara want to vomit. "Yeah?"

French came in. "There are several constables and an Intelligencer here for you, sir."

Flynn turned back to Kara, kissing her brow. "You know."

She bit her lip to keep from crying again. What she was feeling from him—Ugh! He was none of those things! "I do, and I love you, too."

His smile was forced as he left her.

When the door opened again, she wasn't expecting Cal.

"How you feeling, Karabelle?"

She wiped her eyes, smiling at the nickname. "Physically, much better. Whatever this stuff is, it works."

He grunted, dragging over a chair, and settled down with a stack of papers. "Should've called it in sooner…" A faraway look passed over his face and then he was back. "I'm gonna need you to sign these."

"What are they?"

He lit a cigarette. "The forms to transfer House Jester's vote to Nora. Your contract with Flynn already grants you full rights to House Scot's. Boy was damned firm on that point. His mother's influence, no doubt."

"What does that mean?"

"Means you're one of the few women up here legally able to assume control of your House's interests without your husband being dead. This goes sideways, it might be enough to save our vote."

Kara chewed her thumb, hearing what he wasn't saying. "He's not coming back tonight, is he?"

"No. They denied him bail before he'd even set foot in the station. He'll be spending the foreseeable future in lockup."

Kara swallowed the lump in her throat, pulling zero. After the little he'd told her about prison, what this was going to do to him…what having another reel of him out there was going to do to him…

She was going to kill Julia.

"If I sign this, will Nora be able to go with me tomorrow?"

"I'm counting on it, and with Flynn gone, if you want her to come stay the night, I won't tell."

Her eyes got misty and she nodded. "Please…but not in here. He'd be so upset…"

"I'll have French set up something in the North Wing. Deirdre hated it over there. Too dark to grow anything."

Kara took the pen from him, scanning the document. The legalese made her head swim. She gave up, flipping to the last page and signing it. "Thank you. Why didn't you ever tell him about Dionis? It might have given him a measure of peace to know the man that killed his mother was dead."

Cal blew out a cloud of smoke and stood. "Because sometimes it's easier to let people believe what they want than to show them what you are. You've seen more of that than he has, and I'd like to keep it that way."

"Easier for you, or for them?"

"Easier to bury them when you need to." He took the papers from her, his voice hard. "Audrey will be in with another tray. Suggest you eat it this time, before someone decides to floss with you."

Kara watched him leave, everything he and Audrey had said a muddle. Who was she up here? Source Kara wanted to lock herself in the bathroom until all of this was over, and the Kara that'd bouted at the Pony wanted to eviscerate Julia. Beat them at their own game… She gave a sad laugh. How, when she didn't even know the rules?

The door opened again, and this time, Audrey came in with a massive stack of papers.

A grim cast of determination set Kara's jaw. She needed to learn them, fast.

ROGAN SAT WEDGED in the cleft of an ancient hemlock, a sea of Sons churning beneath the trees. They'd infested the wide valley around the rail line, and it wasn't the only route they were taking north. This was the third company he'd come across behind Glynfyls's retreating troops.

The wind kicked up and his thighs tensed, riding the swaying limb as it creaked and shuddered. His expression was grim, counting campfires.

Logistically, there were too damn many.

He leaned back against the bole, a sinking suspicion in his gut. It was proven out when another chapter of Sons popped into existence at the top of a rise. How the hell had they gotten hold of gating stones? As far as he knew, none but the original Fetch and Finder could wield enough talent to make them. And aside from the monstrosities up in Glynfyls, he'd thought Elize and Richard had only made enough of the little ones for the seven of them, the weight of his own hanging on a chain against his sternum.

Christ, who the hell knew what Elize had actually done, but Richard? Shit, he'd been as solid as they came. He wouldn't have dicked around on the side with something like that. They were too damned dangerous.

And now Richard was too damned dead.

Rogan glanced down at the crunch of boots in the snow, going still. Two men approached, heads bent as they scanned the ground for firewood.

"You see it?" the one in a blue coat asked the other wearing a scarf.

"Yeah, man, it's the real deal. Skin's all peelin' back like his damn skull's pushing it out. They say being chosen by the Mother's better than bangin' on coke, but Jesus…"

Blue coat nodded. "Ain't pretty, not that Victor was to begin with."

They both snickered, gathering up fallen limbs.

"Hittin' one of them big houses next," Scarf said. "Hear they're loaded with loot—"

"Ain't gonna let us take none till the job's done. Wants us at that plateau by Tuesday. Shit'll just slow us down. 'Sides, how you gonna carry it all?"

"I got pockets, and the convoy ain't far behind." Scarf shrugged, hefting up a load of wood. "Judgement Day's on a Tuesday?"

"How the hell do I know? Ain't like Easter, and it's a far cry from spring." Blue Coat squinted up at the sky. "Smells like a storm's coming."

"Guess we better hit more than one of them big houses then. Plenty already got frostbite bad. Storm'll fuck us…"

They trudged back towards the fires, and Rogan let out a long breath, looking out over the valley, the haze of smoke sour at the back of his throat.

He wasn't getting involved.

His eyes closed and he swore at himself. Christ, that was exactly what he was doing. All that shit with Phyllis, witnessing the trials, talking about that damned shield… And here he was, up a tree, playing fucking scout—

He was already hip-deep.

One of the captains ambled into the bracken and dropped trou, squatting.

Rogan pulled his blade. Might as well start a rock collection while he was at it.

CHAPTER SIX

Slide [slīd] *noun*

1. *A phenomenon unique to gestating Breaker females during which a subtle swing of personality traits is evidenced. Indicative of the inevitable loss of control over their bloodlust, it manifests at various rates, recommending the practice of sedation after impregnation, preempting succumbing to the pheromone.*

– Excerpt from A Treatise on Talents, Third Edition

"A Fetch's talent is predicated upon their ability to keep in contact with the item they're shifting, and requires knowledge of the location they want to move it to, either by personal experience, or via the imprinting of a locale. The more talented the Fetch, the larger the mass and farther their range of translocation. Interestingly, this ability is limited to fixed positions. Shifting into a moving object, such as a vehicle, is beyond their abilities, as is shifting to a living being..."

– Lord Hamn, Preceptor of Talent Theory,
Academy of Glynfyls

FITZ KNOCKED at the servant's entrance and stepped back, trying to ignore his throbbing head. The garden and the street beyond was all flat without energy overlaying it, but dread spiked up the back of his neck thinking about the auras inside Kristine's. Weren't making that mistake again.

The door swung open, just missing him.

Her butler frowned, most like because it had. Giles were as nasty as his mistress. Shite, most everyone drawing a check from the Prydees were.

"Alms are given before ten," the man rasped nasally.

"Sisters wanted t'see me." Damnable prick knew who the hell he were.

Giles frowned, and the door slammed shut.

Fitz slouched, digging his hands into his pocket, though he didn't need his coin to know this were a louse of an idea. Were as chill as the air. Still made him feel better to rub his thumb across it. He'd cleaned himself up and stopped drinking around noon, not that it would make a wit of difference—*Christ, Cajetan, help me get through this in one piece...*

The door swung open again, his jacket flicking back in its wake.

"They'll see you." The butler's lip curled to rival a bulldog's scowl as Fitz passed him.

Well, weren't that just tits. He slunk into the kitchen, and Giles's boney hand slapped down on his shoulder.

Colors ran.

They shifted into the music room. Cretin pinched his shoulder numb before he shifted out. Fitz bit back a grunt, knowing better than to rub it.

The shitty floral perfume Kristine bathed in seared his nostrils, and his knackers crawled up inside him. Damn room were rank with it. Was miserable hot to boot, too, a fire raging in the hearth. Velvet draperies swathed the long windows, and everything were upholstered into lilac muffins.

Twelve of the sisters was arrayed around a low dais, broods scattered amongst them. One of the younger girls sawed away at a violin in the middle of the room. She hit a sharp when she saw him and scowled. The rest ignored him, drinking their tea from china so fine you could read through it, yammering about Kristine's stupid birds.

"They really are exquisite, how long did you have to breed them to get that mauve?"

"Well over a decade. It isn't found anywhere else, and I've buyers around the globe. We refurbished the estate on the advances. It's quite a lucrative hobby."

Kristine gazed adoringly into an elaborate, gilded cage running the length of one wall. Exotic birds flitted about, trying to avoid the little girl stabbing at them with a fire poker. Prydees was all born vicious. One of them were probably his ma's. Couldn't tell by looks; all of them was butcher-plump with the same dark hair, brown eyes, and that wide Prydee mouth.

All of them save his ma, sitting in the corner looking like she were about to fade away she were so slight. His oldest half-sisters, Pauline and Claire, sat at her side, pointedly ignoring him the way you pointedly ignored someone that'd just ripped one in church. The other three had to be somewhere around here. Three, four? Shite, could be five. Didn't matter. They all hated him.

He closed his eyes, teeth grinding at the girl hitting another sharp. Christ, a blindfolded monkey could play better with its toes.

Giles came in with a trail of servants, delivering trays of dainties. Fitz's stomach rumbled. He ignored it, trying to read the titles of the books surrounding the granite hearth at the far end of the room. At some point they'd get tired of looking at him and decide to make this experience more miserable than it already—

The sawing stopped, giving way to a round of polite clapping. He tried not to look too relieved.

"What's the matter, Fitzpatrick? Didn't you enjoy Stella's playing?"

Shite.

His eyes flicked to Patricia's sour puss. They'd crucify him whatever he said.

Something jabbed into his back, that floral stench enveloping him. Kristine stepped from behind him, her deep-set eyes cold. "Patricia asked you a question."

"Eh…ya. It were real f—"

The back of her bloated hand took him across the face, rings slicing his cheek. "Speak like a human."

He looked away, wanting to throttle her. "It w-*was* lovely." Words tasted worse than her perfume.

"Girls, Giles has cake in the conservatory," she said over her shoulder, her eyes not leaving his.

Double shite.

The one with the poker started to whine. "But we want to watch you make him sorry—"

"Go."

The little battalion stomped off to listen from the hall.

"Show me your palms." Kristine said when they'd gone. He held them out. "Perhaps you're not as stupid as you look."

"Not possible," another quipped. The rest tittered.

Kristine's nasty smile was back. "Rebecca, didn't Fitzpatrick used to play violin?"

His mother's reply was too low for him to hear.

"Do you still?"

"No."

"No what?"

"No, me—*my* lady."

"Pity. Such fine, long fingers. Wasted on a piece of filth like you. Don't you agree?"

"Most everythin' is, ain't it?"

Kristine grabbed the front of his trousers and shifted his bits.

White light exploded behind his eyes. Fitz dropped, struggling to breathe. He dry-heaved, curling up on the thick carpet.

"What was that?" the evil harpy asked.

Spittle flecked his lips with every burst of tortured breath. Fuck, she weren't letting up—

"That's enough, Kristine," Constance said around a mouthful of something. "Let the pinchling go."

The vile bitch dropped talent and sniffed. She wiped her hand off on a bit of lacy nothing, and returned to a chair at the side of the room. Fitz gulped air, tears streaming down his cheeks. Fuckin' cunt… Six sets of gleeful eyes peered around the doorframe at him.

Constance dabbed at her too-red lips. "We wanted to make sure you were very clear that you're not to pledge to Laughlin Scot, and if we even suspect you've shifted from the city on an errand we've not sanctioned, Kristine will personally take great pleasure in removing that pitiful dangle between your legs, understood?"

"I'll take more pleasure in shifting the guts out of that vile harpy he's so fond of. How is your gran, Fitzpatrick?" She smirked malevolently. The pain in his knackers just beat out the surge of icy rage running through him. If they touched one hair on her head—

"And the next time a scion of this House tells you to bring someone to us, you will obey. You've cost us a rare opportunity."

Constance tsked. "I'm sure he had no idea of the implications—"

"That doesn't excuse it!"

"Of course not, but now he knows what he did was wrong, just as a dog does after you beat it for piddling on the rug. That should be enough to curb his behavior in the future."

They watched him writhe. Christ, he were fuckin' dinner theater, and his gran…shite. He needed t'suck it up. His breath came in sporadic bursts, and he fought not to moan. Wouldn't give 'em the satisfaction… He swallowed his hate along with the rising bile, packing it down tight with everything else they'd ever done to him. *Cajetan, ye promised t'make 'em pay…*

"Angry, isn't he?" one of them remarked like he were the weather.

"Mmm. What of it? He's as impotent as the pathetic beast that spawned him."

"I still don't understand why he's breathing."

"You don't need to." Kristine snapped open a paper, a sly grin sliding across her face. "Everything falls into place in its own time. Today's front page is a lovely example."

"Do you think it will stick?"

Patricia tapped her spoon on the side of her cup. "That little fool Miriam's beside herself about it. Between that and having to abandon her hovel outside of Hamlin—"

"Did they raze it along with the town?"

"Not last I heard; the wards on it are impressive. What she lacks in sense, she makes up for in talent. Pity it's wasted on her. Unless someone stumbles across the place with a nullifier…"

"We could always point them in the right direction—"

"No." Kristine were firm. "We're to steer clear of antagonizing Caliban Scot, and Miriam's upset enough as it is. She's been having fits over that missing boy of hers. The flighty goose won't leave her rooms. How she allowed herself to become so attached—" She narrowed her eyes at Fitz, gone still, pain reduced to an agonizing throb. "Get up."

Were she fuckin' serious? He met her gaze and a stab of fear lanced through him. If he didn't, were a good chance he wouldn't.

He'd see them in the ground first, his knackers be damned.

Fitz tried to uncurl, and his guts rebelled, vomit splattering across the thick wool carpet. Wrenching pain jolted through him again, and he curled back up. Women shrieked and the little girls in the hall squealed. He groaned. Served 'em fuckin' right.

"God, he's disgusting!"

"What did you expect?"

"Ugh, just get out, you filthy animal!"

Fitz were happy to oblige. He shifted back to his tenement, then pulled talent again, shifting the pain from his groin to one of his toes. He took a great gasping breath of air, clutching at himself and sprawling onto his back. Bitch had almost gelded him.

He relaxed his sight, staring at the peeling shiplap ceiling, waiting for the nausea to subside and taking some modicum of satisfaction that he'd pissed on their parade taking that lady of Scot's to Pithy. Didn't care why. Who the hell knew why them witches did anything? Just liked making people miserable far as he could tell…

He were keen on returning the favor.

His hand went to his pocket, fondling his coin and thinking. It grew warm, and he grinned, standing gingerly. Toe throbbed so bad it felt broke. He pulled talent, shifting to the 'Pipe.

Place were dour. He limped to the bar. Marl were hunched over his whiskey, watching the reels. Fitz threw down his last few units, and Molly replaced them with an ale.

"Who died?"

The old man snorted. "Them fuckers charged Lord Scot with being a split."

"The hell's that?"

"Some kind of twist ye don't know ye are 'til it happens."

Fitz grunted into his tankard. So that's what the sisters had been going on about.

Marl frowned, finishing off his glass. "That bitch Charlotte Maisey works for's saying he did know, and them hillies is in a froth. Naught but slander t'edge him out and stick it t'us for getting the better of 'em. Folks is fit t'be tied. Hear tell streets around the constabulary is packed again. Ain't nothing about this is gonna end well."

Never do. Fitz took a long pull. Adelaide sidled up to the bar, and he put the stool between them.

She flicked her hair over her shoulder like she didn't care. "Ye should've heard the shite Lotte used t'spill about that Cree woman. Ye'd think she confused her with a confessional, and the way Lotte run her mouth before she got all high and mighty, there ain't no way we wouldn't have heard about it, along with every stain she had t'scrub out of her lady's knickers."

"There many of 'em?" Fitz asked, sipping his ale.

She rolled her eyes. "Aye, ye pig, 'cept for the time she swore the woman was in the family way. Might've been true, way she clammed up and kept t'the hill after."

Little chance of that, way them hillies was. "Thought ye was working at the Pony?"

"Told ye, s'under new management, that fancy lord, Patton. Got plans for it. Don't want me till me face clears. One of ye boys in need? Do ye for half, if I can shack up a few nights."

Fitz adjusted himself, green just thinking about it. He swished a mouthful of ale around, washing the taste of bile from his teeth. "I'm set."

She looked like she was gonna hit him and stomped off to the other side of the pub. Christ, why'd she always have t'be so damned prickly, weren't like it were his job t'do right by her. Fitz patted his pockets, needing somewhat stronger than ale. Had t'be a unit or two he missed…

"I ain't one t'get involved in your affairs—"

"Then don't." Marl raised an eyebrow, and Fitz sighed, glancing at Adelaide cozying up to a sketchy bloke. Woman were a damned Breaker, she could take care of herself, most times at least. "Sorry. Them fuckin' Prydees—ye know where Steg is?"

"What the hell d'you want with a ratter?"

Fitz shrugged, draining his tankard. Bloke had passed, and she were on to the tables.

"I expect I don't wanna know, but'll hear about it plenty after the fact. Guild hired him t'clear up warehouse five."

"Thought he were on the hill."

"Nah, lost the contract t'Willems. Other's ain't keen on it neither. Hear tell he made some deal with them Intelligencers for the privilege."

"Always figured him for a nark. Well, I'll be off then." Fitz clunked his tankard down and shifted.

Warehouse five were at the end of the easternmost jetty where the trawlers docked. Fitz hunched against the wind. What it weren't whipping away stank like motor oil and yesterday's catch. Should've been more people about. Must be a right crowd at the constabulary. He hobbled down the weathered planks, gait roiling like the waves out in the bay. Storm were coming in.

Steg were right where Marl'd said he'd be, messing with his cages of weasels. They was full of the sleek critters chirping away. Cute, for all they stank. The man turned as he came in, pulling the rough woolen cap from his bald pate to scratch at it.

"McCreedy, what brings ye out? I ain't owe ye."

"Nah...ain't like that. Heard what happened, and thought I'd pass on some luck. Adelaide's looking t'shack up. Offering half price for the pleasure."

The dumpy little man licked his lips, eyes going to his cages. "Adelaide, ye say?"

"Aye." Fitz pulled at his crotch. "I'd take her up on it, but got meself in somewhat of a predicament, and I know how ye fancy her." Feeling weren't mutual, but any port in a storm. The wind kicked up again. One were definitely coming in.

Steg chuckled. "Been messin' with them dirty whores on Barris Street, have ye?"

"S'failing of mine. Adelaide were at the 'Pipe just now. Ye hurry, ye can catch her."

"More's the pity. I can't leave me beauties alone out here."

"Eh…don't blame ye. They is sleek. Which one's the best hunter?"

"That one there with the white on her nose. Bring's 'em back like one of them hillies's hounds."

Fitz pursed his lips and crouched down, considering the weasel. "That right? Vicious beastie, is she?"

"Nah, lovin' as a kitten, but that little one there, she'll shred ye soon as look at ye."

"This little one? Seems a lamb."

Steg snorted. "Ye put a finger any closer ye'll find out."

"I'll take your word for it." Fitz stood, dusting off his trousers. "Ye know, I got some time. Wouldn't mind sitting with 'em while ye set somewhat up with Adelaide."

The man's eyebrows rose. "For true?"

"Eh…ya. Don't like the thought of her out on them streets after she got messed up, and with the weather turning… Only don't tell her I sent ye. Wouldn't want her t'get the wrong idea, like I cared or nothing."

Steg gave Fitz a knowing look he didn't much like. "'Pipe ye said?"

Fitz grunted an affirmative.

"Shan't be long then. 'Preciate ye thinking of me, McCreedy. One good turn'll gain ye another." He jammed the hat back on his head and shifted out.

Right then, that outta the way…

Fitz subtly manipulated the energy around him, building a bubble to hide what he were about to do. He turned to the vicious little weasel Steg had pointed out, his halos glowing as he focused on her zipping about the cage.

Took longer than he'd like to get a lock on her, but as soon as he did, he shifted her into the middle of Kristine's birds.

Were like an M80 went off in a pillow factory.

Didn't have anything against them, but Kristine were another story, and it went a hell of a lot quicker than being poked to death. His breath hissed out, locking on the beastie again and shifting it back. Were a pity he'd not be able to see Kristine's face when she found them, but there were pleasure in doing a job.

He dropped talent, ignoring the hunger pains stabbing at him and smoothing away the energy he'd manipulated, none too soon.

Steg shifted back with a wide grin on his stubbly face. He slapped Fitz's shoulder.

"I owe ye, McCreedy. She were right amiable—ye feeling okay?"

Fitz wiped the sweat from his eyes. "Eh…them damned whores… think I'd best get meself t'Pithy."

"Aye. Ye look a fright."

Felt one too. Were basic math moving yerself place t'place. Doin' it from afar, that were fuckin' astrophysics with a side of quantum equations. Not t'mention impossible, and if anyone found out, he'd be at the bottom of the bay along with his da and little sisters. He needed an alibi, 'case any grew wise. Fitz rubbed at his coin, considering the options. Damned thing burnt so hot at the last, he yelped.

Pulling again, he shifted to Meddleton.

———

CAL STRODE down the foyer steps, a cloud of smoke billowing behind him. Talking to Kara had gone smoother than expected, especially with that shit pumping into her. He sighed, hoping she took to it better than Shane had. Damn woman had almost taken his head off more than once, and he knew full well Kara had her sights set on Julia. He exhaled another plume. What the hell had happened to her?

Granted, Flynn had treated the Cree girl like shit, but she'd been keen to take it. Why she'd turned up her nose at Leo… Cal snorted. Stupid question. Given the option he'd do the same. Little shit was as shifty as they came, and half Prydee to boot. No one in their right mind would get entangled with that damned family…which was ample explanation as to why Jon had done just that.

Boy was brilliant, but he didn't have the sense God gave a flea, and twice the nervous energy. At least Miriam wasn't the worst of the lot. Could the Prydees be that Northern connection Flynn had been talking about? Cal chewed his cigar. Didn't feel right. They'd never given a shit about anything aside from feathering their own nest—

A lanky blond kid appeared in the middle of the foyer.

Cal paused on the step. That was quick; he'd just sent that message to Markham.

"Didn't expect you so soon. Office is this way. We're still waiting on someone."

The kid shoved his hands into his pocket and fiddled with something before following him down the hall. Cal kept an ear cocked. Looked like the Fetch would make off with the silver otherwise.

"Scotch is on the sideboard, might be a spell…didn't catch your name."

"S'Fitz," he mumbled, pouring a full glass. "Ye got somewhat t'eat?"

"Potentially." Cal plunked down into his chair's divot. "You the same Fitz that picked up a package for me?"

"Eh…ya. Lord Scot told Markham I should come collect me pay."

"Did he now?"

The kid threw back half the glass like it was water and smacked his wide lips. "Aye."

"Well, I suspect I should pay you then." Cal counted out a stack of units and set them on the desk. Didn't look like he'd know what to do with a check, or be able to sign it, for that matter.

Fitz limped over and rippled the edge of the stack with a thumb. "S'more than ye owe."

It was, but not by much. Interesting that the kid had caught it, never mind brought it to his attention. Ran contrary to what Graham had to say about him. Up close, he didn't look so hot and was older than Cal had taken him for. Early to mid-twenties, if he had to guess. Fitz shrank beneath his scrutiny. Shoulders rounding, hiding behind that curly mop…

"Think of it as incentive to finish the next one. Take a seat. I'll have French bring something up. Anything in mind?"

"Eh…I ain't particular."

Cal rang down to the kitchen for a steak. "So, you're Rebecca's boy, aren't you? Miriam's youngest sister?"

He shrugged, draining the glass and staring forlornly at the bottom. Cal leaned over and poured the kid another. Looked like he needed it. "Don't happen to know where Leo is, do you?"

Fitz snorted. "Probably out fuckin' someone over."

Wasn't wrong about that. "If you see him, do me a favor and let me know. Preferably without him finding out."

"Owe ye money?"

"No. He owes me a goddamned explanation."

Kid grunted. "Ye said somewhat 'bout a job?"

"I did. Thought you were—"

French cleared his throat in the doorway. "A Fetch has arrived for you, sir."

Cal kept his eyes on Fitz. "You know which one?"

"A Joseph Dashell."

Boy scowled, and Cal took a long drag of his cigar. "What do you know about him?"

"Eh…" Fitz pulled on the scrap of beard beneath his lip. "Works at the customs house."

"That all he work for?"

"I ain't a narc."

That'd be a no. "Never said you were, but I figured you'd want to earn that incentive."

Boy wet those wide lips of his, hand going to his pocket. "He's a bully boy for the Prydees…does some sniffing for them Intelligencers."

Cal looked at French. "Don't think I'll need him after all. That steak coming?"

"Yes, sir."

"Throw a potato on the plate, and I need you to make up a room in the North Wing. Invite Nora for a sleepover. Kara shouldn't be alone tonight."

The butler inclined his head and left.

Cal stared at Fitz. After what Flynn had said, dodging that bullet had been a close thing. They had enough shit going on without handing Crandall ammunition. Keeping this kid close abruptly seemed wise.

"Why do you think Markham sent him?"

He shrugged, looking at his empty glass again. Cal had the feeling it was the equivalent of Flynn counting ceiling tiles. He stubbed out his cigar. "If I'm gonna be paying you, I expect you to answer when I ask a question."

Fitz glanced up at him through that tangle of hair, his eyes flashing, defiant. Yeah…boy was Original House all right. He did one hell of a job burying his pride, but it wasn't dead. "Are ye paying me then?"

"How's two hundred units a week sound?"

"What for?"

"Answering questions to start."

"I told ye, I ain't a narc."

"You also don't seemed too enamored with the Prydees or Crandall."

Fitz's hand went back to his pocket. What did he have in there? Cal opened a drawer and flipped two hundred more units on the desk.

Kid tugged on that stupid patch again, frowning. "Both of 'em got Markham by the short hairs. I'd say someone heard ye was lookin' for a Fetch and wanted t'know why."

Cal poured himself another three fingers of scotch. He pulled out his tobacco pouch and sat back, thinking about that. French came in with a tray, and the kid attacked what was on it like he hadn't eaten in days.

"Make up another."

French nodded, shooting Fitz a pitying glance. Cal made sure the same expression wasn't on his face. Didn't think it would go over too well.

"The recipient of that other missive regrets their inability to personally attend to your needs at the present moment." The butler removed a small velvet bag from his vest pocket. "If this is insufficient, they believe they will have some availability tomorrow evening."

Cal snorted, taking the bag. God, he hated dealing with Finders. He emptied it onto his blotter. A crystal shard the size of his thumbnail bounced onto the front page of this morning's paper.

"You know how to work one of these?"

"Might of seen one once." Fitz shrugged, chewing.

Cal grunted. Kid was about as forthcoming as a Shade, but he could appreciate that. "Think you can pull the imprint from it?" Wasn't something Cal excelled at.

"Mayhap." Fitz glanced back at the paper, a still of Flynn front and center. "He in the nick?"

"Yeah."

Kid's jaw slowed, watching Cal's face. "Commons don't give a shite what he is, and one of me acquaintances knows Lotte, that maid of Mistress Cree's. Said she were a right confessional for the lady, an' if it were true, way she run her mouth, thems would've heard about it."

"Yeah? This acquaintance of yours ever hear anything interesting?"

Fitz dredged the last bit of meat across his plate. He'd inhaled the damned thing. Cal hadn't even seen him eat the potato. All that was left was a bit of bone.

"Just the usual from thems that work on the hill." He popped the last bite in his mouth. "Were good, thank ye."

Cal licked the flap of his cigarette closed. "You got another one coming. Enlighten me with the usual while we wait."

"Ye really want whore's gossip?"

"You gonna tell me how to spend my money?"

Fitz shrugged. "Said she whinged about every stain she had t'scrub out of her lady's knickers, 'cept for the time she swore the woman was in the family way, and that it might've been true, 'cause Lotte went mum after."

Cal stared at him. Un-fucking believable. That had to be it. "Where the hell did you come from?"

"Eh…why? What've ye heard? Thems was her words, not mine."

Cal tossed him another hundred units. "Then give that to her."

"Ye serious?"

"Yeah. Now see what you can do with that shard."

Kid was on a roll, and Cal wasn't about to cash out.

OTTO STOOD in a shale cavern lined with crates of munitions. It was part of the extensive network riddling the shores of Casmot's Bay and extending beneath the city, throughout the plateau. The portion of the tunnels that Titus's operatives occupied had become quite cozy. A cot in one of the natural stone chambers beyond this one was calling Otto's name, but as always, business before pleasure.

This was a bit of both.

He frowned at the ratty little man Titus's cell had just hauled in, caked in his own filth. It had only been a matter of time before they hunted him down. Otto didn't believe in loose ends, and Arileo's mind was as shifty as the rest of him. He had just enough Breaker in his lineage to make coercing him challenging at best.

Fortuitously, the pettiness of his core persona made up for that.

It'd latched on eagerly to the majority of Otto's suggestions, and in some cases modified them into even more deviant behaviors. That sex reel that had driven Scot from Glynfyls was a prime example. Mother had wanted something to tarnish House Scot's reputation, and Arileo had delivered in spades.

Otto toed the Fetch's side, and he groaned, unable to move away from his slick of vomit.

"Please…" One of his hands rose weakly, beseeching him.

Otto laughed, crouching down. "Need a fix do you?"

The man whimpered in the affirmative.

Ah. One of the delightful side effects of coercion. As a directive faded, it created symptoms not unlike withdrawal from one of the more virulent narcotics available. Something to do with the stimulation of the pleasure centers, dopamine, blah, blah, blah. Otto hadn't paid much attention to the theory, save that it was extremely unpleasant, and could last for weeks.

It also interfered with a subject's ability to use talent.

Otto cocked his head, enjoying the man's misery. "No. I don't think I'll oblige. Things above are playing out just as I'd like, and you, my friend, have a tendency to over salt the soup." Leo sobbed raggedly as Otto stood, turning to the Breaker waiting in the shadows. "Throw him in a hole and keep an eye on him."

The man grunted and grabbed one of Arileo's ankles, dragging him across the coarse sand, out of the chamber. Otto's lips pursed to whistle, following in their wake. No, Arileo discovering Julia in her current state would risk him spilling all out of spite, or triggering her demise. Pity Mother didn't want him put him down yet. He was like a dull knife, as likely to slip and cut the hand that wielded it as not.

Several days stewing in a hole was just the thing.

They littered the tunnels, constantly changing their geography. Some of the sinkholes were small, mere depressions in the earth. Others had swallowed vast tracts, creating dimples in the plateau above or flooding below. A subterranean sea lay to the west, strange fish and creatures the likes of which Jules Verne had never imagined lurking within its midnight depths.

Arileo was unceremoniously dumped in one of the holes roughly the height of a tall man and a quarter of that wide. It was only slightly damp. That wouldn't do much to improve the chills he seemed to be experiencing, but it wouldn't kill him either.

Otto would take great pleasure in doing that himself when the situation allowed. The Breaker capped the hole with a round of iron grating pilfered from the sewers. They abutted one of the tunnels nearby, allowing for easy access into the city, and the rankness of the effluent kept the proliferation of smugglers and degenerates that haunted the labyrinth clear of their lair.

"Paper has the Sons two days out. What does Titus want us to do?" the Breaker asked, dusting off his hands. Those cramped around a small table playing cards raised their heads to listen, the others sprawled around the room on cots and crates coming to attention as well.

"He anticipates mobilizing once they hit the plateau. His troops will crush that filthy cult between them and the city. A flare will signal you to begin the offensive behind the walls."

A sub with deep pockmarks spoke up. "Engineering Guild's close t'activating the shield. Got some Binder bitch in there with enough talent t'make the weaves work. Big Breaker with her. Been talking with the proctor about bots."

Mmm. That would be Nora Jester. Otto glowered. She and the

Commandant could prove to be problematic, but Mother wanted her alive, and Titus just wanted her period.

Perhaps it was time to set that in motion.

FLYNN SAT in a drab room at a shitty little table facing a pane of two-way glass. The chair across from him was empty, and had been since they'd brought him in here. Merchant was somewhere on the other side of the reinforced steel door, running interference with the constabulary and every camera in Glynfyls.

The little barrister was one of the better ones Cal had hired over the years. He'd bullied his way right through the mob of press, and had gotten Flynn into an interrogation room, instead of letting him languish in the center of the station, or in gen pop.

He rubbed at his wrists, nerves still jagged from when they'd cuffed him. A flush crept up his neck, heart rate speeding just thinking about being put in a cell…a cage…locked up again like a fucking animal. He took a slow breath…

…Accepting hardship as the pathway to peace…

Christ, he'd always thought that line was bullshit. Fucking serenity now.

Flynn scratched at his beard and sighed, tipping back his chair, looking at the ceiling. It was one of those crappy suspended ones. Someone had tried to paint over the brown watermarks a couple times. Hadn't worked, and funk was blooming through the cracked latex.

Sooner or later, the ugly always bled through.

The door chunked open and Merchant came into the room, sounds of a muted crowd behind him. "I suggest you cloak this conversation. We have five minutes before you're to be remanded into the Intelligencers' custody."

Flynn's halos flared. "The Intelligencers?"

"Tensions in the city are worrisome, as is the crowd that's gathered outside of the station, demanding your release."

"You serious?"

"You keep asking me that. Do I strike you as a jocular man?"

He did not.

The barrister pulled out the other chair and sat, placing his briefcase on the table. Sliding it to one side, he snicked it open and retrieved a stack of papers. "Start signing."

Flynn scanned the first document and handed it back. "No."

"What do you mean, 'no'?"

"I knew I was a split a couple days before it happened. I won't lie about it."

"You knew, or you were told?"

Flynn ignored the pen on the table, staring at his hands.

Merchant sighed. "Laughlin, I do a great deal of research on potential clients before I accept a retainer. Helps me sleep. I almost didn't take Master Scot's commission, given your reputation, but then I had your juvenile records pulled."

Flynn eyes snapped to him. Those had been sealed.

Merchant didn't blink. "One of the first charges against you was for assault. There were several witnesses clearing you, but you wouldn't speak in your own defense. Not in that instance, and not in any of the others." He riffled the edge of the documents in front of him. "You did, however, admit your guilt, rather vehemently on several occasions."

"If I did it, I did it."

"And if you didn't, allowing someone to slander you is a crime in and of itself. Knowing and suspecting are two very different things."

Flynn chewed the scar on his lip. "What if I did know? What if I've always known?"

"This is not the time for philosophical introspection. I've viewed the holo. It's a grainy shot of you using Breaker talent. The sound bite has you admitting you're a split, and that Master Scot had prior knowledge of your status."

Of course it did. Christ, he couldn't fucking win. "What'll happen to Cal?"

"I don't know. Due to the unique circumstances under which a split is created, it could be argued you may never have developed a secondary talent, making his foreknowledge meaningless. They'll counter that ambiguity doesn't change the fact that you're dual-talented—"

"And Overlord is supposed to pull all six." What a bunch of fucking hypocrites. Flynn snorted, picking up a copy of Julia's testimony. His temples throbbed as he read. "You gotta—really? She didn't disclose earlier to save my House's reputation, in light of our past relationship? This is all fucking lies."

"Regardless, the Assembly is scheduled to vote on your eligibility to hold a seat while legal matters progress."

Flynn laughed. That hadn't taken long. He looked down at his hands, fingers flickering with talent. Christ.

Merchant took off his glasses, polishing the lenses. "For what it's worth, I don't think they'll be able to push it through, given the state of the commons, however, your denial of any foreknowledge would go a long way to sway anyone on the fence."

The door chunked open again, and two Intelligencers came in. "Time."

Flynn dropped his cloak and stood, leaving the pen on the table.

"SO, TELL ME ABOUT LAUGHLIN." Nora scooped at the sides of a massive ice cream sundae between her and Kara. They were in a darkened room, snuggled together on a u-shaped couch, a vermillion curtain-framed screen in front of them. One of Albanach's ridiculous pre-Surge movies involving a man-sized lizard and an inept woman with huge breasts was playing. Nora couldn't understand why they never took off their high-heels before they ran. Maybe women before the Surge were mentally deficient.

"Well, he hates being called Laughlin," Kara said, licking fudge off her spoon. She was too thin, her cheekbones angular in the flickering light.

"Flynn?"

"Flynn." A smile tipped up her lips and was replaced by worry. "He didn't know… Tell me about Deirdre."

Nora took her time carving off a spoonful of banana. The woman on the screen had become tangled in bracken, thrashing about wildly, her clothes artfully torn when she gained her feet again.

"She was striking, especially for someone not engineered, but tiny. Five feet, maybe? There was something, I don't know, wild about her. She had these blue points of light in her eyes. I've never seen anything like it, before or since, and she sang so beautifully…"

Kara plucked the cherry off the sundae. "Where did she come from?"

"Here, I thought. We weren't close, spoke mostly about politics. The reunification of our people. She was passionate about that—"

"But she wasn't a Talent."

"No, but she wanted a better world for Laughlin, just as I wanted a better one for you, and I fully believe that day will come, quite soon, in fact." Although whether anyone was ready for it…

"I don't see how that's a better world." Kara's eyes rolled. "Can you imagine all of them up here? Ugh, it'd be like dumping sharks into a pond full of piranhas."

Nora laughed. "At first, perhaps, but it needs to happen. The Source is close to becoming defunct. If Titus's harvest fails, they'll liquidate stock, culling or selling off Talents after they're sterilized. Reunification is the only way to save them."

"I still don't see why Flynn's mom would care. She wasn't a Talent, and no one else up here seems to. I'm not sure I do. How did she die?"

Nora took a slow breath. The lizard-man was closing in on the woman on the screen. She balled her fists up before her chin, eyes wide and terrified. "Albanach brought her down to see you after your halos had come in. It was during the second day of your trials. The first had gone so well…" And she'd been so proud. So stupid. "He was delayed in a meeting, and I was impatient to show you off. I took her to the Creche. Dionis was there reviewing his Talents. He wanted her. She objected, and he slit her throat."

Kara chewed her thumb. "Then you didn't kill her."

A scream pierced the air, and they both glanced at the screen. The lizard-man had gotten hold of the woman. She beat weakly at his chest, then went limp. Kara snorted, shaking her head.

"No, but she trusted me, and I led her to her death. That's worse, don't you think?" Nora watched the creature carry the woman back to his lair, unable to meet her daughter's eyes.

"I don't know. Since I left—maybe it's worse not having a conscience to tell you it's wrong. The other night, I wanted Riegel to die, and I wanted him to suffer before he did."

"Whatever he got, he deserved." Nora wouldn't shed a single tear for that monster.

"You said you didn't know Deirdre. Maybe she got what she deserved, too."

Nora stared at her daughter aghast, and Kara shrugged again, still chewing her thumb.

"I can't believe that to be true."

"I told Flynn what Cal did to Dionis, and he couldn't believe it either. Said he didn't think he had it in him."

Nora twisted her ring, her eyes going back to the flickering screen. The woman had woken up in a bed of bracken and was watching the lizard-man tend a fire, something sinister roasting above it. The things Cal was capable of…Dionis was the least of it.

But how well did anyone ever really know someone? Marcos was the most loving, gentle man, and at the same time, he'd led armies that'd subjugated hundreds of thousands of people across the globe. As to what he himself had perpetrated in the field? She'd never asked and never planned to.

And what did it say about her that she loved them both?

"I think a great deal of what you're feeling can be attribute to your genetics—"

"Pardon me ladies," French broke in, "but Mistress Glass has just arrived."

"Thank goodness!" Kara laughed. "I don't know how Cal stands these movies. I would've stabbed that lizard with my stiletto an hour ago."

Nora didn't doubt it, but attributed her daughter's relief more to not wanting to continue the discussion. Kara had always been so reticent about her Breaker heritage, though Nora could hardly blame her, given the stigma against dualities, both here and at the Source—

"Kara!"

The lights flicked on and a rotund blonde woman with a

prominent, aquiline nose bustled into the room and threw her arms around Kara. She laughed, hugging her back. Nora's eyes misted.

"My God! You were so fierce! Did the leathers wear well? You like them?"

"Yes, of course! There's one seam that split, but they were perfect otherwise, thank you!" She hugged the woman again.

"They were Laughlin's idea…what happened? You look like hell."

Kara laughed, dabbing an eye. "Thanks for that. I'm tired of everyone lying to me."

"Well, if you can't trust your couturier, who can you trust? I'm sorry, we haven't met. Reggie Glass." She held out a hand stained a faint blue to Nora, and they shook.

"Nora Jester, Kara's mother. You two are friends?"

Kara beamed. "Yes."

"Then I'm so very happy to meet you, Reggie." She blinked back tears. After everything Kara had gone through at the Source…

"So. What can I design for you?" Reggie took a satchel from her shoulder and pulled out a sketch pad.

Kara laughed. "Everyday Grecian."

It was an accurate description, and the woman was extremely talented. She had a serviceable wardrobe sketched out in fifteen minutes flat. Another ten took care of Marcos's, and all that remained was taking his measurements. Reggie turned to Kara with her tailor's tape.

"Ok, your turn."

Kara looked surprised. "Me?"

"You. If I don't take in the gown I made for your luncheon, it'll hang on you like a sack."

"I—but Flynn—"

Reggie sighed. "Listen, this is the way things work up here. You have two options. Hide or pretend nothing's happened. The first is as good as admitting Julia's telling the truth, which leaves you with the second. You've got to go through the motions. It sounds harsh, but regardless of what becomes of Laughlin, you have the rest of your House to think of."

Kara's hand drifted to her abdomen. "Do you think they'll nullify him?"

"The way the city's talking, it's more likely we'll be overrun with Sons before the courts decide anything." She shrugged, playing the tailor's tape. "But even if they wanted to, they can't until that baby's born. So. Put on your big girl panties, and let's not give those bitches anything else to chew on at this luncheon."

She motioned for Kara to stand. Sighing, she did. Nora's fingers drifted to her ring. Kara had lost so much weight…she needed to speak with Jon about upping her caloric intake.

"So spill it. What are they saying?"

Reggie jotted down some numbers, avoiding Kara's eye until she finished. "What you'd expect. Half the hill is ripping you to shreds for knowingly bonding a twist, the other half is horrified he tricked you into it. Personally, I couldn't care less if Laughlin was blue." She smiled, waggling her fingers. "I'll be back tomorrow. In the meantime, eat something."

"Cal already told me someone was going to try to floss with me," Kara said wryly.

"He's not far off." They embraced, and she left.

"She seems like a very good friend."

"The best." Kara's smile faltered, her gaze going to a neat woman coming through the door carrying in a milkshake.

"Jon's latest addition to your regimen," she said handing it to her.

"I was afraid of that."

"Beats a feeding tube."

Kara glowered, sipping through the straw. "I liked you better when you were a snob." From her expression it wasn't as horrible as she'd expected, but it wasn't good either. The woman smirked and cleared her throat. "Oh, sorry. Nora, this is my secretary, Audrey. Audrey, this is my mother… Do I really have to go to Bea's luncheon?"

Nora couldn't help but smile at Kara's whining. Her dread of duty certainly hadn't changed.

"Pleased to meet you, my lady, and yes. You're expected to carry on as usual." She squeezed Kara's shoulder and turned to Nora. "Master

Scot has asked me to give you an overview of Assembly protocol. He wishes you to attend tomorrow to take up House Jester's vote."

Nora nodded, not prepared for it in the least. If only she had more time…her gaze went to Kara, fighting to finish that milkshake.

There was no time.

"Of course. I'm at your disposal."

"Wonderful. I'm sure Lady Scot will benefit from this as well. Shall we begin?"

Nora smiled at Kara's grumbling, but it was tempered with the foreboding that if the way this pregnancy was progressing didn't change, she wouldn't be hearing it for much longer.

CHAPTER SEVEN

Insighter [in-sīt ər] noun

1. *A rare Finder ability to glean surface thoughts of an individual.
   Shades are resistant.*

– Excerpt from Glynfyls: A History

---

*"…faced with unprecedented censure from the international community, the
Corporation is demanding a complete accounting of your global operations
and troop placement. Failure to comply will result in unfortunate
legalities…"*

– Transmission to T. Merkel, Director of Armed Forces,
The Source

THE INTELLIGENCERS BROUGHT Flynn to Crandall.

He sat in a windowless room behind a desk devoid of paperwork,
an empty chair across from him. The walls were lined with beige filing
cabinets. Stale tobacco and the dusky tang of old newsprint hung in

the air. A fluorescent light flickered overhead, not doing any of it any favors.

Flynn glared at the man as they undid his cuffs, and the smug motherfucker smirked around his pipestem.

"Laughlin. I apologize for having to restrain you, but unfortunately, that bit of theater was necessary. Can I get you a coffee? Cigar? Something to eat?"

Flynn rubbed at his wrists and jerked the chair across the green-speckled linoleum floor to sit. "Yeah. Necessary for who?"

Crandall glanced at the men that'd brought him in, and they left. "I suspect that's entirely dependent upon your perspective."

"Huh. My perspective is that you let Riegel run rampant hoping he'd take me out. When that didn't happen, you figured you'd try and bury me with legalities to save your slice of the pie, and now you're fucking with me for fun."

That smirk didn't fade, and Flynn wanted to put him through a wall.

"It is fun, but we both know not a crumb will remain after our enemies have feasted."

"Then what the hell was that at the Pony?"

"My attempt to reveal the larger plot." Crandall poked at the smoldering bowl of his pipe. "Julia's only a piece. For quite some time, it's been apparent that a systematic influence generating discord has been at work in the commons. It pains me to admit that despite my not inconsiderable resources, we've been unable to root it out. I had hoped to tip their hand by creating a situation in which they'd expose themselves."

Flynn chewed his lip. That didn't sound like Markham's doing. "It work?"

"We were able to verify that the Source has a cell operating within the city. As to where they're based, your guess is as good as mine. The one's we've detained have been resistant to talent, presumably outfitted with technology similar to what Lady Scot mentioned during Assembly."

Shit. "Their halos bleeding?"

"No."

"Then it's not the same." And thank God for that. "So what, you've been scanning crowds for people you can't find, and looking for vermin-free zones?"

"That, and combing through the tunnels, but all we've found so far are dozens of illicit ways into the city. I've begun working with Markham and Carl to shore them up."

Un-fucking believable. The door opened, and an Intelligencer came in with a tray. Flynn helped himself to the coffee and a Danish. He flicked the walnuts from it onto the desk. One bounced into Crandall's lap and his lips pruned.

"Your nomination, and Markham pledging, curtailed any further progress on tracking down the cell, though perhaps that was for the best. I had expected a riot or two, but not the organized front they presented, nor the current situation. Your legal difficulties are coming at an inopportune time."

Flynn snorted around his mouthful. "Tell me about it."

"Very well. The vote on your eligibility is scheduled for tomorrow, and will be decided by Quorum, locking the Shades out of the vote. They're rather miffed about that." The prick smirked. "That drops the required votes to revoke your seat from four, to three."

He paused to repack his pipe, letting the words hang in the air. Flynn grabbed another Danish, adding walnuts to the pile. He felt the "but" coming. Shithead was getting off on making him wait for it. God, he hated Finders. Especially this dick.

"As of an hour ago, there's only one whom I've gleaned will do so."

Flynn coughed, choking on his bite. That was one hell of a "but." Was this asshole seriously admitting to being an Insighter? That was right up there with phazing…

"The Binders are rabid about their line's purity. I can't tell you how shocked I was when they pledged to you based on your impending offspring. Their logic is…well. A Binder's. This however, has sent them over the edge, and they'd gladly see both you and your lady hang."

Flynn tamped down his surge of rage. If they fucked with Kara—
"That doesn't surprise me; the rest of you voting it down does."

Crandall tapped out his pipe. "We each have our reasons, and

Phyllis…well. She's just there to look pretty, now isn't she?" Man was way too fucking smug over that little tidbit.

"Sure she'd love to hear you say so." And would beat the shit out of him for it. The thought improved Flynn's mood. "So what's that like, sneaking around in people's heads?"

"Not as exciting as you think, unless you've a penchant for grocery lists and musings about what's been left on or unlocked. It does, however come in handy during depositions."

Flynn paused lighting his cigar to look up at him. Christ, he was smug.

"Usually, thoughts are like bits of vegetable rising to the surfaces when soup simmers. Messy, churning things, with emotion flavoring the mix. But Julia's…" Crandall fiddled with his pipe, his greasy brow furrowing. "They were akin to a communion wafer floating in a vacuum. No fleeting thoughts, no background noise, and zero emotion. It's all been stripped away, leaving an unnaturally dispassionate single-mindedness."

Flynn tapped his ash onto the floor. That sounded too much like what Kara had done to Mick. Shit. Could someone have coerced Julia? It made a hell of a lot more sense why she was working with the Source if that were the case…but Julia was a Talent. Was Kara wrong about coercion working on them? He took another drag, fighting to keep his hand steady.

"You know something."

Flynn exhaled a line of blue-grey smoke, betting that bitch Nora did, too. "Yeah, you buy cheap cigars."

Crandall snorted. "The inability of a Shade to disclose never ceases to amaze me. Is it physically painful, or does your delight in being an ass outweigh the good of the city?"

"It's usually fifty-fifty. Currently, I'd stake the latter at around ninety percent."

"Well, mission accomplished." Crandall's mouth curdled. "I disclosed in the hopes of establishing a modicum of rapport, and in that same spirit, the higher placed Sons that we've apprehended suffer from the same phenomena. Not to the degree Julia does, but there's no question in my mind that theirs have been tampered with as well."

Flynn chewed on the end of his cigar. That didn't make any sense. Sons didn't truck with Talents, period, and from what Kara said, the only Binders capable of coercion were Source bred. There was no way the Sons were working with them, or vice versa. Shit, they'd bombed the facility more than once—

"Everything points to a third player, and I'm sure that reel was leaked to mask their agenda."

"Kind of like you used me to keep Julia busy?"

The man shrugged with zero remorse. Dick. "Turn about's fair play, and I'm reluctant to show my hand until I have a handle on what we're dealing with."

Flynn laughed. Christ, he couldn't catch a fucking break. "Which equates to me sitting here, whether you think I'm guilty of knowing my 'status' beforehand or not."

Crandall tapped the bowl of his pipe on the table, the air in the little room thick. "God helps those who help themselves. Refuting the allegation would be a good start."

"No."

"Even knowing you're playing into the enemy's hands?" Flynn looked away, and Crandall shook his head. "A Breaker and a Shade walk into a pub. Bartender says, 'Taps are down, all I have are bottles. What'll you have?' "

Flynn snorted. "You're telling me a joke?"

"I am, but I doubt you'll find it funny. It ends with neither of them getting served, because the Shade won't answer the question, and the Breaker won't compromise. Their black and white view of the world is almost as frustrating as a Shade's reticence, and here you are, the best of both."

Asshole.

Crandall packed away his pipe. "I'll have them escort you to your cell. You'll be staying with us for the duration. Plenty of time to think about what I've said, not that I anticipate you using it wisely."

Great. As if a being in a cage wasn't gonna be bad enough, Crandall was holding the key.

KARA GRIPPED Lot's arm as they made their way to the Assembly chamber, the whispers and stares assaulting her just like being back in the Source. She tried to pull zero, but her nerves were raw—especially after last night. She'd been so alone, even with Nora in the same room. Her hand drifted towards her abdomen. Using that tiny bit of talent to look inward, she was still in disbelief. How could she possibly be having—

Lot took her hand in his, and she flinched, blinking back tears. Another of those IVs had been waiting for her with breakfast. Her exhaustion had faded to weariness, but whatever that stuff was had her keyed up. Her bloodlust simmered, and she had the feeling it would be a very, very bad thing to tap into it. Trying to deal with it and the crowd—ugh. She didn't have a choice.

Flynn's concern streaming through their bond didn't help. He'd spent the night detained by the Intelligencers after they'd cited him as a flight risk. The papers were rife with speculation about that, given the fact that he could phaze through the wall if he was so inclined.

They were also filled with the city's turmoil. A market on the fourth rung, ashes. People beaten in the street. Rallies turned to riots.

Glynfyls was eating itself.

Kara put a hand to her mouth, hiding the sob, aching to see him. What she felt beneath his worry for her… She bit at her lip, trying to focus. Just get through this, and then that damned press conference Merchant had scheduled. Beyond the thudding in her ears, her stomach clenched at the low roar of the angry mob outside.

Her knees went weak as they passed the Breakers manning the mangled doors, into the murmur of chambers. Whispers stopped, then started again. All the eyes… She continued down to Flynn's box, her heart a trapped bird buffeting against her ribs.

How was she going to do this?

Lot opened the little gate, then helped her to her seat, settling himself behind her. She blew out a breath, trying to steady herself, Julia's reptilian stare from across the room unnerving. Her hair was done up in complicated braids, like something a tribe in the Deep South would wear. It was bizarre paired with her corseted gown.

Kara fumbled for a waltz in her head, that blackness licking upwards. She met Julia's eyes—

Emptiness stared back at her.

"You sure you want to go through with this?" Lot whispered in Kara's ear.

She raised her chin in the affirmative. She could, for Flynn. Her mother nodded at her from across the room as the speaker took his seat. He offered her a small smile of consolation before banging his gavel.

"Chamber is in session. Well, I suppose our first order of business comes as no surprise. The Binders have put forth a motion to strip Lord Scot of his seat on the basis of him being dual-talented, and have requested the vote be taken up by Quorum. The other lines have agreed, less the Shades, as Lord Scot has been recused from these proceedings. If you're ready? Ah, Lord Ketsing, if you'll start us off?"

The Binder First stood, not looking at her. "Yea."

"Lord Markham?"

He rose mopping at his prodigious chins. "This may be an unpopular stance, but the commons couldn't give a pig's fart about how many talents the man has, and in case you haven't noticed, there's a great deal more of them than us. I vote nay."

Murmurs sprang up, but the room was silent for the most part. Lord Riggs moved on. "Lady Breakspear?"

"The council has ruled on this matter. Despite the evidence, until our line has an Alpha, Laughlin Scot is not a Breaker. Nay." She didn't seem particularly thrilled about it. The rest of the room wasn't either.

Riggs banged his gavel for order. "Lord Klein?"

"Nay. This vote is premature. Legalities need to proceed before we can make an informed decision—" The room erupted, and Kara wiped her sweaty palm against her skirts, light-headed. If they weren't taking his seat from him, maybe there was a chance—

"And Lord Crandall," Riggs shouted above the clamor.

"Nay." The chamber quieted, unable to believe what they'd just heard. The little man smirked. "I find it short-sighted to discard anything that I can point at an enemy. Lord Scot has stated on several occasions that the Source would only get its harvest over his dead body. I'm assuming the same applies to the Sons' aggression. Why on earth would I disenfranchise someone so eager to offer up his life for his country? I say we give him the chance."

Lot's hand fell on Kara's shoulder before she was halfway out of her seat. She bit her cheek, choking back her 'lust. The rest of the Assembly way too amiable to Crandall's rational. How dare they! Flynn wasn't some expendable—she fought to pull zero, her breath ragged—

Riggs's gavel fell. "Well, that's that, then. Measure fails to pass. Next up, an emergency addition to the agenda. We have a motion for Lady Scot to temporarily take over House Scot's vote until Laughlin's, ah, legal issues are resolved. All the paperwork appears to be in order...discussion?" Lord Riggs looked around the room and raised the gavel.

Julia stayed seated, emotionless through all of it. Kara swept a stray lock from her brow, confusion calming her. What was wrong with the woman?

"Wonderful. All those in favor? Motion passed. Now this is a bit of chicken and the egg...ah, I'm sure you've all noticed we have a new face in the Binder's section. It's been given to me to introduce Lady Jester." Riggs read from over the top of his glasses. "The details of her ascension and arrival have been classified as a House Matter...ah, well, I suspect that's that, then."

A low hum of discontent roiled through the Assembly as he scanned its members. "Discussion? No? Well then, welcome, Lady Jester. Moving right along...ah, we were supposed to have an update for Lord Stonefist? Is he, ah, yes, sorry, there you are. Bit confusing with the seating changes. If you could proceed?"

A grizzled Breaker stood, straightening his jacket. "You've all read the papers. We've abandoned the border and are returning to the city, trying to deal with the influx of Sons wantonly destroying everything in the lower territories. They've razed the majority of settlements, working north. As soon as we think we've cleared an area, they're back. I've no idea how they keep getting behind my troops, and no matter how many we stamp out, there are always more. At this rate they'll reach the plateau by tomorrow night or the next day."

A panicked frenzy of whispers began, and Kara's anxiety jumped, her mind flashing back to the train crash and the pack of muties attacking her on the plateau—

"And what about these damned trials we've been hearing about? Do we even have an army anymore?" a man called out.

"The trials won't interfere with our ability to protect the city," Stonefist said. "The council has spoken its will; in lieu of a hierarchy, all Breakers that've pledged fall beneath the purview of the lord to whom they've given their oath."

The room erupted.

"Damn your council!"

"Sending him out to die is one thing—"

"…ridiculous prejudice…"

"How can you possibly follow a twist?!"

"He's innocent until proven guilty—"

"They've got him on a reel!"

Kara's pulse raced, her eyes flicking to each allegation as it was spewed. The concern from Flynn ticked up. She needed him here! Lot's hand settled on her shoulder again, anchoring her, and she gripped his fingers.

Riggs glanced at her, his face grim. He banged his gavel. "Order! Order! That's quite enough! This matter has been tabled!" The room settled petulantly. "Now, Lord Stonefist, given your report, have you any recommendations?"

The Breaker glowered around the room before answering. "The way they're hitting the towns and outlying estates…the rest need to be evacuated and the city prepared for a siege. Our forces are spread too thin. My focus will be on securing Glynfyls and assigning Hexes. Any who want to leave, need to do so now—"

"I disagree," Crandall interrupted, his face sour. "The Sons have made their presence known in the cities we've been shifting people to, persecuting alleged sympathizers as well as Talents. As of two days ago, I'm afraid that's no longer an option."

Concerned whispering ping-ponged throughout the room.

"Perhaps farther out? The Eastern continent—"

"Ah, unfortunately the Source discovered the anchored ships we were using as jump sites," Markham said, mopping his neck. "I'm afraid we've no longer any viable routes that don't go through the Outside, which would be considered aggression, triggering their military response." The whispering broke into discussion.

"And the status of the wall?" Riggs asked above it.

Klein stood, flipping through a notebook. "All of the breaches have been repaired with what we've repurposed from clearing the circumference. As of now, we're shoring up the tunnels and making repairs to other defensive structures, such as the barbican. I'm not sure where Lady Mayfield stands with the shield."

"Ah, I've one last thing to add," Markham said. "I've received some disturbing news through one of our friends in the Deep South. The Source has recalled a large number of military units—"

"And redeployed them to our border," Stonefist finished for him. "We're trapped up here like rats, and they're sitting down there letting the Sons corral us into the city. Once they're storming our gates, I expect the Source will mobilize. They'll exterminate them and harvest us, all in one stroke."

The chamber disintegrated into chaos.

Riggs banged his gavel to no avail and gave up, dismissing the session. Kara clenched the arm of her chair. What happened now? Would they let him go? Flynn's concern streaming through their bond just made her miss him more. She wiped her eyes.

Lot was at her elbow. "Let's get this done."

Kara blinked back tears, nodding. Yes. Before she lost her nerve. Her mother broke away from speaking with Lord Ketsing to join her on the step, looping an arm through hers. Kara leaned against her. Glory, she was falling to pieces…

"Don't let them see you upset, Kara. Jackals like these feed on it." Nora smiled at a leering group of women, and they huffed, snapping up those stupid fans.

Kara took a deep breath, shaking. Lot walked ahead of them, running his hand through his hair. Her chest ached at the mannerism. Merchant was waiting for them beside a massive pair of brass-bound doors, a swell of angry voices behind it.

"Lady Scot. Are you ready?"

No. "Yes." Her voice was the barest thread of a whisper.

"All you have to do is read the statement I've prepared."

She nodded. "Will there be many people?"

"Only the entire fucking city." Lot snorted.

Kara caught herself against the wall. This was for Flynn. She could do this. For him…

His concern had become frantic.

The little barrister led her through the doors, outside, to a massive staircase spanning the width of the building.

Lot was right. Glynfyls stared up at her, waiting.

The wind tore over the landing, flecks of damp ash turning the blue velvet of her skirts into a cosmos of weeping stars. Flashbulbs, like at the train station…the promenade… Her chest ached, and she put a hand to it. Her 'lust churned, feeding on her anxiety. It would be so easy to let it come up…

She swallowed it, along with her angst, and approached the lectern, its microphones spearing toward her.

Merchant handed her a piece of paper. Its marks didn't make any sense, and her fingers left moist splotches where she gripped it. She scrunched her eyes shut, the pounding in her ears so loud…

For Flynn, for Flynn, for Flynn…

She could do this. The print came into focus, but the meanings were lost. Her words muffled by the beating of her heart, the roar of the wind slicing them from her lips. There was a pause when she reached the end, then people started yelling out questions, flashbulbs going off like bombs.

Merchant hustled her back into the building. The door closed, and Kara sagged against him. What just happened? Lot put an arm around her, and his resemblance to Flynn broke her down completely. She collapsed, sobbing. Lot scooped her up and carried her away from all of it, down the hall to the gate.

BARTON STOOD IN THE DOORWAY, Adlothian Scot whisking Kara past him. The girl's mother scurried close behind. Assembly members moved to the side and let them pass, whispers following in their wake. They disappeared through the gate, and the corridor exploded into a flurry of speculation.

Barton swept a wrapper into his dust pan, unable to reconcile the predator that had bitten off a man's tongue with the broken woman who'd just been carried out.

It wasn't logical.

He moved through the crowd, unobtrusive, unnoticed… unimportant. Gathering snippets of conversation to gain understanding.

"Can you believe she had the nerve to show her face? I would've broken from him—"

"And that other one, brazen, wasn't she?"

"…took a lot of guts…"

"Did you see her face? Poor dear was destroyed, it's so terribly romantic!"

"…travesty that this prejudice has been allowed to proceed as long as it has…"

Barton frowned. Emotion confused him, wasn't logical. How was it possible to have so many reactions to a single event? The variables didn't differ. Only perception. Assigning feeling to fact was flawed.

The most probable reason for the disparity in Kara's persona was the slide Titus had warned about.

There was limited time remaining to harvest her.

Barton worked the broom down the edges of the hall, lingering by a group voicing their opinions of the charges against Scot. It made little difference, aside from occupying him while Barton made the grab. The trials would distract the Breaker who had interfered at the Pony, and in her current state, Kara would be easy prey.

He pulled his hand from his lips, running it over the thickened seam of his sleeve, an ampule of sedative secreted within. The Sons were coming, and Titus was within days of mobilizing his troops. Barton needed to be clear of the city with the girl before that happened.

A group of ladies passed, discussing their gowns for a luncheon being held in Lady Scot's honor. Barton hid a smile as he swept. That might provide him with just the opportunity he needed.

FITZ SAT AT THE BAR, staring into his tankard of ale, two empty plates of fish pie at his elbow.

The thick roll of units in his pocket bothered him. Felt too much like being bought, and no matter what his damned coin said, weren't no good gonna come of trucking with hillies…but Markham were right, he owed Scot—

"Somewhat on yer mind?" Marl asked, raising his empty glass for another. Pamela were behind the bar for the lunch crowd. She delivered it, leaning farther over than she had to, collecting plates.

"Ye off soon, love?" Fitz raised his gaze from her generous cleavage to wink at her.

"Not as soon as I'd like. Get ye another pie?"

"Aye, I could stand another."

She gave him a coy smile and disappeared through the tattered curtain into the back.

Marl sighed, shaking his head. "Ye McCreedys got the devil's own luck."

Fitz shrugged, draining his tankard. "Eh…what I got's a right crisis of conscience."

"Have anything t'do with a certain lass?"

"Not a damned thing."

"Then mayhap somewhat regarding weasels loose on the hill?" He tipped back his glass. "Hear tell a certain lady's prize birds was slaughtered."

Fitz raised his tankard. "That a fact? Thought them flats was warded for vermin."

"'Parently weasels don't qualify. Hauled poor Steg and every other ratter in over it, inventorying the beasties. Not a one missing, but Willems lost his contract."

"Suppose someone had t'take the fall." Fitz pulled at his patch. "Mighty peculiar though."

"T'is at that."

Pamela came out from the kitchen with a pie and refilled his tankard. He dug in. Hadn't eaten this good in ages…his nose twitched. All that talk about weasels had him smelling 'em—

"Yer a shite, McCreedy."

His jaw stopped mid-chew, and he choked down his bite, shooting a glare at Marl, snickering into his whiskey. Fitz spun on his stool to face Adelaide. She stood with her hands on her hips, thin red halos around the blue of her irises flickering. Gah, she were pissed. He was gonna kill Steg for squealing on him.

"Eh…ye look real fine today."

"The hell ye say. Think I don't know what I smell like?" She poked her finger into his chest, then smacked him upside the head. "I ain't got enough for a room, never mind a launder and a bath. Only custom that'll have me in such a state's on Barris Street!"

"Ye didn't have t'say yes—" Behind him, Marl hissed past his teeth as Adelaide pulled back to slug him.

Fitz shifted behind her, pinning her arms. Gah, she were rank. He laughed. "Ye didn't let me finish! Got somewhat for ye."

She stopped struggling. "I'm listening, but ribbons ain't gonna get ye clear!"

He moved in front of her, slipping units into her kirtle. She glanced around the bar, fingering the bills.

"S'hundred." Fitz dipped his head close to her ear. "Should keep ye flush 'til that job at the Pony kicks in." He smoothed his thumb over the last bit of green bruising her cheek. Adelaide's eyes went all glassy, searching his, and he kissed her before he thought better of it.

Her fist caught him in the gut, doubling him over, and he almost lost them pies.

"Yer a shite, Fitzpatrick McCreedy. A right shite." She stormed out, pushing past people to the door. Fitz winced, blowing the curls from his eyes as he climbed back onto his stool. Christ, he should've known that were coming.

"So, tell me 'bout this crisis of conscience…"

"Ain't that." He frowned at Marl, picking his fork back up. "I owe a man somewhat. Ain't keen on paying it."

"Best just t'be done with. Owed favors is like fish. Longer they linger, worse they stink."

Fitz grunted around a mouthful. He'd taken the imprint from that shard, and after shifting to them books the old hillie were lookin' for, he'd asked around for Arileo. He weren't the only one trying t'track him down, and the shite knew it.

Fuckin' Radiant. Been using that damned Prydee extra t'manipulate energy and hide hisself. Were doin' a piss poor job of it though, leaving a mess everywhere he'd been. Only reason the sisters ain't found him yet was they were too high and mighty to step a toe off the hill. Well, that and they didn't think Fitz could do much more than pick up an odd aura or two, else they'd have him hunting the shite down.

He sat back, chewing. If he could deliver Arileo t'that old hillie, he could wash his hands of the Scots. His hand went to his pocket, fingering his coin. *Ye up for a game of hot and cold, Cajetan?*

Coin went hot, and Fitz grunted, finishing his pie.

"Most like yer right about that favor," he said to Marl, pushing away from the bar. "Eh…give Pamela me regrets. Got somewhat t'take care of."

Man raised his glass in the affirmative, and Fitz shifted to the nearest mess of energy. Coin stayed like ice until the fourth. He looked around the rumpled room. From the tilt to the floor, he was somewhere just shy of the Pinch, and weren't a soul in sight.

He rubbed a thumb over the coin, kicking garbage out of his way. Closer he got to a pile of filthy clothes, warmer it got. You'd think a Prydee would have regular laundry service.

"Shite, I gotta dig through that mess? Christ, there better not be a body under there…" He sighed, pulling out his pigsticker to poke at it. Coin just about seared his fingers through as he went to flick away a pair of crusty trousers. Grimacing, Fitz checked the pockets and pulled out a cube. *This?*

The coin flared hot again.

"If ye say so." Weren't Arileo, but if Cajetan said it were important… Fitz tossed the nasty garment away and shifted to Meddleton.

The foyer was deserted. Fitz ran a hand through his curls, smelling weasel. Too late t'do aught about it now. He made his way to the hall, grit from his boots crunching loud on the shiny floor. His scalp prickled with sweat. Energy in this place were as bad as any upon the hill… Voices was coming from the office. One of 'em were Miriam's. He swallowed the lump in his throat, feet froze to the floor. Woman hated him more'n most. Knew he didn't want her to find him here sure as he knew his own name…

"I won't have it, Caliban Scot!" she shrilled. "I'm at my wit's end! This House cannot afford one more scandal! Nora Jester, of all people! Lord above, if anyone found out—"

"It's a House Matter, Miriam, House *Scot,* and the only way that'll happen is if you start yapping. Flynn sure as hell isn't gonna say anything, and neither is she. You'll keep those damned sisters of yours out of it."

"My heart can't take this…as if this mess with Laughlin isn't enough, don't you even care that my Leo's missing? What if they caught him out there!"

Fitz rolled his eyes. Cry me a fuckin' river, would serve the bastard right.

"I happen to care about that a great deal. Been trying to find him as a matter of fact, and it's like he's completely non-existent. Something you want to clue me in on?"

"I—I don't know why you're asking me. Sounds like a Shade's involved. Maybe you should ask Graham—"

"I did. He swears it isn't so. Leo's not real popular with our line."

Fitz suppressed a snort. Shite weren't real popular with nobody.

"Well, then I—I'm sure I don't know anything about it." The clack of her heels stormed towards the door, and Fitz shifted into the old hillie's study just as she cleared the jamb. He stood with his back pressed against the wall as her footsteps faded farther into the estate.

Fitz let out the breath he'd been holding, and the old man chuckled around his cigarette.

"I can relate. You got something for me?"

"Eh…mayhap." He walked over to the desk, digging into his pocket and set the cube down. "Went t'where he'd been, looked around a bit. Dunno what's on it, but seemed likely."

The old hillie grabbed it up and flicked it on. Some perky blonde and Scot.

"Jesus H. Christ—" He shut it down quick and went to open the drawer he'd pulled them units from last night.

"Nah—that squares us." Fitz laid out the extra cash the man had given him. "Gave me friend the rest, like ye said, but I ain't earned this, and I ain't gonna."

He shifted away, certain someone other than the old hillie called him an idiot as he did.

CHAPTER EIGHT

runes [ro͞onz] noun

1. *A physical manifestation of a Breaker's honor. When called into being, they are seen as intricate traceries of talent surrounding the individual, giving another of their line the ability to "read" their history and intent.*

– Excerpt from The Way of Honor

"Request to engage. Unidentified craft sighted entering into the Northern Territory's air space from the south. Attempts at communication have failed…"

– Br873, "Kyles", Source Military Adjunct,
Transmitted Field Report

"Request denied. Let the Sons do as they will. We'll put them down soon enough…"

– T. Merkel, Director of Armed Forces,
The Source

VICTOR TORE the last mouthful of turkey off the drumstick gripped in his meaty paw, mud from his boots soaking into the fine linens on the table. Men had made short work of the rest of the feast that'd been laid out. Now they looted through the big house, draped in furs and jewels, draining bottles thick with dust from the cellars.

Storm outside raged, wind slashing hail through the busted windows at the far end of the room. He'd put a stop to that right quick. They could raze the place on the way out. Right now, it was the only thing keepin' them alive, though the close quarters weren't keepin' them happy. Men were packed into the rooms of riches closer than his bolo could shave.

Well, until he walked in. Ain't nobody save Sam stuck around since he'd been chosen. Soon as he went in a room, they pushed into another like a piston pumpin' hydraulic fluid. His hand rose to the clear gemstone protruding between his brows. Damned thing itched somethin' fierce. A wave of pleasure pulsed through him as his fingers met its facets. His eyes fluttered, basking in the Mother's favor. It radiated outward, the hair on his body raising. His vision wavered, and the drumstick thumped to the floor.

Everything went black, and then he was in a garden.

Victor stood upon a path of crushed shells, bleached bone white from the blazing sun. It rode too close in the azure sky above, the air thick. Faint ocean waves broke upon the stillness. A gull screamed, and he turned at the sound.

She sat on a stone bench surrounded by broad leaves of verdant green. Clothed in gauzy robes and light, her long gold hair done up in a crown of snowy orchids. Victor fell to his knees before her, shells slicing his jeans.

"Mother..."

A smile tipped up her rosebud lips. "You've done well, my son. Through the stone on your brow, I see as you see, and know the good work you do in my name. Approach me."

He was overcome. Stubble stained by tears, he crawled across the sharp shards, leaving a blush of crimson cresting the furrows of his passing. His elbows shook with the enormity of her favor, mouth dry and panting. He fell back on his heels before her, raising his bloodied palms in supplication. She placed her fingertips upon his temples, as light and dry as a butterfly's wing.

"Your heart's desire is close to fruition." Mother smiled. "Revenge against the man you call Wolf will be yours, and to further your goal, I give you a gift."

Victor's mind was flooded with images. At the last, he looked out from a woman's eyes. She carried a tray into a dandy room of big house. Talents dressed in finery sat around a table, children playing at their feet with a kitten.

"Divide your forces amongst the places I've shown you. The last was Anafeild. Exterminate all but one to bring word to the city. I will come to you again when it's time."

Her lips pressed against his brow, and a blinding burst of white sent him reeling.

"Goddamned freaks live like kings," Sam grumbled, his knife thunking rhythmic as it scored the table between his fingers.

Victor dropped his feet and went to scrub at his face, pulling his hands back like he'd been burnt. Bits of pink-tinged shell studded his palms. Sam spun the blade, then drove it home into its sheath, still talking like nothing had just happened.

"Road to hell's paved with gold." Victor's voice was a rasp, bloodied hand shaking as he lifted a crystal-cut decanter to his lips, smacking the syrupy liquid back. "And bodies. Any more turn up?"

"Nah, whoever was poachin' us tucked tail when the storm come in. Think they was after them stones. Got maybe a handful more, but we done burnt through most of 'em gettin' everybody under cover."

Victor grunted. "Ain't gonna be a problem. We're right where we need to be."

"How you figure?"

He looked up at his second, images from the Mother flickering through his mind's eye. "I can see it all laid out like it's supposed to happen."

FLYNN'S CELL was six steps wide, and he was about to take the two hundred and ninety-fourth.

He turned on his heel, counting as he paced. Aside from the toilet bolted to the wall actually flushing and a thick wool blanket, it was a carbon copy of every other cell he'd had the misfortune of ending up in. There were only so many things you could do to gentrify a concrete box with bars.

The emotions coming from Kara ate at him. What the hell was she doing? There was no way she was at home in bed where she should be. Christ, if Cal and Merchant had her at the fucking Assembly—of course they had her at the fucking Assembly. He should be there with her, not trapped in this goddamned cage.

Grimacing, he leaned against the bars. He'd asked for something to read, but it was slow in coming, despite the fact that there were three books sitting on the Intelligencer's desk not ten feet away. Asshole had his boots up next to them, perusing the morning edition.

"Hey," Flynn called. "You mind bringing those down here?" The guard kicked one off the pile in his direction and turned to the sports section as it thudded to the floor.

Flynn's temper flared with his halos. Fuck this. He phazed out of the cell and stalked down to where the man sat, smacking his feet off the desk and grabbing the sad little pile of books. The Intelligencer fell out of his chair, the scent of piss tinging the air.

Flynn rolled his eyes and went back to his cell. He sat on the hard bunk and flipped through the titles. Out in the hallway, the guard scrambled to his feet, door slamming behind him. Asshole.

A cheesy romance, a detective novel he'd read when he was eight, and some crap about Feng Shui. Christ. You'd think they could find something decent. He scrubbed a hand over his face. Feng Shui it was. He pulled the blanket over and stuffed it behind him as he leaned against the concrete wall. Shit sucked the heat right out of you.

The door opened, and a different prick took a seat, glaring at him, sans paper.

Flynn didn't give a shit.

Kara's anxiety ratcheted up. He squirmed on the bunk, gritting his teeth. Counted the blocks on the far wall. Halfway through his second pass, he broke out in a cold sweat at the surge of her despair. What the fuck'd just happened?

He pushed off the bunk and paced, then dropped, doing pushups until her emotions settled and his arms shook. Fuck. Exhausted, he rolled onto his back, hating himself.

Just say you didn't know…

He didn't know if he didn't know. He'd sure as hell suspected.

…surrender to His will…

Yeah. As soon as God opened up his trap about what he wanted, Flynn would get right on that.

Fucking serenity.

The door opened again.

Flynn stood as Stonefist entered the room.

"Lord Scot." He glanced back at the Intelligencer. After a tense moment, the man huffed, leaving.

"You know they're still gonna listen."

Stonefist grunted and commandeered the chair. "Doesn't mean I have to make it easy for them. I'll admit they have their uses, but the whole damn line makes the back of my neck crawl. Mangleshield informed me of your terms. I find them acceptable."

"How'd Phyllis take it?"

"As her due." The Breaker exhaled heavily as he sat. "I hear you're a cigar man. Thought you might appreciate me smuggling in some contraband." He pulled one out and leaned forward to pass it through the bars with a book of matches.

"Hey, yeah, thanks." Flynn snagged them and lit up, his nerves mellowing as the smoke cut into his lungs. He fiddled with the half spent book. "You here with an update?"

"Other than you still having a seat, I'm sure it's pretty much what you expect. Sons have started ransacking estates, and the Source is massing at the border. I put out the suggestion to evacuate everyone to the city, but no one wants to hear it. Don't expect that will happen until a scion or two get flayed."

"Markham shifting people out?"

"No. We've been officially penned in."

Flynn grunted. "Then the Source'll wait until the Sons are at the walls, banking on crushing them between us when they deploy to harvest."

"That's my read on it."

"You assigning Hexes?" The small groups comprised of each talent would be their most effective stratagem against the Source and Sons alike.

"As of an hour ago."

"There's someone you should talk to, if you haven't already. Kara's mother—"

"Yes, they were both at Assembly today."

Goddamn it. "She—how was she?"

Stonefist's face softened. "She didn't look...hale. Lot had to carry her out after the press conference."

Flynn's temper spiked. "They had her do a fucking presser?!" He slammed a hand against the bars, turning away. That motherf—he was gonna kill Cal. No wonder it'd felt like she'd fallen to shit. All those people... Christ, and the fucking Source knew she was pregnant while he was stuck in here. Talent crackled around his fingers, and he jammed them in his pocket, snuffing them. "Where was Rogan?"

Stonefist pinched his nose, sniffing, his brow furrowed. "Lord Firestorm? I don't know."

"Find him. She leaves Meddleton again, I want him with her." As much as he hated the fucking prick, he'd keep her safe.

The Breaker blanched. "You want *me* to tell the Alpha Prime—"

"I don't give a shit what you call him, he needs to do it, and you need to sit down with the fucking Commandant to get a handle on what the Source has planned." Flynn snorted at the Breaker's incredulity. "Yeah, I know the feeling. Apparently he defected and hitched a ride up with that bitch."

"Who's leading their forces?"

"You're asking the wrong person."

"I suspect I am," Stonefist said, chewing his lip. "That could change things considerably."

"Yeah. He's staying at our flat in the city." Flynn passed the matches back through the bars. "Here, you can save them the trouble of frisking me."

The Breaker grunted and stood, taking them. "I'll keep you abreast as things evolve."

Flynn nodded, returning to the bunk as the man left. He sat back, head against the concrete and exhaled a long plume of smoke. Thinking about the phrase scribbled on the inside cover of the matches. The one he hadn't heard since he'd been with his squad in Diytan.

Devil's on the loose.

NORA SAT in Cal's office, watching Kara's hands shake around a cup of tea. The girl was haggard despite the IV dripping God knew what into her. They'd tried to get her to go upstairs, but she'd refused to budge from the settee by the fire. Nora was afraid to push her on it, let alone suggest she heal her. Kara had that stubborn set to her jaw that used to signal an impending tantrum. They were bad enough when she was a child, and her health was too fragile to risk one now.

She glanced up and caught Nora staring. "Stop it. I'm fine."

Her chattering teeth said otherwise.

"No, you're not. You need to be in bed."

"No, I have to go back. You said it yourself, they'll feed on this, and if I'm to have any hope of surviving that damned luncheon—"

"She's right, Nora. Let the girl alone, I called you in to pick your brain, not a fight," Cal said around his cigarette.

Nora bristled. Whatever agenda he had, Kara collapsing wouldn't achieve it. She opened her mouth to argue, and his expression seared it from her tongue. Damn the man...

"I got my hands on a list of genealogies from Titus's stable, and there's a few entries that are sparse. I'm curious about this one in particular. Says you were the attending medic. Remember anything?"

Nora flipped through the file he handed her. It was from several years ago. Male Talent, Fixer/Fetch, no further pedigree listed, and the typical stacks of metrics missing. What about this was she supposed to

—wait. The infant had been premature and in crisis. That she remembered.

"I wasn't there for the birth, they called me in to stabilize him. His lungs hadn't finished developing. When I went to put in a request for his metrics, the boy was gone, and there was no record of him in the system."

"You never said anything?"

She met his eyes. "I wish I could tell you it was the only time it happened."

Cal grunted, lighting another cigarette. "So what's your theory?"

"That Titus bred a wild Talent and induced them," she said without pause. The practice hadn't been a secret, though no one had discussed it. "He eschewed the use of the Laborium, and none of the instances occurred with an in-line mating. If he'd contracted with another Patron to create a twist, there would've been paperwork, and the child would've remained in the Creche to observe for flaws." Why did Cal care?

"That's where my mind went. Interesting that it happened towards the end of the timeframe Julia disappeared. This ring any bells?" He tossed over a still.

It did.

"Yes...she was brought to the Creche for self-inflicted wounds around the same time. I didn't treat her, but I remember her weeping. Source Talents don't cry like that." God, that had haunted her for months.

"That doesn't make any sense. If he bred her, why would he let her go?" Kara asked. She'd finished her tea and stopped shaking, half the IV bag of mysterious gunk gone.

"Makes perfect sense. Julia disappeared for almost a year, and no one has seen her father since, though he was always a recluse. The boy's the sole heir to House Cree, and the way that girl's biological clock was ticking before shit hit the fan...well. Puts everything she's been doing up here in a completely different light. I'd wager she sold her soul trying to get him back."

Kara chewed her thumb, and Nora sympathized with her

confusion. Most parents just walked away from their children at the Source and never looked back. Those that did, seldom did twice.

The laborists made sure of that.

Cal glanced over like he knew what she was thinking. "As far as why Titus let her go," he said, taking another drag, "it gave him the perfect pawn to sway the Assembly with. The rest of the world will do anything for their children, Karabelle. I pray you'll feel the same when the time comes."

His eyes met Nora's. Letting her see that he cared, desperately.

She still wasn't sure about what.

Regardless, there was little information she could give him. Jon already had Kara on the standard nutritionals, and the ones Nora had been prescribed during her pregnancies had arrived as needed from Titus's tower. She'd never questioned them. God, that was the problem wasn't it? Lemmings, all of them. Following in lockstep whatever directives were handed down from the powers that be...

Kara must've seen something pass between them because she tensed again and snatched a paper from the coffee table, that stubborn set to her jaw back. Cal asked a question about the Laborium and Nora answered absently. The side effects of whatever was in that drip—

Kara took a sharp breath, and they both looked at her.

"Did you see this? The constabulary is looking for help in identifying a dismembered body found in a footlocker at the Painted Pony," she read. "Female Finder, 5'8", black hair, blue eyes, barcode right wrist...that's Ielle."

Nora blanched. "What? She was in Glynfyls?"

"News to me." Cal took another drag, leaning back in his chair. "Last I knew, she'd been transferred to Titus a week or so ago. That lame excuse he's got for how Riegel slipped his leash isn't gonna fly with the both of them up here. I'll put in a call to the board and the Constable Major on it. Nora, I'm gonna need you to meet with Merchant."

"Lord Ketsing has invited me to dine with their line—"

Kara laughed, and Nora flinched at its alien bitterness. "I'm sorry. Janice is awful...like Serra Hess awful, but without anything to back it up."

Nora's stomach dropped to her shoes. Another harpy as vile as Serra? "Sweet Glory, please say you're kidding me."

Cal cracked a smile. "Shame you can't plead a headache."

She glared at him. "No, but I may have to leave early to check in on Kara. Are you feeling better?" The flush to her daughter's cheeks worried her as much as the pallor had.

"Yes, I—my nerves have just been really raw since starting on this stuff." She discontinued the IV, applying pressure and bending her arm, "What is it?"

"Breaker Business." Cal shrugged, ignoring their glowers to dig through his files. "If you're going back for the afternoon session, I suggest you get a move on. Doors close in five. Hand this to one of the pages when you do. While back, I had Merchant draw something up in anticipation of Julia overplaying her hand. It's a little vague, but should be enough to get the ball rolling."

"The doors don't close at all anymore," Kara said sweetly, batting her lashes at him as she stood to grab it. She looked it over, a feral grin spreading over her face.

"There's my girl. Go give 'em hell."

Nora's brow furrowed. Kara's response to the intravenous treatment was concerning. The way it propped her back up again, masking her symptoms…she needed to be in bed where the underlying causes could be addressed. "You sure you want to do this?"

"Trust me," Kara said, a vicious smile curving her lips. "There's nothing I want to do more."

MARCOS SHOOK Lord Stonefist's hand as they sat across the table from one another. His counterpart's estate, the study in particular, was spartan enough to suit Marcos's own tastes. Done in neutrals, the furniture was functional and in good repair, maps adorning the walls. The single exception was an intricate coat of arms above the fireplace. Waist-high bookcases filled with military tomes and memorabilia lined the rest of the room.

Nothing like the Scot's monstrosity of an estate. Marcos had never seen such a display. Even after being exposed to the Source's decadence, the wealth they so casually exhibited was nauseating. Not for the first time, he tried to reconcile Lord Scot with Kendall's second. There was an angle he was missing, and the concern he felt from Nora didn't improve his opinion of the man. There was something very wrong with Kara, and Scot was to blame.

A slight woman brought in a coffee service with a tray of sausage and cheese. Marcos helped himself to a cup, and Stonefist followed suit.

"You'll have to forgive me for the abruptness of this meeting, but after Lord Scot suggested it, I didn't see the point in waiting. The intel I have on the Source's capabilities is sparse."

Marcos sipped his coffee, smug. "Good to hear. I worked hard to keep it that way. I'm assuming you're the one who sent that Finder to keep tabs on the Hexspar operation several months back?"

"No, that was Crandall," Stonefist said sourly, making up a plate. "I counseled against it."

Marcos grunted and silence stretched. He'd met many a foe across a negotiations table, but never with the intent to join them. It didn't sit well, no matter the rationale.

Stonefist sniffed, pulling at his nose. "I'd prefer not to begin this conversation calling your honor into question, but with what you're putting out—"

"Eau du dick in the dirt?"

The man chuckled, grabbing a wedge of cheese. "Yeah, that'd be it. Mind if I ask to see your runes? Honor and intent will suffice."

Marcos's brow raised. "You don't show halos, but those you flash?"

"It's considered the polite alternative to 'lust."

"If I were a woman, I'd slap you."

"If you were a woman, I might like it."

Marcos cracked a smile. "You show me yours, I'll show you mine."

"Fair enough." Stonefist pulled talent, and a sparking web of candy-red lines surrounded him.

Marcos did the same, reading the man…his conscience eased. The Northern general was not so different from himself, and as wary of a turn-coat showing up at such an opportune time as Marcos was of turning said coat. They dropped talent. "Satisfied?"

"No, curious. Why'd you go rogue?"

Marcos frowned, rolling a slice of sausage beneath a finger. Now wasn't the time to be coy. "Titus gave me access to the redacted files from the last incursion in preparation for this one. They weighed on me, especially after stumbling across confirmation he's violated the terms our forebearers agreed to in exchange for our service by running a blacksite. I can't even imagine how the hierarchy's been perverted—"

"You're telling me he has more troops?" Stonefist swore at his nod. "That explains the sudden influx at the border…then why the guilt?"

Marcos poured himself another cup of coffee before answering, still trying to work that out in his own head. "In part, because I left good men down there. Titus syphons 'lust from our Alpha and keeps him in stasis. We—they're—answerable only to him, and he's done a fine job of greying our honor."

"I'd wondered. Some of those ops in the South…" Marcos couldn't meet Stonefist's eye, the coffee on his tongue more bitter than it should be. "So what's the rest of it?"

"I got played." Gah, that burnt his craw. "He cultivated my disillusionment, then infected me with tech so he could sniff out how Kara escaped and implicate her patron."

"Trojan horse, huh?"

Marcos grunted and took a slice of cheese. "Have you been briefed on the bots?"

"I have. Jesse had several of us down there, trying to recreate the weave you put on the guild door, without success. You and Lady Jester are going to be very busy until whatever she's fiddling with comes to fruition. They need to be installed over as many gates as possible."

He'd been afraid of that, but it wasn't surprising. Until he'd met Nora, he'd never dreamt of working with a Binder, let alone being bound to one. A smile ghosted across his lips, feeling her through their connection. It faded at her anxiety. Over Kara, no doubt.

"How many gates are there?" he asked.

"Just shy of five hundred. Crandall's providing a list of the most frequented, and the Fetches have offered to shift you around. I'm not sure how much talent you've got in the tank, but I suspect we'll find out." Stonefist pulled over a map. "What can you tell me about how this is going to develop?"

Marcos indicated a point on the border. "They'll advance from here. Twelve thousand men, about fifteen hundred qualify as Peacekeepers."

"That include what he's recalled from the South?"

"Some, not all. I've zero intel on that blacksite, and it sounds like he's pulling from it already. The jump sites he's upgraded are oversized for the Talents he has on the books by almost double." And who knew what their capabilities were. If Stonefist's dour expression was anything to go by, he was thinking the same thing.

"Damn. What about Fetches? How soon can he be on our doorstep?"

"He has a dozen in his stable that can shift an average of three hundred men per jump. He was reluctant to say whether or not he'd be leasing Talents from any of the other patrons, and wouldn't disclose if any of them had a route north imprinted." Marcos kicked himself, damning hindsight. Titus's recalcitrance on the subject should've thrown up more of a red flag. He took a bite of sausage, mouth puckering as the unfamiliar spices lit him up.

"I'd prefer to err on the side of caution and say he does." Stonefist's eyes crinkled at Marcos's quick intake of breath.

"That would be wise…gah, what's in those?" He wiped a sheen of sweat from his brow. Damned thing burnt all the way to his gut.

"Greberian peppers." Stonefist grinned. "They're somewhat of an addiction up here. Who has command now that you're gone?"

Marcos took a slice of cheese, hoping to kill the burn. "Must be an acquired taste. Pax was being groomed, but doesn't have the temperament yet. I wouldn't be surprised if Titus had someone else in mind. I wasn't privy to who."

"What about their tech?"

Marcos poured himself another cup of coffee. Damn, that stuff had legs. "I was wondering when you'd get to that. It's finicky, especially in extreme climes. Most of the men prefer to use talent, field retrofits are cumbersome. The warming jackets for the plaz-cannons are loud and triple the recharge time, essentially making them one hit wonders.

I'd worry more about nullifiers. A well-placed mortar armed with one will take out half the city."

"You might be surprised." Stonefist smirked. "We've got one hell of an Engineering Guild."

"You do at that." But he still wasn't convinced, despite the man's nonchalance. "Jesse seems to think she'll have that shield up and running in the next few days."

"Good to hear." Stonefist popped a sausage into his mouth with a quick pull of talent, then chomped on it like it was nothing. What had he—"You need to break the heat." Man smirked at his scowl. Would've been nice to know that before he'd seared his guts. "Well, after hearing all that, I could use a bout. You look like you've beaten me to it. Anyone I know?"

Marcos fingered the bridge of his nose. "Lord Scot and I aren't on the best of terms. He laid me out."

"Uppercut?"

"Cross."

Surprise flitted across Stonefist's face. "Witnessed?"

"Not by anyone who can vouch for our rungs."

"That'll need to change. No time like the present. You up for another bout?"

"Potentially more than one. I get the impression the Breakers up here don't suffer from twitching the way we do down south." The miserable affliction was rearing its head, Marcos's muscles beginning to cramp and seize. He needed to work them out before it got any worse.

"Can't say that we do, but it's opportune at the moment, and I'd hazard you'd sleep better with a rung to ascribe to."

Marcos inclined his head. He would at that.

KARA SAT in Flynn's box at the Assembly, taking slow, deep breaths to keep her bloodlust in check. Lot was behind her, his face radiating disapproval at her attendance. Nuts to him and her mother. Nora was in the Binder section across the floor, deep in conversation with Lord

Ketsing. He—and the rest of the line—were clearly enamored, but what wasn't there to love? She was perfect. Janice was going to have a fit.

Ha.

Kara smirked, wiping her palms on her heavy skirts. The speaker made his way down to his podium, the rest of the Assembly filing in behind him as they returned from lunch.

Riggs smiled at her. "Lady Scot. I'm so happy to see you. Your fortitude after such an ordeal speaks highly of you."

Kara smiled politely. It was more vindictiveness than fortitude, but he could believe whatever he wanted. The surprised glances and ensuing whispers as people trickled in grated at her nerves. Her 'lust churned beneath it all, along with Flynn's concern. She clenched her jaw, trying to concentrate on the waltz playing in her head, not imagining stabbing Julia in time to it. That wouldn't accomplish what she needed to.

But it would be really satisfying.

Riggs banged his gavel and picked up the agenda. He scanned through it, his eyebrows rising to his hairline. His eyes met hers. She gave a curt nod, and he ran a hand down his face.

"It pains me to present a grave matter to you all. House Scot is leveling a charge of treason against House Cree for colluding with the Source."

Julia's face remained impassive in the silence that followed, the members surrounding her conspicuously edging away.

Riggs regarded Kara gravely, and her heart thumped loud in her ears.

"Lady Scot, you must have hard evidence in order to make this claim. It is a most serious allegation. In the entire history of the Assembly, we've never had a member charged with treason. Why would Mistress Cree work with the Source to undermine the city of her birth?"

Kara wiped her hands on her skirt again, praying no one would see them shake. It wasn't nerves...her damn bloodlust was churning, licking up over the strands of the music in her head, warping it with a discordance of fury—

Nora stood. "They have her son."

The color bled from Julia's face, and she seized violently, falling to the floor. The room erupted into chaos.

"She needs a Binder!"

Julia's seizure intensified, her back arching as she foamed at the mouth. Nora ran to her, pushing through the crowd. She knelt at Julia's side, pulling talent, and laid a hand across the woman's forehead. The seizure stopped and Nora's face grayed. Kara helped her to stand.

Her mother sagged against her. "Someone scoured that poor woman's mind…" she whispered hoarsely.

"Did they?" Crandall asked from behind them.

Nora paled, and Kara was sure she did the same. The Intelligencer's black eyes bored into them, and she fought the urge to punch him.

Lady Ketsing burst into the room with a shorter man, both in medic grays. "Let me through, what's this I hear about Mistress Cree? Oh, Lord have mercy." Her halos flared, confusion marring her sharp features.

Nora drew herself away from Crandall. "I've stopped the seizure, but she needs to be monitored. Her condition's highly unstable."

"Best to do that at the infirmary—"

"If you don't mind, I'll accompany you," Nora said.

Janice frowned, then gave a reluctant nod. The stocky man that'd come with her pulled talent, and the four of them shifted away.

Leaving Kara with Crandall.

"I think we're over due for a chat, you and I—"

She flushed, pulse racing, battling to keep her 'lust in check—

The gavel sounded. "If we can all return to our seats?"

Kara fled to Flynn's box, their bond rife with his worry. People trickled back to their places, unsure of what else to do with themselves. She sat, gripping her skirts to still her shaking hands. The adrenaline that'd accompanied the anticipation of confronting Julia and then Crandall was gone, leaving her a jumble of emotion. That Julia just collapsed like that—

"Lady Scot, can you explain what just happened?" Lord Riggs asked.

Kara shook her head, not looking at the Intelligencer. "I have my suspicions, but I—I'm unwilling voice them until I speak with my—with Lady Jester."

"Very well. Regardless of Mistress Cree's unfortunate reaction to the charges levied against her, Assembly protocol demands a vote be taken, no matter how distasteful." Riggs's lips pruned as he scanned the chamber. "Those in favor of opening an investigation of collusion between House Cree and the Source?"

The room was unanimous.

"In all my years as speaker of this esteemed body..." He sighed and banged his gavel. "Passed. Next order of business. Lord Stonefist, you've requested to speak?"

He stood, dour. "Yes. We've just received word that as of an hour ago, the Sons attacked several estates. The sole survivor from Anafeild—"

The uproar drowned him out.

"But that's so close!"

"House Cheryi is gone?"

"How did they get that far already?"

"Why aren't you doing something about it?!"

Kara's heart rate doubled, her mouth dry. Every section save the Breakers' was in a frenzy. The speaker pounded his gavel for order, and the room begrudgingly gave it to him.

Stonefist continued. "The outlying estates need to be abandoned. The Sons have divided their forces and are gathering en masse, not only on the southern lip of the plateau, but in the east and west. As far as I'm concerned, they can rot out there. My concern is Glynfyls."

The room disintegrated into chaos. People shouting, and several making for the doors. A slight woman in the Fetches' section stood, her shrill voice carrying above all of it.

"What about the weasels?"

The clamor broke off, and people turned to stare.

Riggs adjusted his glasses. "Excuse me?"

"Weasels. They're running rampant through the hill, slaughtering—"

"That was an isolated incident, Madame Grey." Crandall sighed wearily. Several people snickered, and her face hardened.

"But you haven't caught them! I won't put my parakeets at risk! I've entered a proposal and demand a vote this very moment!" She thumped her boney fist down on her skirts, thin lip thrust forward. The Speaker flipped through his papers, and pulled out a packet.

"Ah, here it is, and cosponsored by House Prydee, of all... The creation of a Commission for the Advancement of Rodent Control Enforcement is being proposed to...you do realize the Ratter's Guild—"

"They're part of the problem! How else would a rogue nest of those vile creatures exist, except through their negligence? I can just imagine them down there in those beastly caverns—More oversight is required!"

Across the floor Stonefist scrubbed at his face. Kara bit back a laugh. The Sons were coming to exterminate them, and that little twit was worried about weasels? Worse, everyone was taking her seriously. The room was filled with idiots. No wonder Flynn was always so annoyed after session.

"Shall we vote then, on the creation of this, ah, weasel commission?" Riggs asked.

It passed. Kara fought back another manic burble of laughter.

Lady Breakspear stood. "Not that varmint mitigation isn't of the utmost importance, but the Sons are on our doorstep, and the Source is right behind them. I'm calling for a vote to institute Quorum on all issues related to the war effort until those matters have been decided."

A rumble of discontent rolled throughout the hall, and the Speaker banged his gavel again, calling the matter to the floor. It passed by a wide margin.

"Well, per protocol, that will divide our days, all issues related to the war effort will be seen to by Quorum in the mornings, and administrative affairs such as the, ah, weasel commission, will be the province of the Assembly in the afternoons. Small bit of bookkeeping, I will need the name of the lord or lady overseeing those efforts. After the accountability issues with the Pinch Beautification Commission, I will remind you, whomever is nominated is required to be on site, directly involved with the, ah, hunt, as it were."

Kara snorted at the sudden lack of eye contact around the room. Happy to pass mandates, none of them keen to get their hands dirty. Seemed par for the course.

"Yes, and I'm sure we'd all like to be kept abreast of any further weaselry," Crandall said. He didn't bother to hide his smirk and wasn't the only one.

The elderly man missed it, shuffling his papers. "I'd expect no less on such a serious matter. Well, I think we've made good progress for today. I'll see you all tomorrow." He banged his gavel, and the Assembly stood, breaking into smaller groups and exiting the room.

"A goddamned weasel commission. They'd find plenty of them in this room," Lot grumbled, his eyes on Crandall approaching. Kara's heart leapt to her throat, the steps congested with gossiping members. Lot put himself between her and the Intelligencer.

"Adlothian. If you don't mind I'd like a word with Lady Scot."

"I do mind. She's had enough to deal with without you stirring the pot," he growled, members moving away from them.

Crandall was undeterred. "Lady Jester's comment—"

"Should be taken up with Lady Jester," Lot said, looming over the smaller man. The knuckles on his right hand popped, clenching into a fist.

People pulled back, intent on the drama playing out. Kara slipped between them, leaving the two men on the stair. The hallway was just as crowded, a gauntlet of leering eyes and jagged smirks. She swallowed her rising anxiety, smoothing a hand across her stomach—

A hand closed around her bicep, and Rogan caught her fist.

"Where the hell is Lot? You shouldn't be here by yourself."

"I—Crandall—"

Rogan's nostrils flared, scenting her 'lust. His lips flattened into a scowl. Damn it.

"Right. Let's go."

Kara nodded, trying to shake off the lingering blackness and failing miserably.

CHAPTER NINE

"With the genetic enhancements to the Breaker line's physicals, it quickly became evident that bloodlust was especially problematic for females. Gestation inevitably resulted in them succumbing. The tipping point was different for each of them, and the impossibility of predicting, or curing the condition required sedating them as soon as they were impregnated, then culling them after they'd whelped. Faced with a deficit of breeders, adjustments were made to ensure the viability of the program. The most successful innovation was increasing their predisposition for multiples. If we had to expend a bitch for each birth, we would gain a litter in return. Markedly ramping up the gestation speed further improved production efficiencies, allowing us to cater to a wider clientele base..."

– L. Merkel, Head Geneticist,
The Source

OTTO SAVORED his late lunch in a corner booth of the Gilded Pearl, one of Glynfyls's more prominent inns. The lamb was exceptional paired with a pinot noir. Around him was abuzz, the others in the exclusive room chewing over Julia's collapse with more relish than their meals.

Pity that had happened so quickly. He probably should've taken more care with her directives, but honestly, it wasn't like they were going to get that much more mileage out of her. Especially not with the Triam's breeding records turning up. Awfully convenient, that. Titus had to be positively gnashing this teeth.

Otto swirled the liquid in his glass, wondering where Caliban Scot had gotten ahold of them, but then, he was nothing if not cunning. Why Mother refused to out him as a board member...she must have something particularly nasty planned for the man and that Breaker he palled around with. There was history there, and it wouldn't do to spoil it for her.

Not if he wanted to keep breathing, and he most assuredly did.

Otto smirked, watching a group of women through the pretext of inspecting his wine's legs. They sat at a small lace-draped table, blushes and rosés in hand, their cheeks pinked with the same and the fervor of their gossip.

"A son! Can you imagine?" A blonde in a very low-cut gown tittered behind a milky hand. She dropped her voice to a stage whisper. "Do you think it's Laughlin's?"

The doppelgänger beside her rolled her eyes. "No, who would want to bond that?"

A brunette in green didn't discount it. "He certainly was drunk enough...and a twist! You know you can't trust their kind. Degenerates, all of them."

"Mmm, especially Tyrel Sweet," the doppelgänger drawled. The brunette flushed.

"You're so bad, Caro!" The blonde put a hand to her breast. "I bet that's why she accused him. Waiting all this time only to be jilted—What if he was down there trying to get the baby back?"

"And met that Binder instead!"

The table gave a collective gasp, and Otto tried not to chuckle. If nothing else, Glynfyls was entertaining. He fully expected their speculation to be on the front page of the late edition. Barton slid into the opposing seat of the booth, and he tuned them out to attend to business.

"What's the delay?"

The assassin gave that rolling blink of his. "Big Breaker was there."

Otto frowned, allowing a waiter to refill his glass. The man took Barton's order and left.

"They'll let Scot out after this. Titus won't be pleased you've squandered the window." Neither would Mother. Otto sipped at his wine, troubled on more than one front. How had Nora connected the boy to Julia? Even with a Binder's intellect, it was troubling. The woman was far more dangerous than she looked.

"Another will open." The assassin pulled his fingers from his mouth, one blooming claret.

"I suggest you be there when it does, else you'll be flying out of one."

The man made a choked sound Otto took for amusement. The women at the other table began squealing about rampaging weasels. What was that about? His eyes flicked back to Barton, and he shrugged.

His plate was delivered, the meat upon it having only a tangential acquaintance with flame. The assassin sawed at the raw slab, his delight apparent. Otto sipped his wine, his mind going back to Nora. If she'd been clever enough to connect Julia with the boy, she could very well have deduced Otto's own involvement, and she'd be able to identify him. He'd need to take precautions. Whether or not Barton obtained the girl, dealing with her mother had gained precedence.

FLYNN WAS ON HIS BUNK, staring at the same page he had been for the past hour, when another surge of anxiety and shock from Kara scored through their bond, her bloodlust surging. She was barely keeping a handle on it, and with her riot of emotions… He tossed the book away and scrubbed at his face in frustration. Not knowing what was going on—

He should be with her.

He paced the tiny space, dragging a hand through his hair, then gripping the cell's bars. Damned things heated up, warping—Christ, this fucking talent was too close. He took deep breaths, trying to send her—himself—calm. The blackness licking at their bond made his stomach cramp.

He needed to be with her.

The door chunked open, and Crandall stalked in. "Binders have the ability to insight?"

Flynn straightened up, blinking. "I dunno, I'm not a Binder."

If there hadn't been bars between them, he was certain Crandall would've taken a swing at him. Flynn grinned.

"Listen, you infuriating prick, Julia Cree just went into seizure at the allegation she's been colluding with the Source because they have her son."

Flynn dropped onto his bunk. Fuck. That punch had landed. "She has a son?" His shock mollified the man.

"So Nora Jester says. She spirited herself off to the infirmary with Julia. They won't let me in the room until she's stable, and Lot prevented me from questioning your lady."

"Good, she doesn't need anything else on her plate."

"Then answer the question! You know something—" His halos flared and there was a questing at the edges of Flynn's cloak…

He laughed. Christ, he'd never seen Crandall lose his shit. It was definitely the highlight of his week. "So, is it physically painful not to be able to shove your nose up someone's ass, or do you just delight in being that much of a weasel?"

Crandall blustered. "Weasels—" He glared at the Intelligencer snickering by the door. The man tucked tail and left. "God, I hate Shades. You're not going to disclose, are you?"

"I've nothing to say, and trust me, the feeling's mutual."

"Not even if I guaranteed your confirmation will unlock this cell?"

They stared at each other. Shit. Did he really want to let Crandall know about a Binder's ability to coerce? That would open up Kara to way more scrutiny, and if it was possible to coerce Talents… No. She had enough of a stigma from the Source without people wondering if she was messing with their minds. He picked up the book he'd been reading.

"Toilet should be on the other wall. It's impeding the energy flow for cooperation."

Crandall wasn't amused. He unlocked the cell door and pushed it open. "In light of the allegations brought forth by Lady Scot, Merchant's negotiated your bail until the rest is sorted. You're free to go." Man looked peeved as hell about it.

The air went out of Flynn again, his head light. He raked a hand through his hair and stood, pushing past Crandall on his way out.

"At some point we're going to have to come to a detente, Lord Scot."

"Soon as your line pledges, I'll think about it."

Merchant stood outside the door, eyes on his pocket watch. He snapped it shut when he saw him. "On the button. I'm assuming you didn't answer any of his questions?"

"No. Get me the hell out of here."

"With pleasure." Merchant escorted him past desks of Finders, and out a steel door at the end of the room. A gate was on the other side. Flynn stepped through it into Meddleton's foyer—

Kara's arms were around his neck, her legs encircling his waist. "Don't go away, never, never, ever again." She sobbed, kissing him.

"No. Never again." God, she felt so slight—"Have you been eating?" A flood of her emotion broke over him, and he fell back, sitting on the floor. "Shit, Kara…shh…it's okay, I'm here…"

Merchant motioned to Cal's office, and Flynn bristled. His grandfather could wait. Kara needed him. Shit, he needed her. He sat, stroking her hair as she cried. All her hurt and fear from the past few days resonated through their bond. Goddamn, he was an asshole putting her through this. After a long while, her tears subsided and she curled in his lap, limp; a bone-gnawing exhaustion eating at her.

Flynn brushed back her hair to kissed her brow. "Come on, I gotta see Cal, and then you need to be in bed." He picked her up and brought her into his grandfather's study. Not a chance he was getting her to go upstairs without him. He didn't want to leave her, either.

The haze in the room was so thick he could hardly breathe. Instead of behind his desk, the old man sat in front of a dying fire with his feet up on the andirons, looking ancient. He flicked a cigarette butt into the coals and it flared. Merchant was in the straight-backed chair by the desk, and Nora Jester in the other. Flynn snorted at the woman's presence. Whatever.

He settled into one of the recliners with Kara, needing her close. She tucked up under his chin, the physical contact soothing them both.

"You want to go first or shall I?" Nora asked the barrister. He gestured for her to proceed. "I examined Julia at the infirmary. Her psyche's been completely stripped away. I've never seen anything like it. Everything is gone, save for her basic functions and an overlay of composite memories built to defame—"

"But she's a Talent," Flynn interrupted. "Kara said that wasn't possible."

Nora twisted her ring. "In most cases it isn't, but I suspect there is one of our line who possesses the ability as an extra."

"Otto." Kara breathed.

Her mother nodded. "He's a Binder from Titus's stable, and is in one of the few memories Julia has of the past two days. Mentioning her son triggered something and collapsed the structure he'd built. She won't recover."

"How the hell did he get ahold of her?"

"Your guess is as good as mine," Cal said around his cigarette.

Christ, none of it seemed possible. "Would Leo know? I figured he'd be over there twenty-four seven after I cleared out."

"He's still in the wind. I'll be damned if I know how, but that Fetch, Fitz, turned up the full reel of the night before you left." Cal sighed, pulling a cube from his shirt pocket. He tapped it on the arm of his chair. "Leo orchestrated the entire affair. I didn't think the boy had it in him."

Flynn had, but kept his mouth shut.

"Lady Jester has agreed to examine Julia's maid, Charlotte, to see if she can discover anymore information to help our case. There's only two other servants at Julia's estate. It's in shambles, which leads me to believe that this has been going on for quite some time," Merchant said, standing. "If you're ready?"

Nora nodded and followed him out.

Flynn released a deep breath, a sob escaping with it. He held Kara tighter, looking at the ceiling with glassy eyes. "Then I was right about him making the reel." Christ, why did that hurt so much?

Cal snorted, lighting another cigarette from the butt still clamped between his lips, then flicking the spent one into the coals. "It pains me to say that you've been right about a lot of things concerning that little shit. My own goddamned blood…"

He held out the cube.

Flynn eyed it like it was a snake before taking it, tamping down his anger. He rolled in his hand and the fucking thing started to melt. Jesus —he threw it into the fire, trying to remember a time when his cousin didn't hate him.

He couldn't.

"What did I ever do to him?"

His grandfather started rolling another cigarette. Flynn hadn't seen him chain-smoke like this since his mother died. "Jealousy can twist a man. When you were younger, I'd have said he resented the way Miriam doted on you, or you being heir. Now I'd bet it was more you knowing he was in love with Julia, and messing with her just because you could. Didn't mean a damn thing to you, other than a new way to spite Lot and piss him off in the process."

Flynn grunted. Cal wasn't wrong. The old man's hands shook as he took a drag.

"And if that's the case, I'd put money on him tipping off the Source's troops on your way up here, which means he's probably the one behind the border abductions as well."

Jesus fucking—"You really think he's working with the Source? Leo's a dick but—"

"Yeah. I think he's in deep. Titus never was one to waste an opportunity, and Leo…" Cal frowned, picking a bit of tobacco off his lip. "Leo's Leo, and on top of which, what would you do to get your wife and child clear of them?"

The air went out of Flynn like he'd been gut-punched.

"It's his kid?"

"Paperwork said Fixer/Fetch. I'm not discounting the possibility, no."

Flynn's arms tightened around Kara. He knew exactly what he would do to get her and his kid back. What he would become.

And it wasn't fucking pretty.

———

THE TWO OF them left the room, and Cal stood, feeling every single one of his years as he crossed to his desk. He plopped down into his chair's divot and pulled out a bottle of scotch. Nowhere near enough was left in it. He raised the last of it to his lips, then called up French to bring him another.

Goddamn. Why the hell couldn't he ever see what was right in front of him?

This was gonna kill Miriam and Shelby. Maybe the little shit would have the decency to stay away, and they'd never have to know. He grabbed one of his cigars. Chances of that happening were slim to none. Boy would turn up. Bad pennies always did.

French came in with a bottle and the evening edition. Cal grunted his thanks. He settled back and put his feet up, flicking the paper open—

Bile seared his throat.

A head shot of Julia Cree filled the front page, her hair done up in an intricate braid he hadn't seen since before the Surge. Elize had worn it like that to his senior prom. He upended the bottle, letting it burn down his throat.

Hearing the threat as surely as if Jane were whispering in his ear.

Christ, it wasn't Otto. It had been her.

How much did Titus know? Cal pulled at his hair, everything falling to shit. He needed to make some calls to the board. Sons and Flynn's status notwithstanding, it was time to stop dicking around and bury that son of a bitch once and for all—

"One of those days?" Rogan asked, strolling in and heading for the sideboard. He sniffed. "You burning plastic?"

"Flynn was just in here." Cal flipped the paper over and poured himself three fingers. "Yeah, it's one of those days. Where the hell've you been?"

Rogan slapped a handful of milky white pebbles onto the desk. "Somehow, the Sons got ahold of gating stones. Granted, these fizzle out after a couple uses, but I thought it best to remove temptation. Somebody else is busy removing them."

"You gotta be shitting me. Who?"

"Merc outfit. Where is she?"

Elize. He tasted bile again and chased it with what was in his glass. "You know damned well I haven't seen her in centuries. What outfit would be up here hunting Sons? Assembly would've had to sanction something like that."

Rogan glared at him, halos sparking. Man was pissed. "Don't care, and not what I asked. If you're holding out on me and Elize is out there making these fucking things—"

"How the hell can she without Richard?" Goddamn it—he'd suspected Jane could harness the talent of those she'd bound, but—

"Somebody is, and your ex-fucking-wife is the only living half of that equation!"

Cal glared back for half a second before the fight went out of him. He fell back in his chair, fingers trembling on the lip of his glass. Ex-wife. They'd never quite gotten around to hammering that out. He raked his hair back. Should just fucking tell him. Spill his guts and all the dirty goddamned secrets. Let Rogan know what a piece of shit he was—

He'd walk away and let all of it burn.

Maybe he'd be right to, but it wasn't a goddamned option.

"I dunno know where she is, her or Enoch. Woman could always find a way to avoid me when she wanted to."

"You're full of shit."

They sat there glaring at each other. Cal dropped his gaze first to pick up one of the stones. It wasn't as refined as the older ones. Not surprising. Using another talent wasn't easy, though he would've thought fixing and binding were similar enough. He sighed, opening a drawer and pinging it in.

"You still have one?"

Rogan pulled a chain from his shirt and dangled the little stone at him. "You lost yours, didn't you?"

"Maybe." He knew right where it was, but couldn't use the damned thing until the weave it powered was triggered. But at the rate things were going? Should be any day now and what a shit show that was gonna be.

"You're such an asshole. What did you do to piss her off this time?"

"Same old. Fell in love with someone else."

"That'll do it." Rogan leaned forward to refill his glass. "Sending hordes of fanatics to wipe out the city seems a little excessive though, even for her."

Not if he knew all of it. Cal's eyes drifted back toward the paper and he reined them in. " 'Heaven hath no rage like love to hatred turned, nor hell a fury like a woman scorned…' " he muttered. And that was applicable on every goddamned level of this mess. "Now what's this about a merc outfit? They don't typically work pro-bono. Somebody must've called them in."

"Wasn't me. They showed up yesterday, taking out scouts and stragglers. Whoever they are, they're good. No clue if the Sons know they're bring poached. Lot of them gated out right before the storm hit. Mercs hunkered down in their craft."

"Sons hit a handful of the estates ringing the plateau. Wiped the damned things out. Suggest you claim your room at the flat, we're gonna be at capacity, even with Lot shacking up at Phyllis's. Far as that merc unit goes, I was thinking more along the lines of the Northern connection Flynn mentioned. I take it you didn't introduce yourself."

"I'm not getting involved any more than I already am. When'd they let him out?"

Cal snorted, not about to get into Rogan's commitment issues. "Half hour or so ago, and I plan on keeping it that way. Mock my record keeping all you want, but it's gonna save his ass. Merchant couldn't find a damned thing related to Dual-Talents prior to the Great Incursion. What wasn't destroyed was picked out, and some bigoted assholes wasted no time pushing their agenda."

"Still doesn't justify holding onto those Micky D's receipts by the sideboard."

Micky—Cal caught himself looking and threw a cigar at the Breaker. "Asshole."

Rogan laughed, lighting up. "And Kara?"

Cal squirmed, and Rogan's eyebrow raised. After the pass he'd given him on Elize, he wasn't gonna give him another. "Mangleshield's pumping the same stuff into her as the others."

"I wondered. She was way too keyed up after Assembly." Rogan frowned into his scotch. "It's risky. She's got a taste for the 'lust, and the kid sure as hell doesn't have a grip on his. I don't know if she can handle it. You know what all that distilled talent did to the rest of them."

"Don't think we have much of a choice. Titus altered his females to have multiples."

"Not the worst thing for a Breaker. Pregnancies are hard for them to come back from."

Cal poured them both another three fingers, the lip of the bottle chattering against the glass.

"Spill it." Rogan's voice was deceptively soft.

Cal's chest ached, Christ he didn't want to say it. Would make everything too goddamned real—"Ones at the Source don't. I'm praying her Binder genes mitigate the worst of it."

The Breaker stared at the amber liquid in his glass, knuckles going white. He threw it back. "Might. Might not. Without exchanging runes, I don't know how he's gonna pull her from the 'lust, and if she goes, she's taking him with her. Damn it, Cal, you should've clued me in—"

"Oh, cut the shit. After what happened with your brood, you honestly expect me to believe you'd come up here for Flynn? Wasn't gonna touch that with a ten-foot pole. Took enough arm twisting to get you to train Kara. Blame me all you want, but half of it's on you."

Rogan scowled, grabbing the bottle. "Regardless, kid's a time bomb, and people are gonna get hurt. I didn't make any fucking promises, and that's what's going to put the both of them in the ground, right next to Shane."

Cal winced, but it was the truth. "Baby makes it, he might be able to shake it off…"

"Bullshit. You know what that's gonna do to the kid."

"Yeah, I've got a pretty good idea," Cal snapped. "Times ten, and if I can—"

"He's not you."

"No, but he's got one hell of a vindictive streak. Wonder where that came from."

Rogan's eyebrow quirked. "That ain't just me, and if things go the way you want, he's going to have all that power to pull on. What would you have done if you were still Overlord when you lost Sarah and the kids?"

Cal exhaled, running a hand through his hair and taking another drag before answering. "Damage."

KARA LAY against Flynn's chest, her consciousness drifting with its rise and fall. He stared listlessly at the canopy, his fingers tracing circles on her bare shoulder.

"Stop thinking so loud. You're keeping me awake."

He snorted. "Sorry. I just—how can he be that much of a dick?"

"You tell me, he's your cousin," she murmured. Glory, she loved the way Flynn's voice rumbled. She snuggled closer, her hand running over his pecs.

"I'm not surprised he screwed me over, but Graham... Christ, he handed his brother over to the Source. If you hadn't kicked Pax's ass..."

Kara had a vague understanding of why that made it especially offensive, but didn't ask for clarification. Every time she had a question like that it just made him sad, which pissed her off. She was too comfortable to be irritated.

"I guess I thought he had more honor, though I'd do a hell of a lot worse if I was in his position." He rolled over and brushed a lock of hair from her cheek, his hand coming to rest on her abdomen.

She bit her lip. Now was the time to tell him. She put her hands over his.

"What do you feel?"

His brow crinkled. "Like through the bond?" She nodded. "What am I looking for?"

"I don't know how to explain it. Just—try."

He closed his eyes, and she felt him questing through their link. A broad grin split his face, and then his eyes sprang open, searching hers. "Wait, there's—Jesus fucking Christ, no wonder you've been so beat to shit. How long have you known?"

"That night you were gone. I felt so alone, and…" she laughed, tearing up, "I guess I'm not surprised. I mean, there were rumors. Either Breakers at the Source had litters, or Titus was cloning them…" Her heart ached, afraid to tell him the rest. The way everyone had been tip-toeing around her, all the stupid looks between them, they must think she was an idiot.

She wasn't. She knew this pregnancy was going to kill her.

Flynn broke down. A mishmash of terrified joy streamed through their bond. His thumb traced over her cheek, and he looked at her like she was his everything.

"I'm so afraid." Her face crumpled, and he kissed away her tears.

"I won't let anything happen to you. Any of you. It will be okay, I swear it." Those blue motes in his eyes churned, and she wanted to believe him—

A sob choked her. How could she? He couldn't change her stupid biology, what she'd been engineered for…to be a vessel for the next iteration. Not a wife or a mother, not even a person—

But she had now. They had right now.

"Please, Flynn, make it go away. You know how, and I've missed you so much…"

"Shhh…I'm right here, baby," he murmured against her lips, hand sliding to cup her hip and pull her close. "I've got you."

"Promise?" She tangled her fingers in his hair, the moisture on her cheeks mingling with his.

"Promise." His beard prickled across her jaw, down her throat. Tongue teasing, tracing her areola, lips nipping to pull its peak taut. He pressed her breasts together and inhaled along their seam. "You smell so good," he rumbled, drawing her other nipple into his mouth to suck. Kara cried out, a line of fire shooting through her to ignite her core. Her 'lust surged and he inhaled again, groaning. "Mmm. So fucking good…"

So did he. Like heat, and spice, and that musk that was just him.

His 'lust twined with hers, stoking their desire. It thrummed through their bond, their echo building. Her hand closed around him, sliding silken flesh over steel, thumb gliding along the underside of his cock to swirl the dew of his desire around its crown.

"Christ, I wanna do dirty shit to you, Kara… It's been so damned long…" Flynn groaned, his mouth finding hers again, hips pressing toward her. That subtle hum of talent between them teased the edge of her hearing. Lips on hers, breath heavy, his fingers played between her thighs, gathering the slickness within her folds to roll over her clit. "Tell me no," he murmured.

She pushed him onto his back, trailing kisses over his pecs, down the ripples of his abs, following the line of dark curls from his naval to his cock. "How about you tell me what you want instead," she murmured, kissing along its side.

"You sure?" His hazel green eyes searched hers.

"Yes, sir."

Lust surged through their bond, his hands burying in her hair as she licked him root to tip. "Put my dick in your mouth. That's right, just like—" He groaned as she took him deeper, sitting up to fondle her breast. He pinched her nipple, thrusting as she gasped at the delicious bite of pain. She fought not to gag, eyes watering, thighs sticky.

Flynn's chest rumbled, her wantonness and his carnality reverberating between them, building… His other hand fisted her hair, pressing her face down as his hips rocked up. Kara moaned around him. "Good girl. Take what I give you…fuck. What you give me…"

He groaned, pistoning between her lips, taut and tinged with salt. She rolled her tongue over him, across and down, again and again.

Her, feeling him, feeling her.

Losing herself in it, in him.

He panted, fingers tightening, hips insistent. His moan a sliding octave, and the surge of the sea at the back of her throat. "Yes, Christ, that's it, eat it…"

She obeyed, swallowing and sucking, lapping him clean.

Flynn pulled her up his body, licking the taste of himself from her mouth, and then she lay beneath him. His lips traveled her body, pausing to suckle and nip. Mouth hot against her skin. A rumble of pride at the slight swell of her belly, their bond suffusing with joy. He kissed beneath her navel reverently, then moved to nibble on her hip bones.

Kara's legs floated open for him, fingers tangling in his hair. His hands cupped her rear, spreading her cheeks wide. Head dipping, the pointed tip of his tongue pressing against her back hole. Lapping gentle and then with urgency. She cried out and he growled, pressing deeper, feasting on her ass. His thumb slid around to circle her clit—

She pulled him up by his hair, wanting him. All of him. To feel their echoes entwine. He slid between her thighs with a low groan, hooking her leg over his hip. Filling her and then taking himself away.

The hum of talent at their periphery built, his forehead dropping to hers, halos throwing a golden verdigris across the sheets, talent building around them, wanting, begging.

Kara gave.

She opened herself to it, letting the ethereal force stream through her like she had the night of the fight; washing away her fear and nourishing the life inside her. It spilled over, healing her in turn, and laying bare everything that she was for him to see.

That she wasn't afraid to show him anymore. She wanted him to see, to know, before the inevitable.

Clinging to him, her back arched, waves scintillating through them, heightening sensation, their echo a reverberation of cresting desire. The tips of her breasts tightened to aching points, he gasped through gritted teeth—

And still, the talent wanted.

Him.

A sob tore from Flynn's lips. "I can't..."

"It's okay."

She kissed him fiercely, her desire tipping passion, biting at his jaw, his throat. Teeth raking his collar bone. They sunk in, his fingers gripping painful. She shattered around him, his blood on her tongue as he buried himself deep, crying out with her.

The pulse of his throat was loud against her ear. Their breath. He rolled to the side, gathering her against his chest and kissing her temple. She snuggled against him, feeling the best she had in—

A muscle in her cheek twitched.

Her biology reasserting itself.

Along with the knowledge that it was only going to get worse.

A SERVANT in taupe livery escorted Nora into a dining room of golden oak and burnished bronze. A dozen or so couples were seated around a well-laid table, laughing and sipping on thin flutes of bubbling liquid.

Her steps faltered. This was the entirety of the Binder line's Original Houses? She swallowed her shock, the conversation dropping off as she entered. The men stood. Lord Ketsing pulled out a high-backed chair at his right hand, and bade her to sit. She inclined her head, heavy with the weight of her coiffure, and glided to her seat, very aware of the animosity the women hid behind the fans they'd snapped up. Did they know how ridiculous they looked? That they'd left the house in those hideous gowns argued against it. Apparently, the renaissance fad hadn't passed since the last time she'd been up here.

Nora thanked Louis as he pushed in her chair, and returned to his own, the rest of the men following suit. Directly across the table, Janice's gaze flicked over her and then to a woman seated further down the table. The corner of their eyes crinkled, as if sharing a private joke.

Piranhas indeed.

Nora laid her napkin on her lap, the trajectory of the night clear. Kara's comparison of Serra and Janice was apt, as was her not having anything to back it up. The woman's performance at the infirmary was a bare step above what a sub could do. If this was the state of their line up here, they were in trouble unless Pithy and that enclave in the commons could be brought into the fold. No wonder Cal wanted Serra and the rest of her cabal up here.

The cold reception didn't deter Nora from smiling brilliantly at Lord Ketsing. "Thank you for having me. I'm eager to become acquainted with you all." She met their eyes in turn, or attempted to. My, this was a hostel nest of bitches.

"Think nothing of it." He smiled back, jerking like he'd been kicked under the table. His eyes fluttered and he took a deep breath. "Janice was quite complimentary about your skill dealing with Mistress Cree. Do you have any idea what could have caused her condition?"

There wasn't a chance Janice had ever been complimentary about anything.

Nora took the proffered glass of whatever they'd been drinking, the servant blushing as she thanked him. "How kind of her. I believe Mistress Cree suffered a considerable shock that led to an epileptic episode, but without seeing her medical records, that's just supposition."

"An impossibility, I'm afraid," Lord Ketsing said. Servants came in with an amuse-bouche. Some kind of ceviche in vermillion oil. Nora had never seen anything quite like it, which she'd hazard was the point. "When the Sons attacked several years ago, the infirmary was destroyed. We lost our First in the blaze, and his wife soon after."

"How horrible. They've struck at the Source several times. Such a waste of life." The man beside her picked up a set of chopsticks and attempted to eat. Whatever it was looked slippery.

"Aye," Lord Hinswich said. His prodigious black beard made him easy to remember from chambers. "Though I'll not mourn for any of their Breakers."

"You'll be glad enough for them when they roll over the hordes of Sons between us and the border," another said.

"Yes, right up until they're at our walls," the woman at his side retorted, snapping her fan shut to take up her utensils. Their dark features were too similar not to be siblings. She poked at what was on her plate. "Do we really have to bring up such a beastly subject?"

"I don't see how burying our heads in the sand is going to do any good, Fiona. The way this city carries on as if it will all disappear if no one looks—"

"I agree with Fiona." Janice sniffed. "We're here to get to know Lady Jester, not to sling politics. Is geoduck not to your liking?"

"Actually, darling, politics is exactly—"

"After dinner, Louis!"

What a shrew. Nora smiled, taking hold of her chopsticks. They were silver, and heavier than she'd expected. "I haven't tried it. What did you say it was?"

"Geoduck." Lord Hinswich smirked. "Huge clam they dig up on the shores of the bay. Looks like a horse's—"

"Seth!" The woman beside him blushed and smacked him with her fan, giving Nora a pretty good idea of what he was about to say. The rest of the table alternately tittered or chuckled. "You'll have to forgive my husband. He spends so much time in the commons, he forgets what proper conversation should sound like."

"Oh? What do you do?" The clam was slippery, and the smooth metal of the chopsticks an issue. Nora pulled a whisper of talent to bind the stuff to them.

"Lately nothing but wall repairs. That damned barbican should be taken down, but there isn't enough time with the Sons on the move. Worst case, when it shears off, any of them stupid enough to be standing at the gate will get flattened."

Nora popped a bite into her mouth and immediately regretted it. Across the table Janice's face had gained a decided smirk. It had to be that spice Marcos warned her about. Nora drew more talent and bound the heat from her mouth into the heavy metal chopsticks. They warmed pleasantly in her grip.

She took her time chewing to spite the woman. "This is very good. I've never had anything like it. Are there many structural Binders in Glynfyls?"

"Ah…yes, most of us, in fact," Lord Ketsing said, watching her finish what was on her plate. The air shimmered above the chopsticks when she'd finished. "Janice is the most accomplished at healing…"

Nora blotted her lips with a napkin, feeling their eyes. She took a sip of her drink. It was similar to kir, but had more lemon overtones.

"Right then, you've had your fun, and she's bested you." Lord Hinswich chuckled. "I've not seen anyone able to bind heat like that since my gran. You'll want to save it for the next time you're out and about the city. One hell of a storm's blown in. Now let's get on with the rest."

Janice started to object, and voices raised around the table. Nora sat back, sipping at her drink. That had been a test? God, they used to play tricks like that on each other at the Creche. At least it hadn't been ground glass bound inside her stockings or a slice to the hamstring.

The reunification was going to be a very rude wake up call. The thought wasn't displeasing. Marcos's concern at her anger streamed through their bond, and she had to wonder at it herself. What did she care about these people, about what they thought?

Nora sighed. She cared because she had to. This was the next step, and she owed it to Deirdre's memory to make the reunification a reality. Her eyes fell on Lord Hinswich. He and several others had been silently watching her while Janice and the rest of them argued. Perhaps they weren't all malicious children.

He held out his palm and golden knot of talent appeared above it. Intrigued, Nora sent out a weave, pulling it closer to inspect. Janice's shrill voice faded into the background.

It'd been partially undone, but the knot was a clever construct, held together by different binds, some of which she was completely unfamiliar with. The weft and warp tangled back amongst themselves, a single strand spidering into several. She was completely engrossed, solving their paths individually, binding them to prevent it from re-entangling before they became one again, and at the end—

It faded from existence.

"Bravo," Lord Ketsing breathed, his voice heavy with relief.

Nora looked around the table, blinking away a strange hypnogogic state. Dishes were being cleared. Janice and several of the other ladies were gone. Lord Hinswich and the group that had regarded her silently remained. Nora ran a hand across her cheek, that satisfaction she always got after solving a particularly difficult puzzle lingering. A servant set a plate of orzo in front of her, and she grabbed up her fork, starving.

"Was that another test?" she asked.

"No." Lord Hinswich chuckled. "That was *the* test. Lord Brody's Gordian knot."

"He was First before me. None of us could solve it." Lord Ketsing grinned, toasting her. "Congratulations, you've just become First Binder."

Nora swallowed a mouthful with her shock—to have her ultimate goal so easily met... there was a catch somewhere. Innocence seemed the best course until she figured out what game they were playing now.

"I—I don't know what to say... I can't imagine my history at the Source is going to make me particularly popular." Her eyes went to Janice's empty chair. "I'd hoped to contribute in a more ancillary role."

"Perhaps not, but the logic bears it out." Lord Ketsing fretted. "Our talent may be lacking, but as Lord Brody's knot just demonstrated, our cognition is not."

Nora took another bite. He wasn't wrong there. The knot had been comprised of talent, but solving it required intellect in equal parts. They'd had similar Daedalian puzzles at the Source, but that had been far more challenging than any she'd come across there.

"There's nothing to say but yes." Hinswich's voice was firm. "Despite the dissenting opinions of some, this rift in our line has only served to make a mockery of us. If we're to regain our standing, allowances for those of the Southern persuasion must be made."

"Allowances?"

Lord Ketsing wrung his hands. "I'm afraid there are those who feel Sourcies—ah, Talents originating from the Source—shouldn't be considered Original Houses. My lady chief among them." Nora's eyebrow rose, and the man squirmed beneath her gaze.

"Our codes have strict language regarding genetic purity. Only those born of 'natural means' are fit to ascend." The bearded lord spat in contempt. "In the Assembly's infinite wisdom, they left that definition up for debate. You could argue anything short of birthing in a cave—"

"And how will my ascension affect those from the Source already in the city?"

A ripple of unease swept across the table. "Ah...they're not particularly inclined—"

Hinswich snorted at Ketsing. "No, they told me to bugger off."

Aha. The catch. "You're hoping by elevating me, they'll change their minds."

"Aye. Aside from your obvious talent, that's the long and short of it," Hinswich said, running a hand over his beard. "We'd hoped Scot's bairn would suit, but with this splitting fiasco, and finding out she's a damned duality…your blood's a hell of a lot purer. A Sourcie's one thing, but none of us can stomach a mongrel in that seat. As far as propriety's concerned, Louis would act as advisor."

Nora smiled, the man's casual prejudice rankling. She took another bite, making them wait. The division of the line was an issue she hadn't foreseen, and once Serra got up here…

"I'd be honored to accept the position of First."

"Wonderful!" Louis crowed. "You'll need to create your knot for whomever comes after you, though I can't imagine you'll have any challengers."

Now wasn't the time to tell them how wrong they were.

CHAPTER TEN

"…The unaffected survivors of the Surge embarked on a what is now known as the Great Migration, abandoning the Northern hemisphere for the Deep South. The cataclysm decimated civilization, and for decades, only those affected were able to withstand its lingering toxicity. The advent of plaz changed that, allowing the Corporation to lay claim the Southern portion of the continent. However, it soon became clear that the cure was worse than the disease, creating a wasteland inimical to lower life forms, and save for the Source itself, the rest of the territory has remained devoid of any significant population…"

– Lord Talos, Preceptor of History,
Academy of Glynfyls

FLYNN WAS UP BEFORE DAYBREAK. Roles reversed, Kara slept soundly, curled into a little ball in the center of the bed. He smiled. She was worse than the cat when it came to taking up space. Hiss was on the other side of her, flopped out like he owned the place. The furry bastard cracked an eye, daring Flynn to do something about it.

It was a battle he wasn't gonna win. Flynn stretch his arms over his head, smile still on his face, questing through his bond to Kara, and to the little bundles of energy nestling in her abdomen. His chest got tight, emotion rising in his throat.

She was having his kids.

Shit, he'd never thought...his vision misted and his jaw set. He needed to keep them safe. Assembly hadn't pulled his seat, and he was gonna do something with it while he could.

When the hell had that changed? He bit the scar on his lip. Kara was right. Feeling the babies made everything more real. Shit, *he* needed to be real. He looked at the line scabbing across his palm. That's what had gotten him those pledges, not playing at lord. It was time for the gloves to come off.

He was gonna be a dad.

His grin stretched to his ears, and he bit back a laugh, afraid he'd wake her. All that talent last night had been like an infusion, taking care of the awful debilitation dragging at her, but she was still too damned frail. Christ. All that talent. Last night, after the fight...he rolled onto his side, spooning around her.

He'd felt it, what it wanted, and there was no fucking way...but she'd let it lay her open, let him see... God, she was so beautiful, inside and out. That awful stain of self-doubt and the hurt she carried just made him love her more, and how she saw him...

She was delusional.

His stomach dropped, thinking about the note on that book of matches. If she knew the half of it, she'd run screaming, and that prick Rogan would be right there. Not a fucking chance that was gonna happen. Flynn held her close, breathing her in until she grumbled, pushing away in her sleep.

He worked his way out of bed and threw on some clothes. Riffling his hair as he left the bower, he ghosted through the sleeping estate. His mom had loved this time of day, before all the hustle began.

He found himself in the Green Dining Suite at the patio doors, looking out over the gardens like he used to. Waiting for her in his jammies, toes ice against the floor. She'd suddenly appear between the hedges. Cheeks pinked from the cold, lifting him up and laughing, those blue motes in her eyes churning.

Playing at wild things. She'd promised to take him someday.

Lot had ended that.

Flynn put his back to the garden, needing a cup of coffee. A noise from the ballroom drew him in that direction.

Shelby was there, turning forms in her nightgown, dark hair swishing a step behind her. He watched his cousin for a moment before she noticed him. She slowly came back to earth, her feet settling flat, arms and shoulders drooping.

He went to her, putting a hand on her waist, and raising the other for hers. "I couldn't sleep either."

Her smile was sad. She gave him one of her earbuds and took his hand.

It was a foxtrot and she was merciless. After the third time through, he was drenched.

Shelby laughed at him. "Better. You're getting the hang of it again, though your feet are sloppy. Paul's are so sharp—" She blushed.

"That the red-headed guy at Kara's Introduction?"

Shelby nodded, taking pity on him and changing the track she'd been listening to over to a Viennese waltz. "We've been studying Latin dance." Her cheeks colored again.

Flynn laughed. He'd tried to help her out with those, but their attempts had always ended awkwardly. Now if Kara wanted to learn…

Shelby pinched him, rolling her eyes. "I know what you're thinking about. Knock it off."

He laughed. She wasn't wrong. The track ended, and they went into the dining room. A servant was setting up breakfast on the sideboard. Both of them grabbed a plate.

"You really love her, don't you?"

Flynn chewed his lip. "Is it weird?"

"Yes and no. Have you told her yet?"

They sat, and he fiddled with his fork. "Yeah."

"I'm glad." Shelby squeezed his arm. "You've always needed someone, there just wasn't anyone up here that was right. I like Kara. She's nice. You two fit, like Graham and Celine."

"They serious?"

"Oh yes, I'm sure he'll ask for her bond soon."

Flynn's eyebrows rose. Miriam must be having kittens. No way that Fetch fit in with her Prydee sense of propriety. "And Paul?"

Shelby played with a bit of egg. "He's heir, and his House…it's a tangle."

"Yeah, I'll bet," he said around his toast. "Peterli Morris is the most bigoted asshole up here."

"Paul's mother is really nice."

Flynn snorted, like that was gonna make a difference. The prejudice against Dual-Talents was ridiculous. His temper jumped. That someone would deny her bond because of it—Shit, if anyone did that to his kids—

"How are you doing? I know how hard it is when you first find out."

He shrugged, not wanting to talk about it. "It's a complication I don't need." He got up and grabbed another plate of eggs. Shelby kept poking at hers, and he felt like a dick. Flynn set his plate down and called talent, crackling it around his fingers. "It's pretty cool though."

She gave a very un-Shelby like smirk. "It suits you. You know, there's more of us than you think…this lawsuit, it's important. It could change things, Flynn."

Great, just what he needed, to be the poster-boy for twists everywhere. Fuck, he really didn't want to talk about this. "Let's wait and see if I can get out of this without being nullified before you start talking revolution."

She raised her orange juice. *"Vive la résistance!"*

"You've been reading *Les Mis* again, haven't you?"

"Mmm. Jean Valjean reminds me of someone…"

"Not even close." He snorted, fiddling with a piece of bacon. None of the shit he'd done had been even remotely altruistic. "I'm sorry. About how I was, before."

"I get it. Everything that goes along with being heir…" She shrugged, looking out the door to the portico, the sun just beginning to stain the drifted snow gold. They must've gotten three feet last night. "You know, Leo thought it would be him. That maybe Cal had mixed up his metrics with Graham's. Then our talent came in… I'd hoped they were wrong, too." She gave him a sad smile.

His bite turned to ash. Christ, she knew. "Who told you?"

"I heard you were released and came down. The office door was open." Her eyes welled up.

Shit. "Shelby—"

"Don't. I know it's true. He's always been spiteful to you. We had Jon and Miriam. Each other. Deirdre and Lot—you were so lonely. Angry. Especially when Cal took you away. Leo never saw any of that, just that you had what he wanted, and everything with Julia, if he hadn't been so mean…" Her face crumpled, and Flynn gathered her up in a hug.

"Shh, it's done."

She pushed back, her expression fierce. "It's not. Graham and I can't feel him like a true bond, but there's a sense—since the Introduction, something's wrong. Like he's really sick. I don't understand why he hasn't come back or gone to the sisters…"

Flynn finished what was on his plate. Even if Leo was working with Titus, she had a point. House Prydee was rabid about their own. Without more proof, they could claim it was a House Matter, and as long as he didn't leave their estates, no one would be able to touch him.

"I dunno know, but he'll turn up." Flynn forced a smile. "Took him almost a month to poke his nose out after Cal caught him skimming from the books."

Shelby dashed her hand across her cheek. "You up for a jive or a quickstep?"

He groaned at her plaintiveness and stood; either one was gonna kill him.

The sun was up when Kara appeared in the doorway with a cup of tea and a funny smile on her face.

Shelby pinched him as his attention wavered. "Flick your feet!"

Flynn scowled. Flick his feet—he could hardly lift his feet—he soldiered through it, collapsing to sit on the floor when the music ended. He tossed the earbud back to Shelby.

"Same time tomorrow?"

"Not a fucking chance. I'd rather let Rogan beat the shit out of me."

She laughed, grabbing them both a bottle of water and tossing him one.

"That looked intense," Kara said, coming over. "I'll stick to figuring out the foxtrot. I've never seen you move so fast."

"You've never seen him with a lobster."

Flynn shot Shelby a dirty look and chugged his water. Kara lowered herself beside him, nose crinkling as he put his arm around her. "You need a shower, Assembly's in a half hour."

Everything in his stomach soured. Christ, he didn't want to do this. "You coming?"

Her face lit up. "You want me to?"

"Yeah. I don't want you out of my sight."

"I have that stupid luncheon Bea's throwing for me." She scowled, and then her face brightened again. Goddamn he loved her. "You want to ditch the old guys to join me?"

Assembly was suddenly looking pretty good. "Nope." He laughed, and she smacked him on the arm.

"Audrey says you're supposed to make an appearance at the end. You better rescue me."

Christ, on a good day the last place he wanted to be was in a room with all the ladies of Glynfyls, and after splitting—

Kara narrowed her eyes at him. The shadowing beneath them wasn't as livid as yesterday, but she still looked wan.

"Yeah, I'll be there." Damn it. "How d'you feel this morning?"

"Well enough to be twitchy. I'll probably run for a while after I eat something."

That had to be a good sign. He kissed her forehead. "Come on, I need another cup of coffee." He led her into the dining room and grabbed a cup, watching what went on her plate. Didn't seem like enough, but he wasn't gonna badger her. Some weird shake was waiting at her seat.

"Doctor's orders." She sighed, forgoing the straw and downing half of it with a grimace.

Good. She needed to put on weight. Flynn sighed at the clock. Christ, this was gonna suck.

Kara smiled at him askance, buttering a piece of toast. "You're cute when you pout."

"I don't pout."

When Cal came in she was still giggling. The look on his face cut it short. He grabbed a coffee and a plate of bacon before joining them.

Flynn's stomach cramped. "They make a ruling?"

"No. Merchant's presenting this afternoon. Still can't wrap my head around the level of shenanigans that went on after the last Incursion. How they got half the shit passed that's on the books—"

"Weren't you there?" Kara asked.

His eyes flicked to her and she wilted. Christ, he was prickly lately.

"I'm bringing hives up. Availed myself of Dorian yesterday. He found two bots transmitting. One in here, and one in the foyer. Bees will let us know if we're compromised again, but assume everything Leo knows, the Source does, too."

Shit. "So does Shelby. She came down to see me, and the office door was open. She thinks he's sick and says he hasn't gone to the sisters."

Cal swore. "No. Miriam wouldn't be in the state she's in if that were the case. Makes no damned sense—"

"It does if he's fighting the coercion," Kara said. "If Nora's right and that's Otto's extra…" She glanced between them. "When I was applying for that program, they told us we were going to be rehabilitating people, but some of the directives… I didn't—I tried to be, I don't know, gentle isn't the right word, but the coercion didn't stick and they fought it." Her face greyed and she toyed with the straw in her shake.

"Their symptoms were analogous with detox. Sweating, shaking. Violent stomach cramps and headaches. The same happens if the subjects aren't refreshed periodically. They can get out from under it, but it's a debilitating process and takes weeks. If he's going through that, I'm not surprised he doesn't want anyone around."

Flynn ran a hand over his mouth. He knew exactly how that felt and he wouldn't even wish it on his shithead cousin. DTs had left him a fucking mess in prison.

Cal's lips pursed. He'd finished his bacon and was tapping a cigarette on the table "You're gonna be late for Quorum—"

"Quorum?"

"Yeah. They passed a measure yesterday. Quorum deals with anything war related in the morning, and the rest of those jackasses can suss out weasel-gate in the afternoon."

Weasel-gate? Nope. He didn't want to know. Dealing with the Firsts was a hell of a lot better than the lot of them.

Cal snorted. "Don't look too relieved, it's shaping up to be a banner day. Papers have you bonded to Julia, and the Sons hit Anafeild yesterday. Wiped the entire estate out, save for a single servant to tell the tale. Rogan tells me there's a merc unit picking them off when they're not looking. You wouldn't know anything about that would you?"

Flynn shrugged. He did, but not enough to open his mouth.

Cal glared at him. "And after you deal with that shit, I need you back here. What we talked about? It's happening today."

Jesus fucking Christ, when it rained—Flynn checked the time again, Cal was right, and he still needed to shower. He stood, a banner fucking day was right.

FITZ THREW his legs over the side of the bed, head pounding worse than usual. He scratched at his stubble and grabbed a half-finished bottle of whiskey from the floor, downing a goodly portion. Retox were preferable t'detox. A hand slid down the back of his shirt to his bare hip.

"Gotta piss," he muttered, shrugging it off. He stumbled into the bathroom, taking another pull from the bottle, then stretched his jaw. Felt like he'd gotten into it with somebody. Sidling up to the commode, he kicked a pair of lacy knickers out of the way. Must not've been able t'find his wallet. His snoring usually drove them out quicker than nits in the sheets.

Sunlight streamed through the sides of the shade. Looked like it were gonna be a beautiful fuckin' day. He grabbed the bottle again. If dreaming of chocolate cake were any indication, it could bugger itself. Staggering back out, he pulled a slice of day old pizza from the box and took a bite. Fitz squinted through the gloom, the whore in his bed rolling over. Didn't particularly care who he'd brought back last night, but it were time for her t'leave.

"How much I owe ye?"

"Yer in a shite mood this morning."

Christ, it were Adelaide.

She sat up, her dirty blonde hair sleep-tousled around her face. There weren't no arguing, she were a right fine looking whore and knew it. She laughed, lounging back against the yellowed wall. "Ye don't remember a bit of last night, do ye?"

"Eh...nah." Save his luck had turned t'shite ever since he'd given that old hillie back his pay. Adelaide being here were just more of the same.

"S'all right. I remember every word." She stood, raising up on her tiptoes to kiss him. He shut down his sight, the roses and golds flicking through her aura making him sick.

Weren't just the way they churned. Shite, what had he told her t'make her so head over fuckin' heels? He leaned against the table, riding its sway until it hit the wall. She hummed, gathering up her clothes and shrugging into them.

"Ye get me kirtle?" She put her back to him, holding up her hair. His fingers went to the ties without thinking. "Nice and tight. Starting at the Pony today. Said they'd give me somewhat, but want t'look me best." She spun around with a smile, pressing against him. "Bet ye'd fancy a bit of breakfast."

"Look, I dunno what I said, but—"

She put a finger to his lips. "Don't spoil it. I've loved ye me whole life, Fitzpatrick McCreedy, and if the only way I can have ye is by playing that I don't, then that's what I'll do."

Shite. He barely made it to the bathroom.

When he came out again, shaved and showered, the room were tidied and a plate of eggs waiting where the pizza boxes had been. He cracked the fifth at its side. What the fuck were he gonna do? He pulled the coin from his pocket and tossed it on the table. It landed on its edge.

"You're a right shite," he said to it, shoveling down a forkful of eggs and glowering at the extra helping of kippers. "Fine. Ye want me t'know I fucked up? I fucked up. Won't be the last time."

Sure as hell weren't the first, neither.

His eyes went to the empty stretch of board in front of the window. Christ, what day were it? He flipped open the paper and snorted. Like being a twist weren't bad enough. Now they was trying t'smear Scot with a paternity scandal. Least Fitz weren't the only one with shite for luck.

Tuesday. Marl needed that damned map. Fitz finished his breakfast and snatched his coin, for all the fuckin' good it'd do him.

He sighed, snapping up the blind. Under a minute flat, the widow across the way were flashing him her nasty bits again. He waved and she blew him a kiss. Dirty old hag. Weren't a chance he'd dip into that.

He pegged paper to his board and set his margins, inks aligned on the sill. Rickety chair creaking, he sat back and stared out the window.

Fuck it.

He pulled talent, the geography of the bay flowing into his mind, through his fingers, and onto the page. Storm that'd blown through had changed what lay beneath the waves, bits of earth swallowed, others spat up from the depths. He compared it to what lay in the book of memories he held in his mind, morphing it to match.

Map bloomed beneath his fingers, marked off proper by fathom. The curve of a shoal, outline of a wreck. His worries disappeared beneath the swirling lines of lead and ink. Reds and blues, last a compass rose of silver and grey. His mark, with the shimmering rhiolan of House McCreedy.

Fitz ran a finger over the crest and sat back, his guts eating themselves. Sun had risen to the middle of the sky, the morning lost. He winced, dusting the page with pounce, then tapping it clean.

It were a thing of beauty. Hundred times better than the shite they sold in the city.

And he couldn't give the fuckin' things away. His hand clenched on the page and he tore it up. Goddamned every last one of them Prydees. He ran a hand up the back of his neck, head hanging.

All his days stretching out before him. One just like the other, and not a fuckin' thing t'show for it.

... "Comes a point when shoving all of who ye are's gonna eat at ye somewhat fierce... feels like yer dying a little piece at a time, and all them shites just make it worse..."

Fitz knuckled at an eye, missing his da worse than a limb. He took out his coin, fingers tracing its edges. Cajetan had promised revenge, not any kind of life while he were waiting for it. Were better that way. Less for them shites t'take. Christ, his gran... He dashed a hand over his eyes again, shoving the coin in a pocket.

Blight 'em all. Marl needed somewhat.

A couple minutes later he had a rough copy of what he'd made. Should've done it in fuckin' crayon. He rolled it up and shifted to the 'Pipe.

Lunch crowd were just starting to swell the place. He grabbed his stool, nodding at Pamela coming over with a tankard.

"Ye still feeling some kind o' way? Ain't got no fish pie t'cheer ye, but the mutton ain't bad." She brushed her dark braid back over her shoulder and winked.

"Mutton'll be fine," he muttered into his ale. Her face clouded and she left him.

A hand clapped on his shoulder, and he jerked from it, hand going for his pigsticker. Marl stepped back, his wrinkled brow raised.

"Shite, sorry. Bit on edge." Fitz passed him the map.

The old man took it and the seat beside him. "Ye don't say. I'll have me one of them too," he said to Pamela as she set a plate on the bar. They shared a look, and she went back to grab him one. "This mood of yers have anything t'do with Markham looking for ye again?"

Fitz shrugged, his mouth full. Didn't wanna talk about it, and Markham could bugger off.

"Denis used t'get in right black tempers. Always 'cause of them hillies. Suppose it's t'be expected with yer majority looming like a 'berg in the bay." He sighed, smoothing the map out on the bar. "This here's right fine work, Fitzy. What do I owe ye?"

"Not a fuckin' thing. I'll take another," he said as Pamela came back with Marl's pie.

Fitz ignored the old man's eyes, lifting his tankard. Still feeling that hole inside him and all the mutton in the world weren't gonna fill it.

SCOT WAS TEN MINUTES LATE. Marcos frowned at the gilt-framed clock above the Assembly's still listing doors. Save for the speaker at his podium and the Firsts, the room only had a smattering of others, all similarly annoyed. No ladies were present, every last one of them wrapped up in this luncheon of Kara's.

Which apparently meant that Stonefist got to sit in the box in front of Marcos as proxy for the Breaker line. Marcos didn't envy him that, or the dandy of a shiner he was nursing. Their bout had solidified that the Breakers up here were not the same echelon as those at the Source. That first punch had sent the Northern general reeling. To his credit, he'd gotten right back up and come at him. Marcos had been more judicious with his blows after, but the end result was the same.

His rung was back where it should be, and there was little question it would remain there, despite the outcry. Few were pleased to have a Sourcie rank above them, but the council had spoken its will.

Might made right.

Marcos supposed he should feel grateful, but all he had were questions, and that worn tome Mangleshield had given him just gave him more.

The Way.

Bits and pieces were familiar, like that inscription in the back of his drawer, axioms elder troops parroted to grunts. The meanings lost, spirit broken, but none-the-less passed down.

From Breakers harvested from the North.

His thumb worried against his forefinger at the possibility of having a House instead of a designation.

Footsteps skipped down the steps two at a time, and what little conversation there was dropped off. Marcos's lips pruned. Laughlin Scot descended into chambers with a shit-eating grin on his face, sixteen minutes late. What an arrogant son of a bitch. He got to his box and flopped into a chair like he'd just finished a particularly satisfying meal.

The gnarled little man at a podium called the session to order.

"Well, first order of business, I'm sure you've noticed Lord Scot is back with us while his legalities are sorted—"

"Yes, and you'd think he'd be more contrite, not to mention punctual, given his…status." Lord Ketsing sniffed. What a fop. Not that he was wrong, but the tone of his voice set Marcos's teeth on edge.

"You mean now that I'm a split?" Scot snorted. "I don't see the issue. Aside from being able to pull another talent, how does that change who I was last week when you were begging to pledge? Ironic that anyone elected to Overlord has access to all six…" The gaunt man sputtered, and that grin of Scot's widened. "Lemme know when you figure it out with that Binder's logic of yours."

Stonefist chuckled under his breath, and Marcos bit back a snort. Boy had a set on him, that was for sure. He had to admit, it was entertaining when he wasn't bearing the brunt of it.

The dotty old man at the lectern was oblivious. "Yes, truly a regrettable situation all around…" His tone didn't state his feelings on the subject one way or another. From their expressions, the rest of the room was less sanguine. "Do you have anything to say before we begin?"

Scot tipped back in his chair. "Nope. I got the rundown. I'm here solely on your sufferance."

"Well now, I don't know that—"

"Binders want me out, Markham's afraid to piss off the commons, Phyllis can't buck the council, Carl's waiting for the courts, and Crandall wants me to hang around to take a bullet. That about cover it?"

The speaker blinked several times. "Ah…yes. I'd say that's the gist of it."

"For being so well informed, you're awfully nonchalant."

Scot shrugged. "Shit happens, Carl. What is the status of the commons?"

"Strained," Markham said, twisting his handkerchief. "I've no doubt that cell Crandall's been muttering about is responsible for whipping them up."

"Any progress on that?"

"No," the Intelligencer frowned, "but we continue to discover a veritable warren of tunnels running beneath the city, the majority of which are being utilized for illicit means." He shot a glance at Markham, who was very busy trying to look innocent and failing abysmally. Across the floor, Klein's expression hardened. No love lost there.

"As far as the commons are concerned, the lesser heads and union leaders I've spoken to have been doing their utmost to quell tensions, but they persist." Markham mopped his chins. "The outcome of the current legal proceedings is highly anticipated. I'm afraid riots are inevitable if the ruling doesn't fall in Lord Scot's favor."

"And if it does, the outcry on the hill may be worse." Crandall smoothed two fingers over his goatee. "I wouldn't rule out a House War."

Scot snorted. "Then I propose we vote to suspend those until these other two pan out."

"I'll second it. All you damned civs have got your heads up your asses between this and weasels." Stonefist and the other Firsts glared at Markham, and he shrugged.

Scot's chair legs dropped to the floor. "What's this about weasels?"

"The sisters are convinced the city's infested with them after an unfortunate incident with Kristine's birds," Markham said. "They've created quite a frenzy amongst Glynfyls's ladies. The Assembly's created a weasel commission in response—"

"Are you f—"

"Not in the slightest."

The speaker shuffled his papers, peering at them from above the rims of his bifocals. "Ah, officially it's the Commission for the Advancement of Rodent Control Enforcement."

"FARCE? Sounds about right." Laughlin ran a hand over his beard, smirking.

"No, it would be CARCE, wouldn't it? Yes, I have it as that right here…"

"Regardless of the appropriate acronym or its suitability, I've been working with the other lines to get materials to plug the tunnels they're supposedly plaguing," Carl broke in. "The Guild wants to maintain the composition of the surrounding stone. In theory, that should allow the shield wall to operate below grade, if we can find all the damned holes."

Crandall frowned. "All talent has a limit, and I'll be blunt, we're close to ours. The porous nature of the plateau makes it impossible to find every ferret hole down there."

"You mean weasel," Scot snickered.

"There's been no sign of anything save rats and smugglers. We've been concentrating on the southeastern portion of the city, trying to improve that time frame, but I'm anticipating it'll take us the better part of a week to shore up the tunnels we know about," Carl said. "I'll keep you all updated as things progress."

"Very good." The speaker dottily scanned his papers. "Any update on our defenses?"

"Hexes have been assigned and are manning the walls," Stonefist said. "The way the Engineering Guild talks, if we had more capable Binders, the shield would be operational already." Ketsing stiffened and so did Marcos. Nora was doing her damndest, but there were only so many hours in a day... "We're moving forward under the assumption it won't be. Perhaps I'll be pleasantly surprised."

The general's tone said otherwise, and Ketsing sniffed again. Stonefist ignored him. "Both I and Crandall have people in the field monitoring the Sons. They've razed a total of seven estates, leaving no survivors, and I'll be damned if I know how they're getting to them. If I didn't know any better, I'd think they were using the gates or shifting."

"Unlikely. They eschew the use of talent, and Anafield wasn't equipped with a gate, nor was Klafford," Crandall said. "We think they're utilizing some kind of technology. They've plenty of regulated weapons scattered amongst them, including plaz-cannons."

There was a moment of shocked silence, and rightfully so. Never mind the damage, the resulting radiation poisoning could take out the city, and that was a bad way to go. Tombago had been a nightmare, and karma wasn't a concept Marcos was eager to become familiar with.

"They won't be able to use them at this latitude without warming jackets, and you'll know it if they do," he said. "The keening they give off sounds like a craft initiating. Should allow plenty of time to site them and take them out with talent. That wind out there will push the fallout away from the city, mitigating radiation exposure—"

"I'm sorry, you are?" the speaker asked.

"Stonefist's right hand." Scot said.

Marcos glared at him, and the man grinned. "Up until a week ago, I was Br2, Commandant of the Source's military division. Familiarly, I go by Marcos."

"I'm assuming you've vetted him?" Crandall asked.

Stonefist looked at him like he was an idiot. "Regardless of how the Sons are moving, we should be prepared for their imminent arrival, and God help us if it's smack dab in the center of the city. Without that shield operational, we're sitting ducks, and even then, the Flats are on their own."

"Not necessarily. A mercenary outfit has been very busy picking off Sons," Crandall mused, gaze riveted on Marcos. "Any insight into that?"

"Potentially, what's their blazon?"

"They're not advertising one."

"The better question is who hired them," Scot said.

Crandall's attention slid to him. "Is it?"

Scot rolled his eyes. "Yeah. If they're mercs, doesn't matter who they are, what matters is who's paying them. I'll tell you flat out, it's not House Scot."

Marcos kept his mouth shut. Scot was right, to a point. There was only one outfit that's lack of blazon was their blazon, and this was just the sort of sideways op Kendall would get involved with. But if Scot hadn't hired them, who the hell had? The more likely scenario was that Titus had contracted an outfit to lead the vanguard, and they were running dark. If that were the case, the city had less time than he'd thought.

Marcos worried his thumb against his forefinger. He needed to stop back at the Engineering Guild and see what progress Jesse had made.

Without that shield, birds weren't the only thing in this city that were going to get slaughtered.

KARA SAT in an ethereal Art Deco chair, trying to act like she knew what a onesie was and found them fascinating. The weasel attack someone was talking about behind her was of far more interest. For the umpteenth time in the last hour, she consciously relaxed the death-grip on her teacup. The china was so thin she held her breath as she sipped. It was beautiful, but a misplaced sneeze would spell disaster.

That was true of the rest of the room as well. The walls were done in pastel silk moire, light diffusing through curtains more mist than cloth. The iridescent tables set around the mosaic floor of abalone and ivory were like flattened soap bubbles, the lacy swags draped over them pink gossamer. Impossibly tiered trays of dainty delights scattered artfully upon each…the kitchen had to have used a shrink-ray to get them so perfect.

Kara snorted. A shrink-ray. She'd been watching too many of Cal's dumb movies…though a number of the vapid women milling about could've starred in one of those. Dressed in rich silks and velvets, the keyhole bodices and plackets of lace Luann had tried to foist off on her were suspiciously absent. Instead, bared shoulders and swaths of bosoms flashed skin throughout the room. The skirts were still those big ballooned affairs, creating a strange hodgepodge of incongruous style. Well, more like lack there of. Kara wasn't particularly impressed with any of them.

Glynfyls's ladies didn't seem impressed with her, either. She swallowed a smirk. At least they had something in common. Her "gown" was a deep burgundy, high-necked and cap sleeved, its wide, black-striped trouser legs giving the impression of skirts. She didn't want to completely rock the boat, but by the eyes tracking above those stupid fans, she was making waves.

A scant few had approached their little group, for all this was supposed to be her introduction into society. Would this have been her fate if she'd accepted any of those other invitations? The idea of them inviting her solely to be seated in a corner somewhere for people to gawk at—

Whatever. She tucked a tendril of hair behind her ear, not caring. All of this was ridiculous, and from the half-smile on Nora's face, she felt the same, though somehow, her mother fit right in with her flowing emerald goddess-wear. Because of course she did.

Bea was sitting to her right, hugely pregnant. She literally glowed, keeping a hand on her swollen belly and providing a constant stream of consciousness. "…the midwives think it'll be any day now. I'm so sorry I missed the Introduction, but until they figured out my nutritionals, I was a mess." She paused to slurp at one of those milkshakes. From her face, she wasn't a fan either. "We figure the baby will keep developing at the same speed once he's born, then progress regularly once he hits three. Hopefully, that means he won't be in diapers for long!" Her laugh was brittle. Kara smiled in the same vein, trying not to see Phyllis making her way over.

"I think that's everyone, Bea. We can start whenever you're ready," the Breaker said.

"Oh, let's, I'm starving!"

Kara helped her to stand. Glory, she was huge, and that was just one. She brushed a hand over her own midsection, straightening her skirts. She was going to be a house—A smile flitted over her lips, thinking about how happy Flynn was.

It didn't last.

"I'm glad you were able to join us last minute, Lady Jester," Phyllis said, looping her arm through Nora's. "I've heard so many good things from Janice."

Her mother's serene expression didn't waver at the bold-faced lie, and she returned one of her own. "How kind of her. We had a lovely dinner last night, she's such a decorous hostess."

Their smiles were like crossed swords, and Kara bit her tongue to stop from laughing. Ugh! The longer she was up here, the more it was like the Source. All the petty, backstabbing—

A bell rang, and women started finding seats. She trailed after Phyllis and Nora, wondering how Miriam was. She was conspicuously missing, though she'd seen Shelby earlier... They found a table, and Kara absently pulled out a chair, still searching the room.

Then stifled a groan when she realized all of the Ladies were seated at it.

Bea clinked a spoon against a crystal goblet and motioned for Kara to come stand beside her. The room fell silent. Too many eyes abruptly focused on her. Her heart leapt to her throat and a trickle of sweat slid between her shoulder blades. She plastered a smile on her face, hoping she didn't look as nervous as she felt.

The elfin woman put an arm around her. "I'm so glad all of you could join me today in welcoming my friend, Lady Kara Scot, to Glynfyls. Without her..." Bea teared up and wafted a hand at her eyes with a little laugh. "Well, you all know. I hope that you'll be as gracious to her as she was to me."

She looked at Kara like she was supposed to say something.

Crap.

"I—Thank you. I hope to get to know each and every one of you ladies."

Someone tittered behind her. "Laughlin has a considerable head start in that regard. Perhaps you can split the difference."

Several women laughed. Kara turned to them, tamping down her bloodlust. A brunette several years older smirked back at her. Her posture screamed Breaker. The women around her showed varying degrees of amused embarrassment.

"Shh! Quiet Natalia!" one of them chided.

Natalia. She was the one that'd propositioned Flynn at Assembly.

Kara's 'lust ticked up, and her smile went feral. "Natalia? How nice to put a face to the name. After reading your letters to my husband, I already feel as if we're intimately acquainted."

The woman's cheeks flushed, and there was a shocked outcry. Kara wasn't sure if that was from the disclosure of her relationship with Flynn or Natalia's impropriety. Probably the former, considering the rest of the missives he'd been receiving. Ugh, they were so stupid up here. Ignoring their manufactured horror, Kara tapped a finger against her lips, her eyes sweeping the room. "In fact, I can't wait to meet all of Glynfyls's burgeoning authors of erotica. Some of you are so gifted at vivid prose…whereas others are decidedly lacking. Some advice? Your time would be better spent critiquing each other's work than propositioning married men."

Natalia's eyes narrowed.

Reggie laughed at a table in the back, and there were nervous titters. Kara shot one more glance at Natalia before taking her seat. Ugh, she needed to calm down. That bitch wasn't worth it.

"Don't let her get to you," Bea said. "She rubs everyone the wrong way. I've got to play hostess, if you'll excuse me?" She flitted away before Kara could open her mouth.

Abandoning her with the Ladies.

Across the table, Bernice looked like she was having palpitations. Evie and Alice both shared a smug smile. Phyllis was grimmer. She turned to Nora.

"Lady Jester, allow me to introduce the Ladies Crandall, Klein, and Markham. Their husbands are the heads of the Finders, Fixers, and Fetches, respectively. I represent the Breaker faction." She pursed her lips at the last, and began to pour tea. "I hear you've been elected to do the same for the Binders."

"I have, though I don't believe it's official yet. Lord Ketsing will be advising me. Things are quite a bit different up here. I'm eager to become familiar with your culture."

Kara filled her plate, struggling to keep her face bland as they sized each other up. This was going to be more politically charged than she'd expected. Couldn't anything be simple? Her stomach churned. "Miriam's still not feeling well?"

Bernice sighed. "The past few weeks have been too much for the dear. You know she was the one that found Kristine's birds—" Her lips pinched down, and the rest of them made consolatory noises. She went on to discuss the gruesome particulars at length. "Fainted dead away. Giles was afraid she'd been attacked by the beasts."

"It's a crime that son of hers doesn't come home," Alice said, running a finger around the rim of her cup. "I'm sure that would go a long way towards setting things right." Her absinthe eyes met Kara's and she shivered.

Evie cleared her throat, breaking the spell. "I'm just going to lay it out, since we've already talked it to death between us. Despite Laughlin's questionable status, we'd like to welcome you to our little sorority as the Lady Shade. The way you maneuvered him into First, handled Julia and Natalia just now… I don't think there's any question you've earned a place at our table, contingent upon a term or two." She patted her platinum curls, a cat in the cream.

Kara's pulse jumped. "What does that mean?" She tried to sound breezy, and it came out as a squeak.

"Ostensively, philanthropic work in the city. More importantly, keeping a firm hand on Laughlin," Evie said, perusing the crustless sandwiches. "We all do our part to guide our husbands' decisions and the rest of the city's. Am I right that Lord Merchant is presenting evidence in Laughlin's case today?"

Kara went cold. "He is."

"I believe your brother-in-law, Youssef is presiding, isn't he, Bernice?"

"Yes, and I'm afraid he's quite torn. My sister, Constance, says he's been impossible to live with. If it were only the semantics of the case… but how can he not take politics into account? Given Laughlin's past, well…" She met Kara's eyes from over the rim of her teacup. "Unless Youssef can be assured of a steadying influence, I'm afraid he's going to err on the side of caution."

"Mmm." Evie plucked off a jellied triangle. "That would be a shame."

Kara choked down a surge of 'lust, unknotting her fingers from her skirts and smoothing them. These bitches had her over a barrel and knew it. Her teeth gritted together. "What do you want me to do?"

"Oh, come now, you'd think we were demanding something vulgar!" The blonde woman tittered. "All we ask, is that you keep us informed, and heed our advice in guiding him."

All they ask. Kara's 'lust jumped again, and Phyllis squirmed on the other side of the table. Why was she suddenly so silent?

"Guide." Bernice snorted. "Kyle wouldn't know which leg to put in his pants first without directions. You need to start by tempering that boy's swagger."

Kara concentrated on her plate, steadying her breath. Music ran through her head, pushing back her rage. How could they expect her to spy on him? To try to make him different? If it saved him from nullification and exile, how could she say no?

"I disagree." Alice smirked. "I think him having Deirdre's charisma is an asset. I've never met a woman that could win over a room so completely, and he has the same gift." She turned her intense green eyes to Nora, sipping at her tea. "Wouldn't you agree?"

Kara tensed. Did they know the details of what had happened? If not all of them, she was certain Alice did. The woman's double-speak made her head hurt.

"I don't know him well enough to comment, but she was an exceptional woman," Nora returned smoothly, taking a petit four.

Evie airily waved a spoon. "Charisma or no, you must know by now that Laughlin gleefully earned himself a scandalous reputation, even before this split debacle. I'm assuming between his status and your little display with Natalia, he won't be continuing the trend?"

Kara laughed, tamping down her 'lust. The latter she could guarantee, and as far as his status, Glory, if she heard that one more time—"Only if he wants a certain portion of his anatomy removed."

"Speaking of which, what do you intend to do about that nonsense in the paper?" Bernice asked.

Nonsense what—oh. Julia's stupid son. "Nothing. It's ridiculous."

"I have to agree," Phyllis said. "It will burn itself out, all the sooner after announcing you're bred. It's been the cause of too much conjecture, and would go a long way toward quashing some of these rumors, and securing your social standing. There are already far too many whispers that with Bea's pregnancy, Jacques should've been named First, and Laughlin's status—"

"None of which matter, because the Shades know *my* status. As far as his is concerned, if people have an issue with him being dual-talented, I'd love to discuss it with them," Kara said sweetly, tired of being spoken down to. Across the table Alice's smirk deepened.

"Well, I—" Bernice huffed. "The longer you wait, the more the rest speculate—"

"Let them. We haven't discussed it."

"Discussed what?" Flynn asked, coming over to the table. He

kissed Kara's cheek and took Bea's empty seat, helping himself to the spread. Kara made a concerted effort not to slump against him.

"They want to know when we're announcing."

Flynn got that Cheshire cat grin of his, and put an arm around her. "Oh, that. Yeah. Did you—"

"No."

The Ladies looked between them, but she didn't have any intention of telling anyone how many children they were expecting until she wrapped her own head around it. Bernice's eyes unfocused, and Kara bit back a stab of anger as the woman read her energy. Bernice sat back like she'd been slapped, huffing.

Flynn leaned in close, pulling talent. "They can't hear us. What happened?"

She sighed, fiddling with her napkin. "Is it that obvious?"

"Yeah. You've been seething for the past hour, and the tension in here was stupid, even before I walked in. Lemme guess. They're trying to rope you into something, and you met Natalia. What did you do to her?"

Kara went limp at his assessment. "She said something bitchy, and I might've mentioned reading her letters…and the others."

Flynn laughed, way too amused about it. "That it?"

"Other than a riveting conversation about cloth verses disposable diapers, way too much about a weasel attack, and the Ladies blackmailing me into joining them, it's been the highlight."

"Cloaking at the table is incredibly rude, Laughlin," Phyllis said between sips of tea.

He ignored her. "Really? Shit, Kara, you gotta take them up on it. That's huge."

"They only want me to do it to keep an eye on you."

"I'd rather you kept other things on me." He nuzzled behind her ear, and she went scarlet.

"Laughlin!" Bernice hissed.

He glanced at her with that grin of his. "And they're full of shit, they keep tabs on each other and feed it back to their husbands."

"Wait, you know?"

His eyebrow quirked. "Yeah, and they're right. We need to

announce." He raised his head to look around the room, smoothing a hand over his beard.

"Now?" She put a hand on her stomach, wishing she hadn't eaten anything.

Flynn shrugged. "Might as well."

"All of it?"

"No. They'll have to wait for that, but I'll give them something else to chew on." He took her hand and stood, drawing her to her feet and dropping talent. "Ladies!"

The room quieted, turning to them. Kara wanted to crawl into a hole. What was he up to?

"Thank you for welcoming my lady. We wanted you all be the first to know that House Scot is expecting an heir in the coming months." There were gasps and polite clapping. Flynn's arm settled around her waist and he pulled her close, beaming down at her.

"And to commemorate her elevation to Lady Shade, I'll be donating a million units to the commons infirmary in her name."

That got a much larger reaction.

"What did you just do?" she whispered below the clamor.

"You just accepted the Ladies' invitation. I rubbed everyone's nose in it, pissed off the Binders, and one-upped the other Firsts," he said, grinning. He raised his voice again. "Right, you've all had her for long enough, now it's my turn."

Kara took his proffered arm and inclined her head to the Ladies. Only Alice and Nora returned her smile. What was going on with him? "Any particular reason you're dripping swagger all over the room? I'm supposed to curb that."

His grin got bigger. "For the first time in my life, I've got bigger things to worry about than what these assholes think. If they wanna crucify me for what I am, then I'm sure as hell gonna do what I want. I'm tired of playing the game, Kara." He led her back to the gate.

Her pulse sped up, and she stopped to look at him. "So you're taking your ball and going home?"

"Nope. I'm making them play on my court." His hands encircled her waist. "If Crandall and the rest of them expect me to put my ass on the line, they're gonna have to take me as is. I'm done trying to be something I'm not."

She searched his face, feeling his contentment radiating through their bond. Her heart leapt. Wept. Why did things have to happen this way? Her abdomen felt like it was full of lead, dragging at her, and he…

He was so happy.

Tears pricked her eyes, and he cupped her cheek. "I'm gonna be a dad, Kara. There's no way I'm gonna make our kids go through the same shit I did. No more hiding and trying to be what I'm not. I'm a split, and most likely they're gonna be dual-talented, too. It's out there. I'm gonna own it." He laughed. "And a bunch of other shit. Come on, I gotta go see Cal. You up for checking out the wall after?"

"Sure." She wasn't, but didn't want to hang out for more etiquette with Audrey either. They passed a woman with a striking resemblance to Bernice. She couldn't tell the difference between them from the back. "How many sisters does Miriam have?"

"Like eighteen or something, and two brothers. Well, one now."

Kara stopped again to look at him, incredulous.

He shrugged. "It's not that uncommon up here. People usually have kids until they can't. After the triplets, Miriam couldn't have anymore. My parents having me was kind of a miracle. Jon and Lot are actually from Cal's second family. He had nine or ten kids at one point. They all died in the Great Incursion."

"You said that happened over two hundred years ago."

"It took him a long time to get over it. He really loved his first wife."

Kara gave him another funny look. Binders had been extending Patron's lives since they'd discovered it was possible, but that kind of weave was visible as soon as you pulled talent.

And Cal didn't have one.

NORA EDGED AWAY from a servant who had an odd rolling blink. He set another pot of tea on the table, and stood beside her seat, taking his time bussing their dishes. Something about the innocuous little man made her skin crawl, though she couldn't say what. She tried to ignore it. As soon as Kara and Flynn had left, a flurry of debate had sprung up over his donation and the suitability of it.

"A million units to the commons!" Bernice scoffed. "He might as well throw it in the bay for all the good it'll do. As if they'll know—"

"You're missing the point," Evie murmured over her cup. "He's paying them for their support, and no one can object after that little speech."

Nora looked between them. Bernice she'd met briefly years before, and hadn't liked her then. She didn't much now, either. Evie was falling into the same category. "Perhaps he was just trying to do some good—"

The Ladies collectively rolled their eyes.

"Not a chance. He was intentionally stirring the pot." Phyllis sighed, pouring another cup of tea. She raised an eyebrow at Nora. "His donation isn't going to go over well with your line. They've been trying to raise funds for a serenity glade in one of their wards up here. That donation going down the hill—"

"You're going to find the Binder line less than cohesive," Bernice tittered.

Phyllis shot her a look. "They've been a mess since the Brodys passed, and with Laughlin killing that Original House proposal of theirs, there's no excuse for it. You're going to have to intervene."

"I'm aware of the situation." And intervening had been a foregone conclusion. Nora glanced at the alabaster clock in the corner. In roughly an hour, that was going to become exponentially more complicated. The servant brushed the last of the crumbs from table and retreated to the kitchen. Her breath came easier. What had that been about?

"Well, binding is what you do..." Alice drawled, smirking over her teacup. "Pity some things need to be broken first, and then they never go back together quite the same. Always a piece or two that somehow doesn't fit anymore."

Nora smiled back, repressing a shiver. The woman's pupils had dilated at her like a serpent's. "Then it's fortunate I'm exceptional at puzzles. I never have an odd piece left, unless I choose not to include it."

Alice trilled out a laugh, the room pausing for a heartbeat. "That's good to hear, considering the scope of the one you'll be tackling."

Nora's breath caught in her throat. Cal had told her the woman's extra was precognition, but she hadn't really believed it until now. The other Ladies looked between them. Bernice made a noise of disgust. Alice's smirk grew, her gaze flicking to the dowdy woman and dismissing her.

Evie rolled her eyes at them. "Well, spill it, Bernice. What did her energy say?"

"Multiples." She sniffed. "Though I couldn't get a read on how many through that burst of anger. I'd hazard it's more than two, the way they're sucking the talent right out of them both."

"You think she knows?"

Bernice snorted at Evie. "I'd say they both do, considering how smug he was."

"She's tamed him." Alice ran a finger around her saucer. "Which is what you all wanted."

"I wouldn't say that. Leashed, maybe. He reminds me of my Richard with his intensity." Phyllis's lips pursed at the last, as if not entirely pleased by her own comparison.

"He does have a Breaker's passion, doesn't he?" Nora smiled, putting her cup down. If she drank anymore, she'd spring a leak. "I'm happy for Kara. Being loved by a Breaker is no small thing."

Phyllis returned her smile. "No. Nothing a Breaker does is small." The two of them laughed. "I look forward to meeting your Marcos. They tell me he's been making quite a showing on the sands."

"I figured as much by the number of bruises I've bound. It's nice to know the Breakers don't suffer from the same prejudices my line has fallen prey to."

Phyllis frowned. "That's not entirely true, but the hierarchy prevails. It's a bitter pill to swallow, but most medicinal things are, along with harsh doses of reality. Kara's performance the other night certainly qualified. There isn't a Breaker up here that can do what I saw her do. Between her and Marcos…is that what we can expect from Titus's troops?"

Nora spun her ring. How much should she disclose? She needed these women on her side for the reunification to be successful, but they were definitely not her friends.

Or each other's.

"Marcos's metrics are more typical, though at the upper end of ability. Kara is…special. I'm afraid there's going to be a great deal of casualties when the time comes." The women fidgeted uncomfortably, the chatter from other tables filling the silence between them.

"Well, then I suspect it's a good thing we've been so busy preparing the shelters." Bernice scowled at Alice. "Though why you've insisted the basement of the Assembly Hall be set up the way it has…if we ever need that many cots, there won't be anyone left to protect the city, never mind attend to them all."

The seer sipped her tea, then turned to Nora. "Would you like to inform them or shall I?"

Nora glanced at the clock, her stomach twisting at the woman's foreknowledge, but Alice was right, and she was going to need all the help she could get.

FITZ RAN a hand down his face. What the fuck had ever possessed him—bugger it all. His luck had gone to shite, and things was just going from bad t'worse.

"Are ye serious?"

Markham sat behind his desk, fingers laced over his gut, looking for all the world like he were. "Assembly bylaws stipulate each commission be led by a scion of an Original House."

"I ain't a lord."

"Perhaps not yet, but your father was."

His fuckin' father—"Aye, and he's dead. Were such an important man, they sent him t'the bottom of the—"

"Fitzpatrick!" His uncle's hand slapped down on the desk, pens jumping. "The sisters are adamant that you serve in this function, and won't be swayed. They're well aware you inherited the Prydees' mapping extra, and if anyone can find their way around down there, it's you."

The fuckin' sisters. His teeth ground together. Prydees was worse than that rat-fuck dog of Gran's when they got somewhat betwixt their teeth.

"Find me way. I ain't a fuckin' Intelligencer, neither." And there wasn't no weasel nests...but he'd be damned before he admitted to that. Shite. He were damned either way.

"Crandall's men have all been allocated to the southeast finding smuggler's tunnels."

"And think it's bullshite."

Markham shrugged. "Eh..."

Fitz grabbed the decanter off the desk and downed a goodly amount. He grimaced at the nasty sweetness cloying his throat and set it back. Hated port. "So what the hell d'they expect me t'do? Just wander around till I happen upon the beasties?"

"More or less. They've allocated enough funds for a several men to assist you."

His eyebrow quirked. "S'paying job?"

"It is."

Fitz settled back in his chair, tugging at his patch. So they was gonna pay him t'wander around them tunnels with a bunch of blokes? Nah. Had t'be a catch. "What men, and for how long?"

"A week, tops. I believe Joseph Dashell has been asked to assemble a crew," Markham said, squaring his blotter. Fitz groaned, and his uncle glanced up from beneath his brows like he were asking if that were gonna be a problem and not caring either way. Bernice must be riding him somewhat fierce.

Damn it. Them Prydee boys was more likely t'beat the shite out of him and leave him in one of them holes than anythin' else. 'Specially after he nicked that job from under Joey's nose. "And what happens if there ain't no weasels?"

"If that's the case, I'd imagine Joseph will corroborate your findings."

Like hell he would. Fitz's hand went to his pocket. Coin were dead as a smelt. He were gonna fling the blighted—goddamn it, he weren't getting out of this, and them fuckin' Prydees had already threatened Gran.

"Fine." His teeth gritted together, spitting out the words. "Where they at?"

"Custom house, I believe."

Course they was.

Three hours later, well into trudging through the sewers, Fitz trailed after the group of thugs, shoulders slumped, hands jammed into his pockets, fiddling with his dead coin. His stomach churned. Cajetan had forsaken him. Were the only explanation for his current predicament. Forget about the sisters, he were gonna slit his own wrists if he had to spend much longer at this. Were the fifth time they'd come down this stretch.

Ahead, Joey and the rest stopped t'argue about which branch t'take.

Fitz just caught himself from leaning against the moldering brick wall. Tunnels was gettin' nasty and low closer they got to the stockyards, shite wicking up the cuffs of his trousers. He scuffed his boot in the fetidness. Damn Marl, too. His fuckin' majority. There was two weeks t'the blessed event, and all of 'em could choke on it.

"All right McCreedy, you're the sewer rat, where to now?" Shite knew they was lost.

Fitz shrugged. "Eh…left?" Didn't matter, they was in a loop.

"Ye asking me, or telling me?" Chuckle-heads behind Joey snickered.

"If I were telling ye somewhat, it'd be t'fuck off."

"That's real fine." He came closer, knuckles cracking. "Cause I'll be telling the sisters we found that nest of weasels. Hundred of 'em down here, rooting around, and yer dumb ass scattered 'em before they was caught. Pissed us off somewhat fierce, didn't it, boys?"

Seven sets of teeth glinted in the lantern light, moving to pen him in. Two of them shifted to grab him, Joey hauling back a fist—

Fitz was quicker, shifting from the loop into an offshoot they'd come through earlier. Figured that was how things was gonna play out. They'd smear him t'the sisters, but that were gonna happen regardless. He'd come down here like they'd wanted. Should be enough t'keep them off his gran. They'd already done enough t'the poor woman.

He relaxed his sight and started walking, energy from the earth outlining everything in ghostly colors. Wanting t'shift the lot of it and bury the fuckin' city and hisself. Christ, he weren't in a fit mood t'be around nobody.

Fitz sighed, kicking stones from his path. Timbers propped up boards, holding back falls of scree shaken loose long ago. Hadn't been down here in a spell, and he could see where the stones had shifted, dark places where a hole were gonna open. Everything overlaid what were in his book of memories, updating the underground schematic he held in his head.

Joey had taken them down a manhole by the custom house, and after debating whether weasels ate shite or was water critters, they'd been skirting the fuzzy divide between the caverns and the sewers, moving to the northwest, away from where them Intelligencers was nosing out smuggling routes. Think they could've looked for weasels while they was at it…

Fitz slowed at a branch tunnel that would take him under the stockyards at the outskirts of the city. Weren't too far from a bootlegger's drop. With all that'd been going on, chances was good there might be a case or two unattended…

Getting shitfaced by his lonesome sounded like just the thing.

He tugged his patch. Probably'd be a bust with his luck of late, but were worth checking out. He resigned himself to walking. Things below changed too quick. Weren't careful, and he'd shift into a hole or somewhat just as nasty.

Not that this stretch weren't. Tanneries drained into it, and it stunk t'high heaven. Didn't run, but he moved quicker than he ought otherwise. Tunnel branched, he took the right, curving towards the bay. Bunch of offshoots was flooded, and it weren't with water. He buried his nose in the crook of his elbow. Shite, it were foul—

He paused, squinting. Wiped his watering eyes.

Were a light ahead. Voices…sounded uppity, like that shite that'd tried t'shanghai him. Tunnel ended in a recent slide of scree, too new for the dirt to trickle down and fill in the spaces around the edges. Light flicked from them, along with the smell of roast chicken teasing through the foulness. Fitz's stomach rumbled, and he tensed.

"—beg for it." Laughter.

"A waste. He's just going to puke it up."

"Please, I'll do whatever you want—"

Shite. Fitz felt like he were gonna puke. Knew that voice. Were a nest of weasels down here all right, and Arileo were one of 'em.

TITUS FLICKED THROUGH HIS MISSIVES, pausing at the numbers from Brix. The last of the troops bivouacked in the Deep South were en route, only the few with active commissions unaccounted for. Most countries had terminated long-standing contracts, citing ethics concerns.

He snorted. As if hiring mercenaries to pillage their neighbors wasn't questionable to begin with. He raised a hand to his aching temple. No matter, when they came crawling back they'd find rates had doubled. He ignored the last missive from the board; he'd be called on the carpet soon enough.

His eyes went to the clock. Still some time before that delightful interlude began.

No doubt the meeting was to grill him over the complication of legalities following the discovery of Ielle's corpse. That, or the growing number of troops stationed at the border. By now, even Rache would've noticed there were far more than what was on the books.

Whether Salist was unable or unwilling to clue him in to their agenda was mildly troubling, though not unexpected. The man had either been excluded from the board's off-record grousing due to their familiarity, or he'd turned coat. With the amount of money sitting in escrow, Titus found the former more probable. Salist was merely sitting back and enjoying the show.

Titus didn't take it personally. He would have done the same.

He pulled up the feeds from Glynfyls. Excellent. The number of hosts his bots had infected was steadily climbing and now included

Original Houses, offering up an entirely different perspective of the city.

In particular, the new owner of the Painted Pony was a gold mine. Not only did he have an impressive smuggling ring with a multitude of off-book ways in and out of the city, he also had a seat on the Assembly. Between the two, it gave Titus a well-rounded perspective of Glynfyls's siege readiness, or lack there of.

He smiled wryly; it was going to be a bountiful harvest.

A communications orb pulsed blue. That would be the board. Titus slicked back his hair, accepting the transmission. Nine screens materialized.

None of the faces populating them looked pleased.

"Well, let's get this wrist-slapping over with, shall we?" he said, baring his teeth.

"With pleasure," Plumm replied. Now that was surprising. He was in charge of legal, and very rarely involved himself with the board's infighting. "After your failure to address our most recent missive, the board has voted to censure you, and demands redress for injury to the Corporation's reputation resulting from your actions."

Had they? Titus laughed at the notarized documents Plumm transmitted to his server. "Because it was oh so pristine up until last week. Please—" Titus laughed again. They were serious. The international community must really be tightening the screws. Nothing for it then. "Very well, what would you consider equitable restitution?" A billion units or so should get him clear—

"Damage is done. Only way to recoup and protect our other divisions is with a complete separation of assets and a major restructuring. We need to shut genetics down," Albanach said, flicking a long column of ash into that damnable birdbath.

Heat flushed through Titus. What had instigated this about-face? "You're mad. I've far too much invested in this venture, and quite frankly, with the military resources I have at my disposal, that's no longer your call to make. Nor should it ever have been, given your involvement with the Northern Territories."

Old man didn't bat an eye. More concerning, save for Rache, neither did the others.

"Thought that might be the case. Whelp, have it your way. Don't say I never gave you the chance to walk away. Mad or not, I'm taking my Talents as payout and liquidating my stock…" Albanach smiled at something off screen. "Ah, yes. There it goes."

Titus blinked. The man couldn't be serious—

Rache's piggy little eyes bulged. "He's dumping all of it!"

What?!

The effect was immediate, prices tanking as the market was flooded. The coveted shares were being snapped up for pennies on the —Titus ran a shaking hand across his mouth.

It wasn't just Albanach.

The others were doing the same at a ridiculous loss—what the hell was going on?

He fell back shaking.

Ruined.

Another holo popped up above his desk. Vector alarms screaming, unsanctioned shifts across the facility, all ending at the Creche—A massive flow of talent, and the visuals—

It was gone.

The entire complex had disappeared.

The rest of the board, party to his financial evisceration or not, was shocked.

The old dragon leaned back in his chair, puffing on his cigar. "I don't bluff."

Titus couldn't even begin to acknowledge his rage.

Yin recovered first, salivating. "The majority of share holders' divesture of interest constitutes as a vote of no confidence, doesn't it, Plumm?"

"It does," he said, fiddling with something off screen. "And I've just filed the paperwork creating a separate legal entity. Once it's approved, we can finalize the sale of concrete assets… unless you have the capital to buy what's left of the Source yourself, Titus? As a board member, you are entitled to first right of refusal."

Titus glared at the man.

Yin laughed, clapping her hands together. "It is a shame your father was so adamantly against the criminalization of insider trading.

I think you'll find the board's new chair even less reasonable than Albanach."

The man kept smoking his little cigar, not a care in the world.

"New chair?" Titus growled.

Albanach flicked his ash. "Mmm. Part of that restructuring I mentioned. I'm stepping down in an official capacity, but will act as proxy for the foreseeable future. Boy's got a lot on his plate right now."

Titus tried to focus past the building pressure in his skull. There had never been a time when Albanach, or someone of that name, hadn't been on the board.

He looked past the communications orb again and muted them for a moment. "Sorry about that, just tying up a loose end or two. You all should receive my paperwork within the hour." Albanach's eyes tracked away from the orb again and he smiled. "That'll do it. Come here, boy, meet the board."

Laughlin Scot moved to stand beside the old man, smug.

Titus laughed. "I was right, you've been working with them all along to sink the division, haven't you? This is absolutely preposterous!"

"No, I've been working to diversify our leadership. It's the only move that's gonna save our asses after all the shit you've pulled. Well, not yours, but none of us are crying about that." Albanach grinned. "Lord Scot has agreed to help us out of this PR nightmare by assuming my chair in exchange for the release of any and all Talents under our purview."

"And what do the rest of you get out of this?" Titus snarled at six other gleeful faces. Rache looked as sick as he felt.

Yin gave him a nasty smile. "Plausible deniability, and rid of you."

"Walk away, Titus," Albanach said, flicking his cigar.

Titus bared his teeth again. "No. I don't think so, and really, I should thank you. This hostile takeover has removed any fetters I may have otherwise had. In rendering the Source a non-entity, you've voided any treaties preventing me from mobilizing my troops."

The man took a leisurely puff of his cigar. "You don't have the funds to mobilize or the balls."

"I don't need funds when I have my Elites." Titus seethed. "And rest assured, I'll be leading them north. All of them. And when I do, I'm going to rape, pillage, and raze everything in my path. If I can't have the Source, I will have Glynfyls. Make no mistake about that."

Titus cut the transmission and pulled at his hair.

"Where's my bourbon!" A cowering sub ran over, drink in hand. Titus snatched it from him. "Bring me the goddamned bottle and get out!"

He was going to war.

CHAPTER ELEVEN

"DO you think it was wise to bait him like that?" Kara asked, staring at the space where the communications orb had just been. She drew her knees to her chin, scrunching up in the chair across from Cal. He blew out a plume of clove-scented smoke and dropped his cloak, the color bleeding back into him. That was so weird, like a sponge sucking up color.

"It was necessary. The international community needs to see him for the despot he is. That last bit should already be streaming, giving the rest of Corporation the deniability it needs to maintain dominance in this hemisphere, and keep anyone else off us. Without them as a buffer, the Deep South will be up here faster than you can blink."

"Surviving what's coming is gonna be hard enough. They need to figure out that damn shield wall," Flynn muttered, lighting one of Cal's cigars.

"Nora and Marcos should be acclimating the Talents I just gated up, but you're gonna need to do the same with the Firsts to get them ready for the next round. I've arranged to have the rest of the Talents sent up via air transports. Meantime, Source Binders'll help with the shield, and tracking down anyone infected with those bots. Unless I deliver on the iridium, Orin's not budging on them. You need to move forward with getting the remaining lines pledged."

Flynn snorted. "You really think they're gonna make me Overlord after all this shit?"

Cal pursed his lips. "Stranger things have happened."

Kara couldn't understand the dread she was feeling from Flynn. Neither man would meet her eye.

Flynn jammed his hands wrist-deep into his pockets. "Is Miriam gonna be able to set the wards on Meddleton?"

"Yeah, she's settling in at one of the sister's flats and then and she'll be back. I'll take care of the cloak. French is getting you two packed up, but no one can catch that damned cat of yours."

What the heck were they talking about now? She tamped down her irritation. "Are we going somewhere?"

Flynn's brow furrowed. "Yeah. The Sons are slaughtering random estates, and everyone's moving into the city—no one said anything at the luncheon?"

She laughed. "That would have been too many levels above vapid. Seriously?"

"Yeah. Sorry, I would've—"

"No, it's fine. I'll get Hiss and be back down. You should ask Nora to cure that clove allergy of Miriam's. Those cigars smell so much nicer." Cal's eyebrows raised at the suggestion. Kara left the room, feeling Flynn's annoyance at the mention of her mother's name and shrugging it off. She couldn't do anything to make that better.

Hiss was hiding on top of the bed's canopy. He jumped right down for her and spat at the maid holding a carrier. Kara gave him a kiss and pushed him in.

"Come on, you little monster."

She dodged the servants carrying boxes, and went into the bower despite Hiss's protests. Flynn was right, cats were weird. You would've thought he'd love it out here, but he'd just sulked in their bedroom since they moved in, avoiding the indoor garden like something in it was going to eat him.

And now they were moving out.

She stopped to sit at the lip of rock surrounding the little pond. A manufactured breeze stirred the leaves, the calming scent of growing things filling her lungs. It seemed like every time she got used to a place it was ripped away. Hopefully they'd be able to come back. Her hand brushed at her damp cheek and fell to her abdomen. Hopefully she'd be able to come back.

Even if it wouldn't be for long.

Her fingers trailed through the surface of the water. It was colder than she thought it would be. A tingle travelled up her arm, and she shivered, rubbing it. Hiss started yowling, and she picked up his carrier. He was such a baby.

Flynn was waiting for her at the gate when she lugged the cat into the foyer. His brow knit. "You okay?"

She couldn't tell him. "Just going to miss this place."

"You've no idea how much." He laughed, taking the carrier, and offering her his arm. They walked through the swirling mists into a stark, square room higher than was wide, then passed a doorway with a thick iron gate, and into another room lined with drab couches.

Boxes were stacked everywhere, servants busy shuffling them about. The floor was covered with a grubby carpet. She couldn't even begin to guess its original color. Vertical windows slit the walls let in light, but not much else. The room's most decorative feature was a large hole punched in one wall.

After Meddleton, it was…jarring. Flynn hadn't been kidding, it was a dump. Maybe the rest of the place was nicer, but she wasn't going to hold her breath.

She turned back to the gate. "How does it do that?"

"What makes you think I know?" He flopped down on a couch, sending up a cloud of dust.

She wrinkled her nose and sat beside him, poking a finger in at Hiss when he mewed plaintively. He swiped at it. What the heck? "I'm getting the impression that you know a little about everything."

Flynn fidgeted, insecurity jolting through their bond. "They're relics from when the city was founded. No one knows how they work. Well, maybe Cal, but good luck getting him to tell you." He smiled. "See, I don't know everything"

"You know a lot more than most people."

Flynn chewed his lip. "Is that a bad thing?"

"No, it's pretty hot." She kissed him, and the cat started yowling.

"Always messing up my game," he murmured, catching the attention of one of the men in livery. "Can you put him in our rooms? Make sure he's got a box, last thing I need is him crapping in my shoes."

Kara giggled. Hiss would do it, too. The man reluctantly took the growling carrier, and she curled up against Flynn, hoping he couldn't sense how tired she was. Multiples. How was this even happening? One child was surreal enough—

He tipped her chin up and kissed her.

She smiled at him. "What was that for?"

"Do I need a reason?"

"Mmm, maybe it was an apology. A board member, really?"

Flynn shrugged. "It's part and parcel with the whole reunification he and my mom planned out. People can't know about his involvement with the Source, and now that all those Talents are up here—"

"Seriously?" The idea of Tamara Hess lurking around made her want to vomit.

"Yeah. I don't know the details, but expect I will sooner than not. Hey, he doesn't expect me to do much, and the plan is for him to take it back over as Cal. I'm just the temporary front man."

Kara gave a weak nod, unable to shake the feeling that nothing good was going to come of it. A servant approached with a tray, and Flynn grabbed a sandwich from it. There was a shake for her. She sighed and chugged some of the foamy cardboard down. Ugh, it was gross. She ran her tongue over her teeth, thinking about that stupid luncheon.

"The Ladies hold a lot more power in this city than most people think, don't they?"

"Yeah. It's a big deal they asked you to join them. It's not just being the First's wife. All of them are really smart. They change policy up here, and do it a hell of a lot more effectively than the Assembly. You know those assholes voted on a fucking weasel commission?

"Oh, I heard all about it. One of Miriam's sisters is in a lot of debt now, something about advances she received for those birds that were killed." Kara glanced at him, playing with her straw. "The Ladies said —well, insinuated—that if I do what they say, they'd have the court rule in your favor. Bernice's brother-in-law is the judge."

"Of course he is. Prydees have strings on anyone with influence up here, and aren't shy about using it. You need to be careful around the sisters, Kara. They're way vindictive, and will make you pay every perceived slight back with a pound of flesh. Bernice and Miriam aren't terrible, but the rest of them are snakes."

"Like Leo?" His chewing slowed, and the mash of his emotions made her sorry she'd asked. "Do you really think they can do it? Get you clear?"

"Yeah, and they're gonna want something above and beyond what the Ladies asked you to do." He chewed some more, and she finished her stupid shake. Forget about Meddleton, she missed the coop. Why was everything up here so convoluted?

"You ready to go check out the wall? The guild's trying to get the shield up and running."

She gave the affirmative and went with him to the gate. They passed back through the opalescent mists and came out in the middle of a small stone room. He walked over to a door with a portcullis over it, and knocked through the bars. A wicket snicked back and forth, then the bars raised before the door could open.

Kara laughed. "A little much, isn't it?"

He shrugged. "Whoever shifted this portion in must've had a thing for medieval architecture. You gotta admit, it's impressive."

It was. They entered a narrow courtyard. Massive stones rose up on either side. Flynn nodded at the guard manning the door, then gritted his teeth, hugging the wall up the steep stone steps. At the top, he flattened himself against the parapet, running a shaking hand through his sweaty hair. Kara's brow creased. His face was pinched, and he had to work at regulating his breathing. What was wrong with—

"Wait, you're afraid of heights?"

"No," he growled. "I just don't like them."

She laughed, and he flushed, moving down the walkway with his shoulder scraping the parapet, pointedly not looking down, or at her. How adorable! He stiffened when she caught up and tried to walk beside him.

"Not so close to the edge," he squeaked, grabbing her arm.

What? She laughed again, the walkway spanning the top of the wall was easily ten feet across. A waist-high balustrade surrounded the inner edge before it dropped to the city below.

"How can you stand the bower?"

"It's different." He glowered and kept walking. Jesse was up ahead. Flynn wiped his palm against his pants before holding it out to shake. He kept the other on the parapet. Kara tried very hard to keep her face neutral.

Especially when she saw the Creche in the middle of the plateau, backlit by the setting sun. She tugged on his sleeve. "Flynn…"

He followed her gaze and swore.

"Oh my…" Jesse breathed behind them. "That wasn't there a moment ago."

"What's the status of the shield?" Flynn asked, turning back to her like it was nothing.

She blinked, unable to tear her gaze from the complex. "I—It needs a considerable amount of binding…"

People in the outer city were filling the streets, staring at the glaring white conglomerate of cylindrical buildings against the grey of the wind-scoured landscape. Kara's stomach cramped.

Tamara was in there.

"Are you feeling all right?" Kara jumped, but Jesse was looking at Flynn.

He wiped the sweat from his brow. "I'm fine. Aside from the binds, is the shield ready?"

"Theoretically, yes. Once they're set, we can lay the rest of the weaves. I don't anticipate that taking long."

"Good, we won't have long. Any progress on the bots?"

She brightened. "Yes. They're the most incredibly clever delivery system, and the tech embedded in them is fascinating. I've made several modifications, chief among them replacing the plaz circuitry with iridium. The results are promising, especially in regard to the negation of a Finder's talent. The change in power source has permuted it into a frequency annulling that of a nullifier within its sphere of influence."

Flynn's jaw dropped. "You can nullify a nullifier?"

She laughed. "There are several limitations inherent to iridium, but as I said, it's promising. I'm hoping to have a prototype in a day or two. The existing ones will still require frying, and I'm afraid I've been monopolizing Nora's talent trying to get these binds set. There's not enough hours in the day, and she's the only one with enough ability to recreate them."

"Not anymore." Kara's eyes were glued to the tower. A hard lump settled in her stomach. Everything she wanted to forget, who she was, how she'd been...all of it had followed her up here.

Just like Riegel.

Flynn put his arm around her. "It'll be okay," he murmured into her hair.

He meant it, but she didn't believe him. He couldn't save her from her biology, and he couldn't save her from what was in there.

***

NORA STEADIED herself against Marcos as they shifted onto the plateau before the Creche.

It stood roughly a mile from the city, and up close, it was even eerier the way it abruptly jutted from the stoney tableau. The ground floor was partially embedded, the building canted, leaving no obvious ingress, and the mirrored windows made it impossible to tell what might be looking back at them. A web of protective binds shimmered over its surface.

Those shouldn't be there.

She huddled down into the collar of her jacket, filled with dread, but there wasn't anything for it. This was what she'd come up here to do. The reunification had to succeed, and for that to happen, she had to get the Binder line firmly beneath her before the others from the Source arrived.

Be the ice queen… Nora took a deep breath and released the weave of talent preventing the Fetch Bernice had commandeered from shifting inside, then nodded to him.

Colors ran.

The grand foyer took up a quarter of the main building's ground floor. Intended as a meeting space, it was littered with sitting areas, all empty and in shadow. The steel staircase leading to the balcony above was a sinister slash of black. Why had the power been cut?

"Hello?" Her voice echoed back at her.

Nora's lips thinned and she pulled talent, calling up a scintillating orb of golden light, her breath fogging in its glow. The instructions she'd left had been for everyone to gather here, so she could bring them up to date. No doubt Serra had overruled them as soon as she'd left.

She started up the steps, her jaw clenched. The Fetch followed, with Marcos bringing up the rear, grim. She felt his unease and shared it. Something wasn't right. Out of the corner of her eye, she caught his hand drifting to his sidearm, well aware they were in enemy territory.

"Nora?"

She turned at the voice. "Jolie?" An umber-skinned woman in tawny Binder's scrubs glanced anxiously at the balcony as Nora came back down to meet her. "What happened?"

"What do you think? As soon as all of Albanach's Talents assembled, Serra put the facility into lockdown. That cabal of hers bound the portlock controls. I can't get into the wards." Jolie wrung her hands. "The infants—"

"And she left you out here so I'd know exactly what she'd done." Damn that bitch! Nora turned to the Fetch. "Take this imprint, and shift the manual release. Marcos can break the bind. Once the doors are open, tell everyone to gather here, as they were instructed."

Marcos put a hand on her shoulder, and she shrugged it off.

"Don't. This is Binder Business."

He frowned but stood down, shifting out with the Fetch and Jolie.

Nora went upstairs.

The door to the administrative office was open, emergency lighting streaming into the hall. She took a deep breath and entered the room.

Serra sat in Nora's chair, flipping through a Talent's private records. More lay strewn across the desk. Her handful of sycophants alternately rifled through people's desks or lounged in the other cubicles, looking thoroughly bored.

Serra tossed down the folio and smirked at her, the chair subtly rocking left, then right, and back again beneath her ample rear, like a cat getting ready to pounce. She set her elbows on the desk and templed her fingers, tapping together gold-enameled nails, too long to do anything other than cause trouble. Not for the first time, Nora wondered which one of the brown nosers in here wiped her ass.

"Well, Nora, we've followed your instructions, and now we're in the middle of nowhere freezing to death. What's the next part of your fantastic plan?"

"My instructions were for everyone to meet in the foyer so I could share that. Perhaps if you'd used the generators to power the heat instead of an unnecessary lockdown, you'd be more comfortable." In her peripheral, Talents had moved to either side of her and were closing in. Mmm. Not wasting any time, were they?

"Did you? I must have missed that part."

"You'll miss the rest if you're not down there in the next five minutes." She turned to leave, and a bind whipped out, holding her fast. Serra laughed, hefting herself out of the chair. She sauntered over, hips swaying beneath her tight leather sheath.

"You know, I can't help but think that this little exodus means that all those silly rules we had to abide by are null and void." She smiled, her curved nails scoring down Nora's cheek.

"If you think you can take First, you're welcome to try."

Serra moued. "I don't think I can, I *know* it."

The bind tightened, and Nora pulled talent, batting it away. Serra was strong but—

Another's bind settled on her, knocking the air from her lungs.

The cabal had joined the fray.

Sweat dotted Nora's brow. Against all of them, she didn't have a chance… A smile flickered over her lips. But all those silly rules were null and void, weren't they?

She pulled talent from Marcos, and threw out a weave similar to the initial one they'd used on the bots, this one just shy of completely debilitating.

The cabal writhed, and Serra screamed, her body juddering. Nora held the weave, smoothing her dress and flicking a lock of hair over her shoulder before dropping talent. Serra and her cabal fell to the floor, juddering. Nora sniffed. They could bind the damage themselves.

Or not.

"You have five minutes before I begin." She glided from the room, not letting herself shake until she turned the corner. Marcos was there.

"You all right?" She nodded, burying her face against his chest. "What about whoever's back there?"

"They'll survive."

"That sounds unfortunate."

She laughed, wiping her eyes. Damn Cal. She would have rather purged that nest of vipers. They wouldn't give her another opportunity like that, but she was sure they'd give her cause to regret letting them live.

"Forcing the lockdown's killed the reserves. I'm not sure what your plans were, but powering the facility's off the list."

Nora took a calming breath. Alice must've seen this. The Assembly hall had beds ready. Perhaps not enough for everyone, but the children in the lower wards could be evacuated.

She nodded and took Marcos's arm, going back to the foyer where Talents milled about. Conversations dropped off and they looked up at her. She stood at the balcony's rail.

"The Source has been liquidated, and all contracts null and void. Lord Scot has negotiated with the Corporation to bring us to Glynfyls, the Northern Territories's capital city, and for our freedom. In that city on the horizon, Talents are the masters of their own destinies. We've been invited to join them, and become one people again, as we were in the days following the Surge—"

"It's a frozen wasteland, and that city looks like it's about to fall over," Serra rasped from behind her. "If we're free as you say, why shouldn't we go where we like?"

Nora gripped the rail, biting back her first reply. She kept her back to the woman. Marcos had her sited. He arched an eyebrow, glancing at Nora and brushing a hand against his sidearm. If only.

"Because, Serra, Glynfyls is the only place on the planet where Talents are not currently being exterminated."

Her shrill laugh cut through the frigid air. "Do you really expect us to believe that?"

"No, but I expect you'll believe this." Nora took a cube from her pocket and tapped it to stream news clips from around the globe.

The room watched, stunned.

When it had finished, Serra wasn't laughing, and the upturned faces had become fraught.

Nora wet her lips. "We'd hoped to house you here, but the unnecessary lockdown you were subjected to has drained the facility's reserve power. I'm afraid you're going to have to endure until—"

"Endure?!" Serra's incredulity crackled through the air. "My status entitles me—"

"To nothing," Nora said sweetly, wanting to rip her face off. "If the Fetches can take this imprint, we'll begin shifting the infants and juveniles. Others from the city are poised to help. In the meantime, feel free to thank Ms. Hess for your current circumstances, and bundle up."

The crowd murmured darkly as the few Fetches in Albanach's stable came forward.

Serra faded to the back, glowering at her from the shadows.

CAL WALKED into the flat's dining room and shook his head.

Rogan was in his seat at the head of the table, feet up, munching on a skewer of chicken like he owned the damned place.

Hell, if he wanted it, he could have it. Place was a shithole and claustrophobic as hell after the estate. Cal passed through the bars of weak light striping across the table's chipped paint to pull out a chair, shadows penning him in.

Wasn't real cheery.

But then, nothing about this damned city was. God, he hated it. Just being here put his back up. Every time he landed between these walls some Christ-forsaken calamity occurred.

This time wouldn't be any different.

He scowled at Rogan. "Is it physically impossible for you to keep your feet off the furniture?" he asked, sitting beside the Breaker and motioning to the servant for a cup of coffee.

"When you're around? Yes." Rogan said around a bite. "I'm assuming that monstrosity on the plateau's where you've been squirreling away that gating stone of yours. What'd you do, daisy chain it to a bunch of Fetches' weaves?"

"Something like that." Cal pulled out his pouch of tobacco. "Corporation'll keep the Deep South off our ass while Titus takes care of the Sons—"

"There's less than you think. Before the storm, that horde down there divvied up, east, west, and south. The one that stayed south got scotched, along with the estate they'd staked out. Those mercs have got a real thing for explosives. Kid know anything about them?"

"Yeah, but he's not talking. My money's on it being Kendall, but as to why his outfit's up here?" Cal shrugged. "Boy doesn't need that morsel of culpability floating around, and that Northern connection he mentioned…whole situation's trouble waiting to happen." He licked his cigarette closed. "What the hell have you been up to, other than playing scout?"

"Breaker Business."

Cal rolled his eyes. That usually equated to drinking, whoring, and brawling. "The holy trinity, huh?"

"Two out of three," Rogan said, munching on his skewer. "Brawling's been a bit lacking without knocking Flynn on his ass every morning. It's too bad. He was coming along quicker than I would've expected. Kid was born to beat on people."

Cal lit his cigarette and gave him a long look. "Dare I say there's a note of approval in your voice?"

"Wouldn't go that far. He holds himself back. If he could get over that goddamned reluctance and learn how to use his talent, he'd be a veritable force of nature. As it is, he hits harder than any of the Breakers I've come across." Rogan pursed his lips. "You think they're gonna vote him in?"

Cal inspected the tip of his cigarette. "Every line but the Finders and Breakers have pledged—"

"You know what the Investiture's going to do to him."

"Yeah," Cal said, taking a drag. "He'll be able to handle it. It's good to see him stepping up. Him and Kara are down at the wall now, and by the way, thank you very little for siccing Jesse on me. Damn woman's worse than Miriam when she gets something between her teeth."

Asshole looked tickled with himself. Cal glared at him.

"Anyway, regardless of this potential clusterfuck with that merc unit, Flynn showing restraint is the last thing you should be complaining about. Him going south was a godsend. Gave him some discipline."

Rogan quirked an eyebrow. "Discipline?"

"Yeah. Boy's always had a chip on his shoulder, but after Deidre died...it was bad without her buffering him and Lot." Shit, it was bad *with* her buffering him and Lot.

"That's got nothing to do with discipline, that's the hierarchy. It would've set the two of them up for one hell of a power struggle. From what I've seen of Lot, he'd be lucky to make grunt." Rogan sighed, scratching under his topknot. "Damn it, Cal—"

"Haven't we been over this?" He didn't want to get into it again.

Apparently, Rogan did. "Shane suicided by default instead of admitting she was wrong—"

"The hell she was, the rest of you—"

The Breaker's feet slammed to the floor, and he loomed forward.

"Don't go there. It's done, and all of us fucked up, but goddamn it, Cal, who in their right mind—"

"Never said I was, but okay, let's play what if. Say I'd asked you to come up and take a hand with the boy, and by some miracle, you did. What then? There was already too much twist bullshit going around. Bringing him up as a Breaker would've disqualified him as my heir."

"If you hadn't made that fucking promise—"

Cal snorted. "What, you would've made him yours?"

Rogan's jaw clenched as he looked away.

Damn it. That'd been low. Cal stubbed out his cigarette, feeling like an asshole. "In retrospect, he might've been better off," he allowed.

His best friend grunted, hearing the apology behind his words. "How the hell did all that twist bullshit get started anyway?"

"Not the foggiest. It was after the last Incursion, I wasn't exactly in the position to add my two cents. Regardless, even if the court rules in his favor, it's gonna be an act of God to get him invested as Overlord. Damned politics in this city…between Crandall and the Prydees, unless Flynn pushes the issue, there's no way they'll go through the ceremony to invest him with all six lines of talent."

"He won't strong-arm them." Rogan tossed the skewer onto the table. "But, the kid could come into power the same way I did. Sure as hell is pissy enough, and he's got the control. Every now and then when we'd spar there's—"

"There's what?" Cal looked at him sharply.

"Something. Just below the surface. Those blue specks start churning…whatever it is, he buries it cold, like he's afraid to use it."

Cal pull out his pouch and rolled another cigarette. Pretty certain there was a good reason for that.

VICTOR HANDED the binoculars back to Sam. They crouched at the edge of the plateau, staring out at the complex that'd just appeared.

"Where the hell do you think it come from?"

Victor spat a stream of chew to the side, hunching inside his heavy coat. "Looks like one of them Source buildings, all white and shiny."

"Think it's full of them freaks?"

"Most like." The wind flung up a wave of stinging grit, and they retreated back to the truck, kicking their way through the brush. Rest of the men he'd brought up were crammed into vehicles or lean-tos. Cut the wind, but cold was gonna screw them regardless. Big house they'd left a smoking ruin behind them. Mother'd been firm on that point.

The truck doors chunked shut, and Victor blew on his smarting hands, fingers tipped black. Sam teased the engine to turn over. Goddamned cold made everything want to curl up and die.

"So what now? Ain't gettin' any warmer, and the chapters we left down south missed check-in. You want me to blow one of them stones and have a look?"

Victor sucked on the wad tucked into his lip, knowing what he'd find. Weather wasn't the only thing pickin' them off. "No. Pass the rest of 'em out to our boys. Things is about to get real, and if it goes sideways, tell 'em to use them stones to regroup at the chapter house."

Sam glanced at the gem studding Victor's brow. "What about her?"

Victor looked out the window. A line of vehicles and transports fogged up the frost-blasted landscape, not enough fuel to do more than idle. Sons shivering lumps, jammed around fires so close nobody had eyebrows.

Judgement day might've come, but the Messiah was late.

"We do the Mother's will, but she done promised that shit stain Wolf is mine, and I ain't checking out before I punch his ticket. If they're lettin' us this close without hittin' us back, them freaks is plannin' on sittin' pretty while we freeze to death. Time we force the issue. Them plaz-cannons ready?"

"Yeah, they're in the transport keepin' warm. Got maybe three bursts between 'em before they freeze. Where you want 'em?"

"Pointed at them freaks. Round up who's able while I get orders." Victor sat back, cracked pleather creaking beneath his bulk. He raised his fingers to his brow, biting back a moan as they caressed the gem's hard facets. The driver's side door opened and shut right quick.

White fingers of warmth tripped through Victor's mind, caressing his thoughts.

Mother was before him, astride his lap, her blue eyes boring into his. He shifted his hips and her rosebud lips curved into a smile, pleased with him. Her hand rose to his cheek, thumb grazing across his stubble.

"My Son. All this conflict in your thoughts. Do you really think my promises empty?"

"I serve your will." But it felt like the feast he'd been shown had turned out to be paper mâché and wax.

"You do. Admirably. Even while seeing what others don't." He looked away, and she raised his face back up, catching his eyes with hers. "The purpose of the Sons has ever been to prepare the Messiah's way. The work you do here accomplishes that. Not a single wild Talent exists outside of the city, and when the time comes, Scot will be yours, and it will be as I have promised. This life is a lie. Your true fate awaits in the next, and begins with his death."

"Have you seen it?" Victor rasped out.

Her expression became distant, alight with a holy glow. Victor's chest swelled, her belief buoying his. "I have. Men as God intended, without this stain of talent. Living as they had before the Surge, as it was meant to be."

He trembled, images flashing before his mind's eye of a tangerine-skied utopia. "What do I gotta do?"

She blinked, long lashes dusting her cheeks. "Attack."

FITZ SHIFTED to Markham's office, still getting wafts of shite despite his shower. Why talent were so finicky with smell—the hell? Place were packed. Fetches shifting in and out with stacks of paper, yammering about supplies and housing. Somewhat must've happened. He mussed his damp hair over his face and grabbed a sandwich from a sideboard that'd been set up.

"Fitzpatrick!"

Shite. He turned, chewing. His uncle came around his desk, tugging at his waistcoat, sleeves rolled up to show forearms hairier than an ape's. Weren't nothin' compared to the rest of him.

"What in God's name did you think you were doing? The sisters—"

"Found Arileo."

Markham looked like he'd been slapped, then laughed, the room turning to them. "You—in truth?"

Fitz shrank beneath all the eyes and shrugged, chewing.

"I'll be back with you all in a moment." His uncle grabbed him by the arm, pulling him away from the hubbub. "Where the devil is he?"

"Northwest tunnels, near them bootlegger's caverns."

"Bootlegger's caverns? The ones by pier eight?"

"Nah. These is past the stocks—"

"I'm not familiar." Markham mopped his brow. "You have no idea what good news this is. With everything that's been going on, his absence is a distraction I can ill afford. Give me the imprint and I'll collect him."

"Ye said somewhat about pay?" Fitz asked around a mouthful.

Markham raised an eyebrow. "If this results in bringing Leo to heel, I'll double it."

"Nah…" He took another bite and spoke around it. "Ye can owe me in kind."

Markham's eyebrow arched higher. "Very well, an obligation of equal weight." He held out his hand, and Fitz shook it, then grabbed another sandwich. "Now, the imprint?"

"Eh…thing is, he weren't alone." Fitz tugged at his patch, and Markham's eyes narrowed.

"Who was he with?"

"Dunno. Talked like that shite that tried t'shanghai me. Were more than a few, and he weren't with 'em 'cause he wanted t'be."

Markham inhaled sharply, drawing himself up. "That has to be the cell Crandall's—"

White light seared through the dusk-darkened windows.

A boom knocked Fitz's feet from under him, the room shaking. Men shouted, pictures falling from the walls, crashing to the floor. He shook his head, hands and knees on the carpet, the fuck—

"To the wall!" Markham yelled, hauling him up by an arm. "Stay close!"

Colors ran and they was there. His uncle dragged him to the

parapet. Air had a funny tang, like battery acid and ozone. Fitz's skin started itching. On the plateau, smoke poured from a complex of ruined buildings. Lines of men and vehicles studded the landscape behind berms of scavenged shite. Gunfire rattled sharp through frigid air, mowing down strangely dressed people. Where had—screams—so much fuckin' screaming—shite, there was kids—

The Flats beyond the wall was chaos, people choking the streets, rushing the gates, all of them trying to get to the inner city. A shrill alarm cut through all of it, Hexes popping up along the ramparts.

Breakers was shifted to the edge of the Flats, drawing fire. Dogs started baying, a pack running out behind the line of attacking men. The enemy split their focus, firing randomly. Bodies thumped down onto the barren landscape. Shite. Shades had cloaked a company of Breakers—

"So much for any fucking warning. Markham!" They turned, Lord Scot stalking over to them with two ladies in his wake, one of them a dark-haired angel. Lord, she were a picture—

A shrill whistle split the air, and Scot's halos ignited. Another massive explosion tore across the sky. Searing light crackled across an invisible barrier, the mitigated force throwing Fitz to a knee, his vision spotted.

Christ, the energy…he shut his sight down quick. His hands came away from his ringing ears bloody.

An old Breaker were there with one of them man-buns, him and Lord Scot arguing with the angel, their voices underwater. Fitz got back to his feet, scratching. That stink had redoubled, his exposed skin the color of rhubarb pie. A strip sloughed off beneath his nails and he froze, mouth dry with horror.

"Let me help!"

"Kara, you can't—"

"I don't need talent to suture!"

Scot looked pissed, but nodded. "Fine, but Rogan stays with you, and I swear to God, if you pull any fucking talent—"

"I won't, I promise." The angel's arms was around Scot's neck and his face went all soft, kissing her. Breaker didn't like that too much. "Be careful."

Scot grunted and glared at the other man. "Hill infirmary. She starts looking like shit, take her straight home."

Breaker handed him a holster and a gun. "Try not to do anything too stupid." He took the angel by the arm, and herded her to the stairs. The other lady trailed behind them.

"Evacuate that building," Scot said to Markham and the group of Fetches that'd followed them from the office. He shrugged into the holster like he knew what he were doing, his eyes falling on Fitz. "Get me behind their line, then help with the evac."

Fitz glanced at his uncle, and Markham gave a curt nod. Shite.

He pulled talent, taking him.

Scot fired before Fitz had gotten his bearings, his halos ablaze. "Go!"

Fitz went.

He shifted in front of the building, staring at the carnage. A little girl ran past—he grabbed her and shifted back to the wall. More poured from the smoking ruin. Boys, girls, men and women…

He pulled talent, bringing them to safety, going back—bullets tore a line through the turf in front of him, and he sprinted for the building.

Side of it were cracked open like an egg. Bodies littered the ground, some moving, some not. His stomach heaved. Someone grabbed his arm. A woman, globe of golden light over her shoulder. She were bleeding, side of her face smeared crimson.

"The infants—"

"Where?"

She ran deeper into the building, down a hall. Smoke clogged the air, flames licking up a doorway. He tripped over rubble, a body—

Cries up ahead. Shrill and weak.

The room were in shadow. Part of the ceiling had collapsed. A line of swaddled infants on the floor, squirming like larva—

"This all of 'em?" She shook her head. "Need t'be t'gether." He ran for the nearest bassinet, recoiling at what was inside. *Jesus fuckin'*—the next held something he could recognize. He brought it back the rest, her doing the same.

"There's more, in the next ward—"

"I'll come back." Christ, where could he—

He shifted them to the Dove. Whores looked at him like he were a ghost. Didn't have time t'explain, they'd figure it out. He shifted again. Woman stood by the door, face streaked with tears in the dying light.

"Where next?"

She brought him to another room. Talents on the floor, parts of them elsewhere. Bassinets tipped over, crushed. Gunfire ripping through their wails. Building shook, stark light searing the room, leaving it blacker as it winked out. God, he didn't want t'see—

Fifth or sixth room were the worst. Blast had taken out the wall and burst a water line. Cold had killed as many as the explosion. Blue and stiff—Fitz shook, gathering up the little bodies still breathing. Woman stumbled, falling to the ground. Water wicked up her pants. She were done in. People ran down the hall. Fetches by the silver of their halos. Help.

"Hey! In here!" A head popped in and swore, going for the infants.

Fitz slapped the woman's cheeks once they was clear.

"How many more?"

"I don't know," she sobbed. "This whole floor—"

An explosion sent him skidding across the room, pain lancing through his ribs. He sprawled on his back stunned, staring through a hole to the sky. A discordance screeched through his mind. Hurt too much t'be dead. Black grit fell, and he blinked it away, vision swimming. He tried to roll over. Agony in his side. Sharp click of a knife snicking open. Woman screamed and then she didn't.

Boots came close.

A man over him, looking down. Spat on him and squatted. He dangled the knife, dripping red. His smile were stained and broken. "Well now, what we got here?"

Fitz pulled talent—

And it wouldn't come.

CHAPTER TWELVE

Plaz-Cannon [plaz ka-nən] noun

1. *Ballistic weapon capable of projecting condensed charges of a
   radioactive ionic suspension over a broad area resulting in
   widespread devastation and lingering environmental
   contamination. Usage has been regulated by international treaty
   classifying it as a weapon of mass destruction.*

   – Excerpt from Keog's Modern Tactical
   Armament and Warfare, *Twelfth Edition*

---

*"They came during the dead of night with nullifiers, rounding up Talents
from the Flats outside the main wall. By the time the alarm was given, three
transports had already been filled and could be seen leaving in the distance…"*

*– Lord Talos, Preceptor of History,
Academy of Glynfyls*

FLYNN HOLSTERED his sidearm to wrap a makeshift bandage
around his bicep, dissonance scraping through his mind with Kara's

concern. Assholes had timed that last grenade with a nullifier, and his cloak had vanished as it hit. He'd taken shrapnel from the blast and the big piece he'd dug out wasn't all of it. He should've known better, and now people were dead.

Fucking bloodlust.

The squad he'd hooked up with had decimated the Sons' flank, routing them toward the main body away from the Flats. Behind his shield, nothing had been able to touch them, bodies littering the field in their wake—that blackness, a siren's song of destruction singing through his veins, the torrents of force channeling through him to mow down swaths of men—he'd gotten caught up in it, and the Sons had pounced. Christ, was that what Kara had meant? If she felt every time she fought, no wonder Rogan thought it was a fucking problem—

A line of fire tore a furrow of earth to his right.

Goddamn it. He pressed against an overturned jeep, teeth aching at the frigid air hissing through them, pulling the knot tight. So was the lack of cover, and now they were out gunned. If they sent up another one of those charges, the city was fucked. Where the hell had they scored plaz-cannons?

A grenade went off, rocking the vehicle. He dug his feet into the frozen tundra, skidding under its weight—*Don't fucking tip*—

A group of Sons ran past, disappearing into the smoldering building. Screams and the pop of a semi. Shit. He grabbed up the sidearm and tore after them. Shots fired, Flynn hit the ground, crawling on his belly through the gap, puffs of stucco whipped away by the wind, window crazing fractals—

Inside, breathing heavy, his back to the wall. Christ, it was dark. Wet. He squinted, waiting for his eyes to adjust.

Bodies. Smell of cordite and death. The ever-present gale shrieking through the holes ripped through the building. Smoke hanging in low ribbons, and water splashing farther on. An explosion shook the ground, chunks of ceiling crashing, cement peppering down around him. Gun shots and bursts of muzzle flash illuminated a hallway. He got to his feet and made for it.

A woman screamed. He edged up to the doorway as her body hit the floor, water stained scarlet, soaking a pile of tiny swaddled bodies.

That blackness in him licked up, the animal cresting to the surface.

Man was crouched over someone prone, his back to him. Three steps and Flynn's hand raked him up by his hair, bullet speeding through his temple, grey matter and crimson gore spattering the far reaches of the room.

"Shite! Don't shoot!"

That kid was on the floor staring up at him, eyes wide in his soot-streaked face, hair plastered to his head. Flynn snorted and shoved the corpse away, sweeping up the bolo it'd dropped. Only one chapter issued these goddamned things. Fucking Victor. He should've killed that son of a bitch when he had the chance. He shoved it through his belt and held a hand out to the kid. He took it, wincing.

"You hit?" It was a stupid question. A spreading stain of scarlet bloomed across his side. "How bad?"

"Eh…dunno. Feels pretty bad…" He staggered.

Flynn swore, his breath streaming out in a cloud. He ripped a sheet from one of the bassinets into strips. "Arms up."

He wrapped the kid as best he could, fingers numb with cold, fumbling at the knot. He needed a medic. Flynn grimaced, that goddamned dissonance in his head…

Gunfire cut through it, and the whomp of something big catching flame. His eyes met the kid's. Whatever that'd been, it wasn't good.

"Fitz, right?"

"Eh…ya."

"See that gurney? Get under it." Fitz winced again, moving to the patch of dry ground. "I'm gonna pile a bunch of shit around you and go find that nullifier. Soon as it cuts out, shift to the infirmary." Kid nodded, his face gray. Flynn dropped a sheet over the stretcher, hiding him. "If I can, I'll check back to make sure you got out."

Both of them knew what it would mean if he didn't.

———

NORA STOOD in the doorway of the shelter that'd been set up in the Assembly hall's sub-level. Despite the expansive space's shiny linoleum floors and bright white ceiling tiles, it felt like the room was crushing in, the beige Lally columns only delaying the inevitability of it snapping down.

Far from the joyous event she'd dreamed of, a pall of despondence hung in the room. Children sat at the edge of their cots and against walls staring blankly. Older Talents milled around, speaking in hushed tones, glancing at her askance. Aid workers were on the other side of the room, huddled around the coffee service. The food set out remained untouched, and rows of beds, empty.

Rows of cribs.

So many of them were still out there. Abandoned and unable to fend for themselves... maybe half the children had been evacuated before the nullifier kicked on. She twisted at her signet. If the facility had been in lockdown when the blast hit, the explosion would've been mitigated. If she hadn't been so eager…how many lives had her vitriol against Serra cost them?

How many more if they'd followed her instructions and had all been gathered in that room instead of in the process of shifting out? A familiar hand settled on her shoulder accompanied by the scent of tobacco.

"Busy beating yourself up?"

She turned into Cal's embrace and let him hold her.

"As nice as this is, Nora, I'm gonna take a raincheck. As First Binder, you need to be out there, setting an example. Things aren't going well, and the fallout from that damned cannon's got half the Flats puking out their insides. You need to rally your line. All of them."

She wiped her eyes, nodding. He was right, and wallowing wasn't helping anyone… God, cases of radiation poisoning were going to show up for months, only the worst would be clamoring for attention now—

And they wouldn't be on the hill.

She collected every Talent in the room with medical training.

"Take us to the commons."

MARCOS CROUCHED against the blackened side of the Creche, heading the battalion Stonefist had sent out. They were scattered amidst the rubble, another inside securing civilians. God only knew what was going on in there, but what Stonefist's men lacked in hand-to-hand combat, they more than made up for in guerrilla warfare, and if the random blasts coming from the Flats were any indication, they had urban combat expertise as well.

Would've been a hell of a lot more effective if they had a solid chain of command instead of the middle being mush. If this was any indication how things were going to go when Titus got up here, they were screwed.

The sun had dipped below the mountains in the west, sky streaked a dying azure gold. It bled into the velvet juniper ink of the shadows softening the plateau. Dusk. Should be a moon—how much of one he didn't know. They'd be running dark until it rose. The fire that'd started was on the wrong side of the facility to lend light, but it sure as hell wasn't being stingy with the smoke. Oily, black, and too heavy for the wind to do any more than thin it out, it hung lank at ground level like treacle webbing.

Marcos ran a hand over his stinging eyes and spat, tasting fuel oil. Plaz reserves heated up and they were going to have an entirely different problem. His hand tightened on his sidearm, and he gave the signal for the Breakers to advance. It was time to address the body of Sons pinning them down from behind a line of vehicles.

He broke cover, sprinting to the next pile of debris.

A semi racketed, and Marcos fired above and to the left of the muzzle flash. A popping line of fire arched skyward—

"Incoming!"

The blast of a grenade threw him forward. The ground rose up for him to kiss, and he emptied his clip as he fell. Breakers surged past him, drawing fire. He rolled, catching his breath behind a hillock of twisted metal, and ejected the spent magazine for a new one.

His last one.

He flipped onto his belly. Breakers crashed through the line of Sons, and things devolved to hand-to-hand. It would go quickly. Hierarchy or no, they were still Talents against subs—

Lights flared behind him and he turned, shading his eyes.

Another mass of vehicles was rolling across the plateau.

KARA APPLIED pressure to a Talent's leg, the wound spurting. The infirmary was swamped. People bloodied and dazed, crowding the hallways, lying insensate on gurneys and curled up in corners. Pervasive moans and weeping clawed at her ears, twisting her insides. She wiped her cheek against her shoulder, hands slick, the man's life pulsing past her fingers.

She bit her lip, fighting the urge to pull talent. Others were worse off, the children huddling together silent. Eyes wide and frightened. She closed her own, trying to un-see. Hands slapped down on hers, and the warmth of talent spread. A Binder, nameless, her face haggard, and then she was gone. All they could do was the bare minimum. An artery repaired, holes left gaping. Kara took up the suture kit, finishing the job through her tears.

She called for a cryo-vac, and a Fetch came over, shifting blood into the man. His color improved. Maybe he would make it.

So many wouldn't.

She wandered through the crush, triaging as she went. Shock. Superficial lesions. Broken arm. Second-degree burn. Gut wound smelling of viscera and bowel—too far gone.

A little boy, separate from the rest. Grey as a medic's uniform, he cradled his hand against his sunken chest, sleeve a sodden, dripping red. Kara stopped, and he looked up at her with eyes devoid of emotion.

"Show me." She held out her hand, and he reluctantly offered it up.

His hand flopped, a wash of scarlet throbbing from the wound. She gripped it and caught the hem of a medic's skirt as she rushed past. "Help him!"

The woman's mouth curdled. "Commons don't have priority."

A black rage washed over Kara and the woman's face was abruptly inches from her own. "Help. Him." The Binder swallowed and her hand shook as she touched the boy, healing him. "Triaging patients does not include social status, do you understand?"

The woman's eyes flicked toward the end of the room where Janice stood, caring for a man with a dislocated jaw.

While others bled out.

Kara slapped her bag of supplies against the woman's chest. "Finish the job."

She was across the room and Janice was jacked up against the wall, her eyes like dinner plates and piss pattering to the floor beneath her. Kara's breath caught at Flynn's frenzied concern, shocking her back from the blackness surging through her. She gritted her teeth swallowing the urge to destroy. The room had gone silent behind her. Even so, she made sure to speak up so they all could hear.

"The definition of triage is to sort and allocate treatment to patients to maximize the number of survivors, not to treat only those whose social status you deem worthy of attention, you pretentious cunt. If I see one more person conveniently overlooked because of some fucked up elitist agenda, I will personally make sure you suffer the exact same injuries, and are left to suffer them." She dropped the woman and turned to address room, staring at her agape. Rogan stood in the doorway, his face a careful blank. "Questions?"

There weren't any.

Janice cowered in the puddle at her feet, and Kara resisted the urge to spit at her before she stalked through the abruptly energized room.

"That wasn't wise, though I couldn't have said it better myself," Rogan murmured, draping a blanket across Kara's shoulders.

"I don't care."

"I know. That's why it's time to go, before you do more damage than they can heal."

"Not yet." She went back to where the little boy was, checking to make sure he'd been cared for properly. The bandaging looked adequate. He peeked at her from beneath a grubby fringe of bangs. "What's your name?"

"Gil, m'lady." His voice was a thready whisper.

"Gil." She smiled at him. "Who do you belong to?"

"M'da's the baker on Quai. Was giving alms—" His bottom lip poked out trembling, and her heart broke.

"Let's get you home, then." She met Rogan's eye as she said it, and he grunted. Not happy, but not gainsaying her, either. Good, because she wouldn't be. Not on this.

If she couldn't use her talent, she'd be damned if she couldn't set at least this one thing right.

VICTOR GRINNED, sucking on the wad tucked inside his lip. Dark had set in, and the conflagration at the back of the building had grown, throwing light all the way to the city. It was answered by random pockets of destruction across the Flats, buildings flickering like birthday candles. To the east, a sea of lights advanced. That'd be Dale's men comin' in, right on schedule. He turned to Sam.

"Set 'em loose." Metal squealed at the back of the transport, and a chorus of baying went up, paws pounding out across the frozen tundra. Victor added his voice to the mix. "Yeah! Dinner time, doggies! Go get 'em!"

The muties sped past, dim lights flashing, a black stain spreading across the flame-lit landscape. Beasts would flush out any freaks left, and shred the ones that was too slow. Howling and slavering, starved into a frenzy, they set upon whomever had the stink of talent. Goddamned freaks weren't nothin' without their devilry. Was time to send 'em all back to hell.

Victor laughed, gunfire sounding from the east, and a scream—

His smile died. Weren't no scream, that was thrusters. His eyes searched the sky, moon yet to rise.

The craft came in low, a striking shadow, slicing above Dale's men, line of fire blooming in its wake. Vehicles exploded, gears and metal torn asunder, sticky blue flames eating steel. Smaller bursts of orange and red flared, gas tanks going up, men thrown clear, rolling on the ground, lying still—

"Gimme that goddamned cannon!"

Sam shrank back. "Dale was bringing—"

Whomps of searing white light in tandem, a heartbeat of false dawn, wind whipping it towards them, tingling, then a burn—

Shit.

The craft was banking, coming back for another pass. It shot over the city, swooping in their direction.

"It's done gone sideways," Sam rasped out.

Victor's hand shot into his pocket, gripping his stone.

Nothing happened.

FITZ PRESSED a hand to his side, breath clouding in jagged spurts. He couldn't stop shaking, the gurney above rattling with him. Only thing warm was what was trickling out his side. His clothes was stiff with rime, skin sloughing away where it'd been exposed when that bomb went off.

Shite. If he were gonna die, be nice t'get on with it—

Rhythmic clicking came from the hall, striking counterpoint to the gurney's rattle. He tensed up—*Jesus, Cajetan, I didn't mean…*

Pulsing points of dim light, red and green, glowed through the sheet thrown over the gurney. One set, then two, bobbing knee-high. Edging into the room.

Click click.

Fitz scrunched his eyes shut, hand squeezing the fabric of his trousers around his coin—Fuckin' muties! He was gonna get eaten by fuckin'—

Snuffing. His eyes snapped open.

Click click.

A crash, skittering back—

Click click.

Advancing. Lapping and the shake of metal tags.

Click.

The sheet rippled.

Fitz's breath caught, scream bound up and choking him. Snuffing and the imprint of a muzzle pressing against the sheet. A low growl. The other set of lights came close…

White light flared through the room, silhouetting the muties. Floor shook, and a godawful groan—

Fitz was thrown back, sheet ripped away, billows of grit and dust turning everything grey. He coughed, agony searing through his ribcage, colors bursting across his vision, darkness eating inward. He fought to stay conscious, taking spastic, tortured breaths.

Fuck, it hurt…

Wind swept in and his teeth chattered. Room were lit by an eerie blue flicker, glittering on the particulate grey still afloat.

Wall, muties—gone. Out on the plateau, fire burned lines of ghost light, studded by blooms of red and orange.

It were pretty.

Fitz's breath fogged out. Tasted like blood. His head lolled.

Black.

FLYNN DEACTIVATED ANOTHER NULLIFIER, and swore at the pounding in his head. How many of the damned things did they have running? That'd been the fourth he'd pulled off a Son's belt. He flung it away and grabbed up the man's sidearm, jamming it into the back of his pants.

This wasn't getting him anywhere, and Kara was losing it. If that asshole hadn't gotten her back to the flat by now… Damn it. Jesse needed to get a jump on those modified bots. He looked up at the squad of Breakers awaiting his command and pointed to the guy missing an ear.

"You're with me. Rest of you rendezvous with the others." They saluted and took off. Flynn went in the opposite direction. It looked like they'd wandered into admin. Should be a quick job to finish clearing this level. Most of the survivors had been in the wards.

Most of the casualties were, too. Christ, the kids—

A woman screamed, and he took off running, leaving the one-eared Breaker in the dust.

The last explosion had just about done in the building. It groaned beneath his boots, portlocks rolling across doorways and walls listing. Sections of ceiling hung free, wires and rebar dangling, partially blocking the hall. An I-beam had crashed down and black gaps of floor were missing. Smoke hung oily and thick, flames providing just enough light for him to know he didn't want to see any more.

He spat, trying to get the taste of death out of his mouth, knuckling it from his eyes—the tap of nails on concrete and low growls sounded behind him.

You gotta be—

Flynn's head turned slow, glancing over his shoulder, hand tightening on his sidearm.

Muties.

There were four of the mutated beasts, and no question they'd been culls. More machine than animal, their implants pulsed red and green, reflecting off bits of metal beneath torn fur, slick with gore.

The woman screamed again, and one sprang at him, the others rushing past. He fired, dropping it, and spun, taking out another before the other two disappeared into a room ahead. One of the muties yelped, the sound fading—Flynn caught himself right at the lip of a gaping hole.

Talents were on the other side, crammed onto a crumbling spit of floor in one corner. Looked like the ceiling had collapsed and kept going, taking out a chunk of wall with it.

The mutie was edging around the jagged rim of the room towards them. Flynn fired and dropped it. The other Breaker caught up, panting. Now how the hell were they gonna—

"Are you two supposed to be the calvary?"

Flynn's attention snapped to the voice, temper flaring. An older woman in a leather dress sneered at him. Was she fucking—

The ground shook again, and the younger women screamed. There was a whomp of sapphire flame out on the plateau. Baelfire, LaVeil's calling card. Kendall and the rest of them were up here, all right. The flickering blue light back-lit two figures. One of them had a mohawk.

Victor.

"Yeah. We'll be right back. I forgot my trumpet." Flynn bared his teeth and wrenched the portlock closed. The Breaker snickered. "Take your time getting help. They're not going anywhere, and I got somewhere to be."

NORA PUSHED the hair from her eyes with the back of a hand, moving through the crush of bodies. The medics she'd brought were spread out amongst the cramped wards, triaging and sending those most in need back to the rooms with beds. Too many people clogged the corridors with panic attacks and superficial wounds. The ones seriously injured cringed in heaps, faces pale, shaking at their sloughing skin. She paused to send talent to a woman, knees drawn up on a gurney, rocking. Eyes wide as the flesh dripping from her fingers became plump and pink again.

Nora moved on, they needed a better system—

There was no time to implement one.

A Binder was up ahead, struggling to take hold of a man thrashing on the floor, a little island of space around them from his flailing limbs. She rushed to their side, throwing out a weave to bind him. Some type of neurosis...the Binder pulled talent and the man went slack. They dragged him to a wall and propped him up, dazed and drooling, but calm.

The Binder stood, much taller than she'd taken him for. He was bald, half his face hidden by large silver goggles, making it impossible to tell his age. It had to be the man Marcos said treated her.

"Pithy?"

He nodded, his fingers moving in an elaborate dance.

"I'm sorry, I don't—"

He motioned for her to follow, and they moved down the hall, a rhythm developing between them as they paused to help those in need. His talent complimented hers, binds setting smoother, weaves made stronger. It was bizarre under the circumstances, but something in Nora relaxed working beside him.

He brought her to a break room filled with Talents in medic greys huddled over steaming cups of tea. He clapped his hands and made a circular motion in the air. They rose as one and headed back out into the fray, glancing at her curiously as they passed.

He stopped a pretty brunette woman several years younger than Nora. That dance of fingers again. She was somehow familiar. His offspring, perhaps? Her fingers danced back, and she turned to Nora.

"He says yer very skilled, and thanks ye for bringing people t'help." Haggard medics trickled past her into the room, expressions creased with that unique cast signaling they were coming to the end of their abilities.

"How could I not?"

Her mouth soured. "Easily."

"Whatever prejudices have existed need to end."

"Ye mean that, don't ye? Good luck." She laughed, holding out a hand. "I'm Umari."

"Nora."

"I know. After this we'll have to make it a point t'become better acquainted. I've always fancied what me sister was like, but I sure as hell didn't think she'd be like you."

———

CARPET FIRE BLANKETED THE PLATEAU, the craft banking for another strike. Its initial attack had given Marcos and the other Breakers some breathing room. They'd been scattered by the second contingent of Sons coming from the east, each scrambling for a defensible position.

Marcos could use one of those right about now. He'd taken a hit to his right calf. Bullet had gone clean through and missed the artery, but it throbbed like hell. He hobbled towards the building, hobbled by the damned thing—bomb strikes hammered behind him, the impact throwing him forward—

His shoulder clipped an outcropping of debris, spinning him to the side. He landed atop a body and pushed off, panting.

A cylinder glinted beneath it.

He wrenched the corpse away and grabbed the nullifier, deactivating it. The shrill keening in his head abated. Thank God—

bullets whizzed past his ear, snicking into the building's facade and raining concrete.

Marcos pulled talent, sending out a wave of force and furrowing the earth to cover his retreat. He hefted himself up and limped for cover, needing to find someplace to hunker down. With the nullifier cut, reinforcements would shift in. He just needed to stay alive until they got here.

Just.

Inside the building was blacker than black, flames sending sporadic flickers of light through the gaps. The stench of wet iron and smoke hung in the foyer. Frigid water pooled ankle-deep in the room, not doing a damned thing for his leg. He waded through the slush, pushing past floaters, feet numb, stumbling on submerged debris. Outside, intermittent gunshots.

Inside, nothing.

The hallway was drier. He shambled down it, to where the wards branched off. A mutie bayed, and he put his back to the wall, sidearm at the ready. Three rounds left. Getting a clear shot was going to be dicey, but outrunning it wasn't an option. The nails tapped to a splash, then a whine, tags jingling and the loping sound of it running back the way it'd come. Marcos let out the breath he'd been holding. Say what you will about the mechanized beasts, but they weren't stupid.

He started picking down the hall again. Place was destroyed, each corridor more of the same, and at the end, the entire back wall of the building had been blown off, doorways open to the plateau, wind whipping through—

A moan and something glinted silver. Marcos crept closer. A gurney, crushed against a ridge of wall, and a young man sprawled beneath. Marcos squinted, sure the faint cloud of breath was his imagination—how in the hell?

He searched the shadows. An ambush? Nothing moved. Cursing himself for a fool, he went in, recognizing the boy by his wide mouth as he got closer.

It was that Fetch…Fitz. He was breathing, but wouldn't be for much longer. Marcos slapped his cheeks, and the boy started with a yelp, clawing at his pocket and coughing. The damned thing was steaming—

He garbled something, his lips flecking crimson.

Marcos sat him up. Sounded like he was drowning in his own blood. "Can you shift, son?"

It took him several tries, his halos weird splinters of light through his irises. What the—

Colors ran.

<hr>

"WHAT D'YOU mean it don't work?"

Sam's face was as pale as a fish's belly in the blue glow. They'd taken cover beneath the bullet-riddled transport, and Victor was trying to figure out how the hell they were gonna get out of there. Smoke roiled across the plateau, and he turned his face from it, choking. Oily grit coated his tongue, searing the back of his throat. He rolled to the side and fumbled at his pocket, pulling out his stone. It was still whole, ain't a goddamned reason why it shouldn't—

A sinking suspicion started in his gut.

"Try it again, looks fine to—what?"

Victor spat to the side, feeling sick. "What if the damned thing uses talent?"

Dale's men were all dead, and the chapter they'd left south of the plateau. God only knew how many of his boys had gotten nixed, and here they were using devilry in the Lord's name. Weren't no surprise he was strikin' them down. Otto had given them the stones and they ain't seen hide nor hair of him since. Victor stopped his fingers halfway to the gem studding his forehead.

She must've known. Sanctioned it, even. *None shall bear the taint of talent…*

"How you figure?" Sam's brow knit, trying to suss it out.

"Worked fine till we switched on them nullifiers, and it ain't gone to dust like the others when they was spent."

Sam looked as sick as he felt. "Think she knows?"

"Nah. S'one of them high laws."

The words tasted worse than the lumps of ash sticking in his craw, and using the damned thing was the only way they were getting out of here. If he was right. Never said how they worked, maybe she'd known he'd been plannin' on tuckin' tail and was lettin' them swing for his lack of faith. Was only one way to find out, once them nullifiers went down.

If they went down before them freaks found them.

They both stared down at the little stone, then up at the scream of thrusters. Craft was making a landing. Troops in fatigues jumped down with semis, taking cover behind the berms thrown up by the explosions. Weren't no one left to pin them there.

Sam and Victor edged back. A mountain of a silhouette was coming up fast from the building's ruins, making a beeline for them, and one hell of a target against the blaze.

Wolf.

Victor drew a bead on him and fired before he'd even had time to think about it.

Bullet hit dead center, and there was a ripple across him like something done ate it. Wolf raised his piece—

Sam slapped his hand down on the stone, and they gated away.

FLYNN'S SHOT tore into empty turf.

He swore, riffling his hair and turned to the craft, ears ringing in the absence of battle. Random shots still studded the gale, but it was clean-up at this point. Mercs had put down any serious resistance. Three of them were headed his way. An old man in a flak vest, flanked by a lanky man with dreads, and a shorter man in an aviator's cap, flames reflecting off the thick lenses. Flynn's chest got tight.

Kendall, LaVeil, and Bates.

Shit. How the hell was this gonna go down? That fucking Northern connection… He looked at the sidearm in his hand. Unchambered the round, and holstered the piece.

Kendall stopped a few strides away, sucking his teeth. He already looked half frozen. Had to be a rude awakening after the Deep South.

"You must be Lord Scot. You're bigger in person. H. Kendall." He came forward and extended a hand. Flynn shook it. If his old CO wanted to play things like this, it was fine by him.

"Not that I don't appreciate it, but any particular reason you're laying down so much firepower on our account?" Kerns had come up beside Bates and LaVeil. Her long blonde braid was gone, and her close-cut hair spiked up. She smirked at him behind the collar of her parka.

"Business down south's dried up as of a few days ago. Decided to take a contract to hunt Sons up here." The wind kicked up, and the group of them edged closer together. "Would've charged more if I'd known how miserable it is."

"Confidentiality one of the terms?"

"Not on this one. House Carmody's footing the bill, but tips are appreciated."

House Carmody—Flynn gritted his teeth. Fucking seers. God, he was an idiot. That made way too much goddamned sense—

An Intelligencer and a Fetch appeared, and Bates's sidearm snapped up. Kerns smacked the muzzle down before he fired. The Talents were oblivious.

"Lord Scot! The Assembly—"

Fuck the Assembly. "You got a cigar?"

The man blinked at him. "Ah...no."

Flynn turned at a crinkling to his right. Kendall held out one of those little cheroots he used to burn through by the case. "Thanks," he said past the lump in his throat, turning it over. "What d'they want?" He knew, but needed a minute.

"An explanation of events. The other Firsts are already there."

Flynn nodded. He lit up and blew out a long plume of smoke, addressing Kendall. "Where you billeting?"

"Someplace called the Manse, heading there now to negotiate a contract extension."

That was the Carmody's estate, way out in the western mountains. He glanced at the craft. "Good luck parking. Whatever you were gonna charge, double it, then report to Stonefist. He'll need a rundown on your capabilities unless you plan on babysitting out there."

The wind kicked up, a blast of smoke and grit making them all hunch down into their collars, sporadic flames flaring amongst the wreckage scattered about the plateau. Christ, what a fucking mess.

"Roger that. You sure you don't want me to tag along now?"

Flynn shook his head. It was gonna be enough of a shit show as it was. "I'll handle it."

"Where've I heard that before…" LaVeil muttered. Kerns elbowed him, and the Intelligencer's eyes narrowed.

Christ, Crandall was gonna jump all over that shit. Flynn sighed, nodding to the Talents.

Might as well get it over with.

CHAPTER THIRTEEN

Rhian [rhi-an] noun

1. *Tattooed markings across a Fetch's back and upper arms comprised of two distinct patterns indicating their maternal and paternal Houses. Completed in increments from birth to majority, and added on to for significant life events, it is believed to portray a Fetch's soul.*

— Excerpt from Glynfyls: A History

"…Though extending our support at this time is impossible, should your ambitions prove fruitful, there are those that would not be opposed to the procurement of any livestock you may have to offer…"

— Encrypted Private Transmission to the Source,
Origin: Deep South

NORA SAT at the break room table, exhausted. Her fingers traced the cracks in its worn Formica top. No matter how many people she'd healed, she was bailing against the tide. None of the procedures in place were geared for the sheer number of people clamoring for attention, and the supply shortages…

She wiped her eyes, doubting they were suffering similarly on the hill. She needed to address that sooner than not, but had zero energy to deal with Janice at the moment. Pithy set a teacup before her, and she wrapped her hands around its welcome warmth. He went back to the thermocoil, stirring a pot of something. She watched his lean back, Umari's words clattering around her skull.

Was he her father? She'd spent the past few hours stealing glances at him, trying to see herself in his features, mannerisms… Nora's files listed both her dam and sire as deceased, but it wasn't outside the realm of possibilities.

Damn Cal. Why wouldn't he have said anything?

She ran a hand over her face. Because he was Cal.

The door opened with a wash of the clamor behind it. Umari came into the room followed by a little tattooed man. She twisted a plain band encircling her ring finger, and Nora's lips quirked. Check one for mannerisms.

"We've a problem. Some idiot shifted laud knows how many infants and children t'the Dove. They're overrun, and I ain't got no idea where to put them—"

More had gotten to safety. Nora stood with a hand to her throat. Her eyes hot. "There's plenty of space at the Assembly Hall. I can show you." Umari traded glances with the little man and colors ran.

Nora stood amidst a sea of eyes. They'd shifted into a grand salon, the worn couches and mounds of pillows awash with children tinted pink by fixed globes of light above. Large burlesque fans of grey feathers adorned windowless walls of plum paper and erotic art. A curtained doorway was at the back of the room behind a marble-topped bar.

Pretty women were scattered about, rocking and soothing the inconsolable wails of squirming bundles. Older children had been conscripted to help, holding their younger brethren awkwardly, but the majority of infants had been laid in rows like sardines. Those too young to help grouped together silently in their pods, their whites torn and soiled. So many—the breath went out of her, and Nora fought back tears, paralyzed by relief. Umari hurried to check on the infants.

The little Fetch was at Nora's elbow. "Ain't no time for that now, m'lady. Ye have an imprint for me?"

"Yes, I...let's get the children not helping with the others settled." Nora wiped at her cheeks and cleared her mind, giving the man the location to shift them to, then approached the first pod.

Shock, a sprained wrist. Scrapes and bruises. The Fetch shifted out with them, and she went on to the next. More of the same. She bound a fractured fibula and a nasty slice to one girl's arm—

A muffled screamed and a door slammed somewhere within the building. Footsteps pounded down steps. Heads turned to the curtained doorway, a middle-aged woman in a scanty robe bursting through.

"A Binder! I need a—"

Nora was at her side, and the woman grabbed her arm, pulling her down a long hallway of closed doors, then up a dark wood staircase. The room they came to was done in soft pinks and beside the bed—

"Marcos?"

"Later." He stepped to the side, revealing a crumped form on the coverlet

Nora pushed past him, her halos washing the room in gold, binding the young man's shattered ribs and repairing the damage to his lung, liver...the perforation to his spleen...Glory, the damage to his internal organs should've killed him...

He groaned, then took a gasping breath. He was blue with cold beneath the radiation burns and filth. She sent talent to his extremities, salvaging the ruined flesh. His clothes were stiff with ice and gore. She began unbuttoning his shirt, he needed to be in drier—

He scrambled away from her hands, eyes wide. The older woman grabbed him before he landed on the floor. He pulled his collar tight around his neck, chest heaving. Behind him, the woman crooned, lifting her hand to pet his matted curls. "Shh...I've got ye..."

He buried his face against her waist, like one of the children downstairs. The woman met Nora's eye. "I'll take it from here."

It was clearly a dismissal.

Marcos put his hand on Nora's shoulder, steering her from the room. He was limping—

"Don't even think about it," he said as she went to pull talent. "I'll live."

Her lips quirked and she slumped against him, doubting she could've done much anyway. Her channel was raw with how much she'd been pulling. That last bit had stretched her limit. They hobbled down the hall together.

"What was that in there?"

"That was Fitz," Marcos said as they made their way downstairs, steadying one another. "Luckiest son of a bitch—you should've seen where I found him. Wall that came down took the rubber off his boot soles…that and you being here—what are the odds?"

Lucky indeed. With the extent of his injuries and how fatigued every Binder in the city was—they pushed through the curtain, the faces beyond it pinched with exhaustion. Nora closed her eyes. Umari was in front of her when they opened.

"They're looking for ye. The Firsts are being called t'Assembly. Trick can take ye with the next batch." The room had cleared out considerably since she'd been upstairs, with several more Fetches shifting in and out. The quality of their clothes indicated one of the Original Houses had become involved.

The little Fetch that'd brought them wearily bobbed his head. "Right then, shall we?"

Marcos's arm tightened around her as Trick's halos flared and colors ran.

***

KARA SAT with Flynn in chambers, sweating. He chewed on a stumpy little cigar, hair at all angles, totally filthy. His clothes were torn and spattered with who knows what, and a nasty strip of cloth wound around his arm, oozing. Why they'd made him rush here just to sit and listen to them fight amongst themselves—

The same frustration was coming from him. How did they ever get anything done? All of them yelling and talking over each other—half the time they didn't even wait for their questions to be answered before they started on some other triviality.

The temperature of the room continued to rise, and it wasn't just because of Flynn's temper. The chamber was packed with the heads of every Original House and their scions. The Fetches has taken over the upper part of the Binder's sextet, other lines bleeding into the aisles and filling the gallery above. Riggs pounded away at his gavel to no avail, finally flinging it over his shoulder in disgust.

"Right," Flynn said as it hit the floor, "I've had enough." He stood, halos flaring.

The room cut to dead silence.

Mouths continued to move, then eyes widened, hands going to throats. He cleared his own, and everyone focused on him. Kara fought not to shrink back. Ugh, how could he stand it?

"Yeah, that's me. It's temporary, unfortunately. Look, I'm tired and need a shower. Now is the time for purpose, not panic. We've won a decisive victory over the Sons, and I'm calling on my bondsmen to use this respite to regroup before the Source is on our doorstep. The Flats need to be evacuated. Those not assigned a Hex should be at the infirmaries assisting the medics…"

His words drained the tension from the air, his confidence infectious. Shoulders relaxed and hands unclenched. Jaws became determined and there were nods. Kara listened to him lay out everything that had happened over the past few hours, from the Source's dissolution onwards. Who was this man, enough at ease enough to bring them ease? He didn't just gain their attention, he commanded it, had a presence.

Was more.

"…though the threat the Sons posed has been mitigated, the fallout from the weapons they deployed remains. Until further notice, the city is on lockdown. Go back to your homes. I want an accounting from all the Firsts on their lines first thing tomorrow morning. Quorum will decide our next steps. Now, if you'll excuse me."

Flynn turned and offered Kara his hand. She blinked before taking it to rise, his weariness breaking her from her shock. He didn't lift his cloak until they'd reached the Assembly doors, still hanging askew from their hinges.

The clamor started when they were halfway down the hall, and by the time the Assembly sent a runner after them, they were stepping through the gate.

As soon as they did, he turned on her, his temper spiking. "Where were you?"

She jerked away from him, his change in mood setting her heart racing. "I—"

"Rogan was supposed to bring you right back here. I felt you flip out, Kara. What the hell happened?" She started to tear up, and her own anger jumped, cutting into his. He raked a hand through his hair, swearing as it sparked, then sighed, looking at the ceiling. "Fuck. I'm sorry. Today's just been one big shit show."

He went to pull her close, and she pushed him away, mad at him for making her cry. "Janice was only treating Original Houses. There was this little boy—" Her stupid tears burst out, and she let Flynn gather her against him.

"He okay?"

She nodded. "Yes, but he wouldn't have been. I—I told the Binders their elitist bullshit had to stop."

"Seriously?" He laughed at her nod. "Good. It does need to stop… what else?"

She told him the rest, and Janice's reaction.

He was less amused, running a heavy hand down his face. "Where was Rogan during all this?"

"By the door. He wanted me to come here, but I had to take that little boy home—"

Flynn pinched the bridge of his nose. "Where?"

"I—his father has a bakery on Quai—"

"Jesus, Kara, that's the sixth rung—"

"I couldn't just leave him there, and they were so…they were so happy… Is that what it's supposed to be like?" The baker and his wife had burst into tears at the sight of their son, the reunion putting a lump in Kara's throat. Her hand drifted across her abdomen, a strange warmth filling her breast. Flynn hugged her tight, his anger leaving him like a switch had been flipped.

"Yeah, if you're lucky." He sighed into her hair.

"The people down there, everyone was supposed to take shelter, but there were so many huddling in doorways and alleys. Don't they have someplace to go?"

"No. A lot of them don't. It gets worst the farther from the hill you go."

Kara chewed her thumb. "Doesn't seem right."

"There's a lot of that going on up here. Soon as a genocidal maniac's not coming with his army of super soldiers to harvest us, we'll see what we can do."

She laughed. He had a point.

FITZ HUDDLED IN THE TUB, water hot as he could stand, arms wrapped around his knees, shaking. Eyes opened, closed. Didn't matter. All the shite he'd seen were burned into his brain, and it weren't going away. His hand rose, tremblin', skin didn't look like pie no more—

The door to the bedroom opened, and he dropped his shoulders beneath the water, pressing them to the back of the tub. Sarah came in with a tray. She put it down by the sink and raised an eyebrow at him.

"Ye just in there marinating? That ain't gonna do." She soaped up a sponge and crooked a finger at him. Fitz looked away. What'd possessed him t'come here? Everything about this were fuckin' wrong, but every damned time—

The water stirred, rising as she straddled his lap and started working the sponge over his chest. He closed his eyes, her fingers massaging up his neck to knead his scalp. God strike him dead, but it felt good. Weren't gonna think about what would feel better.

He wouldn't, afterwards.

Sarah hummed, her fingers working through his hair, teasing out the knots.

"Could use a cut. Yer girl like it this long?"

Christ, this again. "She ain't me girl."

"She know that?"

Fitz's eyes popped open, going to the tray she'd brought. He craned his neck. "S'there a bottle over there?"

"Aye, full of aspirin. I'll trim your hair before ye go. Denis never let it get so long."

"I ain't me da."

"No. Yer still breathing," she snapped, "but it were a close thing. It'd kill me t'lose ye both, Fitzpatrick."

He snorted, tipping his head back for her to rinse. The tips of her breasts skated across his slick chest, hardening. Weren't the only thing in the tub doing that. He kept his hands on its sides, knuckles white. Should shift t'his own damned—the sponge moved over the unfinished rhian licking around his left shoulder, and he tensed.

"Leave it."

"Quiet. Ain't a damned thing on ye I haven't seen."

And that, right there, were the problem. "I've had enough." He slipped from under her, pushing out of the water and grabbed a towel from the floor. Wrapped it around his waist. "I got an extra skin here?" Felt too exposed without one of his undershirts, whether she'd seen his shame before or not. Bare skin on the right side of his back burnt with it. Unfinished rhian on the right weren't much better.

Her eyes ran over him. "No, but Peregrin sent up some clothes. Left 'em on the bed."

Fitz grunted and grabbed a pasty from the tray on his way past. Sarah came to the door in her robe as he was toweling dry. She set the tray on her little table and tapped a comb and pair of shears against her palm, motioning at the chair with them.

"Sit. Ye can finish what I brought up."

His stomach overruled his good sense. He wrapped himself up again and sat. She started working out the tangles, and he winced between bites.

"Helps if ye comb it, regular like."

"Yes, Ma." She smacked the back of his head, and he choked on his mouthful.

"Serves ye right. I ain't nobody's ma, least of all yers."

He mumbled an apology when he could breathe, grabbing another pasty. Snippets of wheat gold curls pattered to the floor, her hand running up the back of his neck before moving to the sides.

"Ye want t'talk about it?"

"No." Shite, he didn't even want to think about it. "Ye ain't got nothing t'drink?"

Sarah stood back with her hands on her hips, robe gaping. Weren't a stitch under it. Fitz kept his eyes on hers, and her lips pursed. "Yer a stubborn one. Ye get that from him."

She went to her bureau and rooted around in the top drawer. Came back with half a pint. Didn't last, but it were a good start. Sarah sighed as he set down the empty, and came to stand between his knees, tipping up his chin.

"Ye drink too much."

"Balances out the gamblin' an' whorin'."

Her mouth turned down. "Almost done."

He closed his eyes, damp curtain of hair between them. She snipped a line at nose level, then fluffed it out, scritching the sides of his head like he were a dog before tucking it behind his ears. Fitz laughed, way he aways did—shite. His smile faltered.

"I can't do this."

"Ye came t'me. This time, and the last—"

"Aye." He scrubbed at his face. Christ, he were fucked up, and this weren't helping. He stood, shrugging into a shirt and pulling on trousers. Took his coin off the bedside table. "Won't happen again." Her face was ashen, but it weren't him she was seeing. "I ain't me da, and ye said it yerself, ye ain't me ma."

"I should've been—"

"Nah," he laughed, "fuckin' me were the end of that. Ye can't have it both ways. I can't have it both ways." And now he weren't gonna have nothing at all. Every fuckin' thing he touched turned t'shite. He shoved his feet into his sodden boots, trying not to see how pale her face had gone, or the lines creasing around her mouth.

"Denis said the same after he bonded that hillie bitch…but he came back. Ye will too."

No. He wouldn't, and he'd damned well make sure of it. Fitz stood, taking one last look at the woman as he gathered up his filthy clothes. "I asked him once. Why he didn't break from her t'marry ye. Told me it were because whores ain't for loving. Not even ye."

Her hand snapped his face to the side, cheek stinging fierce. "And what would a man without a soul know about love?" she spat back.

"Not a fuckin' thing." He glared at her and shifted away, his insides churning.

———

TITUS CACKLED with glee at the holo coming back from the North. The Sons had broken what little spirit the miserable city had, highlighting just how unprepared they were for an assault. It had left the commons in complete disarray, and the those on the hill cowering beneath their bedsheets. The arrival of that mercenary unit wiping out them out afterwards was icing on the cake. There would be no opposition when his troops sallied forth.

He'd reallocated all but a handful of them from the Triam to the Source in anticipation of his next move. There was no longer any point in subterfuge after the Corporation pulled out of the sprawling facility, and his Elites had been encouraged to pillage and destroy. When they marched, there would be nothing for Albanach and the rest of the board to recoup.

A communications orb popped up above Titus's desk and he smirked, answering it. "I was wondering when you'd come slinking back. Calling to get in on the ground floor of a new genetics conglomerate?"

"A bit over confident, aren't you?" Salist lounged on his chaise of pelts, frowning. "And I'd hardly consider assessing the status of our bet slinking. I'm concerned at your ability to pay up after they've frozen your assets and gotten their hooks into that escrow account."

"I'll admit my liquidity has suffered, but it's a temporary setback." He poured himself a glass of bourbon. "Would you like to pay me now, or later?"

The dark man's lips pursed. "Mmm. Been approached for the spoils of war already, have you? I'm not surprised, but I doubt any of them are willing to float you a loan until you've brought that city to heel. Quite a mess up there, as I understand it."

"Indeed." Titus took a sip, sucking air between his teeth at the burn of it, and the situation. Plenty had expressed interest in procuring Talents to replace those the Sons had exterminated, but none were keen on providing support. International sanctions had rendered his income non-existent, and there was limited time before he beggared himself trying to feed his troops. "But the chaos is all to my benefit. Sure you're not interested in buying a stake now?"

"I'm afraid all my excess capital has been tied up in the Corporation's restructuring," Salist said smoothly. He smiled, giving lie to the statement. "Perhaps in a week or two when things have settled down, though I'm assuming all will be said and done by then."

"It will at that." Titus anticipated storming the city's walls within three days, two if he crippled his Fetches. He wasn't opposed to the prospect. There were plenty up there to restock with. "Was that all you wanted?"

"No, as a matter of fact. I was perusing the registry of Talents ceded to the North and couldn't help but note none of the Breakers from Kasham's stable were included."

Titus took another sip of his bourbon. Where was this going? "No, their services fell under a lease agreement." He had no patience for pimping when there were battles to be fought, but that didn't mean he was immune to the potential for profit. "Why?"

"There was one in particular I'd considering holding back for myself, but didn't get the opportunity."

"Oh?" Titus didn't bother to hide his grin. "Then it's too bad you're so short on capital."

"Sadly, I am. However, I do have access to several off-site warehouses of supplies. It would be a shame if there were a security glitch and they were raided."

"That would be unfortunate. Tell me, which one struck your fancy?" A file popped up beside the communications orb and Titus chucked as he reviewed it. "How many warehouses did you say?"

CHAPTER FOURTEEN

Overlord [oh-ver-lawrd] noun

1. *The elected ruler of Glynfyls, historically held by the Talent with the most bondsmen.*

– Excerpt from Glynfyls: A History

"The office of Overlord was a double edged sword. In becoming a living conduit of talent, the recipient of the title was privy to godlike power whilst in the confines of Glynfyls. However, the farther they strayed from the city, the more their power waned, until they became completely bereft of even the talent they were born with…"

– Lord Talos, Preceptor of History,
Academy of Glynfyls

"LOOK, if you don't wanna go, I can't make you," Flynn said, riffling his hair as he and Kara exited the lift. Despite the early hour, workmen were patching the wall he'd put his fist through over a decade ago. At this point, he didn't understand why they bothered.

Kara didn't spare them a glance, too busy stressing out about the Talents that had come up from the Source. Flynn led her down a dingy hallway to the dining room, not knowing how to make that better. Her hiding from them wasn't gonna do it, but he wasn't dragging her there.

He snorted as they entered the long room running the south side of the flat. Someone had thrown a tablecloth over the chippy grey table for twelve, and the crisp linen made everything else look dumpier. Christ, he'd forgotten what a shithole this place was. Figured Lot was too cheap to keep it up, especially if he'd been shelling out for the bower to be maintained. Flynn still didn't get that, even if it had been his mother's sanctuary. His father hadn't given a shit about it when she'd been alive, why had he cared once she was dead?

Kara went over to the thin windows running the length of the wall. Thick metal plates lined their sides. She ran a finger down one, her brow knit.

"This was one of the first buildings designed to hold off the Source. All the windows and doors have plates to seal them off in the event of a siege. I'm sure Cal's gonna ask Nora to update the binds." Flynn tried to keep the rancor out of his voice, joining Kara at the window.

Flat might be a dump, but it was situated smack-dab at the top of the hill, and the view was something else. A dark line of haze hung over the lower portion of the city, then the buildings on the upper rungs stabbed out like a demented crown. The top of the hill was comprised of Gothic stone homes lining cobblestone streets. Beyond all of it was the plateau, and the mountains in the west. From the roof, you could see the bay to the north.

Kara's eyes were glued to the park across the street, bisected by lazy walkways, free of snow and ice. An ornate bridge crossed a stream, burbling despite the cold. The geothermal spring it ran from was why the city had been built here in the first place.

"That's Compton Park. The homes of the oldest Houses surround it. See that roof down there?" He pointed to a spire in the distance. "Assembly Hall's there, on the third rung. We're on the first. There's one for each of the city's founding members. They get a lot wider as they go down the hill; the number of streets doubles every two rungs.

Once the weather gets nicer, you can take me for a drive." He kissed the side of her neck, running his hands over her abdomen. She turned, smiling up at him. Goddamn, he loved her. Them.

"There's no way I'm operating one of those things."

"A car? Sure there is. You'll love it, trust me."

She rolled her eyes, gaze going past him to the door. Cal came in and ripped back the chair at the head of the table to sit, muttering to himself. They went over and joined him.

"Issues?" Flynn asked.

"Several. First and foremost, the wasp's nest you kicked up with that stunt last night. What in the hell possessed you to swing your dick around and silence the entire Assembly? Damned hill's up in arms about it, and with this lawsuit still playing out—"

"We both know that's fucking theater, Cal. They wanna keep it hanging over my head, fine. In the meantime, I'm gonna do my damnedest to keep it attached to my shoulders, along with theirs." No matter how painful it was. Fucking bondsmen.

His grandfather glowered at him. "Regardless, soon as you left, the debate over the pros and cons of you being nullified versus elected Overlord ran hot and heavy. They postponed ruling on your case, and Merchant's having a bird trying to run interference. Think you can tone it down until that gets sorted out?"

"No promises. Anything else?"

"Yeah. The goddamned Source Binders—You need to take their oaths before you meet with Quorum." Cal glanced at Kara. "I suggest you be there."

She narrowed her eyes at the way he said it, and Flynn pushed back in his chair. "Why?"

"I don't know how they managed it with the lockdown, but someone's given them an earful, and the back biting and social climbing has begun."

Kara scrubbed at her face, her irritated dread coloring their bond.

Flynn looked between them. "What's that supposed to mean?"

"I'm bred. That makes you fair game. Any of them will be happy to step over my gestating body to get to you. I'm sure they're already jockeying to see who gets first dibs at being your second."

"So what the hell is me taking their oaths gonna do?"

"It's gonna slip a leash on them before they know which end is up," Cal snapped.

Christ. Flynn gave a weak laugh and ran a hand through his hair. Fucking Sourcies. Servants began bringing in breakfast. His stomach growled. Nora and Marcos came in and his appetite died. Goddamn, living here was gonna suck. Too bad shacking up with someone like Lot had wasn't an option.

Cal turned his pissy mood on Nora. "You need to nip this bullshit with your line in the bud. If they've already got their sights on becoming Flynn's second, you better believe Serra's jockeying to snag First out from under you."

Nora didn't blink as she sat. "I'm aware of the situation, Caliban. Thank you."

Flynn snorted. What a fucking bitch. Kara chewed on her thumb, staring at her pancakes. Goddamn, he wished he could make this easier for her. "Hey, we'll figure it all out, okay?"

She nodded and picked up her fork, pushing food around her plate.

Damn it. He gritted his teeth and turned to Nora and Marcos. "You two need to set those weaves on the gates, priority on the Assembly Hall and government buildings. I'm assuming the Binders you brought up are capable of helping Jesse?"

"Yes, they should make quick work of it."

Flynn grunted, finishing his breakfast. Nora and Marcos left before he was done, allowing him to almost enjoy it. None of Kara's was gone when they stood to leave. Flynn frowned, about to say something when he realized Cal had followed them through the gate. The hell? His grandfather rarely ventured into the city. Twice in one day had to be a new record.

"Binders are on the lower level," Cal said. "We'll have to find better accommodations for them soon, though I haven't the foggiest where. Damn city's packed as it is. I've got a half dozen air transports arriving the day after tomorrow with the rest of the Talents from the Source, and that bit about evacuating the Flats didn't help."

Whatever. It needed to be done. "They institute the lockdown?"

"Yeah. Assembly's a bunch of idiots, but they're not suicidal. Rest of it went through too, though they're not happy about it. Despite Quorum holding the reins, all of them plan on being there this morning. Suggest you bring your A game."

His A game. Flynn snorted. He didn't give two shits if they were happy or not.

He fell into step with Kara. Her face was grim, and it felt like she was psyching herself up for a fight. Crap. His anxiety ticked up. The empty halls didn't help. It was eerie without the usual bustle of people.

They took a lift down to a large cafeteria. Cots lined the stark room, and people were milling about, eating breakfast. Nora was speaking to a group in the corner. She looked up as they entered, and the rest stopped to stare at them. Flynn stared back.

Every one of them a specimen of physical perfection, and not one of them wearing anything remotely appropriate.

They looked like the cast of a very large porn production.

Glynfyls was gonna have a bird. He shook his head, trying to pay attention to what Cal was saying.

"...Lord Scot, to take your vows of fealty."

Flynn was abruptly the catch of the day. Women, and men alike licked their lips and tried to better display their assets. Kara's agitation was like a living thing in the back of his brain. It completely drowned out the anxiety she'd been feeling a moment before. He cleared his throat, trying to push past it.

"Welcome to Glynfyls. I apologize for the poor accommodations, but we've been rather beset upon of late. I'm hoping your presence will help us turn the tide. As Cal explained, I'll need your oaths in order for you to move freely about the city once the lockdown is lifted. I'd recommend warmer clothing beforehand and will see what I can do to facilitate that." There were a few nods and some discussion.

A handsome, dark-haired man in a sheer shirt and tight leather pants was openly appraising Kara. Flynn put his arm around her, not appreciating him eye-fucking his wife. She snuggled against him, and he tamped down a surge of anger. Cal hadn't understated it. This was a nest of vipers.

"Well, let me be the first to kick things off," Nora said, offering her palm.

Christ, she was the last fucking—whatever. He flipped his knife into his hand and slashed open the pink scar bisecting the other, fighting to keep his expression blank as they exchanged talent.

That prick that'd been staring at Kara was next. He let the man take a good long look at his halos, gripping his hand hard enough to feel the bones shift. From his expression, he got the message. A voluptuous brunette in a short chiton followed him. Shit, it was the screamer from the Creche.

Flynn glanced at Kara, leaning against the edge of the table beside him, her revulsion for the woman like nothing he'd ever felt from her. This had to be—

"Tamara Hess." She held out a hand like she expected him to kiss it, smiling coyly when he didn't. Her gaze was molten sex. So was the rest of her. "I can't overstate how much I'd enjoy being your second."

She went to move against him—

Her hand scrabbled at the golden band of light around her throat, feet kicking for purchase. The room gasped.

Kara's halos burned.

"*He is mine,*" she gritted out. "There are no seconds in Glynfyls. If you've got a problem with that, I'll personally see you left outside the wall for Titus's Breakers."

She dropped talent, and Tamara fell to the floor, taking in great sobbing gulps of air. Flynn ran his gaze over the speechless crowd and put his arm around Kara.

"In the North, the bond of marriage is sacrosanct, and her reaction pales in comparison to mine, should anyone be stupid enough to make a pass at my wife. I suggest you assimilate quickly." He flicked his gaze at Tamara, rubbing her throat and glaring daggers at Kara. "When pledging fealty to House Scot, you're also pledging to her, and if that's an issue, I'll see you outside the gates myself."

"That won't be necessary." He glanced up at the ingratiating voice. It was that bitch that'd asked if he was the calvary. "Serra Hess. I apologize for my offspring's ignorance and promise it won't happen again. Let's move this along, shall we? We're all so eager to be of service. My House in particular excels at healing, which I hear you're in great need of?"

Flynn pursed his lips, wishing he hadn't shot that mutie. "Yeah. Nora can get you registered with the medics." The woman's face pruned, and he didn't give a shit. "Of equal importance is using your talent in the defense of the city. There are structural binds on the wall that need reinforcing. Those with the strongest work ethic will be given priority housing." When he could find some. "Any questions before we proceed?"

They shuffled their feet, but the rest of the oaths went smoothly, if awkwardly. Flynn's hand throbbed to his shoulder as the last was taken, enough to let Nora bind it. Cal smirked at him, and Flynn scowled, pulling Kara close.

"No more talent," he murmured, feeling her exhaustion. She'd skipped her shake along with breakfast, and now that she wasn't all keyed up—damn it. He understood why she'd pulled, but didn't like it. Shit, he didn't like anything about these assholes. "Come on, I need to meet with Quorum."

They left Cal with the Binders, and took the lift with Nora back upstairs. A woman was mopping the floor and a sour smell hung in the air. Someone infected with bots had come through the gate.

"Who?" Flynn asked, stopping in front of her.

She paused in her work. "Lord Patton, sir. He's resting in the lounge."

Flynn grinned, heading in that direction. This he had to see.

Klaus was splayed out in a chair, devoid of his usual grace and smelling like the stomach flu. "Come to gloat?" He took a swig from a bottle of water, swished, and spat it into a bucket beside him. "I haven't expelled my guts so thoroughly since you talked me into sampling the buffet at the Red Skirt. I suspect I should count myself lucky that this won't come with a side of clap."

Flynn snorted. That hadn't been his fault; even he'd given the fish a wide berth. Klaus shot him another dirty look and reached inside his waistcoat pocket. He held out a bank note.

"Here. I'm trying to reconcile the last of Gerrard's books and start fresh. That's what the Pony owes you after last weekend."

"Start fresh?"

Klaus stroked his goatee, smug. "Yes. He took one hell of a bath with that fight, and I bought him out. I suppose I should thank you, but since you're not a fan of flowers, that cheque will have to suffice."

The sum was more than considerable. "Holy shit."

"Indeed. Renting the ring for those Breaker trials is the only thing keeping me solvent at the moment, but a debt made is a debt which must be paid. If you ever tire of this respectability nonsense, I'd love to have you back." He ran his eyes over Kara. "I'd love to have you any way I can get you."

She laughed at the bedraggled man. "Forgive me if I'm not tempted."

"A boy can dream. Now, if you'll excuse me." He hefted himself up and tottered from the room.

Flynn stuffed the note into his pocket and turned to Kara, the chime for Quorum sounding. He ignored it. Wasn't like they were gonna close the doors on him. He ran his fingertips down the side of her face. She was fading again. "Go back to the flat and drink that shake before you end up with another IV."

She glowered at him, but didn't argue. "Thank you for what you said downstairs."

"I meant it, Kara. You're mine and nothing's gonna change that." His lips brushed against hers then kissed her in earnest. Goddamn, she was addictive…

"Ah…ahem…Lord Scot?" A voice interrupted a long moment later.

Flynn sighed, his forehead against hers. "Yeah?"

"They're waiting for you, sir." A man in livery stood in the doorway.

Christ, this was gonna suck. "Duty calls," he murmured, tracing a thumb over her dimple. She smiled, and he jogged down the hall to chambers, wanting to get this crap over with.

The room was packed, and creepy silent, his boots loud on the steps, eyes drilling into him. Shit. Cal hadn't overstated it.

Flynn's throat bobbed. They were gonna hang him. His steps slowed and he wet his lips, halfway to his box—

A surge of Kara's alarm tore through him.

Flynn went rigid, his head snapping around. "KARA!" he bellowed, gasps coming from around him, then Riggs's gavel pounding on the lectern at the outcry as Flynn tore back up the steps, pell-mell, his sense of her dwindling…

He burst into the lounge, heart in his throat, panting—

A chair on its side, spray of blood across the wall… His awareness of her winked out.

No.

Flynn's stomach dropped, head light and cold sweat pebbling his body. *You son of a bitch…* He stumbled back, disbelieving. Frantic rage welling up from his core. Gone. She was gone! How the fuck could she be gone?! *No no no no nooo…* His back hit the wall, vision stained red—

You fucking took them, took them!

A primal scream scraped from his throat and a wave of force exploded outward, blowing through the floor, the wall—the side of the Assembly building vaporized and untempered force erupted into the street and through the Judiciary across the way. Windows shattered, dust and debris graying the air, the Judiciary groaned, shifted, and shook.

Crumbled.

He fell to his knees, numb to the destruction. Unseeing. Unable to feel Kara. The babies. Flynn laughed. *It's my fault, all my fault. I fucking —no. Please, God, don't—*

Cries of terror throughout the building and outside went unheeded. Sirens blared. He gripped his head, keening. *Fuck. You did. You did and they're gone.*

His rage crested. Bloodlust thickened the air, roiling outward to drown the city beneath dank, inky waves of his building fury. Blinding, tearing pain seared through Flynn's temples. He gave into the blackness of his despair, lashing out with another blast of rage dwarfing the first.

What the fuck do you want from me?! Damn you, you fucking prick, take me!

Metal squealed and concrete vaporized. The building behind the Judiciary disintegrated, then the one behind it. Fires erupted. Screams turned shrill. Smoke. Flames blazing across stone, whipping into the air. Glass from the surrounding buildings imploded, peppering the devastation in the streets.

Manic laughter ticked up his throat. She was gone. Kara was gone. Her, his kids—talent plucked at him, inciting his rage—

It could all fucking burn.

His bloodlust redoubled. Blackness welling, the air gelatinous with it. A tornado of flame surged forth, his wrath pulsing raw—

Something snapped.

Talent slammed into him, knocking him down. His hands hammered onto the floor and it buckled with an alarming groan. Flynn screamed, the influx of power scraping his insides raw, searing into him through every bond he'd taken. Talent filled him to the breaking point, and overflowed—

Into Kara.

Flynn's head jerked up, feeling her blaze back at him, talent echoing between them—

Images tumbled through his mind's eye. A squalid room. Kara rigid in a corner, halos burning like twin suns. People falling back from it. A man in Assembly livery, face hidden by a towel.

A growl rumbled through Flynn's chest, and a knife was in his hand.

His teeth locked together, fighting to separate out the power he needed, wrestling for enough control—Getting to his feet.

And stepping through.

Colors ran.

Kara.

THE BOY DISAPPEARED.

Cal sagged against the door frame, wiping at the blood in his mustache, his ears, staggering against the wall beneath the storm of righteous fury bombarding him. Behind him, all the Firsts save Crandall were similarly affected, staring at the spot the Flynn had stood a moment before.

Hadn't taken him long to figure out that trick.

Beyond the ravaged room, Glynfyls burned. Shit. Cal wiped his mustache again.

No fucking promises, all right. Christ, he needed a cigarette.

The Firsts pushed past him into what was left of the lounge, staring out over the destruction, the sky black as midnight, clouds swirling, blotting out the sun. They exchanged shocked glances before quickly looking anywhere but at each other, their halos on full display. Yeah, that was gonna take some getting used to.

Phyllis was just about hyperventilating, as pale as a woman could get this side of the grave. The rest of them weren't too steady either.

"What in God's name just happened?" Lord Klein asked, wobbling against the debris.

Cal struck a match, smell of sulfur thicker than it should've been. He lit up, smoke swallowed by the particulate in the air. "If I'm any judge, boy just took Overlord." He was, but they didn't need to know that. He didn't need to feel guilty about it either, damn it.

Crandall sputtered. "What do you mean he *took* Overlord? The Investiture—"

"Wasn't instituted until after the first Overlord abdicated, breaking his connection to those that'd sworn fealty to him," Phyllis murmured. "The Alpha Prime accessed their talent when he was unable to find the body of his one true love. He didn't need the Investiture."

That's because there wasn't a body to find.

Cal sighed and took another drag, sourly studying his cigarette. Another surge of rage poured through them. That he could do without. Flynn had always been too damned emotional. Was gonna be one hell of an inconvenience until he figured out he had to cloak it.

"Boy's worse than a woman." Nora shot him a look, and Cal shrugged. "No offense."

Phyllis hadn't heard him. She stared out at the destruction, resigned. "Breakers don't do anything small."

Markham shook his head at the sudden bolt of enraged satisfaction jolting through them.

"Good Lord, is he—" Lord Klein swallowed back the question. "Where did he go?"

"To get his wife back." Cal took another drag, wincing at the malevolence battering him. "And I'm gonna guess he's found her."

BARTON PACED THE SQUALID ROOM, darting glances at the unconscious woman in the corner. She'd been more resilient than expected. The dart should've knocked her out instantly, but she'd stayed on her feet a good thirty-seconds after it'd hit.

He swallowed blood, dizzy. Swapped out the gore-soaked towel for another. The bitch had split him from one ear through to the other side of his face with the dart he'd hit her with, severing the carotid artery in his cheek. He needed to find it. Shift the wound.

Couldn't.

She'd done something to his talent and he wasn't able to access it anymore. His hand slapped against the wall. Swaying. Staggering. Stumbling.

Screwed.

And trapped like a rat. He'd sent a message to the Fetch in Titus's cell, but too much time had passed, and something was happening at the Assembly Hall.

Two loud explosions, rattling the windows hard enough to crack glass three rungs away. People running through the streets. Screaming. Pointing. The clouds swirling, noon-time dark as night.

Apocalyptic. Scot was of consequence. Barton's eyes darted to the girl. So was she.

They needed to move.

The towel was dripping again. He rucked up a bed sheet, disgusted. Sloppy. He was never sloppy—

Barton spun, hissing. Two men and a woman had shifted in, angry.

"You're not supposed to make contact, this had better be—oh, shit."

"I'd say that qualifies," the other muttered.

The woman crouched beside the Jester girl. "What'd you give her?"

He pointed at a vial on the table, his vision pricking gray at the edges.

Tasting his death.

"What the hell—" One of the men stared out the window at the swirling clouds.

Kara went rigid, sucking in a great, gasping breath. Her eyes sprang open, halos blazing like the sun. Barton turned away, hiding his face in the sheet—

It went dark and he couldn't move.

Fixed.

Slow boot falls. Sound of a knife singing through flesh. Bodies thumping to the floor.

The sheet was ripped away.

Scot towered before him, his halos a fiery maelstrom. They dominated his eyes with an unworldly malevolence, overtaking his irises. He seethed with rage. It rolled off him in thick, cloying waves, the air too dense to breathe.

The room was stippled and striped vermillion, gore pooling on the floor.

Like the train's engine room, out on the plateau.

Scot licked the spatter from his lips, and ran a blade up Barton's throat, the azure motes in his eyes churning. Azure? What talent—

Not talent. Other. The taste of graveyard midden filled Barton's mouth.

"You're not getting off as easy." Scot smiled and grabbed Barton's collar, dragging him across the room. The corpses on the floor turned to ash as they passed. Scot dropped him to gather the girl up like a child, holding her close, his boot crushing Barton's throat.

Colors ran.

They shifted to the Assembly's lounge, or what was left of it. The western corner of the building, gone. Barton's thoughts raced, pulse throbbing in his cheek. None of this was logical. What kind of creature was Laughlin Scot—

A woman cried out. Quick patter of footsteps. A sigh.

"She's been sedated, but isn't harmed."

"You need to scrub us and keep this one alive." Scot's boot took Barton in the side, flipping him onto his stomach. "For now." A wave of nausea overtook the assassin and he retched, vomit searing his wound. His vision grayed, then was carried back on a wash of golden talent.

A small man with a greasy little mustache squatted beside him, his halos pulsing plum. "Marvelous."

"Don't say I never gave you anything."

"And it's not even my birthday. I've just the place to put him. I have a feeling he'll require more strident questioning than the constabulary will be comfortable with."

An old man smoking sauntered over and flicked his ash on Barton's face, singing the crease of his eye. "I'll go with you. Think I know just how to get him warmed up."

Barton would have shivered if he could. He could tell the old man didn't bluff.

<hr>

ROGAN BROODED, arms crossed, leaning against the cavern's wall and fighting to rein in his bloodlust. He'd leaked enough to create a wide buffer between him and the rest of the Breakers jostling for space. It was in short supply. The conclave was packed, waiting for someone to clue them in on what'd just happened.

It wasn't gonna be him. Putting out that fucking inferno had been enough. Kid had no idea what he was doing, what he was capable of—

Goddamn it. It wasn't his problem.

Rogan hawked and spat to the side, trying to get smoke and the dankness of what the kid had blanketed the city with out of his nose. That cluster fuck at the Assembly Hall had dropped every Breaker within a ten block radius. The shit was still swirling through the streets and creeping into the conclave on people's clothes. Pervasive fingers of dominance bending the knees of every Breaker in the city.

Well, less one.

Rogan made a concerted effort to unclench his jaw. Kid hadn't been challenging him, but the results were the same. He hadn't wanted to beat the fuck out of someone like this in God knows how long.

He frowned as Voss approached.

Man smiled and leaned against the wall beside him with a sigh. Didn't seem particularly concerned about his halos showing, but that had always been a civ hangup. There was no hiding where the hierarchy was concerned, though Rogan had to admit there were more duals in the crowd than he'd expected. Good. Maybe it would put an end to that twist bullshit when people realized how many of them there were.

Not that he'd put money on it. All of it was—Goddamn it. Why was he even here?

Voss's thumb worried his staff, looking over the assembled crowd. "You clue him in, or did he figure it out himself?"

"Which part?"

The old man chuckled. "I was referring to him taking Overlord as you did, but if you want to talk about the firestorm you had to snuff, we can."

"I don't want to talk about any of it." Fucking kid was a goddamned liability, and people were getting hurt. More were going to. He needed—

"He needs a Menot."

Goddamn it.

Rogan's jaw clenched. "Good luck with that."

"And here I was going to wish you the same." Rogan frowned at him, and Voss smiled. "You know, that whole familial mentor thing…"

"I swear to Christ, if you start quoting that fucking book—"

Voss laughed, drawing stares from around the room. He pushed off the wall. "Well, that's as good a segue as any…" The crowd of Breakers parted as he strode forward, then reformed in his wake as he passed through them to the center of the sands. A sinking feeling had started in Rogan's gut that didn't have a damned thing to do with the shitty bottle of liquor he'd downed before getting here.

The Menot pounded the butt of his staff against the sands thrice. "I speak the Way."

"We listen," the room intoned, touching between their brows.

"Then hear the council's judgement. Like the Alpha Prime, Laughlin Scot has taken the power of the Overlord through might instead of Investiture." Excited whispering sped around the room, and Voss's eyes met Rogan's.

Shit.

"In this, the Way is clear. Such power cannot remained unchecked outside of the hierarchy. Blood calls to blood! The council has assigned Lord Firestorm as Lord Scot's Menot to bring him into the fold."

The room stared at Rogan and he laughed. "You gotta be—"

"I believe it was you who reminded me that the trials have knocked everyone from their rung. You're no exception, and have yet to regain your status as Alpha Prime to counter our ruling."

What a dick. The old man smiled.

"So sayeth the Way," the room intoned.

They could all fuck off. Voss raised that staff of his into the air again. Rogan could think of a better place to put it. Wasn't gonna get involved… Christ, forget about hip deep, he was drowning in this shit, and for once, he couldn't blame Cal.

Oh wait. Yeah, he could.

"Hear the council's final will! The Source approaches with their Alpha. Ours must be prepared to meet him, a united hierarchy at his back." Voss's eyes found Rogan's again. "You have three days to meet each other on the sands and submit—"

Rogan turned and left, having written the book on what would happen if they didn't.

FITZ SHIFTED INTO THE 'PIPE, gripping his eye with one hand and his trousers with the other, tripping over the bodies beneath his feet. Somebody swore and pushed him into the wall.

The hell? Place were mobbed and silent as a tomb, everyone focused on the reel playing behind the bar. He zipped up his pants and spotted Scotty in a corner. He waded over and his friend tipped his tam at him, both of them doing a double take.

"Yer flashing colors—"

"Adelaide?"

Fitz grunted, flickin' a hank of hair over the shiner. Didn't want to talk about it. Shite, everyone in the bar was wearing sunglasses or had hats pulled low. "What's all this?"

Scotty looked at him like he'd been livin' under a rock. Between Kendra's thighs were close. He winced, dabbing at the goose egg swelling his face. Was gonna be blacker than original sin.

"Anyone who pledged is flashing colors. Word has it somebody tried t'shanghai Scot's lady. Took Overlord without them hillies giving it t'him t'get her back. Assembly Hall's been blown t'shite, eight blocks is burnt t'the ground, city's on lockdown, and Markham's ordered all the warehouses and public buildings t'take people in. Where the hell ye been? He's looking for ye."

"Eh…around. He say what for?" An old woman in sunglasses shushed them, and Fitz frowned. Reel was showing a pile of rubble. Christ, that'd been the Judiciary. Guess he weren't gonna worry about paying that last fine.

"Somewhat about yer cousin, but that were before this fucking mess. Hear tell all them Firsts is holed up at Assembly."

"Not a fuckin' chance I'm going—"

"Shhh!"

Fitz scowled at the old woman, and she returned it. Rotten old bat. Whatever. Markham could wait. Arileo weren't going nowhere.

"Ye find him?"

"Eh…nah. Keep having t'pick up his jobs."

Fitz spotted Molly behind the bar and shifted to the clear space beside her. She screamed and slapped him right in the goose egg. Stars exploded.

He blinked his good eye, looking up from the floor, face throbbing somewhat fierce.

Molly looking down at him in horror. "Oh! I didn't—" Her eyes welled up, and she ran into the back. Christ. He scraped himself up to sit, head ringing. Marl peered over the edge of the bar, a bevy of smirking onlookers behind him.

"Ye got a problem?"

Old man pursed his lips and sat back, the rest of them snickering from sight.

Molly ran back out with a bundle and crouched beside him. "I'm so sorry, I didn't mean—"

She pressed it to the side of his face and he winced. Ice. Shite, that smarted. He took it from her. "Eh…not that I ain't appreciative, but whiskey would do me better."

Her brow furrowed and she went into the back again. His head throbbed too bad to enjoy her change of heart. Christ, how the hell

Adelaide figured he'd be at the Skirt messing with Kendra… Think she could've put that much effort into tracking him down when he were dying in a ditch.

Shite, that weren't fair. He grimaced, rocking his jaw. Whole side of his face were fucked. An' all on account she'd heard tell he'd shifted to Sarah, not her. Granted, he weren't in the best position t'explain when she'd found him—Christ, why the hell should he? Didn't owe Adelaide naught. Whatever he'd said t'make her think she had a claim on him… He adjusted his grip on the ice, wincing.

Molly came back with a fifth of top shelf. He traded it for the ice. Shite. Maybe his luck were changing—

"Where is he?" Adelaide's voice rang out and the low murmur of voices cut off.

Nope. *Fuck me life.*

Molly stepped close, skirts blocking him from view before he could shift. Now this could be interesting. He pulled his legs up to listen.

"Was here a spell ago," Marl said. "Got slapped and dropped right out o' sight."

Snickers.

"Serves the pig right. Ye see him, tell him he ain't clear, not by a long shot."

Shite. Last time she were this pissed, it'd been a month before he'd been able t'show his face. Every time he'd turned around she'd been waiting t'pound him. Needed a place t'hole up, else she'd sniff him out. The 'Pipe…his room…would've threatened Craig and Scotty on the way out, and her beating Kendra wouldn't make him popular at the cat houses. Weren't desperate enough t'go t'his grans… Eh, maybe he were. He ticked off the days since he'd seen her last. Nope. Not nearly long enough t'suffer though that—

Molly knelt down beside him, her eyes narrowed. "She's gone. What'd ye do?"

Fitz cracked the bottle and took a long swallow. Damn, that were smooth. He met Molly's big green eyes. Fuck it. "Shifted t'me step-ma's after the plateau instead of her. Then she caught me with a whore she ain't on good terms with." He tipped the bottle back again, bracing for another slap.

"It true ye saved all them littles?"

Shite. "Eh…why? What've ye heard?"

Molly rolled her eyes. "Yer the shiftiest Fetch I've ever met, Fitzpatrick McCreedy. Now answer me. Yes or no?"

He shrugged and looked away, cursing hisself for a fool. Shifted too damn many of 'em, but how could he not? Still, thems on the hill got wind of it…nothing good could come of fessing up t'that.

She sighed, her voice soft. "Take this imprint. Stay in the loft, she won't find ye there, nor will me da. He do, and that black eye'll be the least of it. Me shift ends in an hour. I'll bring ye out somewhat t'eat then."

A lump was in Fitz's throat. "Why in the hell would ye do that?"

Her hand brushed the hair from his good eye. "Yer a rogue, but ye can't be half of what ye pretend if what I heard tell ye did's for true. Now take it, before I change me mind." She rested her hand on his cheek giving him an image.

He pulled talent and was there before she could see him cry.

CHAPTER FIFTEEN

Contract [kŏn'trăkt] noun

1. *A legal agreement between Houses, most often associated with a scion's bond, and resulting in betrothal.*

– Excerpt from Glynfyls: A History

"Aging out is a solemn time for any Breaker. Physically unable to compete with their younger brethren, the Breaker willingly relinquishes their rung. Some seek solitude, or the absolution of a glorious death in battle. Others become Menot or Banes, the highest calling an aged Breaker can aspire to. As lore keepers and scholars of the Way, it is their duty to guide future generations, ensuring the honor of our line…"

– Lord Grimmight, Breaker Menot,
Glynfyls

TITUS STOOD on the balcony overlooking the Source's battle plain. The troops assembled below stood at attention in precise formations, paragons of military excellence.

It should have been a satisfying moment, but the last transmission from Barton's bots had sucked the savor from it.

He'd lost the girl, and her retrieval was no longer a delay Titus could afford. Salist's warehouses, stocked as they were, would only buy him a few more days. Titus grimaced, turning to Brix, the Peacekeeper that had replaced the Commandant. The setting sun glinted off a gold hoop below the ragged notch in his ear.

"We deploy first thing tomorrow morning to join those at the border. Weiss will shift the last of our men from the South as soon as they arrive, but I'm not waiting any longer."

The Breaker grunted. "Orders for the Triam?"

Titus's black mood redoubled. He'd pulled all but two squads and put the last of his funds into maintaining services. It had left him destitute. "The females will remain where they are until we secure Glynfyls and assess the situation. They're far too precious to risk on campaign."

Brix grunted again, satisfied. Titus tried to keep a straight face. What would the Breaker do if he knew the facility and its inhabitants were scheduled to be expunged if he didn't countermand his orders within two weeks?

A smile jagged across his lips, and the Breaker looked away.

Titus gripped the railing in front of him. The icy metal stung his hands through his thick leather gloves. Weather modifications had been the first expense to go. He pressed the button for comms, his voice booming out over the field.

"The Source has been disbanded, releasing us from any previous obligations or restraints. Tomorrow, we go north to take what should be ours. Rape, pillage, and rend! Cause havoc! Your orders are to bring the storm out of which a new society will arise!"

The men below gave a single oomph, then went silent. Titus's smile was ice.

Glynfyls would be his.

KARA'S EYES FLUTTERED OPEN, groggy. What had—someone beside her stirred and she attacked, hands crushing around a burly neck, then closing on empty space. What?

"I missed you, too."

Flynn.

She whipped around.

He sat behind her, rubbing his throat. She gave a great sob, throwing herself at him. "I knew you'd find me."

"I told you, nothing will take you from me, Kara. Nothing." He held her close, breathing her in. She pulled back to kiss him and gasped. His halos covered his irises, swirling like a tempest. Glory, they drew her…

He put a hand to her cheek. "Your eyes," he whispered. "They've gone gold."

His lips found hers, talent resonating between them, playing off their bond. Flynn's kiss, first tender, then intense. His need for her searing through there bond, meeting her own desire and redoubling. This man…

Her love.

Dark musk filled the air, setting her aflame. Shirt on the floor, skin on skin, arching against the pillows, his mouth hot through the satin of her nightie, working down her body, teasing…

No, not…not yet. She pulled him back up by his ears, needing—he kissed her hungrily, and she returned his fervor, her 'lust churning. Wanting to dominate. To be dominated. She strained against him, struggling to flip him onto his back. He grinned, capturing her wrists above her head and twining his fingers with hers.

Kara squirmed, unable to break his grip. How…? He chuckled and her 'lust rose up at the implicit challenge echoing between them. Flynn grinned again, releasing her with a gentle kiss. His hands slid to her hips, carrying her with him as he rolled over, letting her take control.

Something between them quickened, and the world contracted.

Kara, pushed up, one hand on his chest. Straddling him, her breath coming fast. Her head dropped back, rolling over her shoulders with a low moan, hair dusting over his thighs. She wet her lips, focus narrowing to her mate beneath her. His pupils blew out, intent on her, mouth parting with ragged breath.

Their bloodlust surged.

It suffused her, seducing. A different flavor of teasing darkness. Her fingers curved to drag her nails down his chest and a growl rumbled from beneath them, his hands bruising upon her hips. His gaze locked on hers, rising from the bedsheets—

Her palm took him across the cheek, snapping his face to the side.

FLYNN GROWLED, the lines of fire from her nails and that slap going straight to his dick. It jerked, hard as fuck and aching to be buried between her thighs. This woman. A goddess astride him. Hair wild, cream satin nightie poured over her curves, nipples erect and begging for his mouth. His nostrils flared, the room thick with her scent, taunting him…

Her pouty lips tipped up in challenge as he pushed up to sit, pulling her onto his lap. "Can I help you with something, Laughlin?"

He grunted, her playful demeanor throwing him. Taking him back to the teasing vixen she'd been in the woods behind the farm…chasing her through the snow… Flynn jerked her hips closer and slid his rigid length against her honeyed core. Wanting to feel that with her again, the animal in him rising. Christ, the things he wanted to do to her… His mouth watered, her scent thick in his nose.

Kara's lips brushed against his ear. "Use your words, and ask for it."

An animalistic surge of passion shot through him. "If you're gonna hit me, I suggest you do it harder, 'cause when I fuck you, I promise it's gonna hurt."

A coy smile tipped up her lips, her anticipation surging through their bond. "Say please."

He tongued a canine, his grin feral. "Please."

She hauled back and slugged him, jacking him against the headboard. Flynn grunted, seeing stars, the air going out of him as he hit, head snapping back, gasping at the heat of her desire searing through their bond—

She was on him. Her mouth colliding with his, devouring, nails raking his scalp, ripping at his hair. She bit his lip, his blood on her tongue, thrusting against his. Emotions tangling, their bond rife with carnality. A rumble in his chest, fire in her core. Her scent enveloped him, a heady perfume. She inhaled along the length of his throat, moaning—

Then sprang away, laughing.

RUN. She wanted to run. On the bed, Flynn's surprise changed to a grin. He got to his knees, crawling across the king-sized mattress, stalking her like a beast. Hair wild and eyes burning with the anticipation of the chase, he grinned, the swirling maelstrom of his irises locked on her. He dropped a foot to the floor, edging around the footboard. Kara backed toward the doorway—

He lunged, and she bolted with a scream, through the doorway and vaulting over the sitting room couch. Flynn crashed after her, flipping it on end in pursuit.

She slipped from his reach and spun, tagging him with a kidney shot and laughing. He grunted, and she lifted her nightie, taunting him. His grin widened, and he rushed at her, trapping her in a corner and pinning her against the wall, arms above her head.

They strained against each other, 'lust washing through them, darkness cresting. Hers twined with his, struggling serpents of desire. She fought and failed to break his hold, shocked and elated. When had he gotten so strong?

His mouth crashed against hers, their kiss tinged copper. "You're mine," he growled, lips dropping to her throat, body tight against hers. Her legs rose, climbing him, wrapping around his waist. He groaned, pressing between her thighs. Kara panted, their need a living thing, bond thrumming with the echo between them.

"Please, Flynn..." Talent swirled through the room, their halos blazing, casting stark shadows, power crackling between them, the darkness in them rising.

"Ask me." His beard rasped against her ear, and she moaned. "Ask me for what you want." His lips teased over her jaw, nipping. "Tell me what to do to you."

"TIE ME UP AND FUCK ME."

Flynn's mouth went dry, his cock painfully hard. "Yeah?"

"Yeah." Her eyes met his. "Take what you want and make it hurt."

He dropped her wrists to grab the top of her nightie, rending it from her body. A rivulet of sweat glistened between her full breasts, nipples taut—Her fist drove into his gut, doubling him over as she slipped away.

Flynn laughed, hand at his belt, after her again. He whipped it free, doubling it and cracking it against his thigh as he closed in on her. Kara squealed and dove behind a chair. He snagged her ankle, dragging her to him. She pulled a lamp from a table and swung it, cursing when he ducked.

Then he was above her, his weight pinning her to the floor. She raised her fist, and he caught it. Her other palm took him across the face before he grabbed it, looping his belt around both her wrists and cinching it tight. She moaned, nude beneath him save for a tiny, sodden scrap of satin between her legs, the tips of her breasts diamond peaks, arching against him.

"Goddamn, you're fucking beautiful," he murmured, capturing a nipple in his mouth and drawing it taut against his tongue. She cried out, her bound hands dropping to tangle in his hair, thighs spreading for him—

He fisted her panties and ripped them off, balling them up. He held them to his nose inhaling. Jesus fuck, she smelled like heaven. "Open your mouth," he growled.

Her eyes blazed defiant, then went wide, his fingers spearing into her wetness, curling against her inner walls to stroke. His thumb circled her clit and her lips pinched down tight, biting back a moan as she rode his hand.

"Naughty, naughty girl," he murmured, feeling her tremble around his fingers, so fucking close... "I said open." He pulled his hand away and slapped her pussy. She gasped and he shoved her panties into her mouth, his palm covering her cry of outrage. He kissed her temple, fingers back between her folds. Her eyes rolled into her head. "That's it baby. Now you're going to come for me. I need this pussy nice and wet for what I'm gonna do to it."

<hr />

OH, sweet Glory...

Kara, rocked against his hand, the tang of her own desire ripe against her tongue, Flynn's hand tightened over her mouth. Breath stuttering, the leather of the belt cutting into her wrists—his fingers swept against her inner walls, twisting then going deep, thumb a speeding circle over her clit, passion rising—

"Keep them in your mouth, and your hands above your head, or I'll stop," he rumbled, his palm moving to her breast. His head dipped to tease her nipples to swollen, aching points, then licked the sweat from her abs and buried his face in her pussy, growling low in his throat. He swept his tongue up her slit and paused, meeting her eye, their bond rife with his dominance.

Kara's speeding breath caught, her bloodlust churning. Caught between wanting to hit him again and wanting to give into the pleasure he was giving her—

Flynn smirked and bent his head to feast.

Glory! He was such a—oh, sweet bliss—talented, talented man... She gave a muffled cry, arching against his mouth, riding the waves of cresting pleasure, white light building, bursting across her mind's eye, core clenching down around him.

Feeling his smug satisfaction at the deluge of her desire dripping from his beard, her thighs limp and shaking. He spread them wide, licking his glossed lips. "Look at all that cream...so fucking wet for me..." He popped the button on his trousers, his other hand lazily pumping a finger into her sensitized folds. She squirmed, and his eyes shot to hers. He raised his fingers to his mouth, sucking them off slowly. "Stay. I'm not done with you."

Her temper spiked and that Cheshire cat grin spread across his face.

Kara bolted.

His hands clamped around her thighs just as she gained her feet, swinging her around to bend her over the overturned couch. Her head hung over the side, feet dangling, the weird angle rushing blood to her head. Flynn's palm cracked down on her ass and she screamed around her panties.

Kara spat them out and sucked in a gasping breath. "Glory, you're an asshole!"

"Mmm. Speaking of which…have I told you how pretty yours is?" He nosed along her crack, and she gasped as he tongued into her back hole, then fingered it, lips back on her clit. Her hips tipped up for him despite herself. Passion rising—

FLYNN SALIVATED as his fingers disappeared into her tight little asshole, feeling it clench around them. He dropped his mouth to her clit, sucking the engorged nub into his mouth and flicking back its hood. Kara gasped, the sound clear. He chuckled, surprised she hadn't spit out her panties sooner. She squirmed, and the taste of her irate lust flavoring their bond was fucking delicious.

His cock throbbed, so fucking hard it hurt. A sticky mess dripped from its tip, weeping in anticipation of her trying to beat the shit out of him the second his mouth left her cunt. Her asshole clenched tighter, pussy oozing cream, begging to be fucked.

Who was he to deny her?

He stood, slicking her honey over his cock. Pressing his broad tip to her seam. She moaned as his crown breeched her folds. Jesus fuck, the way her cunt gripped him, sucked him in…his hips slapped against her upturned ass, sac dusting her clit, grinding himself deep and bottoming out. Pressure from his fingers in her ass making her pussy that much tighter... His free hand pressed an ass cheek back as he retreated, cock glistening, her honey gathered behind the ridge of his crown. She whimpered as he pulled out. Flynn licked his lips, stroking himself, a long line of his pre-cum dripping into her needy little hole.

Fuck, he needed to fill that up.

His bloodlust surged with the urge to see it overflow with his seed, sloppy and dripping milky white. He thrust back into her and she screamed, her bound hands flying up, unable to find purchase. Flynn gripped her hips with both hands, watching her asshole tighten into a little rosette, pistoning into her, unrelenting.

Kara cried out, flailing. Totally at his mercy. He groaned, eyes closing as her bloodlust spiked, driving his cock into her slick velvet cunt, her challenge fading to submission.

"You feel so fucking good wrapped around my dick," he growled, reaching forward to fist her hair.

FLYNN PULLED her back against him. The room spun, blood draining from Kara's head and pricks of darkness spotting her vision. He railed into her from behind, punishing her. His hot breath rasped against her ear, his chest slick against her back, the thick length of him pounding her into submission. He growled, his hand closing around her throat. Kara groaned, her pussy spasming with another burst of desire.

Flynn chuckled. "That's it. Get my dick all fucking wet." He slapped her clit and she screamed, his fingers rolling and pinching it, teeth grazing her nape, nipping just shy of painful. "Does it hurt enough, baby? Or do you want more?"

"More," she choked out. Sweet Glory, with this man the answer was always going to be more—

He picked her up and flipped her over, slamming her against the wall. Plaster cracking. Smoldering, his eyes a tempest. She wrapped her legs around him, lowering her bound wrists around his neck. Feeling his desires war inside him. Needing him to claim her. To make her his. She kissed him softly. Her lips a bare brush across his.

"Hurt me, Flynn. Please."

"As my lady wishes," he murmured. He pressed her against the wall, his hands spreading her cheeks. The damp tip of his cock nudging her back hole's tight ring of muscle. His lips took hers, tongue sweeping her mouth—

Swallowing her scream as he thrust to the hilt, the searing burn of his cock spearing into her ass and lighting her up. Sweat bloomed over her body. She jerked away from him, the buckle from the belt binding her wrists slicing into his flesh. Flynn groaned, his pace unrelenting, blood welling, running down his spine to pool over her crossed ankles and drip to the floor.

Kara's head fell back, thudding against the wall, letting the pain bloom to pleasure, the hurt kindling to passion, desire building. Needing his darkness. Sating her own. Talent building, pricking at them, wanting with them…

Their bond pulsed with their echo, desire amplified by 'lust. Her satiation and his savagery a mirror balance. Giving and taking.

Her, feeling him, feeling her.

TALENT BUILT, the line between them blurring again. Her pleasure, his pain…or was it the other way around? Didn't matter. He drove himself into her, deeper, faster, his balls growing heavy. Slapping with each thrust. Dripping with her desire. Trying to ignore the need to use his talent. Breath heated, coming fast. His hand dropped between them, working her clit. Feeling her pleasure build, tinged with pain. Her satiation dancing on the knife's edge. He felt it. Her. All of it like it was his own. She was. Belonged to him. Was his.

His brow furrowed. No, she wasn't. Not yet. Something was still missing…something he needed to do…

The talent in the room writhed and Kara's arms tightened around his neck, slicing the belt buckle deeper into his flesh, spine sticky with gore. Scent of copper tinging the air. He moaned, wanting to taste it—

"Please…" Kara's head tipped to the side, baring her throat, feeling his need as her own. He growled, licking a long line from her collarbone to her ear. She shivered, her asshole clenching around him, drawing his balls up. Close. So fucking close... A growl rumbled through his chest, and he struck, teeth burying themselves in her shoulder with the next thrust.

Claiming her.

She screamed her abandon. Red-laced talent swirling around them, flickering through the room. His head snapped up at a lamp exploding into a shower of sparks—

And her lips were beneath his jaw, teeth sinking in.

Flynn's eyes rolled back, his head going light. "Oh, fuck, yes." His cock swelled, balls drawing up and a tingle shooting along his spine. He collapsed against her, 'lust and talent jolting through them. Kara cried out, releasing talent and spasming around him, asshole clenching impossibly tight as long ropes of his seed spurted into her.

Fuuuck...

He laughed, flashing back to that night with her at the coop, and let power run through him to join hers.

BLOOD IN HER MOUTH, his moan in her ear. The need to use her talent—her panting sped, building, she cried out, letting it go, a bellow tearing from his throat, halos flaring—

A weave settled over them.

Their breath was ragged, mingling.

He cupped her jaw, making her look at him. "I love you," he rumbled, lips teasing hers.

They tipped up into a broad smile. "I love you," she nipped at him and he chuckled.

Flynn bent his head, lowering her to the floor, and she took her arms from around his neck. Something had just happened. Their bond felt completed in a way it hadn't before. Kara looked up at him, and he kissed her gently, his lips swollen. He phazed the belt from her wrists, running a hand across her cheek with a kind of wonder.

"You feel it too?"

"Yeah." His fingers traced the darkening bite on her shoulder, and he kissed her again, swearing when his lip split. She laughed and raised a finger to bind it.

He pulled back, glaring at her.

"Stop. I'm fine, I feel like I have brand new batteries. I don't know, I can't explain it." Her hand dropped to her abdomen. "That gnawing's gone, I—no, they're fine, I feel them, but it's like they're not eating me anymore." Her stomach rumbled and she laughed. "I'm starving though. All that talent, it did something…keeps doing something. I don't understand it, but it's like…it's like it wants to help."

His thumb ran over the mark he'd left above her collar bone, his brow furrowed. "Okay, but leave scars, like you did for the oaths. On both of us. Whatever this is, it feels the same. Like it's important."

She pulled talent with a soft moan, a fine network of pale lines springing into being. Scars crisscrossing his torso and thickening the one already on his lip, beneath his jaw, and a crescent moon at the base of his neck. He was right. Somehow it was important that they were there.

Kara ran a hand over them, and he shivered. "You'll think I'm stupid, but I like seeing my marks on you…and I miss your old ones."

"Some days I do, too, and this," he traced the silvery oval his teeth had left on her shoulder, "is hot as hell."

"You're so weird." She laughed, looking past him at the room. "And that's a mess."

The room was trashed. Broken furniture and a Kara-sized dent in the wall. A lamp smoked. Flynn unplugged it with a shrug. "Place needs a makeover anyway. Let's get something sent up. I could go for a steak."

He held out a hand and led her back into the bedroom. She curled up on the bed, and he called down to the kitchen, then joined her. She snuggled up against his chest, feeling complete, replete.

"What happened?"

"I dunno." He scrubbed at his face. "After you got grabbed, I lost it."

"Lost it?"

"Yeah. Blew up the Assembly Hall and there was this massive fire

—" He grimaced, guilt washing through their bond. She propped up on an elbow to look at him.

"Really?"

"Shit, Kara, I can't even tell you what I leveled. This fucking Breaker talent…it's too easy to pull. I can't control it. I thought I lost you—something in me broke, and you were there, in that room, like I was looking through a weird doorway. Then, I dunno, I stepped through, and it was real." His arms tightened around her. She chewed her thumb, sharing his awe and trepidation.

"It's all there, each line of talent…it's…I can't even explain it. It's just all there. I think about something, and I can do it. Maybe you're right about the talent wanting to help. It's more of an explanation than I have. None of this shit—it's all ancient history. I mean, I didn't pay too much attention, but I'm pretty sure they didn't get into specifics at the Academy. Especially the part about not needing an Investiture."

"Is that why your halos changed?"

"Yeah, I guess. I dunno why yours did though." He touched her cheek, pulsing his halos and frowned. "Damn, I can't cloak them. I'm gonna have to find you another pair of sunglasses."

She laughed, but he wasn't joking, and there was this creeping fear…"What else?"

He looked away. "I—if all this Overlord shit is really real…I can't leave the city. If I do, I won't be able to pull talent."

She stared at him, horrified. "I don't understand—"

"The talent I have access to now is from all of them. Everyone I took an oath from. The farther away I get, the less I'll be able to access."

"Meddleton?"

He shrugged, playing with her fingers. "I dunno. Look, I know you're not going to like it, but from now on, if you're not with me, I want Rogan with you."

She quirked an eyebrow. "You hate Rogan."

"Yeah, but he's the only other person I trust to keep you safe. I wouldn't put it past Titus to try something like that again. If you won't do it for yourself or me, do it for the babies."

"Now that's just fighting dirty." She scowled at him.

"What's wrong with being dirty? I know for a fact you happen to like some very dirty things."

She gave him a half smile and rolled onto her back, letting him show her exactly what they were again.

WELL, that was embarrassing.

Cal thanked the good Lord above his office was occluded in smoke after having to ride out Flynn's anxiety over Kara's well-being for the past few hours. If the most recent interlude was any indication, she was feeling the high side of fine.

Cal was feeling incredibly frustrated. He adjusted his crotch.

The little barrister across the desk from him coughed and waved a hand in front of his face, cutting a swirling swath through the smog. God bless the man, he picked up right where he'd left off, less the eye contact.

Cal was gonna chalk that up to flashing colors and leave it at that.

"There's precedent that could clear Lord Scot from liability, but the case I'm referring to involved a harbor blockage resulting from a shifted sandbar. Several boats ran aground, but there were no deaths. If I were advocating for the victims, I'd argue the scope of destruction renders that ruling meaningless."

"Even with them violating the lockdown? No one should've been in the administrative complex."

Merchant coughed, waving a hand through the air again. "Granted. However, in light of your desire to settle this quickly, I'd advise against reminding the victims' families of their culpability. A fund for the restoration of the city, and those affected by the incident, would be better received."

Cal grunted. Blood money always was. "Fine. Do what you have to. What about holding office?"

"The judge is still deliberating, and this won't help. A definition was legally established differentiating between a twist and a split, however the ruling is going to take into account Lord Scot's quote unquote fitness for office. Quite frankly, this paints him as a loose cannon, and him assuming the mantle of Overlord without a vote…"

The boy had slipped their leash and they were pissed. Cal sighed. "Get those funds established, and let me see what I can do on my end. You can close the door after yourself."

The little barrister gathered up his papers and made his escape.

What a mess. Between this, settling the Source Talents, and ensuring the board's cooperation, a sizable hole was forming in Cal's checkbook, but it couldn't be helped. Morris and the rest of them were gonna have a goddamned field day, and any potential fires needed to be snuffed out now. Whole reason he'd amassed the financial portfolio he had was for shit like this.

Well, that and he needed something to keep him occupied. A millennium of downtime added up, and he was about to spend more of it. He pulled talent, assuming the persona of Albanach, and called up a communications orb.

Unlike Titus, Salist didn't play games.

"Something I can do for you, Albanach?" The dark man smoothed his rich purple kaftan, looking like a sultan of old reclined on his chaise of pelts. Firelight flickered above a low bowl of stones before him, and played over the mouthpiece of his hookah.

Cal knocked the ash off his cigar. "How does spending some of my money sound?"

"Appealing, should there be something in it for me."

"I can make that happen, provided the details don't go any farther than us."

"A clandestine task?" Salist's teeth were an ivory slash in the gloaming. "Orin owes me. I'd bet him you weren't done with Titus, though I'm assuming I'll have to wait until the conclusion of our business to collect."

"You will at that. Interested?"

"Indubitably." He blew out a thick plume of smoke, the tropical breeze wafting it away. "What did you have in mind?"

"I want the Triam."

Salist sputtered, laughing. "You'll never get it."

Cal chewed his cigar, having expected that reaction, and that the man knew about the damned blacksite. "Care to wager?"

Salist pulled himself together. "No. No matter how unlikely, I've learned not to bet against you. If you've your eye on the Triam, I've no doubt it will end up in your pocket...but considering what Titus's allowed those troops of his to do to the Source, it very well may be a smoking ruin by then. He'll have made arrangements should this incursion of his go poorly."

"You know where it is?"

Salist took a long pull from his hookah, making him wait. "I don't, but have my suspicions it's underground, and I'm sure it's been designed with those vectors lurking above in mind."

Cal grimaced, chewing his cigar. He'd been riding the same train of thought. "2.7 trillion, seventy-two hours. Throw it on the table. He bites, you get ten percent."

"Fifteen."

"No."

Salist laughed again. "It was worth a try. Very well, but I can already tell you he won't, and then what will you do?"

"Not your concern. Call me when it's done." He cut the transmission, settling into the divot of his chair. What was he gonna do? He'd hoped Leo would've turned up by now. If he wasn't dead... Lord knew he'd earned a bullet, but it'd be damned inconvenient.

Someone knocked on the door.

"Yeah?"

Nora poked her head in, then closed the slab after herself, coming to sit. "Any luck?"

"Time will tell." He tapped off his ash, rolling the cigar between his fingers. "You?"

She frowned. "The line is so fragmented, and Serra isn't helping. Her and Janice are already thick as thieves. How she managed to sway that woman with her prejudices against Source Talents..."

"Birds of a feather. I'm assuming harpies qualify."

Nora laughed, then pursed her lips. "Is he my father?"

Cal sighed, not having to ask who she meant. He took another drag. "No."

"Then how is Umari—"

"Veronica had another child after you. By that time, she was too unstable to send to the Laborium. I fudged the records, brought the baby up here. Pithy and his wife raised her. The talent disparity between the two of them, well. Woman was desperate for a child, and he couldn't give her one. She was beside herself when I offered Umari up."

"Then he's not a Jester." She sounded deflated, but there wasn't anything he could do about that. When Veronica had lost control of her talent it'd taken out the whole damned House along with the top of his tower at the Source.

"No."

"Then Kara really is the last of us."

The implications of that statement were a gut punch. "You don't think they'll make it?"

Nora shot him a dirty look. "I'm more concerned about her. When Laughlin brought her back…she's close to twelve weeks. At the rate they're developing, it's more than the talent deficiency or nutritionals. The strain on her… I don't think she can carry them to term, and I'm positive she knows it."

"How many?"

"Four," Nora whispered, her eyes glassy.

Christ.

OTTO PEERED down into the hole, blinking at the stench wafting up. Arileo was in a puddle of his own filth at the bottom, drawing ragged breaths. Damn Barton for bungling the grab so abysmally. It was forcing Otto to play his hand far sooner than his wont, but there was nothing for it.

"Pull him up." The Breaker made a face, but squatted down to grab Arileo by the collar and hefted him onto the sand. Otto put his sleeve to his nose, the man was several shades beyond ripe. He addressed the Breaker again. "You have your orders. Try not to botch it."

The man's face tensed, but he nodded, going back to his troops.

Otto sighed, toeing Arileo in the ribs and gating them to a hovel in the commons.

The monstrous hag he'd hired was waiting beside a tepid bath. He probably should've hosed the louse down first, but it was no longer his problem. She was being paid to deal with it.

"Get him ready."

Her lips tightened, but she obeyed. Otto made his way past a ragged curtain into the kitchen, hand on his abdomen. His stomach had been troubled of late and the effluvia coming off the man hadn't helped. He scanned her meagre shelves for something to settle it, lamenting the loss of Julia's wine cellar. Intelligencers had raided the estate, and he'd be stupid to think they wouldn't have eyes on the place.

Otto popped the cork of a likely looking bottle amongst the rat turds and sniffed. His lips curdled, but it would have to do. He poured himself a clay mug of the questionable brew and eased onto a stool beside the fire. The draw was poor and a haze hung in the squalid room. It suited his mood.

Damn Barton.

How the man had failed…it boggled the mind. His track record had been impeccable—

Otto gnashed his teeth. There was no point in belaboring it. The damage was done. Scot wouldn't let the girl out of his sight, and now he had the powers of the Overlord at his beck and call.

Otto's stomach cramped again, doubling him over. Blast it. He panted through the pain, galled that he couldn't do anything about his condition but let it run its course. Half Binder though he may be, his talent resided solely in the influencing of psyches. Healing was an art which escaped him. Fortunate then, that he had no interest in it, except when it affected his person.

Now was one of those times.

He pulled talent, attempting to look inward—the effort was futile. He downed the rest of what was in the cup, hoping to blunt the agony if nothing else.

"Master?" The hag was at the door.

"What is it?"

"He's prepared as ye instructed."

Good. At least something was going to plan. Otto hefted himself up, wiping the sheen of sweat from his brow, and followed her into the adjoining room.

Arileo was sprawled out on the pallet, stuffed into a rumpled suit of clothes. His pallor would have been concerning if Otto gave a damn. He approached the man, and laid a hand on his clammy brow; it was well past the time he should've checked in.

Doing so now didn't excite him, and utilizing the wretched louse for the task wasn't ideal. Otto sent his consciousness through the fragmenting web of talent linking Arileo back to Mother, damning his Breaker blood.

She was in her garden, overlooking the ocean. Gone was the toothsome girl she had been, replaced by the creature she'd become. Armored in gemstones, the stolen souls of the hundreds of thousands of Talents she'd bound to her flesh throughout the millennium were blinding in the sun. She'd harvested them with ruthless intent—Binder, Fixer, Shade, Fetch, and Finder, all to power her grand scheme and reverse the Surge.

Only Breaker talent was immune to her machinations, though not for lack of trying.

Otto blinked, looking away from her radiance. The thought gave him little comfort. His soul may be safe, but the rest of him was not.

Mother drummed her fingers on the polished coquina wall. "I expected you sooner."

"I had matters to attend to, the Sons—"

"Are not the issue." She turned, her milky white eyes boring into him. "Wild Talents have been eradicated from the South, and those peppering the North have been herded into the city or exterminated. You chose well with Victor. He lives, rallying the surviving Sons to his banner. There will be enough to finish the job. Yours was to guarantee Kara Jester's removal."

"Barton—"

Mother laughed. The dry rasping sent a chill through him, despite the blazing sun above. "Was but a tool, wielded poorly. The onus was on you. Now, how shall you redeem yourself? Delivering her would've put Laughlin under my sway, giving me access to the Breaker line's talent." She didn't seem overly concerned about it, a hint of Jane's playfulness in her voice.

Otto abruptly knew how a mouse must feel when cornered by a cat. He wet his lips. "I should have Nora Jester and the Commandant in hand within the hour. Titus has already deployed a craft to collect them. I'd take them to you directly, but my gating stone won't make the trip."

A smile ghosted across her lips. "Mmm. Pity that. The two of them are a rather poor trade for the girl, and smacks of you trying to save your own skin. Have they outed you?"

Otto tensed. If she already knew and he didn't disclose, things would go poorly for him, but admitting he'd become a liability wouldn't do either…

"I'll take that as a yes." She smirked. "But it's of no matter, nor is Barton's failure." She stressed the assassin's name, and Otto bristled.

Mother leaned against the wall, raising her face to the sun. The largest of her gemstones blazed in the golden band across her brow. Amethyst, topaz, and silvered quartz. The distilled essences of four of the original seven Talents, with bare settings above each temple awaiting the final two. All that talent at her disposal… He suppressed another shiver, her diminutive form at odds with the power she held in thrall.

Overlord in her own right, and as trapped in Halja as Scot was in Glynfyls.

She smirked at him, as if she knew what he was thinking. A cramp ripped through his gut, and the garden wavered, sweat breaking out on his brow with the effort to steady the bind connecting their psyches.

"Laughlin's ascension was necessary, and the more power he amasses, the greater the chaos will be when he's removed. Let them bend a knee. They bare their necks for my ax when they do." Her lips pursed around a smile. "Feeling poorly?"

Dread spiked up Otto's spine at the lilt in her voice.

"Pity there's none of my shard-bearers in Glynfyls. I was able to manifest through Victor and heal the remaining Sons of radiation poisoning, but without a shard to allow me to materialize, I'm afraid you're in a terribly thorny predicament."

His eyes narrowed at her smile. That damned crown of thorns she'd placed upon his brow…

"It shouldn't be fatal, as long as you make haste in carrying out my instructions. Titus is on the move. In three days, I expect you to have the cell prepared to open the city wide at his signal. Your penance is to remain with them until the job is done. You can use the stone in his ring to return to me after. Enoch and Elize will attend to collecting the Jester girl." Her fingers brushed the amethyst stones at her brow.

Otto gritted his teeth, another wave of nausea scouring through him. "And should Glynfyls's preparations prove to be more effective than you've imagined? If Scot's able to utilize the Overlord's power—"

"Oh, I hope he does." Her bloodless lips bloomed into a beatific smile. She approached, her form shimmering with her laugh, and a golden girl stood before him. Jane's palms cupped his cheeks, and she moued at his frown. "Come now, Otto. I do so love games. A wildcard always makes things so much more interesting. How delicious is the prospect of him wiping out all those Breakers? I can't wait for him to discover the Triam. Do you think he'll do it before or after it's destroyed? Either way, the look on his face will be priceless."

She laughed and Otto cringed, pulling away, and toeing the dirt.

"What? No stomach for poetic justice? Well, I suppose you haven't one for much of anything at the moment. Very well, if you're keen on expediting the process, I'd advise you proceed with stacking the deck." She pursed her lips at him again and tsked. "Oh…thought I'd forgotten about that knave, Leo, you've been holding in reserve? You really should know better, but I approve of your foresight. Get on with you, then. Time's ticking…"

She pressed a finger to his brow and he was back, slumped over Arileo. Otto's lips curdled as he pushed away from the man, cursing the duplicitous bitch that'd birthed him. He needed to see this done.

It was time to send Arileo home.

CHAPTER SIXTEEN

"Though a resident's accommodations on Glynfyls's rungs has devolved into an indication of social status, it was not always so. History shows Breakers populating the seventh rung in order to man the wall, followed by the Binders on the sixth, then the Fixers, Fetches, and Finders consecutively, with the Shades on the second rung. Those at the crown were comprised of a mixture of Talents with the greatest ability, allowing them to blanket the city with their power while remaining protected from physical assault…"

— *Excerpt from* Glynfyls: A History

THE DOORS SLID shut on Titus's private transport and lifted away from the Source. The industrial complex receded beneath them, silent and dark for the first time in over eight hundred years. Scavengers were already scuttling through the open gates. Titus hoped they stripped it bare, leaving nothing but its bones.

His Breakers had made considerable headway with that. Swaths of the city were reduced to smoking rubble. The Triam would serve as a fallback point, should he need it. There would be no coming back to the Source.

He had nothing to come back for.

The transport reached altitude, pausing before its thrusters engaged, then speeding north. Save for the one he'd sent ahead, it was the only air-unit he had access to. The rest had been reallocated, moving Talents north.

Albanach's coup had been thorough, but it was of no matter.

Titus's Fetches were working in teams, transporting Breakers via the jump sites that'd been upgraded. If his Fetches lived that long, his army would be within striking distance of the city in less than two days.

He popped several pills, cursing the constant ache in his temples. Shriver, the sole Binder at his disposal, hadn't been able to provide any relief. Not for the first time, Titus cursed himself for sending Otto ahead. The pain redoubled, underscoring his lack of foresight. Titus grimaced, pouring himself a bourbon, and settling into the plush captain's chair, flicking through holos.

The world was watching. Unsurprisingly, the destruction of the Sons hadn't been met with any outcry, but Scot's reaction to the ill-fated abduction had brought the seething cauldron of anti-Talent sentiment to a boil.

How could anyone possibly rest easy knowing the amount of power one man had access to, let alone a city full of the creatures? Surely they wouldn't remain content to sit up in their frozen wasteland, and without the Source to give them pause... Titus smirked, more than willing to cash in on their fears.

Missives of support and offers of aid were pouring in—for a cut of the action of course. He wasn't ready to consider any such partnerships. He would rule Glynfyls as emperor, or not at all, and the city was ripe for the taking.

A communications orb pulsed and he smirked, answering it. "Salist. I'm assuming you're pleased with your purchase?"

"Quite." The dark man ran his hands over the girl at his side as if she were a favored pet.

Titus's smirk deepened. Bertram's litters tended to be distinctive, and her resemblance to the Jester girl was striking. Save for her halos, they could've been twins. It was a pity so few of them remained. After her performance in the ring, a fortune could've been made whoring them out. Alas, aside for the one at Salist's knee, the rest were currently breeding or had been culled.

The man wet his lips and pushed back against the pelts covering his chaise. "She's proving to be quite adept at seeing to my needs. We may have to negotiate further terms."

Titus shrugged, not opposed to the idea, especially if more supplies were involved. His troops were already grumbling about rationing.

"I see you've left. Is tomorrow the day?" Salist asked.

"Not quite, but care to make a wager on the outcome?"

The man laughed. "I'm not sure that I do. If I win, you'll be dead and what's left of your funds tied up in probate. Not the best of odds, and I'd rather not fight your widow for my cut."

"I don't anticipate on dying in either event. I have plans in place to secure my person." Tucking tail and running chief among them, but Salist didn't need to know that.

"I'm sure. And what will happen to your little Eden should your plans fail?"

"Like the garden, it will disappear from the face of the earth."

"Seems a waste."

Titus shrugged. If he was dead, he certainly wouldn't care.

Salist stroked the girl's hair, pensive. "What if I offered to buy it from you?"

"You don't have that kind of money." Titus laughed.

"I've 2.7 trillion to offer for it, sight unseen."

Titus's heart was in his throat. He took a shaky sip of his drink, mouth abruptly dry. There was no way Salist could come up with that kind of capital on his own. "Which power are you in bed with?"

Salist smiled, lifting a lock of the girl's hair to his nose. "I wish I could be more transparent, but anonymity is a stipulation of the offer."

His eyes narrowed. "Forgive me if I'm suspicious of silent partners, heirs, and all things not formally disclosed."

"You have my sympathies in that regard." Salist took a glass of something from the girl. "I did caution you against investing so heavily in a venture where Albanach was the primary stakeholder. Man is a snake. But, be that as it may, I've been authorized to leave this deal on the table for the next seventy-two hours. Think about it Titus."

Titus sipped his drink as the feed went dark, not about to take the man's advice. The only thing he wanted to think about was bringing that city to its knees, along with Laughlin Scot.

***

FLYNN KISSED KARA'S KNUCKLES, holding her hand as the lift descended to the ground floor, a stupid smile plastered over his face. She giggled and he didn't give a shit if it made him look dumb as fuck. He didn't care what channeling all that talent as Overlord was gonna do to him anymore either. It was worth it. She was back to how she'd been when they'd first met. Shit, how she'd been that first night they'd gotten together…a surge of carnality went through him again.

She glanced over, her dimples a mile deep, and laughed. "What?"

"You know."

"Mmm." Her arms slid around his waist to cup his backside. "No idea what you're talking about. You should definitely show me."

"Yeah?"

"Yeah."

The door pinged open, and she squealed as he grabbed her up and bore her down onto one of the long couches. Her hands were in his hair, his lips on hers—

Someone cleared their throat, and she buried her face against his chest. Flynn looked up, grinning. Cal had just come through the gate, a servant carrying boxes in after him.

"You know you do have rooms here."

"We were going to breakfast." Flynn pushed up and took her hand in his again, grin growing at her pinked cheeks.

"Right. Suggest you figure out how to cloak your meals from your bondsmen. Can't say I, or the majority of the city, had a particularly restful night, and I'm gonna warn you now, I walk into a room and see your bare ass pumping, I'm gonna stripe it like you were ten-years-old again, we clear?"

"Crystal…" What the hell was Cal talking—oh. Shit. A multitude of consciousnesses simmered at the peripheral of his awareness, tethered to him by the oath's he'd taken. Flynn laughed and pulled talent, cloaking them. A distant hum winked out. His grandfather grunted.

"Thank you."

Kara went white. "The city?"

"Yeah. Asshole left himself wide open. Anything he felt between five-seconds ago and assuming Overlord, his bondsmen felt too."

She sagged against Flynn's shoulder, and he kissed her temple, glad everyone knew how he felt. Maybe that would stop all those fucking notes she'd been getting.

Kara stared at Cal. "Your halos—"

Flynn looked at his grandfather again. Shit, she was right.

"Side effect. No one who's pledged will be able to hide them. Overlord is a living conduit of talent. You're always open to it, and through you, everyone who's pledged can access more than they would otherwise."

"Christ, this is gonna be a shit show…" Flynn glanced at Kara. Her halos consumed her irises. The burnished gold ringed with that dark line lent a feline cast to her features that was hot as hell. That prick from the Source wasn't gonna be the only one eye-fucking her. She smirked like she knew what he was thinking, a jolt of electricity echoing between them. Goddamn…

"So…" Her lips pursed around the word, and he wet his. "You hide your halos, except when there's an Overlord, whose powers make them a twist, but no other Dual-Talents can hold public office?"

"That's all fallout from the Great Incursion. Things were different before then," Cal said sourly. "Records we pulled clear you to hold office, but the damn judge and a good portion of the city think you're a loose cannon. You'd best give them reason to believe otherwise. Since they didn't give you access to that power, they can't take it away, but they'll nullify your ass quicker than you can blink. Short of that's exile, and the end result's the same. Channeling all that talent's gonna leave you a husk. You might wanna stop vaporizing buildings when you get pissed." He threw the morning edition at him.

SCOT STRIKES DOWN SIX!

Flynn's stomach rebelled and he choked it back, Kara gripping his arm at his influx of anxiety. He scanned the article. Jesus, the entire west wing of the Assembly Hall had collapsed… the Judiciary complex, neighboring buildings…

Eight blocks destroyed, six people dead, and a hell of a lot more injured. What had he done?

"Merchant's been busy spending my money cleaning things up," Cal said, lighting a cigarette. "House Scot's set up a fund for the reconstruction of Glynfyls and for any victims of the tragedy. Do me a favor and try not to piss anyone off for a while. You take down anymore buildings, and I'm not gonna be able to cover it."

Flynn pulled Klaus's crumpled bank note from his pocket. "Here. This'll help."

Cal took it and whistled. "It will at that. This from the fight?"

"Yeah."

His grandfather grunted and slipped it into his waistcoat, turning as Rogan came through the gate. Breaker stormed past, scratching at a day's worth of stubble and scowling. Flynn's hackles rose at the malaise of bloodlust and alcohol he left in his wake.

"Wonder who pissed in his cornflakes," Cal muttered, trailing after him to the dining room. Kara tapped Flynn's thigh and he sighed, following.

Nora and Marcos were already at the table, eating. Well, Nora was. Flynn averted his eyes. Everyone's colors displayed so brazenly was gonna take a while to get used to, and he most definitely did not want, or need, to see hers. Marcos was glowering at Rogan and the asshole was busy ignoring him. Miriam sat across the table from them, her expression severe.

She'd aged in the last week, cheeks drawn and pale. Her mouth pinched down when she saw him, and he was very glad she was on the other end of the table. Same with Rogan. The look the Breaker shot his way made Flynn wanna deck him.

His aunt started in before they'd even sat. "I don't care if you're Overlord, Laughlin James Scot! I'm a God-fearing woman and refuse to stay in this city if you persist in projecting such filthy behavior! As if everyone flashing colors wasn't bad enough—No one needs to be a party to that!"

Shit. He couldn't keep the grin off his face. Kara went white enough for both of them. Flynn laughed, running a hand over his beard. No wonder French had been weird this morning. The man serving him and Kara breakfast wouldn't look at them either, his face a decided shade of red as he set their plates down. Christ, the thought of going to Assembly was just getting better and better.

"How would you know, Miriam?" Cal asked. "Not one of the Prydees have pledged."

"And thank goodness for that! The energy coming from upstairs was quite enough!"

"Why haven't you pledged, Miriam?" Nora asked.

She sniffed, pushing up the side of her glasses. "The sisters have always had grave concerns over Laughlin's temperament. Given the past few days, and that obscenity last night—"

"Wasn't obscene, it was a Breaker's bonding—Witnessed by far more than necessary," Rogan muttered.

"I thought you were staying with one of your—" Flynn's attention snapped from Miriam to the Breaker. "Wait, what?"

Rogan's lip curdled and he swore under his breath, then pulsed his halos, running a critical eye over them. "You both did a fine job setting your runes on each other, for all you didn't know what the hell you were doing, but it's long past time you stop fucking around and come to the conclave. They declare you rogue and all hell's gonna break loose."

Miriam tsked at him. "Annabelle's eldest had to move back in with her brood after the attack, but with that kind of language I still might."

Flynn grunted, not really listening. Cal was glaring down the table at Rogan and the Breaker's knuckles popped. Something passed between them, and his grandfather's hand trembled as he took a drag. What the hell?

"What do you mean, setting our runes?" Kara asked.

"Look at each other with Breaker talent and figure it out," Rogan muttered, going back to his meal.

Flynn scowled, but did. Lines of claret sprang into view. He was covered with them. They crisscrossed his body following the scars Kara had left, surrounding him with a pale nimbus of power. The mark on her shoulder created the same effect, scintillating around her in a ruddy sphere.

"What the fuck…"

"What do you see?" Her face screwed up, halos fizzling with claret pricks of light. She laughed. "Ugh, I can't—that's horrible, there's no order to it!"

"Using another line's talent isn't easy. Some of them harder than others."

Flynn's eyes narrowed at Cal, and the old man clammed up. How would he know?

"It's good you claimed her before you were challenged," Rogan said around a mouthful. "She's more Breaker than anyone suspected. Must be the air up here."

"So, there's a few things I failed to mention—"

Flynn snorted at his grandfather. "A few?"

He shrugged, trading his cigarette for a piece of bacon. "Events got ahead of me. Don't worry Miriam, he keeps things cloaked, those shenanigans upstairs should be it," he assured the overwrought woman.

She didn't look like she believed him. Flynn didn't either. "Should" was a slippery word where Cal was concerned, and the way he was looking at Kara didn't give Flynn warm fuzzies. Her tearing into her breakfast did. She was too frail, having her appetite back had to be a good sign. Maybe all that deficiency bullshit was behind them.

"I'm assuming the Jester's extra is why Kara's halos expanded… that's gonna be interesting." Cal munched on a piece of bacon, pensive. "Wonder if you'll be subjected to the same caveats."

Kara went pale. "You mean I can't leave the city either?"

"You can leave…though I'll admit, things get a bit dicey talent-wise at Meddleton. With everyone crammed into the city, I doubt Flynn'll be able to pull much farther than the gates."

"And how would you know that?"

His grandfather wouldn't meet his eye.

Flynn opened his mouth to press the matter and violet light flickered outside the windows, everyone turning to look.

"Ah!" Nora clapped her hands together. "Lord Scot, your shield wall is functional. The Binders were extremely motivated after yesterday, and Jesse was more than happy to put those with structural experience to work."

Flynn grunted, his eyes still on his grandfather.

"They need to look at those damned sewers." The Commandant growled, startling the servant taking away his plate. "City's sitting on Swiss cheese. You should see where people were popping up once they figured out they couldn't get through the main gate during the attack. Finders had thought they'd ferreted out most of them. Klein's about ready to have a nervous breakdown, and that stick up Crandall's ass just keeps growing."

As much as Flynn enjoyed hearing Crandall was fucking up, he had some sympathy for the man. You could wander around down there for years and never see all of it. Of course, the odds of Titus's troops being able to find their way through it were pretty slim, too. Flynn pushed his hash browns around his plate, smiling at Kara devouring a second helping.

"You get anything out of that asshole I hauled in yesterday?" Miriam clucked her tongue and Flynn ignored her. If he had to put money on it, Titus's cell was probably somewhere underground, especially if Crandall still couldn't find them.

Cal shook out a match. "Not much. He's a nasty piece of work. Man's covered with tattoos of people's faces. Several were recognizable." His eyes lingered on Kara.

Flynn's temper jumped, and he glared down the table at Rogan. "I want you shadowing Kara when I'm not with her. I don't want her left alone."

She sighed, eyes rolling as she chugged her shake. He didn't give a shit.

The Breaker's jaw tightened. "You asking me, or telling me?"

Flynn bristled. What a fucking—"I'm telling you, and I'll have your oath if you plan on staying in this city any longer than it would take you to haul your ass back to wherever the fuck you crawled out from."

"Laughlin James!"

Rogan flashed those fucking teeth of his and a whiff of 'lust cut past Flynn's nose. "That right?"

A growl started in his chest. "Yeah. That's right."

"Seriously?" Kara looked between them. "Why does this have to be a pissing contest?"

"Because he doesn't know how to control his talent, and neither of their rungs are settled," Marcos said, glaring between Flynn and Rogan. He sniffed, running a finger under his nose. "Gah, it's worse than the pre-pubes's barracks in here." Kara laughed. Didn't help. "Look, in case he didn't spell it out enough for you, the council's ruled that you need to submit to the hierarchy or they'll put down."

Flynn snorted. "I'd like to see them fucking try."

"Language!" Miriam slapped down her napkin.

"There is no them, you dumb ass. It would be me," Rogan growled.

"Really! I don't think—"

"Breaker Business," Marcos and Rogan snapped at Miriam in concert, then scowled at one another. The look on his aunt's face would've been funny if the shit hadn't involved him—Christ, that asshole would do it, too.

"The hierarchy needs to be determined. The Sons proved we can't afford to have it in flux when Titus gets up here. If those mercs hadn't shown up when they did, we would've been in serious trouble," Marcos said.

"Any insight into that?" Cal asked, tapping his ash onto the floor.

"Yeah, it's Kendall." Flynn ran a hand over his beard, no point in dancing around it anymore. "House Carmody's the Northern connection. They're billeting at the Manse."

"Christ."

"Regardless who hired them, whatever reluctance you have to place in the hierarchy, get over it."

He glared at Marcos. "I kicked your ass, doesn't that mean you have to shut the fuck up?"

"Wasn't witnessed, doesn't count," Rogan said around a bite, "and if the seers are involved, those mercs need to be up here."

"He's right. Won't be the first time those damn witches have pulled our ass out of the fire, though I'm sure it'll kick up a shitstorm," Cal muttered.

Flynn tossed his fork down, appetite gone. Kara put a hand on his and he blew out a breath. "I'm assuming they expect me at Assembly?" Us. He was serious about not letting Kara out of his sight, especially if that prick wasn't gonna cooperate.

Cal pushed away his empty plate, and a servant whisked it from the table. "You'd be right. Suggest you start trying to control the narrative by sending out a presser on Kara's status. Since the lockdown, people don't know what the hell's going on. You play it right, you might be able to win some support via sympathy."

Flynn sighed, goddamn, he hated this shit. "Fine. Anything else I should be doing?"

"We've just covered that," Marcos said, standing. "Meantime, Nora and I have to get to the Guild before Assembly. Jesse said something about a prototype. Rogan, I'll see you later on the sands."

The other Breaker glowered at him as he left. Flynn tucked back into his breakfast, hoping the two of them would kill each and leave him out of it.

"WAS THAT NECESSARY?"

"Do I really have to answer that?" Marcos returned, helping Nora into her coat. The look she shot him said yes. "Boy needs to get over himself. They both do."

"Or what? You'll put them over your knee?"

He'd been thinking through a wall. "Something like that."

She took his arm and they entered the gate. Damned eerie arches were on a long list of things outside his comfort zone since they'd left the Source. Those bots running rampant were at the top. The security breach they represented was enormous.

The streets were empty, though no less depressing without their denizens. Ash had built up and the slushy mess was ankle deep, random furrows crisscrossing between buildings. The wind wailed through the canted skyline, hurling a stinging gray mess at them. It hit with the hissing ting of ice, static in the silence. Nora pulled her fur-lined hood closer around her face, and he put an arm around her, that spot between his shoulder blades itching again. City was more dangerous than half the ops he'd been on.

"I need to stop at the commons infirmary later today," she said like she knew what he was thinking. "I want to make sure the supplies I requisitioned have been delivered, and the bot infection rate is the highest down there. Those gates should be a priority."

"Sure you're not just avoiding Janice?"

Her mouth curdled, and he had a feeling it wasn't just from the blast of fetidness the wind whipped up the street at them. "No. I can't afford to. Serra's already been whispering in her ear. That damned woman is well on her way to being even more of a thorn in my side. At the Source there was the specter of Albanach's displeasure hanging over her, up here there's nothing to blunt her ambition."

Marcos bit back his temper. If that woman threatened Nora again, he'd put a bullet in her and aim to do a hell of a lot more than blunt anything. He held open the door and she smiled at him.

"I'm perfectly capable of taking care of myself."

"Never said you weren't. Just don't think you should have to."

She laughed. "And they say chivalry is dead."

He pursed his lips. Someone was going to be.

They walked onto the shop floor, the usual bevy of techs and mechanics missing. Jesse was standing over a table, fiddling with a prototype.

"Ah! Just in time." She smiled, coming over to shake their hands. "As I'm sure you can imagine, I've been very busy in my off-hours with these bots. This might seem like a non sequitur, but I'm assuming you've noted healing binds don't dispel when within a nullifier's influence?

The question took Marcos aback, trying to imagine the woman's off-hours. As far as he could tell she lived at the Guild.

"I have, though it was never explained," Nora said, abruptly all ears.

Jesse's eyes sparkled. "I won't bore you with the science, but it has to do with talent being embedded into a living thing. I've predicated my work with the bots using the same theorem as applied to the city, thought I'll admit, this is a much more elegant solution."

Marcos could vouch for the veracity of her claim. He'd seen too many old wounds open up in the field after losing a man, but how the hell would they apply that to the city?

"Which leads me to my request." She clasped her hands in front of her. "I'd like to run a trial. I envision administering them to the army first, so a Breaker test subject—"

Marcos frowned. "You want me to be a lab rat."

Jesse's cheeks flushed. "Inelegant, but accurate. You're ideal, as Nora can monitor you for any side effects. I don't anticipate any, the Source did all of the heavy lifting in that regard…" She tapper her lip, pensive. "And I can't be positive, but it looks like they were originally designed to be powered by iridium. They function utilizing plaz, but it's akin to using a bicycle as opposed to a transport."

"I wouldn't be surprised," Marcos mused. "The Source was betting on that iridium mine in Diytan as being a sure thing. It would make sense that they'd have developed tech ready to bring to market in anticipation."

"Like the boost Riegel was implanted with." Nora frowned, the discussion not helping to convince her. "The prototype utilized iridium. Are the bots still infectious?"

"To an extent. The iridium forces them to adapt to their host on a molecular level. In mice, I've seen cross contamination between littermates, but not across the population as a whole. However, the iridium also curtails the bots' reproductive capabilities. Once administered, I haven't been able to culture them past twelve hours."

The benefits far outweighed the risks in Marcos's opinion, but Nora twisted her ring.

"I suppose we haven't much—"

Footsteps echoed across the floor and they turned. A squat, older woman came towards them, looking lost. "Sorry to bother you… Do you know where I can find Nora Jester?"

"I'm Nora Jester."

"Wonderful!" The woman's halos flared, fixing them and their channels. "I've got them," she yelled over her shoulder, flashing a nasty smile.

A big, red-haired Breaker lumbered down to the shop floor. He stopped to gloat, his hands on the top of a test frame. Marcos knew him. Br83p. He'd been shipped to Hexspar after a court martial. "Titus just wants these two. What about her?" he asked, leering at Jesse.

"Collateral."

"Then I could use some fun." He licked his lips at Nora. "Too bad you're Titus's. I can guarantee I'd give you a rougher ride than him or this geriatric cull."

Marcos's pulse pounded in his ears, Nora's outrage matching his own. He tried to pull, but the damned fix held his channel tight.

The woman frowned and started up the ramp. "Fine, but don't take too long. Otto's expecting us."

Anxiety shot through the bond from Nora, and Marcos wracked his brain. Otto? What did one of Titus's Binders have to do with any of this?

Br83p smirked, looking into Jesse's eyes. "Hmm, Finder. The only thing you're going find is my cock in your ass." Smiling, he glanced over at Marcos. "Maybe you'll get some ideas for your lady friend. Too bad Titus is going to hollow her out before you get a chance to use them."

He flipped a knife from his back pocket, running the blade down the side of Jesse's throat, then methodically sliced the buttons off her shirt. He reached in to fondle her. "Not bad for a skinny old bitch. Aym!" he yelled back at the Fixer. "Let this one go, I want her to squirm."

The fix on Jesse lifted, and she turned to bolt. His fist shot out reflexively, slamming into her jaw. She crumpled to the floor and the Breaker prodded her with a toe, sighing. "Shit. There goes that." He turned to them. "Guess it's your turn."

KARA WALKED into Assembly on Flynn's arm, thanking that God of his she'd been able to bind the flush from her cheeks. Ugh, that everyone had felt them together...the last thing she needed was to walk in looking like a tomato.

Not that anyone would notice. The room was a silent sea of sunglasses, and everyone was taking an abnormal interest in the floor. Kara snorted. They had such ridiculous ideas of propriety. She looked at Flynn through her lashes. His halos dominated his face, taking over his irises and swirling hypnotically. People glanced up, then couldn't help but stare. He met their gazes with his, and none were able to hold it. Was that because of his halos, or because of last night? Kara bit at her lip, her arm tightening on his as he led her to his box.

Her mother and Marcos weren't there. Kara frowned. The Binders were supposed to be voting Nora in today. Had Serra poisoned that pot already?

Lord Riggs looked frazzled. His cheeks flushed when he saw them, and he switched his attention to his papers. Ugh, even him? Kara wanted to find a rock to crawl under, and Flynn had that damned Cheshire cat grin. Jerk. He sat beside her, and she bit back her temper.

"Lord Scot." Riggs rubbed his forehead like it pained him. "I think I speak for all of us when I ask you, yet again, what was that yesterday?"

Flynn stood, jamming his hands into his pockets. "The first battle in the war against the Source was waged."

The room erupted into a frenzy.

The Speaker banged his gavel to no avail. Flynn stood there, rocking back on his heels, waiting for the noise to subside. How did he do that, portray such calm? He made it look so effortless, yet all she could feel from him was frustration and his spiking temper...

The clamor subsided enough for him to be heard, and he raised his voice again.

"Yesterday one of Titus's operatives attempted to abduct Lady Scot, and I'm afraid I didn't react to the situation in the most rational manner—"

"Rationality has nothing to do with the devastation the city incurred as a result of your temper tantrum!" A woman in the Finders' section spat. "Your actions over the past few days have us greatly concerned. We're about to be invaded by the Source, and I, for one, feel that your temperament is a liability!"

Kara chewed her thumb. The woman wasn't wrong, but if it hadn't been for him, those plaz charges would have fried everyone. The fallout had done enough damage to the Flats.

"Concerned?! I'm outraged!" shouted Lord Morris from behind them. "Split, twist, whatever you want to call yourself, you should be ousted from this body immediately! Six people died from that reckless use of talent, and hundreds more were wounded!"

Flynn's temper spiked at the grumbles of agreement spreading throughout the room. Talent flickered around his wrists, and he jammed his hands deeper into his pockets, turning to face the man.

"I regret that people died, but all of you know when talent comes in, it can be dangerous." Their bond churned with Flynn's self loathing as he parroted back the statement Merchant had prepared for him. "I had no knowledge of what I was pulling, let alone what it would do. Their families will be compensated, and House Scot is paying for the damages. Aside from that, the Overlord is a conduit of talent for all six lines—"

"Bequeathed via a vote! Whatever ability you've managed to connive is stolen, and you're not worthy of the title. House Scot's propensity for throwing money to right your ills is disgraceful!" His mouth pruned up like he was going to spit. "Compensated. You're comparing killing people to breaking a window!"

Kara glared at the nasty little man. He was frothing—actually frothing!—at the mouth.

"Yeah, you're right." Flynn scrubbed at his hair, then shrugged. "Fine. Let's get this over with. I'll release any House from their oath who isn't comfortable keeping it." The room broke into animated whispers. Kara looked at him aghast. What was he doing? He raised his voice above the clamor.

"Right now. Figure it out and take a vote. Either I'm Overlord, sworn to defend this city with my life, or I'm not, and under no obligation to assist in its defense when the Source attacks. Next plaz charge they send over the walls, you can deal with yourselves."

Their fervor ticked up.

Kara's mouth went dry. Flynn would never—but they didn't know that, did they? Every last one of them thought the worst of him. Ugh, he should leave them to suffer themselves.

He ran his gaze around the room, conversations faltering. Lord Morris looked like he was about to have an apoplexy. They should be so lucky.

Riggs cleared his throat. "Ah, well then. All those wishing to withdraw their oath of fealty from House Scot?" He scanned the Assembly. A few hands. Most squirmed in their seats, not enough guts to foreswear, thought they clearly wanted to. Kara hadn't thought it possible, but her opinion of the esteemed body dropped even lower.

"Well, it doesn't appear that there's an issue. Very good." Riggs cleared his throat again. "Then on the matter of electing Lord Scot as Overlord—"

A sea of hands rose.

"So be it. Enter it into the record, on this day, Lord Laughlin Scot has been declared Overlord with eleven, ah, sorry, twelve, Houses dissenting. Comments?"

"I have a question," Klaus drawled from the upper reaches of the chambers. "What was that delightful montage last night, and can we expect more of the same?"

Kara paled, a hand over her mouth. She was going to be sick. Members of the Assembly alternately hissed their displeasure or laughed. Flynn got that damned grin again. He looked down, shuffling a foot, then met Klaus's eyes across the room.

"That? Last night was an intensely private situation that neither I, nor the Lady Scot, had any idea we were sharing. As you can see, she's mortified." The room flicked its attention to her.

Kara forced her hands into her lap, seething. She was going to kill him for putting her on the spot. He glanced at her and his grin redoubled. She couldn't tell if it was at her anger or what he was about to say—

"I hope you enjoyed it."

The room erupted.

He was dead. She was going to kill him, bring him back, and then kill him again. Twice.

Flynn laughed and the room settled. "Look, I apologize. That was a side effect of accessing the abilities of Overlord, much like my bondsmen, and myself, flashing colors. The first won't happen again, the latter we're stuck with. Believe me when I say I wish that wasn't the case."

"It certainly ends any speculation as to who has the biggest dick in the room," someone muttered. There were several guffaws and

Laughlin colored. Kara smirked. Good. Served him right. He flopped back into his chair.

"I hate you," she muttered.

He laughed and put an arm around her. "Liar."

Riggs sighed, shuffling his papers until the room quieted. "Well then. I'm glad the lady's safe and sound, though personally, I could've done without the aftermath." He raised an eyebrow at Laughlin, and that damned grin... The speaker shook his head, pulling a sheet from the stack in front of him. "On to business. I have before me an abdication of First by Lord Ketsing. Is that right, sir?"

The gangly man stood. "Yes. After today, I'm stepping aside in favor of Lady Jester's strength of talent, but will be acting in an advisory capacity until she becomes familiar with our customs." Kara bit back a laugh. If Nora's mood after that dinner was any indication, there wasn't a chance he'd be advising her on anything.

The Speaker inclined his head, making a note. "It will be entered as requested. Do we have a second?"

"House Hinswich seconds the nomination."

"I have a written statement of your line's concordance, so I suppose that's that. Enter it into the record. On this day, the Binder line has elected Lady Jester as First by unanimous decision. Ah...where is the lady?"

"I'm not certain, but she's been very much involved with the wall and at the clinics. Perhaps time got away from her," Ketsing said. He didn't look pleased about it, and Kara wasn't either. It wasn't like Nora to be late for anything...

"Ah, that reminds me." Riggs pulled another sheet. "I have a missive from the Guild. Let me see here, ah, yes. The shield wall has been activated. Please be advised that no one will be able to shift in or out of the city. Lady Mayfield goes on to say that the wall should be impervious to both talent and some ballistics. Lovely news, I'm sure you all agree..."

He went onto other intensely boring matters. Kara reached down to rub her calf. Ugh. Twitching, right on schedule. She needed to run. Her mind went to last night and a wave of desire broke over her. Flynn inched closer and she bit back a giggle. That had been glorious.

This—this was painful. She didn't understand how he could sit through—

The gavel fell and people stood. She shot to her feet and he laughed. "Don't get too excited, it's gonna take us another forty-five minutes to get out the door."

"Can't you just shift out?"

He smirked, pulling her close. "Why, did you have something in mind?"

"Laughlin," Lord Markham said, squeezing his bulk through the crowd. He eyed it warily, his voice low. "I've called Quorum. Shall we?"

"What, now?" He looked down at Kara and she shrugged. "Yeah, okay."

Colors ran.

They stood in the conference room they'd been held in. The other Firsts, save Nora, were already seated around the oblong table with Stonefist. Flynn pulled out a chair for Kara, joining them.

"Now that we're all here, I'll be brief. I have a concrete lead on where the Source's cell is." Markham held up a hand, forestalling questions. "As expected, they're underground, somewhere past the stockyards. Unfortunately, before I could get an imprint from Fitzpatrick, the Sons attacked, and now he's nowhere to be found."

A wave of guilt came from Flynn. "Shit. I left the kid out there—"

"He's been spotted in the city since, but..." Markham sighed. "From what I gather, he's in a great deal of hot water with a woman. I'm assuming he's lying low to avoid her."

Crandall's halos flared and the man frowned. "I can't get an image of him at all, and the tunnels are even more of a warren in that sector. Are you sure he's still in the city?"

"I can't imagine where else he'd be...and there's something else you should know. The cell has a hostage. My nephew, Arileo."

Kara put a hand to her mouth, and Flynn leaned forward, a mash of emotions clashing through their bond. His anger spiked through all of them. "Is he a hostage, or working with them?"

"I—" Markham's face paled. "Fitzpatrick said he wasn't there because he wanted to be...but I will admit, Arileo has something of a deceitful nature—"

Flynn snorted. "No, he's a goddamned traitor. I've got proof he's been working with the Source, and is probably responsible for the border abductions. Julia's kid is his."

Jaws dropped around the table, and Markham fell into a chair, the wood protesting beneath him. "Good God..."

Kara was pretty sure whoever God was, he didn't have anything to do with it.

Flynn was pissed. "Forget about the tunnels, you need to find that kid, Fitz."

Crandall's face was grim. "Agreed. I'll let you know when I have him."

FITZ LOUNGED BACK against a hay bale, bored out of his skull. Loft of the barn were too quiet. He played with his pigsticker, tossing the nasty little dagger up and catching it. Snicking rats had lost its charm, bottle were done, pasties ate, and Molly...

Molly.

He grinned, the side of his face aching somewhat fierce. Christ, Adelaide had gotten him good. It'd been 'bout a day since she'd gone off...he pulled at his patch, figuring the odds she'd beat the hell out of him again if he turned up.

Were pretty good, but he were gonna lose his shite if he stayed here much longer, damned shakes was setting in—

Footsteps below, then on the ladder's rungs. Basket came up through the hole, then them glorious auburn curls. His face started aching again, smile to his ears.

"Yer still here."

"Ye sound surprised."

"I am." She pulled herself up through the hole, and came to sit beside him. "Can't imagine yer having a fine time of it. Woman must be a right bitch."

She had her moments. Fitz poked at the basket. Not a drop t'be found, but sweet rolls was still warm. He grabbed one, gobbling up the nuts first, then snagging another.

"I ain't never seen a man so skinny eat as much as ye."

"Ain't skinny. Just lean. Here, gimme yer hand and I'll show ye." Molly blushed, and he laughed. She were warming up t'him right fine. "Didn't want t'leave without saying thank ye. 'Preciate ye shacking me up."

"She gonna hit ye again?" Her fingers swept across his cheek, then lingered.

"Eh…most like she'll try." He'd have to keep clear of being otherwise occupied for a spell. Molly's thumb traced over the edge of the goose egg and he winced.

"Looks a fright." Her voice was a whisper.

He leaned towards her, hoping she'd kiss it better. "Feels one, too."

She stiffened and pulled back. "I'll be late, and hear tell Markham's looking for ye again. What business do the likes of ye have with the First Fetch?"

Fitz started. Shite, she were fresh from the farm. "Eh…he's me uncle."

Her eyes got dinner plate round, and he wished he hadn't ate them rolls. "Yer a lord?"

"Nah—"

"And here I thought ye was just a lay-about! Ye've prospects, could make somewhat of yerself, law! Ye should be ashamed!" She stood, sweeping her skirts from him like he were filth. "Ye deserve that shiner, and if I weren't genteel, I'd be tempted t'give ye another meself!"

She stormed away, and Fitz fell back against the hay, feeling sick. Fuck this. He needed a drink, Adelaide be damned. He stood, pulling talent—

And his talent ran into a wall.

The hell? He tried again, but there weren't no getting into the city. Fitz scrubbed at his head. Shite. Must've gotten that shield working. Suspect he'd have to go through the main gate… Fine sight that were gonna be. Prydees was gonna crucify him for being out in the Flats. He pulled at his patch. Nah. Tunnels was the way t'go.

He shifted below, on the other side of the funk he'd waded through last time he'd been down here. Wall shouldn't be too far on, and once he were past—

Were a light and scuffling steps coming around a bend. He hotfooted it to a cutback, standing still in the blackness, listening.

Murmur of voices, getting louder. Were them weasels. Breakers and some dumpy bat leading 'em. They tromped past, two of them carrying dead weight over their shoulders. Bodies. Shite. Were them two that old hillie had sent him t'fetch...

Fitz's hand closed around the coin in his pocket, praying. *Cajetan, ye shite, ye've gone and left me out t'dry for long enough. Take pity on your poor worthless son, and tell me what the fuck I'm supposed t'do...*

Coin stayed dead.

Bastard. Fitz pulled at his patch. Think, think, think. Ain't nobody at them estates. Can't get t'that old hillie—well, he could, but ain't nobody need t'know that. Markham. He should go t'Markham.

Fitz poked his nose out of the cutback and made a break down the tunnel. Up ahead, a weird shimmering curtain of energy fizzled through the black. Behind him were a shout. Didn't stop to think, he dove through the damned thing and pulled talent.

He landed under the table in Markham's study, air knocked out of him.

"Did you hear that?"

Shite, it were Bernice. Couch hid her from view.

"Hear what?" Kristine. His knackers constricted.

"I thought I—"

A drawer slammed shut. "We don't have time for your paranoia. Did you find anything?"

"No, and it's entirely possible there isn't anything to find."

"Rebecca thinks otherwise. If Kyle's not holding it for him, then that filthy bitch in the Pinch must've squirreled it away." Fitz's mouth went dry at his ma's name, and they was talking about his gran.

Bernice snorted. "If that's the case, you're never getting your hands on it. I don't know why you're so insistent. Even back then, what House would have been stupid enough to contract a marriage with—"

The door opened. "Ladies, did you need to speak with me?" Markham huffed, his footfalls heavy on the carpet.

"Kristine was hoping to learn the status of the CARCE."

"The CA—oh, yes. Ah, it progresses. Never fear, we've people scouring the tunnels for those beasts."

"I should hope so," Kristine sniffed. "Well, we won't keep you then." A moment later the door closed behind them, and Fitz popped his head up from behind the couch.

"Lying bitches was looking through yer desk for a contact for me bond." Weren't gonna find the blighted shite there, and Bernice were right. Ain't nobody would've wanted it. Off chance it did exist, Gran weren't giving it up, and she could take it to the grave with her for all he cared.

Markham's hand flew to his chest. "Good God, Fitzpatrick, don't do that! Where in the devil have you been?!"

"Why, what've ye heard?" He upended a decanter and his stomach rumbled. "Ye got somewhat t'eat?"

<hr>

OTTO PEERED into Nora's eyes, a nasty smile on his face. The defiant fear in them was rewarding, to say the least. He skated his fingers down her cheek, to her throat. The side of her breast.

Exquisite.

The cell had retrieved them without incident, and with luck, it would remain that way. He wasn't feeling up for dealing with drama, or much else. A cramp ripped through his gut and he grimaced, the pain severe enough to unman him.

Th poison from Mother's crown of thorns needed to be dealt with sooner than not, but in the meantime, his abdominal distress did nothing to prevent him from taking a peek into that pretty little head of Nora's. He cupped her cheek and pulled talent, tendrils snaking forth—

A surge of rage knocked him back. Otto blinked, his head splitting. What in God's name?

Past the woman's shoulder, the Commandant glared at him. Ack, it had to be their damnable bond. Cursing the Jester extra that allowed them to share talent, Otto gritted his teeth, slapping his hand against her cheek again and thrusting his psyche into hers. He was prepared for the onslaught this time, and blocked it, delving through the woman's memories. It took very little time to discover pay dirt.

He chuckled, releasing her. If the fix hadn't been holding her up, she'd be a puddle on the ground. Fortunately, neither Titus nor Mother wanted her for her mind.

"Put them in a hole and release the fix. Wouldn't want them to be uncomfortable."

"Are you sure that's wise?" a Breaker asked.

Otto grimaced, the ache at his temples matching the one in his gut. "She's not going anywhere, and I'm sure the Commandant's honor prevents him from any untoward behavior—"

A cramp ripped through Otto, doubling him over. His illness was quickly becoming untenable. Damn that bitch. "If you're that concerned, switch on a nullifier," he panted.

The Breakers exchanged glances, then dragged the fixed couple back into the shadows of an offshoot. A moment later, discordance filled his mind. An ounce of prevention, he supposed...but it exacerbated his throbbing head. That with his stomach...

The craft Titus had deployed to collect Nora and the Commandant couldn't come soon enough. Forget about remaining in the city for Titus's troops to advance. Otto planned on accompanying them to the rendezvous at the border, then gating back to Halja, and begging for Mother's mercy. He could hardly function, never mind ensure the cell would operate as she intended.

Not that he particularly cared about any of it at the moment. His bowels threatened to loosen and his sphincter tightened. Cursing the vile bitch, he hastened to the jakes.

"UN-FUCKING-BELIEVABLE." Flynn ran a heavy hand over his beard and glanced past the Firsts sitting around the conference table to Kara, standing by the window.

She was a goddamned mess. Christ, he wished he could've left her at the flat, but that asshole Rogan was nowhere to be found. She'd already been keyed up about her mother missing Assembly, and finding out Titus's goddamn cell had her upped the odds Kara would do something stupid…which would probably result in him doing something even stupider. Talent flickered around his fingers and he hid his hands under the table, avoiding Phyllis's eye. What those assholes had done to Jesse…

They were gonna bleed.

He tamped down his bloodlust and turned back to Fitz. "You're sure?"

Kid nodded, poking at the bookcases like it was an archeological dig. Shit, it pretty much was. They were packed with old surveys and moldering tomes. A bunch had been pulled out, and Stonefist was poring over the most recent ones of the sewer system.

"How did you happen upon this cell again?" Crandall asked, his voice laced with suspicion.

"Weasel hunting," the kid murmured, flipping through a bunch of old maps. "Intelligencers is on the wrong side of the city. Was up past the stockyards a stretch. Caves there dump out t'the bay." He leaned closer to the map he was looking at, then grabbed another bunch, comparing pages.

Crandall's brow furrowed. "What are you pawing through over there?"

Fitz jumped like he'd been burnt, and put them back. He shoved his hands in his pockets, fiddling with something. Flynn snorted. Kid glanced at him through his tangled hair, then away. Piece of straw stuck out from the back.

"Come sit, Fitzpatrick," Markham said.

Kid looked like he was about to bolt, then pulled out the chair farthest from everyone. He sat, blowing the curls from his eyes. Somebody had landed one hell of a punch.

"If he's right, and there's that many Breakers down there, we've got a huge issue," Stonefist said, following one of the map's lines with a finger. "Especially if they've got nullifiers. Going by Marcos's performance during the Trials, we're not going to be able to take them on hand-to-hand."

Christ, he wasn't wrong, but they couldn't leave them down there either. Who the hell knew when they'd make their move? Wasn't a chance Titus had them hanging out for shits and grins—

"That ain't right," Fitz said, watching Stonefist trace a tunnel on the map. "Ends there. Rest is caved in." He turned to Markham. "Ye said if I came, there'd be somewhat t'eat."

The other Firsts frowned at him.

"Something's being prepared," Markham said, wiping his brow. "Perhaps in the meantime you can update what's there?"

Fitz glared at him through his curls, hand busy in his pocket, that wide mouth of his turned down. "Mayhap, if ye throw in a bottle."

"Done," Markham readily agreed. The kid snatched a pencil from the table, then pulled over what Marcos had been looking at, muttering to himself. "My nephew has an uncommon hand with maps," Markham said to the rest of them.

"Aye, and this one's shite. Easier t'start over—"

"Then do it." Flynn flipped the damned thing to the blank side, and the kid shot a look at Markham. The man gave a barely perceptible nod. What the hell was that about? Kid wet his lips, hunching over the paper. He scratched his head and made a few notes before laying out a grid Flynn would've needed a T-square and a micrometer to reproduce. A faint glow lit his pencil strokes.

Shit. It was his extra.

"Ah, if you'll excuse me, I'll just pop out to get him something to eat." Markham was gone before anyone thought to comment, spellbound by what was coming out the end of the kid's pencil.

"Ain't gonna be gospel," he muttered, sketching. "Eh…got a pen?"

Phyllis and Klein both tossed him one, and he glanced up, shrinking in on himself before he started back up. They all sat mesmerized. Where the hell had he learned all this? Didn't look like he could spell his own name, never mind figure out the calculations he was scribbling out in the margins. And the detail… Christ, the sewers looked like a damned work of art—

"You should see the tide charts he's done with proper materials,"

Markham said softly. He set down a bottle of whiskey and a bowl of pasta big enough to feed a family of four. "I'd ask that none of you disclose his skill…it's a House Matter."

"It's fucking impressive is what it is," Flynn snorted.

Markham's face was sad. "It is at that."

"Otto has to be down there," Kara said, rubbing her arms like she was cold.

Goddamn it. She was right, and if he'd looked inside Nora's head… woman knew way too much. "Give Crandall an imprint of him. We need to put out warrants for his arrest. He's a Source operative, and extremely dangerous."

"Any particular reason?" the Intelligencer asked.

"He's able to coerce Talents with his extra. The wafer in a vacuum? He did that."

Crandall's expression went hard. "Consider it done."

Fitz pushed back, stomach growling. He spied the bowl and dug in without a word to anyone. Stonefist took the map, looking it over, and then at the kid.

"Jesus."

There was a stylized X on a large cavern fed by five tunnels studded by smaller caves and dead ends. One of them stretched out to the bay. If they were gonna try to smuggle Nora and the Commandant out, that'd be the most likely route. Flynn tapped a finger on it.

"Where's this come out?"

"Mile and a half north of the docks, where that spit of shale lie," kid said around a mouthful. He cracked the bottle and washed it down.

"I didn't realize those caves went back so far, but that shore is holier than the Pope," Markham mused. "If I'm remembering correctly, it's possible to slip a skiff in there at low tide if you're careful of the rocks, and I don't believe anyone is watching the bay." Everyone glanced at Crandall.

He sat back, stroking his goatee. "There are, but not many. Most of my men have been reallocated to support our efforts on the southeastern sections of the city. It's possible a skiff could avoid detection."

"So that's what, three, four men in or out at a time? What's the cave look like?" Flynn asked the kid. He played with his pasta like he didn't want to answer.

"Eh…shelf of rock at the back, big enough for half a dozen pallets and room t'work. Passage's tight. Can't bring in more than a case or two per trip, and ain't no one passing ye while ye do. Breaker'd have t'turn sideways."

"A case?" Klein asked. The kid's chewing slowed, mop of hair falling to hide the rest of his face. Half the damned bowl was already gone. He shrugged, tipping back the bottle.

"We'll need to position a squad at the entrance in case they try to make a break for it," Stonefist said, marking the area. "These branches, where do they go?"

Kid shoveled in another bite. Markham cleared his throat, and Fitz's good eye shot daggers at him. Flynn recognized the set to his jaw. Kid wasn't gonna budge. What House Matter could be making him clam up like that? Christ, he didn't have a damn House, and—shit. It had to be the Prydees. Flynn sat back in his chair, fingers tapping on its arm. His halos flared and Crandall swore.

"Did he just—"

"No one's shifted. I'm assuming they're cloaked." Markham frowned.

"Yeah, we're cloaked," Flynn said to Fitz. "Sound too. Look, I don't know what the sisters have on you, but if you don't disclose, there's a good chance that cell's gonna open the city wide when the Source gets up here."

Fitz concentrated on his pasta. "Ain't me problem."

"Yeah, it kind of is. I don't give two shits about most of these assholes, but you see that woman at the window? Unless I man up, she's gonna get hurt, and I'll be damned if I let that happen. Pretty sure there's at least one person somewhere out there that you feel the same way about."

"So are we just supposed to sit here while they have a private tête-à-tête ?" Klein groused.

"Hopefully he can talk some sense into the boy. Fitzpatrick can be fractious."

Kid shot his uncle a look, frowning. "And what if me opening me mouth'll get 'em hurt before any of it?"

"If Leo's down there, I'm gonna bet saving his raggedy ass will win you enough brownie points to keep them safe."

"It's still incredibly rude," Phyllis muttered. "I preferred it when Shades kept their talent hidden."

"Was that back when Breakers kept their opinions to themselves?" Kara asked, batting her lashes. Flynn just about swallowed his tongue. Shit, they needed to hurry this up.

"Now that'd be a cat fight…" Fitz snickered, pulling at the patch of beard beneath his lip. "Wish I could help ye, but Kristine don't give two shit about him, and she's the viper that worries me."

"So find the damned weasels."

Kid's mouth screwed up. "Ain't no weasels."

"Then killing them shouldn't be a problem."

He laughed. "Ye'd cover for me?"

"You get us down there, I'll owe you."

"How much longer do you think this is going to take? I've better things to do than watch Markham sweat," Klein said, pushing back in his chair.

Crandall raised his brow. "Personally, I find it fascinating he doesn't wrinkle into a raisin before our eyes."

"I shift in a great deal of water. This genetic imbalance is the devil, I tell you. Would that it took weight with it."

"Genetic imbalance?" Fitz snorted. "Man's hairier than a bearded ape. Right, fair enough. Ye get that angel t'heal me face, and it's a deal. Me teeth is ready t'fall out after eating that."

Flynn's halos flared again, and he called Kara over. She was scowling. Woman's bloodlust was becoming problematic.

"Will it take a lot of talent to fix his face?"

She shrugged. "I don't know, let me look." She pushed his tangled locks back. "A man shouldn't have curls like this, it's not fair," she murmured, teasing them between her fingers. Flynn's eyebrow quirked.

Kid grinned up at her. "Ye ain't the first t'say so. Way ye ladies like t'run your hands through 'em, I ain't complaining." She snatched hers back like she'd been burnt, and Flynn snickered. Kid was a player.

"I'd say they like clean your clock too, by the looks of this," she said sweetly.

Flynn laughed. "What? A woman did that?"

"Either that, or he pissed off a brawny ten-year-old. Knuckle pattern's too small for a man. It won't take much to heal, if you think he deserves it."

"Nah, not until I hear why."

"Were a differing of opinions." Fitz scowled.

"A differing of opinions?"

"Eh…ya. She didn't want me visitin' a certain lass, and I differed. Found me in the middle of it."

Woof. That had to suck. Bet he hadn't even seen it coming. "Yeah, take pity on him."

Kara rolled her eyes and pulled talent. Kid's face went back to where it belonged.

"Thank ye."

Flynn dropped his cloak. "Map."

"Have you come to a—"

Fitz pulled it over, cutting Markham off. "That one leads up t'the guard shack by the old north wall postern. There goes t'the basement of the 'Pearl, but they got a honking meat locker atop the trap. This follows the tannery sewage line, and them last two is caved in or underwater."

Shit. That was more than he'd expected. "How'd you get there?"

"Tannery line, they got the end blocked off…but there's a branch above…" He chewed on the end of his pencil, then made some marks. "Here. S'higher than the rest. Empties into an old cistern that connects t'where they is, eh…here. Ye can get into it through t'them storm drains by the slaughterhouse."

"A squad needs to be in each of those tunnels and advance as a unit," Stonefist said, reviewing the map. "This one here should run point, driving them down to the bay, and another positioned at the exit to pick them off. There's very little cover on that stretch of shore." He looked over at Markham. "How many men can you shift at one time?"

The Fetch raised an eyebrow. "As many as you need. Just tell me where you want them."

Stonefist grunted. "If that's agreeable to you, Lord Scot?"

Flynn ran a hand through his hair. Sounded as good a plan as any. "Yeah, do it."

"And where will you be?" They all stared at him.

Shit. If he couldn't leave the city… "I dunno yet."

"Figure it out. I'll round up troops and meet you all at the sally yard on the fifth rung." Stonefist left the room, and Crandall turned to them, sour.

"Why wasn't Fitzpatrick conscripted to assist with our efforts in the southeastern sector?"

"S'Fitz."

"House Matter," Markham replied in the same breath.

"And would that House Matter prevent you from providing a similar schematic for the rest of the city?" The Intelligencer asked through gritted teeth.

Fitz leaned back in his chair and pulled at that patch of his, hand in his pocket fiddling again. "Eh…dunno. S'it a paying job?"

CHAPTER SEVENTEEN

*"Dark currents of fury | Funneling down |
A voice, my own | Lost as I drown."*

*— Fion, Breaker Poet,
Glynfyls*

---

*"The hierarchy demands the submission of all Breakers. In this matter, the
Way is clear. Rogue talents threaten the balance of power and must be brought
into the fold, or put down. There is no way but the Way. A Breaker walks
upon it, or not at all…"*

*— Lord Grimmight, Breaker Menot,
Glynfyls*

"IT'S NEVER GOING to stop, is it?"

Kara slumped onto the couch by the gate, her face white. Every
time she turned around the Source was right there, and now they had
Nora. Anxiety crawled up her throat, choking her. They were never
going to be safe—

"Hey." Flynn knelt in front of her and made her look into his eyes.

He was doing it again. Pulling up that veneer of calm when everything inside him was screaming for blood. "Whatever Titus throws at us, we'll deal with. Get out of your head. He's only as big a threat as you make him. We know where the cell is, and how to get to them. Another couple hours, it'll be all over. We'll worry about tomorrow when it happens." He stood, holding his hand out to her. She ignored it.

"You know you can't go out there."

He scowled, running a hand over his beard. "I have to—"

"No you don't. Jesse's going to be fine, and it could've been a lot worse than a broken jaw. Your job is to stay here and protect the city." His 'lust jumped and talent flickered around his fingers. He wiped them on his pants, frowning.

"How the hell can I protect the city when there's a—"

"She's right."

Flynn spun to glare at Rogan. "Who the fuck asked you?"

The Breaker shrugged, leaning against the door jamb. "Look kid, hate to break it to you, but leaving the city's going to do more than strip you of your talent. Feels like you're coming off a goddamned bender, and your performance in the field's going to suffer big time."

"And what makes you such an expert?"

Rogan snorted. "Christ, don't they teach anything at the Academy anymore? Who the hell do you think got suckered into being Overlord in the first place? It's a rotten gig, but there's a way around it, if you're interested."

What was Rogan doing? Kara looked between them, feeling Flynn's curiosity warring with his overwhelming dislike for the man.

Curiosity won out.

"Like what?"

Rogan's eyes fell on her. "Like a Valkyrie. Their original purpose was to use the Overlord's strength in the field as instruments of his divine retribution."

"What?! Fuck no—"

"Why not?"

Flynn looked at her, sputtering. "Kara, you've spent the last few weeks in and out of bed, Christ, you're—"

"I'm what? My metrics are superior to any Source Breaker, and I've been so twitchy—" Her temper spiked. "You know I don't need your permission, right?"

"Yeah, I know. But, goddamn it—" They glared at each other, tempers stoked by their echo, emotions playing beneath it. He was terrified and she didn't care. She could do this, and the fact that he didn't think she could—

"Fine," he spat, scowling at Rogan. "But you're going with her, and I want your fucking oath!"

The Breaker sliced his palm and held it out. Flynn did the same, teeth gnashing as he gipped the man's hand, talent cracking up his arm. Rogan's lips thinned, watching it.

"You need to get a handle on that shit."

"She gets hurt and I'm gonna fucking bury you with it."

Rogan snorted and squeezed her shoulder. "Go get ready, I'll meet you where they're mustering in ten."

Kara laughed, bouncing on the balls of her feet. Yes! She was finally going to get to do something—Flynn's expression wiped the smile off her face. "Do you really not want me to go?" It was a stupid question. She knew he didn't.

He sighed. "I know you can handle yourself, I just...no. I don't want you to go. Christ, Kara, you're so damned frail, there's the babies to consider, and—you sure you can keep a handle on your 'lust? Combat isn't the same as the ring—"

"Breaker females are built for this. I've lost weight, not muscle mass, and Rogan will be there, he—"

Flynn's hand skimmed down the side of her face. "That's not what I asked."

Her eyes misted and she blinked back tears. Dang it. "I think so...I —I feel like I have to do this, Flynn. I'm so tired of all the backbiting and stupid teas. None of it matters, not really. Even at the infirmary, I couldn't—" she bit back a sob. "I haven't been able to use my talent, have been stuck in that stupid bedroom while you're—Ugh! I feel so useless and I hate it! I just—"

"Shh..." He pulled her against his chest, sighing again as she wept. "I'll phaze the babies to keep them safe like we did for the bout. Stick close to Rogan and be careful, okay? Don't take any stupid risks."

She sniffed, wiping her eyes. "Really?"

"Yeah. I fucking hate that you're gonna go down there, but if it's that important to you, then you're right. You need to do it. Go get changed. I gotta let Cal know what's coming down the pike." He kissed her cheek and jammed his hands into his pockets, leaving the room with another sigh.

Kara chewed her thumb, going up to their suite. She could do this. I wasn't like she didn't know how to pull zero anymore. The past few days, it had become second nature.

Which was kind of the problem…

Ugh, whatever. She could handle it. It'd be easier once she was less twitchy. She needed a good workout and this would fit the bill. Once she got rid of all this excess energy, her 'lust wouldn't be a problem. Flynn was just being overprotective. Her metrics were better than any other Source Breaker, it would just be like putting Pax in his place. She pulled her leathers out of the closet and slipped them on, a feral grin splitting her lips. Her heart raced.

With excitement. Not 'lust… *Yeah. Keep telling yourself that, Kara…* she quashed that stupid little voice inside her head and went back downstairs, braiding her hair. She could do this.

Flynn was waiting for her by the gate, puffing away on one of Cal's cigars. "You're sure you can keep it in check?"

"Absolutely." Okay, probably…

He blew out a stream of smoke, looking at her like he knew she was full of shit. She smiled at him, and he shook his head, putting a hand on her abdomen. His halos flared, phazing the babies. "Then let's do this."

They stepped through the gate into a stark grey room. Equipment lined three walls. The other was a row of windows overlooking a training field rucked with hillocks and scorch marks. The sun was dipping below the horizon. Several squads of Breakers, each led by a Hex, waited in formation beyond the glass, casting long shadows.

Inside, eyebrows raised when they caught sight of her. Phyllis's expression was resigned. "You're going with them."

"I am."

Lord Klein was incredulous. "Lady Scot, we've all seen the footage, and don't doubt your ability, but this is unnecessary risk. Stonefist's troops can handle it."

Her mouth set into a line, the man's words hardening her resolve. "I don't doubt they're capable, which is why I'll be going. My mother is down there, and I'm going to bring her out."

He looked at Flynn, and he shrugged, jamming his hands into his pockets.

"It's her choice," he said, sounding way more at ease than what she was feeling from him. Kara's cheeks dimpled. It was what she wanted to hear, even if it wasn't what he wanted to say.

"Only on the condition you're in the rearguard," Stonefist begrudgingly allowed. "Those men have worked together before. I don't need you throwing them off, and you'll stay on comms at all times."

"Of course."

Flynn sighed like he knew that wasn't going to last. She bit back a smile, and he scrubbed a hand over his face, then grabbed a pair of goggles from the wall.

"Here, you'll need these." He looped them over her temples. "Night-vues. Focus them with this." He toggled a little switch on the side. "Got it? Good. Now where's Rogan?"

"Rogan?" Crandall asked.

"Yeah, Kara's bodyguard," Flynn said irritably, saved from further explanation by the Breaker stalking through the gate. Man bristled with weapons. He threw a leather wrapped package at Kara. She unwrapped it. Haladie and fingerless gloves. A fierce grin split her face as she put them on and spun the double-sided knives.

"Right. What's the plan?" Rogan's eyes flicked to Phyllis's and something passed between the two. She didn't look happy, and he didn't seem to care. Lord Stonefist briefed him.

"No. We're in front. I don't want your men in our way," Rogan said.

To Kara's surprise, Stonefist gave a curt nod. She glanced at Flynn. He chewed on his cigar, stoic. Her stomach flipped. Ugh! Now wasn't the time for doubts—she'd committed.

"I'll be on the wall, overlooking the stockyards." His expression said he'd be over it in a heartbeat if he thought she was in trouble, and what was streaming through their bond—He pulled his beanie out of a pocket and shoved it on his head. "Right. Let's get this over with."

He turned away, and Lord Markham shifted them into the tunnels before she could say goodbye. She wiped at her eyes. Stupid…

Rogan squeezed her shoulder. "Head in the game, Karabelle."

He was right. She could do this.

A squad of thirty men were behind them in a pitch-black tunnel, fetid enough to taste. Kara gagged, burying her nose in her elbow. Oh, that was awful. She steeled herself and adjusted her night-vues, everything snapping into focus with a weird green glow.

The tunnel they were in ran parallel to the sewers, walls pockmarked with crumbling steel grates. Then those became fewer, and the tunnel narrower. It didn't branch, just pitched towards the bay, faint noises echoing from the depths. The men behind her were moving single file now, low piles of scree in tumbles across the passage. The stones slickened beneath her feet, then dropped away into a channel. A Shade from the Hex cloaked them as they advanced into the rankness, water splashing soundless.

Kara sank to mid-calf into the stagnant funk before hitting the bottom, muck squelching. Ugh, that was disgusting…new boots. She was going need new boots—

She stumbled, and put a hand out to catch herself, then snatched it back. Stupid fingerless gloves. The walls glistened and wriggled. She brushed the goo on her thigh, gorge rising in her throat. Ugh, what had she been thinking volunteering for this? Something from the ceiling plopped into the water between her and Rogan, and she cringed.

Flynn's voice crackled through the comms. "Everyone's in position. Be careful Kara…you know."

She did. Her lips tipped up, then down. She was also pretty certain that this had been a stupid idea. She was going to kill Rogan for suggesting it. He had to have known she'd jump at it before thinking about what it actually entailed. She flicked more slime from her fingers, tempted to put it down his collar—

A pinpoint of light resolved in the gloom. The echoing noises became voices, two if she had to guess. The tunnel ended at a grate another three, four hundred yards away. Rogan stopped, motioning for her to fall back, and approached the squad leader.

"They've got a nullifier running. Give us five minutes before you advance." The man signaled for his troops to hunker down. "We're going in, lover boy," Rogan said into comms.

Kara rolled her eyes. Glory, he could be a jerk. She crept down the tunnel after him. The walls were drier here, mossy instead of slimy. She stepped out of the channel, onto a narrow ledge running beside it.

A shadow flashed across the tunnel's ceiling, and they froze, a man's voice echoing up at them.

"That craft can't come soon enough. I can't wait to get out of this shithole."

"I don't wanna hear it. We're stuck down here until the vanguard signals."

"Sucks to be you."

Kara and Rogan edged closer to the tunnel's mouth. It came out near the top of the cistern Fitz had told them about. Past the rust-eaten grate, two Breakers were at the bottom, passing a bottle around a fire.

"Whatever, won't be long. Hear Titus's at the border. Rations are supposed to be tight, and suppressant's on that list. Things are gonna get ugly when those Elites start succumbing." A wrapper crinkled.

Kara frowned at the rungs driven into the wall beside the opening. No way was she trusting those, and the drop was going to be a problem.

The grate wasn't. Half the bars ended midway in flaky stumps. The squad wouldn't have trouble getting through, but it would take time. Rogan tugged on the crossbar. It was stuck fast. He motioned for her to stay and crept back to the troops. She kept to the shadows, listening to the men below.

"I still don't understand why Titus wants this bitch bad enough to send up a craft—"

"Cause she cast some fucking bind to make the Commandant defect, that's why."

"It don't sit right. I got respect for the man."

"We all do, but, you know what they say about the power of Binder pussy. They can do all kinds of shit with those weaves."

The other man grunted. "You should've nailed that skinny old bitch."

Rogan slunk back to the grate, and secured a rope around the crosspiece. He ran a section behind his back, bracing it, and handed Kara the length. "I'm right behind you," he whispered.

"She was out cold. That's like necrophilia or some shit. I'm about to start twitching if I don't hit something else, though. You should've seen her drop, I barely tapped her."

"Go a couple rounds with Adams. He's all pent up, too."

Kara gathered a section in her hands and rappelled into the cistern —*please don't tangle, please don't tangle*—

Sand crunched under her boots. Rogan's voice came over comms telling everyone to hold. Heart thumping, she spun to face the Breakers.

"The fuck—"

"Shit, that's the other one. Looks like you've got someone to hit." The dark-haired man looked up at the tunnel. Rogan was nowhere in sight. Kara's pulse pounded, waves of 'lust licking at her. "Stupid bitch came by herself. Let's go a few rounds."

She pulled out the haladie, spinning them. The red-head flicked open a blade.

"We saw what you did to that near-cull. Think you can do the same to a 'keeper?"

"We're going to find out, now aren't we?"

"We are." The dark-haired one wet his lips, and leaned against the wall beside a pitted steel door, smirking. He wasn't as big as Riegel had been, but he looked more solid. She tried to edge around them to put their backs to the tunnel, but they weren't budging.

"Save enough of her to have some fun after."

Kara rolled her eyes. Jerk. The red-head advanced, snickering as he slashed at her. She ducked under his blade and drove hers into his gut, the other finding his throat. The man against the wall came at her before the body hit the floor.

Kara spun just in time. He was a lot faster than his friend. His fist went through the space her head had been as she dropped, sweeping at his feet. It was like hitting ironwood stumps, his center of gravity too low to knock him off balance.

She danced away, pulling zero. He swung and lunged again, a knife in his hand. The tip sliced across her bicep. Kara staggered back, bloodlust surging. His eyes glazed, nostrils flaring, and charged again, arms spread to grapple. She kicked him across the face. His head snapped to the side, and he grunted, his teeth clacking as she drove her blade up under his chin. He crumpled to the ground with the other one.

She panted, fighting to bury her 'lust. See? No harder than Pax, and over. It was over. Listen to the music…it looped through her mind, beating back at the darkness.

A hand was on her shoulder, and she flinched.

Rogan held up a bandage between his thumb and forefinger, giving her a long look.

She snatched it from him. "I'm fine."

He didn't look convinced.

Whatever. She could do this, damn it. The last of the squad assembled in the chamber while she bandaged her arm, then joined Rogan on point.

"First chamber secured, craft inbound for the hostages. Moving forward," he said into comms.

Behind the steel door, the tunnel made a ninety degree turn, pitching upwards. Snoring. They edged into a roughly hewn cavern with a couple dozen cots set up. Half were filled. Stonefist's men ensured they stayed that way.

"Second chamber secured. Dozen eighty-sixed. Count's at fourteen."

Kara wiped her palms against her thighs, the leather slick. The next chamber was the one Leo was supposed to be in, but where did they have Nora?

MARCOS HELD Nora in his lap, running a hand across her brow. Whatever that loathsome little Binder had done to her, she was beyond sedated, the abrupt shift in her emotions when the man had his hands on her…and now she was a blank slate. Marcos didn't know what that meant, but it worried the hell out of him. The damp hole they'd been thrown into couldn't be good for her either, but at least they'd removed the fix—that goddamned crack about his honor…

Honor didn't have anything to do with it. The sheer number of Breakers milling about guaranteed his good behavior. He knew many of them and their capabilities. There wasn't anything to do but bide his time. The fact that they hadn't shifted was telling. They were waiting for something, or someone. Marcos hoped the delay would provide a chance for their absence to be noted and acted upon, though how anyone was going to find them down in this warren…

He tried to convince himself that biding his time didn't mean he was going to Titus without a fight. He had no illusions as to what waited for them there. Marcos pulled Nora's limp body closer, hand at the base of her skull. His mouth went dry, but if it came down to it, he'd spare her that.

A Breaker poked his head over the lip of the hole and tipped his cap. Devlin. He'd been in one of the units Marcos ran early on in his career. He glared at him. Man had the decency to look ashamed as he turned away.

The Fixer took his place. "Stand up, the craft's almost here." She made a disgusted noise when he didn't move and pulled a pistol, pointing it at Nora. "Move, or I put a bullet in her."

"Hand her up, Commandant, there's no point in resisting," Devlin muttered, not meeting his eye.

The hell he would. "Stand back." Marcos adjusted his grip on Nora and vaulted from the blasted pit. He wasn't that damned old. A squad fell in around him, pop of gunfire somewhere behind them. His feet slowed. They'd found them…

"Walk!" A muzzle jammed into his back. The odds that she'd shoot anything vital warred with the possibility of it going through him and hitting Nora. Marcos gritted his teeth and picked up the pace.

The walls of the tunnel closed in, scraping at him. Ahead, men had turned sideways. How the hell was he supposed to carry her through that?

The going was slow. Tight, but not impossible. Water lapping against stone echoed up the narrow passage. It ended in a sea cave, a skiff bobbing beside an outcropping of rock beside the ledge.

Devlin got into the boat and held his arms out for Nora, meeting Marcos's eyes. His grip loosened at what he saw in them. He passed her over, and got in without a word.

FLYNN STOOD on the cliffs by the northwestern section of the wall, just outside of the shield. He'd forgotten the damned thing blocked talent. That was gonna be a major problem when Titus got up here. It'd keep the Breakers from blowing them to shit, but they wouldn't be able to do any damage in return.

He scowled, looking out over the bay, and trying not to lose his shit. Goddamn, he hated heights. He pulled talent, casting out his senses, trying to find the craft that was supposed to be inbound.

Nothing, but he didn't know what the hell he was doing, either.

Finding left a funky flavor coating your tongue. Who knew what a craft was supposed to taste like. Metal, maybe. His luck it'd be fucking Skydrol. The wind whipped away the smoke from his cigar, chilling his sweat-stippled skin. Didn't do anything for his nausea. Maybe that was what Rogan had been yapping about. He glanced over the edge and the ground loomed up at him. Maybe not. His breath caught, knees going weak, back pressing against the wall.

Christ, this sucked. He rocked his beanie lower over his ears, cold cutting through him despite his cloak. The aurora teased the horizon, the light from the city snuffing out the ribbons of dancing color above. His heart ached thinking about Kara. The babies.

His family, down in those fucking tunnels, and he'd let them go.

… "She's not meant to sit on a shelf…"

No. He wouldn't fucking do that to her, but goddamn it, her being down there was a stupid fucking idea. He blinked, then wiped his eyes…something was coming in low across the bay. A small craft, big enough for maybe six people, max. It banked beside the spit of shale, hovering roughly fifty feet in front of where the cave entrance was supposed to be. A skiff rowed into view.

Two big men, one with a woman in his lap, the other at the oars. The Hex sent out a fix and froze the trio on the water, then fixed the craft.

"Hold fire on that Breaker!" They needed one of the assholes alive. A Fetch shifted onto the boat, then brought everyone aboard back. The Commandant inclined his head and stood.

"Laughlin. Nora needs medical attention." Bastard said it like it was his due.

"Fine. Take them through one of the gates to scrub them of bots first," Flynn said to the Fetch. He'd try to do it, but he was worse at binding than finding. As in, he couldn't even pull it even though he knew it was there. Freaking talent was as convoluted as their logic. "Then shift the Breaker to the brig, and the Commandant and...*her* to the Infirmary. Report back."

The Fetch saluted and they were gone.

Shots rang out from the craft, red spatter running down the inside of the plex. Flynn shook his head. "We've got them, and the craft is secured," he said into comms, even if it was gonna be a fucking mess to clean up. It'd also been too easy. His stomach cramped. Somewhere, shit was gonna hit the fan.

What he was feeling from Kara was proof positive of that.

KARA HUNKERED behind a tumble of crates, her irritation at being pinned down and the screeching discordance of a nullifier threatening to break her hold on her zero. The cavern was stacked with supplies and full of enemy combatants.

They'd only been able to take out two before the cry went up.

Element of surprise gone, their advantage had left with it and mayhem ensued. Bodies littered the floor, too many of them from the North. The second squad storming the chamber had given them some more breathing room, but not enough to turn the tide. Maybe half their number remained, and they were all pinned down by gunfire, her superior metrics worth shit against bullets.

Flynn was right, this was nothing like being on the mats.

"I count six 'keepers and a couple others," Rogan growled. He was bleeding from his shoulder and a ragged cut across the bridge of his nose. "The rest scattered. We've gotta take out those snipers."

She nodded, hearing what he wasn't saying—that they were in trouble. Her stomach churned. That last guy had hit her hard enough to see stars, and her body ached. Whatever she'd come down here to prove—ugh! Stupid, stupid, stupid!

Rogan racked his pistol, and her fingers tightened on the one she'd taken off a Breaker. She needed to snap out of it. There was nothing to do but get through it.

"You go right, and I'll cut left. That fucking nullifier is in that alcove by the rocks. We kill it, and it's a whole new ballgame." He gave a three count and they bolted.

Kara made for the next rack of barrels where two men from the squad crouched beside a body—

White hot pain bit into her thigh.

She dove for cover and collapsed, hand pressed over the burn. A bullet had torn through her leathers, slicing a furrow through her flesh. Flynn's panic followed it, and her bloodlust licked up. She couldn't—music beat it back and she hissed out a sob. Glory, that'd hurt—

***

SOMETHING HAD HAPPENED TO KARA. The earth scorched around Flynn's feet, his fists digging into the returning Fetch's shirt, jacking him up on tip-toes. That thing inside him scrabbled at his insides, frantic. "Get us down there, now!"

The man quailed, throat bobbing—"I…I just saw the cave entrance from the boat—"

Flynn growled and colors ran.

He was submerged in icy water. Breath bubbling up, his feet kicked, boots dragging—

Air, slicing into his lungs. Flynn gulped at it, shaking water from his eyes. The Fetch bobbed next to him.

"Get the rest of the squad down here."

Then Flynn was alone, cliffs ahead, moonlight eaten by a dark slash through its face. He swam for it, not waiting for the others, his anxiety fueling him, beating back the nausea, the ugly inside him feeding on it. Voices ahead, slushed by the surf. The tide buffeted him against stone, fingers scraping it, propelling him through the gap.

The cavern was nullified, and full of Breakers.

He swore, gliding through the water, toward an outcropping of stone. One of them had a plaz-lantern. They crowded around it, arguing as he angled behind the rock.

"...when Beritram gets up here."

"Fuck that false Alpha, You weren't there, the 'lust in the streets—"

"No, but I was in the arena at the Source that day, man's a monster—"

"And the Commandant put him down with a tranq. If he's with Scot..."

Gun shots from the tunnel behind them. Flynn eased out of the water, numb and shaking.

Feeling like he'd come off a bender.

He bit back a laugh. Good thing he was an expert at that shit. Effect his performance—he'd fucking perfected his performance hung over. Who the hell knew it would be on the job training? That ugly inside him gnawed at his guts, stronger out here, urging him to act. To do something stupid. Flynn tamped it down, feeling its frustration. Its rage, stoking his own. He put his back to the stone, pulling his sodden sidearm. Water poured from the barrel. Christ, that wasn't good...

KARA TURNED at the sounds of a scuffle. Rogan had engaged with a Peacekeeper, and from this vantage, one of those damned snipers drawing a bead on him was open. She took him out before he could get the shot off, then—Crap. Her magazine was spent.

"Ammo?" she asked the men beside her, tearing a strip of cloth from the corpse's fatigues. She wasn't going to bleed to death, but she was light-headed enough as it was.

"Tapped," the bigger of the two said, watching her bandage her leg.

She pulled it tight, blinking back tunnel vision. Panting. *Don't you dare, Kara. Catch your breath, and keep going.* Heartbeat mellowing...*too long. Keep moving before you don't.* She pulled her haladie. The cavern spun when she stood. Nothing for it—

Kara sprinted to the next pile of supplies, hoping everyone was paying attention to the fight on the other side of the room. A bullet hit the ground behind her. Crap. She rounded a crate, bowling over a woman behind them.

She screamed and raised a pistol with shaking hands—

Her end was quick. Kara took the gun, peeking past the edge of the crate—A bullet clipped the corner, splinters spraying. She flinched back. Damn it. The next stack of supplies was too far...

But the nullifier was just past that.

She looked through the gap between the crates. Rogan had made it to cover and the enemy Breaker was down. Five left—

Sand scuffed, and she hit the ground hard, a blond man on her. He knocked the pistol from her hand and pinned her beneath him, slamming her head back. Her vision prickled, gray nausea rising up—

OUR MATE!

The animal took over, rage suffusing Flynn, dark and black, exploding outward, a dank wave of fury blanketing the cavern. The Breakers spun on his position, staggering, hands faltering on their weapons, dropping to their knees and cowering. He ran forward, snatching a gun from a man's hand, and barreled down the tunnel.

FLYNN'S RAGE burned through their bond and Kara took it up along with his strength, snapping her head into the Breaker's face. The man's nose crunched, and she scrambled away, retrieving the gun. He rolled up into a crouch and her bullet put a hole between his eyes.

Four Breakers left.

She panted against the crates, mouth dry, running an arm over her face. Flynn was close and getting closer. What was he thinking? He was going to get himself killed, and it was going to be her fault—

Unless the nullifier was down. She sighted it and pulled the trigger. Nothing.

Crap, the magazine was spent.

Shots across the room. The sniper was targeting someone else.

She took off pell-mell to the other stack of supplies.

A burst of white fire bucked into her shoulder, spinning her around. The bloodlust she'd been holding back rolled over her, and she put on a burst of speed, making it to cover.

Two Breakers waited for her behind the crates, and she smiled.

FLYNN FELT the bullet hit Kara and the blackness consume her.

He roared with fury, a howl tearing from his throat as he burst out of the tunnel. She was there, two Peacekeepers closing in. Their attention snapped to Flynn, nostrils flaring.

Kara lunged, skewering one of them with that wicked double blade. He fell back but wasn't down. The other went at her. Flynn stumbled at the 'lust pouring off her—she couldn't fight it and them. He charged one of the Peacekeepers, knocking him off his feet into a pile of rocks beyond the crates.

Rogan lay behind them in a pool of blood.

Shit. The 'keeper threw Flynn off him, and he landed on the man. He was still breathing, but wouldn't be for long. Flynn pushed away, facing the 'keeper—

A nullifier was in an alcove behind him. Flynn raised his gun, and a stone struck it from his hand. Motherfucker!

The 'keeper laughed. Fuck, he knew that asshole—

… A knife slides down the side of his face, his limbs held prone by Peacekeepers. He knows better than to struggle. His eyes stay on the one with

the wine-colored birthmark wielding the blade. "You're awful pretty, Inmate 5462. Let's do something 'bout that"...

"Scot! Almost didn't recognize you with that pretty face again. Brix is gonna be pissed when he finds out I got to you first." He lunged, and Flynn scrambled back, tripping over Rogan—

A scream split the air, and Kara launched herself at the Breaker's back, slicing his throat.

Flynn clambered to his feet, running to the nullifier, and turning the fucking thing off. Kara sprang from the Breaker, her attention zeroing on him. His chest constricted. She stalked towards him, eyes molten pools of malice.

It was a knife in his heart, and the beast inside him quailed.

She didn't know him.

He stepped backwards, his hands raised in supplication. "No. Not this, Kara, please..." His voice caught, trying to push emotion through their bond. She faltered and the fury was replaced by a moment of confusion, a flurry of sensation reaching him. He choked on a sob. She was running on pure adrenaline. The bullet had nicked something, and she was slowly bleeding out.

"Fight it Kara, please...please..." He pulled at his hair—

Her head snapped up at the motion, eyes narrowing.

Fuck! He pushed her more emotion, trying to get through to her—

The darkness ate it.

Behind her, the squad poured into the room.

"Fix her!" A flash of bronze and she froze. Flynn stumbled against the wall. God, her rage...she strained against the fix, it wasn't gonna hold her for long...

Pity in the squad's eyes. His composure crumbling.

The Binder was at Rogan's side, halos ablaze. "I've done what I can. We need to get him back to the infirmary—"

Flynn didn't give a shit. He dropped to his knees beside Kara.

"Help her..."

"I don't have enough talent—"

Not enough...fuck that, how...? Everything he got was from his people, and there was a room full of them. Flynn fumbled, trying to pull—his hand snaked out and gripped the Binder, pushing—

The man's eyes went wide at the influx of talent, his halos blazing.

"Take it," Flynn gasped. "Take all of it, just save her. Save them."

The Binder got to work.

Flynn plucked the blade from Kara's hand and staggered to his feet, hollow. Two Breakers were on their knees on the sand, under guard, hands fixed behind their backs. He walked over.

"Any more hostages?"

One of the squad shook his head. "There's a filthy pit, but no sign of whoever they had in it."

Damn it. "These two were in the room?"

The men guarding them exchanged glances. "Yes, sir. The rest surrendered. What do you want us to do with them?"

Flynn laughed and they flinched. The Breakers on their knees glared back, unrepentant.

"Not a fucking thing." He tested the gore-slickened blade with a thumb.

The Source had taken his heart, now he was gonna take theirs in return.

CHAPTER EIGHTEEN

*"Suppression meds became necessary with the advancements in Elite
physicals. Unable to isolate the nucleotide responsible for the adverse effects of
bloodlust without detrimentally affecting a Breaker's development, a serum
administered on a strict regimen mutes the hormone and guarantees
tractability after puberty is reached. The effect of a lapse in dosage in a single
subject results in an increased probability of succumbing across the whole of
an exposed subset. It is, in short, 'catchy'…"*

— T. Merkel, Triam Laboratory Records

KARA EXISTED in a turbulent state of heightened emotion. Pain.
Pain had fueled her, then a golden glow had stolen it away, leaving her
to thrash against violent currents of inky anger. Memory…repressed,
dismissed, explained away—

Reborn.

Her body rigid, she strained against the fix. Whispers surrounded
her. They used her voice, coaxing, seducing…seeking vengeance.

Other voices, underwater.

"I've healed her body, but I can't help her with what she's fighting
now."

A man. His hand on her cheek. Eyes sad.

Weak.

"Please, Kara…come back to me…"

Her lips ached to curl into a snarl, to rake her nails down his face, curls of flesh gouging off beneath them, blood slicking her hands—something pressed towards her, and her pulse sped—

Something…she fought to grab onto lilting notes…

A secondary link of talent appeared.

…*use it*…the whispers urged, gleeful.

Everything else was churned beneath their blackness.

The man's face crumpled.

She pulled talent, chipping away at the fix.

***

"YOU'VE REVIEWED THE FOOTAGE?" Titus asked, grinning around his bourbon at the behemoth in his cabin. Though the loss of his cell grated, the final transmissions he'd received more than made up for it. Hopefully Otto had managed to ooze from the fray, Titus was running low on pills, along with everything else. Why he'd never had the man infected with bots…his hand rose to his temple. Damn these headaches…

"Yeah, 'lust's got her." Brix frowned, rubbing at his oiled scalp as if something about that bothered him. Titus's eyes narrowed. That bizarre thread of compassion needed to be bred out of them. Why should he care if the Jester girl had succumbed?

There was no coming back. The question now became whether they would put her down or try contain her somewhere until she gave birth. It was unlikely, but the possibility of being able to retrieve her genetics was an appealing one. In either event, the end result was the same.

Scot had been unstable before, but this had broken him.

His volatile temper evidenced over the past few days was giving even the board pause. Albanach's assurances and attempts to assuage them were falling flat. So much for their new image. After this… Titus chuckled, forwarding the feed of Scot eviscerating those last two Breakers to every news outlet on the planet.

"The old Breaker with the topknot, any intel on him?"

Titus glanced up, having forgotten Brix was still there.

"Not a shred, which is interesting in and of itself. His performance suggests Elite DNA, but his age disproves the possibility. In either event, I'm assuming blood loss will kill him." Brix didn't look convinced. Titus didn't care. "Anything else?"

"The last of the men have assimilated the boosts and are online. We lost two of them during the integration."

"Can the modules be salvaged?"

"No."

Titus's finger tapped against his glass. Three of the mechanized men would have to do, but five would've been better. "How are the troops adapting to the rationed suppressant dosages?"

"If they can't handle it, they'll get put down."

Not ideal, but necessary. Succumbing had the unfortunate tendency to propagate throughout the ranks if not dealt with swiftly. "Scot remembers you. I'd like you to make the most of that fact."

Brix's lip rose in a feral grin, his canines filed to sharp points. Gah, he was ugly, but too effective to cull on aesthetics. His metrics were superlative, more than earning him command of the Elites, and Titus was well aware of how much the Breaker was looking forward to carving Scot up again.

"When we advance, your squad is to wait with the reserves until an opportunity presents itself. I want him, along with the others on your list."

"In what condition?"

"Able to breed, beyond that he's yours."

Brix rubbed his knuckles and left smiling.

FLYNN PACED the empty sitting room of their suite, raking at his hair. He'd lost it. Become that goddamned animal and fucked up again —His hands shook, caked in gore to his elbows. Didn't matter, he didn't—what the fuck was he gonna do? A guttural moan tore from his throat. He collapsed to the floor, cheeks wet, temples between his palms, rocking.

He should've kept her here. Said no. Fuck, this was his fault. He knew she couldn't handle it, had felt her fucking 'lust...his fingers trembled against his lips, unable to look away...

Kara stood rigid in the center of the barren room, unmaking the fix as fast as he replenished it. He pulled more talent, channel burning, and she answered in kind. What happened when he couldn't pull anymore?

She'd kill him. He wouldn't—couldn't—hurt her.

And then she'd rage through the city, and they'd put her down.

Her and the babies.

His head knocked back against the wall, glassy-eyed, looking heavenward.

Why the fuck would you give me everything I've ever wanted, and then take it away like this? What the fuck did I ever do—

Plenty. His eyes closed. Answering his own question. Christ, *he* fucking deserved it, but she didn't, and the babies...

Fuck this.

He stripped off his blood-soaked shirt, wiping his face and throwing it to the floor.

Going to her.

"Kara..." His hands were on her cheeks, meeting her eyes, trying to make her see him.

The rage of a trapped animal glared out.

His face crumpled and he choked back a sob. "Christ, you need to snap out of it! Don't...don't leave me." He pressed his lips to her forehead, trying to send emotion through their bond—

Nothing, no recognition.

He ripped a hand through his hair and put a fist through the wall, the air around him shimmering with heat. How the fuck was he supposed to bring her back when he couldn't even reach her. She wasn't listening—

Listening.

She played the waltz in her mind to reach zero.

He ran into the bedroom and ripped open a drawer, rummaging— dumped it out on the floor, and snagged her earbuds from the mess.

Back to her. Pushed her hair back, dropped one. *Goddamn it, why do they have to be so fucking small—*

He hit play.

The first few bars of the waltz they'd danced to at her Introduction lilted.

Flynn rested his forehead against hers, eyes screwed shut, holding her.

Please please please please please....

She stopped straining against the fix, and her heart rate ticked up. He pushed emotion at her; a slow give to the blackness, like pressure on cooling tar. A trickle of recognition flickered in her eyes, then was lost again.

Not a fucking chance that was happening.

Flynn picked up her rigid form, holding her close as he spun around the room, over and over again. Certainty building in his gut that if he stopped, he would lose her.

One, two, three, one, two, three…

Hours passed, the darkness ebbing like a tide, little pools stagnant in the shallows, rage crashing further from her consciousness. He released the fix, and she clung to him, burying her face in his neck and sobbing.

Clutching her tight, he wept with her.

He sank to the floor, letting her cry against his chest, stroking the hair from her face, kissing the top of her head. "I thought I lost you. I… I can't do any of this without you."

"I couldn't—I couldn't shake it. That second bullet—the 'lust is alive, Flynn. It was waiting for me…whispering, drowning everything else out. I've never been so afraid. It was so hard to hear your voice, the music, rhythm. I followed it back, but what if it happens again? What if it takes me, and I can't—"

"Shhh…" God, her terror—his arms tightened around her. "It won't. I won't allow it. Train all you want, but actual combat? Never again."

She nodded against him, and he let out a breath. A part of him had been afraid she'd fight him on it.

"Rogan?"

"At the infirmary."

"Did he…did people see me, like—like that?"

"Squad did." And fucking Titus, if the plaz those assholes had bled was any indication. She didn't need to think about that right now. The shame coming off her was enough as it was. He tapped her arm and stood, holding a hand.

"Come on, let's get cleaned up. I'm supposed to be back at the Assembly in another six hours, and I'm sure they're gonna want another explanation. If I don't get some sleep, I might slip and vaporize them."

Her eyes were on his fingers; what was encrusted beneath his nails.

"Something bad happened."

"Yeah, baby." And if Titus had holo of her losing it, he had holo of Flynn doing the same.

OTTO HUGGED the bricks of the alley, pulling the hood of his jacket closer around his face. He'd barely gotten out of those damn tunnels, and used up his gating stone in the process. Warrants for his arrest had been posted around the city. How they'd gotten his image—

A cramp ripped through his stomach, and he doubled over, sinking into a crouch.

Damn Mother and her crown of thorns. He grimaced at another stab of pain lancing through his guts, incensed at the very real possibility that he was going to die from them. Panting through gritted teeth, he huddled in the shadows, waiting for it to pass and considering his options.

There were few.

The city's lockdown had been extended, and no one was getting in or out of the gates. Even the ports were closed. With his face plastered everywhere, there wasn't a chance he'd be able to sneak through, and he was in no condition to wander about the tunnels. That tub of lard, Markham, had sent out an edict to his line forbidding unsanctioned shifts. In any case, Otto didn't have enough units on him to make that happen. With the cell routed, he was effectively stuck here.

He rested his head against the grimy bricks and sighed, his breath wreathing out around him. Even if he still had that damned stone, with the shield up, he doubted it would function. His guts twisted again, this time with anxiety.

All part of Mother's fucking game, he was sure. No wonder she'd been so pleased about his plans for Arileo. Had she known this would happen?

Did it matter?

He jammed his hands into his armpits, slumping. It shouldn't, but it did. His anger buoyed him. After all he'd done, sacrificed—

Another day. If he managed to refrain from shitting out his insides and stayed under the radar for that long, he could present himself to Titus and take the man's ring with the gating stone.

Playing the knave he'd held in reserve would assure that.

CHAPTER NINETEEN

"After establishing your rung, the next challenge will be for your chosen mate. Bloodlust makes it imperative that Breakers share a unique bond borne from the surrendering and conquering found only in battle. No female will submit to a male who can't best her. In order to prove yourself worthy of the chase, you will need to establish your dominance over all others..."

— Lord Grimmight, Breaker Menot,
Glynfyls

FLYNN SCRUBBED AT HIS FACE, wishing he were anywhere but in chambers. Every freaking Original House in Glynfyls was crammed into the room, with the exception of the Jesters. Nora still hadn't recovered, and the Commandant wasn't leaving her side.

Must be nice.

Last night had sucked. The few moments Kara had been able to sleep, she'd been plagued by nightmares. She'd clipped Flynn in the middle of one, and his damned jaw throbbed. Sometime around dawn, she'd finally settled, and if French hadn't woken him, he'd still be in bed. Shit, that's right where he was headed as soon as this circus wrapped up.

Stifling a yawn, he tried to focus. The arguments over bringing the herds in from the Flats had been inane enough, Chase Park was a shithole, who cared if they crapped all over it? He wanted to strangle Lord Crown and his Society for the Preservation of Glynfyls, and listening to Madame Wence shrill about what a piece of shit he was for the past ten minutes wasn't improving his mood.

Loose cannon, liability, threat to society…blah, blah, blah. Fine. Get to the fucking point.

She waved the early edition at him. "It says here that you, and I quote, 'lined them up as if for a firing squad and systematically eviscerated them, tearing their hearts from their chests. With nary a look of remorse, Scot shredded their quivering organs and ground them into the sand beneath his feet.'"

Flynn sighed, wondering if the squad had spilled that to the press, or if Titus had already leaked the holo. Whatever. Either way, it was out there. He stifled another yawn, and ran a hand over his jaw, wincing. "I don't recall that last part, but the first is true."

Gasps. He rolled his eyes and she glared at him.

"Your cavalier attitude regarding your excessive brutality is beyond the pale! There must be a limit to your behavior. Didn't you think there was any intelligence to be gained from those men?"

Christ, he was having flashbacks to Miriam grilling him for staying out past curfew.

"Close to two dozen Breakers surrendered, Madame Wence. How many prisoners do you think we need?"

She sniffed. "We must hold ourselves to a higher standard of conduct—"

"War isn't pretty Annabelle," Phyllis said, rescuing him. "Our troops stormed those tunnels, going against three score of Peacekeepers, with no talent to draw upon. Lady Jester hasn't regained consciousness since she was taken, and Lady Scot was gravely injured in the melee. If that cell hadn't been routed, I have no doubt that they'd planned on compromising the city's defenses when the Source was at our gates. The force employed by the Overlord served as a message to our enemies—Glynfyls will not sit idle while her citizens are threatened."

Madame Wence didn't look swayed, though others did. "I was unaware of those circumstances. However, I still don't—"

Flynn's hands cracked down on the arms of his chair. "For fuck's sake, enough! I'm not here to debate, and I'm done justifying my actions. You elected me to keep this city safe. Last night I did that, though my lady almost died. I'm tired of sanctimonious arguments when we're about to be invaded. All of you knew what you signed up for when you voted me in, now shut the fuck up and let me do it!"

She stared at him, indignant, and the rest of the room was silent.

He stood, done. "All of it ends now. This is no longer a democracy. Titus is at the border running short on supplies. We've got a day—two, max—before he's outside those gates. The herds will be brought in by tonight. I don't give a shit what they're gonna do to the landscaping. I'm not feeding the Source's army while they attack us, and if anyone impedes progress, they'll be arrested and tried for treason—"

"Treason? That's outrageous!" Lord Crown sputtered. "You gleefully murdered those men, but saving a beloved public space is treason?" The man purpled with rage. He puffed up, spewing his earlier diatribe.

Flynn's hand shook through his hair, the smell of scorching wood in his nose. Goddamn his temper, this fucking talent—He needed to get out of here before he did something he'd regret.

Christ, he wouldn't regret it, and that was the problem.

"Lord Crown," he boomed out, startling the man silent. "This is not a negotiation. As Overlord, my word is law. You will abide by it, or face the consequences." He started up the steps, ignoring the man's continued protests, and the outcry from the rest of them. Riggs pounded his lectern for order. Rapid footsteps caught Flynn at the doors.

"Laughlin."

Shit. Phyllis put a hand on his arm and he stopped.

"Are you all right?"

"No, I'm not fucking all right."

She stepped closer, her expression full of concern. Goddamn it. His mom used to—

"I can't do this." His voice broke, and he blinked back tears, pushing past her, and stalking down the hall to the gate.

Shelby was waiting for him when he stepped through. She wrung her hands, eyes pleading. Shit, he knew that look. "Leo's back."

A visceral shot of rage lanced through him. "What? When?"

"About an hour ago, he came through the gate—he's really sick." She broke into wrenching sobs.

Christ. He pulled her into a hug. "Where is he?"

"Cal shielded his talent and put him in the servants' quarters. There's a Breaker outside the door. They won't let anyone in—"

"Miriam?"

"She doesn't know yet."

"Good." Not for nothing, but Miriam would do whatever the asshole asked, and if she whisked him off to the sisters, they'd never get the chance to grill him.

Shelby's chin trembled. "What are you going to do?"

"Get some answers. But first I need to see Kara." He kissed the top of his cousin's head, then took the lift upstairs.

Kara was in bed where he'd left her, curled into a tight little ball. He slid in beside her. She turned and nuzzled up under his chin, her breath hot against his throat.

All he could feel from her was fear and an awful self-loathing.

"Stop," he murmured. "You can't keep beating yourself up about it."

"What if it happens again? What if you can't bring me back?"

"That's not an option."

She lifted her face—God, she was so fragile—but there was no trace of the madness from last night, just the shame and guilt eating at her.

"I was an idiot for going down there. I don't know what I was trying to prove... Is Nora okay?"

"She hasn't regained consciousness yet. They have her at the infirmary. Marcos is playing guard dog so the Source Binders don't murder her in her sleep."

"I wouldn't put it past half of them up here either. I should go see her. Maybe there's something I can do. Is Rogan still there?"

"Pretty sure he left last night." His brow arched. "You feel up for that?"

"No. I feel awful."

"Then rest," he said, kissing her forehead. "I'll take you later."

She sighed, chewing her thumb. "All that was just the beginning, wasn't it? It's going to get so much worse when Titus gets up here."

"Yeah, it is." And if there was an after, the mob would be coming for him next.

"I-I heard them talking. They're running out of suppressant. We're not going to be fighting against men, they're going to be like Riegel— like I was last night."

"We'll figure it out." He sighed, wiping away her tears. She buried her face against his chest, and he wrapped her up in his arms, holding her while he could.

***

FITZ GROANED, springs squealing as he rolled over. Fuckin' couch. He were gonna be a goddamned cripple when he tried t'get up. Pitter-patter of evil little feet accosted him, and a fetid tongue swept across his lips. He jerked back swearing.

Christ, whatever had possessed him—he sat up on the green and gold and paisley monstrosity, his gran's rat-fuck dog jumping into his lap and slobbering on him. He pushed the damned thing away, and it trotted across the packed dirt floor t'piss in the corner, tongue out like it were laughing at him. Fitz scowled, watching the nasty blighter disappear behind the curtain t'his gran's room.

He scrubbed his face, eyes sweeping across the hovel as he tried to stretch the kink out of his back. Were a new slick of nasty coming down the wall by the sink, and the chimney needed t'be stuffed with rags again. Draft coming down were about making him blue. Why the woman wouldn't leave this shithole—

Weren't a fight he were gonna win. Fitz sighed, extracting himself from the miserable excuse for furniture, and limping over to the equally wretched Formica table, clicking on the thermocoil. Smacked it till it buzzed. He stretched, fingertips grazing the bowed ceiling, eyeing it. Needed t'put up another plank before the damned thing caved in.

Locker had a can of hash and a lone egg. She were out of tea. Fitz frowned, fishing a bag out of a mug by the sink. Heddy should've gone t'market for her yesterday. He set about making breakfast.

Christ, he were beat. Fuckin' Intelligencers had him shifting through the night, but it were better than the Prydees coming down on him for usin' his extra and making a map. One he'd done were bad enough. Stink of hash rose up, and he cracked in the egg.

Were ready by the time he'd finished the dishes. He pushed through the faded curtain, stench of his gran's chamber pot hitting him square. Room were pitch, only light the dull glow of her splintered halos. Creepy how she just sat there. Harpy did it a purpose.

He pushed aside a stack of newspapers and set the tray on the bed, fumbling for the oil lamp. Were out. He yanked the curtain back and grabbed one from the other room.

"Heddy ain't been here?" he asked, trimming the wick. Ain't nothing been kept up.

"Not since ye last decided t'grace me with yer presence. Went the way of the last one. Jet been by, brings me the news, but naught else."

Fitz frowned, fucking Prydees must'a run her off. He struck a match. Them were about out, too.

"Don't start."

"I ain't." He moved the tray across her lap, and knelt beside the bed. "When's the last ye ate?"

"Bullshit. I can hear ye thinking from here."

"Thinking ain't saying, but if I were, I'd be somewhat about a decent set of rooms a rung or two higher than the Pinch. Christ—" Couldn't get a drop more into the damn chamber pot—he shifted the fuckin' mess into the street. Her fork rapped down on his head.

"Ow!" He rubbed at the spot glaring.

"Ye think they ain't watching? S'a fine way t'get nicked, use yer goddamned head!" Her eyes narrowed at him. "Let me look at ye."

He pulled back. "Ain't nothing t'see."

"Ye've gone and done somewhat. Out with it!"

Fitz dropped onto the foot of the sagging mattress. "I ain't..." Christ, she were gonna find out one way or another. "Me luck's gone t'shite. Shifted too many of them kids from the plateau, Adelaide's on the warpath, and Markham's got me running for the fucking Intelligencers. Wanted a map—"

She started coughing, and Fitz sprang up, grabbing her a cloth from the bedside, and holding it to her lips. Shoulders were frail as a china doll's, and the way they shuddered and shook… She spat something noisome into the cloth and snatched it away, but not before he saw the red. Dog beside her whined.

"Pithy didn't come neither?"

"Aye, he came." She wheezed, putting a hand on the beast. "Told him t'get the fuck out of me house."

Fitz's jaw clenched. Goddamn it. "I paid him t—"

"And I don't give a shite!" She started coughing again, batting him away. "Sooner I'm dead, sooner ye can get out from under them fuckin' Prydees! Gimme that bottle."

He picked it up and sniffed at the cork. Laudanum, about kicked. His mouth filled with sour, handing it over. "He leave that?"

She dribbled the last of it between her lips. "Aye, and ye can get me some more."

"Can I now?"

"Said so, didn't I? Ye make it for him?"

The map. "Nah. Spent the night shifting t'all them tunnels that need shoring."

"Yer da would be proud." He glanced up at her. "All them kids. Somewhat he would've done. I think yer a fuckin' idiot. Shite like that's what got him killed."

Fitz snorted. "Well, that'll get me out from under them Prydees, now won't it?" She flipped up the tray at him, plate still full. Fitz swore, flicking hash off trousers as he stood. Dog lapped at the mess, and the miserable woman cackled, her eyes growing dull with poppy. "Gah, you're a right bitch."

"Turn down the lamp before ye go."

"Ye see Jet, tell him I'll pay his ma t'take a hand with ye. I'll get ye set meantime."

"Get me tincture first, and no fuckin' hash. Can't stand the smell of it."

He snagged the little bottle from her bedside. "Pity it's in yer sheets then."

She cackled again, and he shifted out.

———

KARA SAT AT THE WINDOW, looking out over the city, alone. Flynn had left to deal with Leo. Hiss was hiding under the bed. Ever since they'd come here, the poor thing was miserable and hated her for it. She pulled a blanket closer to her chin, so cold—

A soft knock at the door. She froze, silent. *Go away, go away...* It cracked open, and she huddled deeper into her nest of blankets. Whoever it was, she didn't want to deal with them.

Rogan slid into the room, his eyes finding hers. Every one of his lifetimes lived behind them today. She looked away. He'd seen. Knew what she'd become. Kara chewed her thumb, his footsteps approaching. One of the chairs that'd been brought up to replace the ruined furniture clunked down beside hers.

He sighed. Sat.

Silence.

"After the cistern, I should've sent you back." His voice was low, rusty with emotion. She glanced over. The old Breaker stared at his hands. "In the beginning, our women would fight alongside us. Glorious. Like Valkyries of the old sagas, savage and beautiful. Then... Christ. I still remember the first we lost. We didn't know what was happening. Something about the bloodlust and whatever changes your body's going through..."

"The babies are doing this to me?"

A slow nod. "And it's been exacerbated by the Source. Cal says the females down there can only be bred once. I don't know if that's because of the genetics they've introduced, or because they don't have strong enough bonds to bring them back. Both, maybe."

Her throat was tight, the truth strangling her. She'd felt it, had known... "A-all of them?"

He shrugged, not meeting her eyes. "He thinks your Binder genes will temper it, your bond... It's strong. Flynn brought you back. I couldn't do that for my wife; she told me it was hearing the baby cry." He smiled, and it reached all the way up to his eyes, a network of fine lines creasing the corners. "James, then the twins. Shane. Each time it gets easier. Still hard, but you survive it once, it makes you stronger."

She snorted. "Easy for you to say you've never—"

"I've succumbed twice. There's no shame in it, Kara, and I know what it takes out of you. Does to you after. First with Jane…then Maria…" He buffed at his knuckles. "Cal brought me out both times. I owed him, which is why I agreed to train you. Why I'm back up here, instead of on my beach waiting for the miracle to happen. Yesterday, I figured I'd tempt fate. I'm tired. Seen too much… However unlikely, death in battle's better than all this fucking lingering."

Kara's pulse jumped. He went down there to die? "Then why did you want me there?"

He ran a hand over his stubble. "The council assigned me to be Flynn's Menot. Kid has no interest and neither do I. There's too much…I can't be—can't do that again—but I know you. If not yesterday, you'd have gone out on that plateau when Titus shows up, and have become an even bigger liability. It was the lesser of two evils, and if Flynn couldn't figure out how to bring you out of it—"

"You'd put me down." His expression was answer enough, and she couldn't fault him for it, but… "But if you had died… You used me."

"I did. Kid needs to get a handle—"

"Then teach him."

"You don't understand what you're asking."

She laughed. "Breaker Business? Cal's secrets? No, I don't, and I don't care. Flynn blew up part of the city because he's got no idea either. He's just as much of a liability as I am, and that's on you and Cal."

His face closed up. "If he doesn't want it—"

"He doesn't have a choice, and neither do you."

Rogan's shoulders slumped. He rubbed his palms against his thighs. "Fine. I'll talk to him, but until those kids are born, you need to stay put."

Kara chewed her thumb. "He's forbidden me from combat." It was stupid. She felt like that should piss her off, but she was just relieved.

"Good. If nothing else, kid's instincts are on point. Men like him, they spend their lives searching for whatever they're missing. If they don't find it, they end up destroying themselves one way or another. From what I can tell, he went pretty far down that path before you came along. Kid needs you, and it scares him shitless. Doesn't know whether to lock you in a room or cosign your bullshit." Rogan stood. "I don't envy him that. I got people to hit. There's a treadmill here, I want you down there running as much as you can take."

"You sound like you know how he feels."

The Breaker's lips flattened. "Yeah, and I chose wrong, both times."

Kara watched him go, the empty room closing in on her, black thoughts teasing at the edges of her mind. Those whispers—She wiped her eyes and got dressed. Last night, Rogan now, it was too much. See needed to see Nora.

The flat was oddly silent on the ground floor. Probably all interrogating Leo. She frowned. That wasn't going to get them very far if Otto had been influencing him, but when Nora felt better she could take a look inside his stupid head.

Kara paused at the gate, glancing over her shoulder. She just needed to envision where she wanted to go, right? Didn't sound too hard… She stepped through before she could talk herself out of it— and into the infirmary's sterile hallway.

It was still dotted with people seeking treatment, but the flurry from a few days ago had subsided. She ignored the questioning looks, and went to the nurse's station. Two Binders she hadn't met before paused their card game. They exchanged a look.

"I'm here to see Nora Jester."

"She's not here." That look between them again.

What? "When was she—"

"Kara."

Loathing spiked up her spine, she gritted her jaw, turning. "Serra."

The nasty woman stood in medic grays far too tight over her curves. Her face smug, inspecting those talons of hers. "Here to see Nora? I'm afraid you won't find her. She's been transferred to the commons infirmary. We all felt she'd be more comfortable there."

Kara ignored the intended insult. Her mother was safer down there if Serra was roaming these halls. "Then I'll need a Fetch to take me there."

Serra flicked her nails at a man standing at their peripheral, and he jumped to do her bidding. Dread replaced Kara's loathing. The horrible woman hadn't wasted anytime expanding her sphere of influence. The man took Kara's elbow, and colors ran.

They stood in a dingy corridor, thronged with people, the smell of corrupted flesh ripe in her nose. Her temper flared. How could they be up there playing cards while all of these people suffered? The Fetch shifted out, abandoning her. She waded through the crowd to the nurse's station. No one was manning it.

Kara smacked the bell on the counter, feeling all of the eyes on her and fuming. Behind her, the din of misery quieted to fervent whispers, people edging away. She fought back tears. This was wrong, so wrong—

"Can I help ye?" A pretty brunette woman separated herself from the crowd, her eyes flicking over her. "Lady Scot." The last was said as if the woman wasn't sure what to make of her. Kara couldn't blame her. Flynn had been right. Original Houses treated the commons like shit.

"I—yes." Why was she so familiar? "I'm here to see Nora Jester, please."

"This way." She led Kara into the bowels of the building.

The crowd had pulled back. Hats in their hands, eyes lowered. Feet shuffling. A woman curtsied as they passed through a peeling archway. All of it was dingy and worn, but there was a warmth to it that was decidedly lacking on the hill. Well, aside from her welcome, but she hadn't felt that up there, either. The stained hallways had drawings tacked up, and they passed a ward where a woman was reading a book, children squealing with laughter.

"We had t'put her in one of the offices at the back. Ain't no room elsewhere." She glanced over her shoulder at her. "And it ain't the hill."

"No, I'm sure she'll be much more comfortable here."

The woman stopped and turned. Her eyes were very blue. "What's yer game?"

"Game? I'm sorry I don't—"

"Aye. All them units. Making them treat the Ferris boy. Ain't no love lost betwixt us and the hill. Ye tryin' t'make it worse?"

Kara stared at her, speechless. How could she explain…her temper spiked. Why should she have to? Nora. They were caring for Nora. "The donation was Flynn's idea, and I'm—Gil needed help and I got it for him. Do you know how he's doing?"

The woman snorted, approaching a door. "Hand ain't gonna turn black and fall off, if that's what ye wanna know."

Bitch. "I'm sorry, I didn't catch your name?"

"Umari." She knocked softly before opening it. "Find me when yer done. I'll have a Fetch take ye back up the hill, where ye belong."

Kara thanked her, ignoring the dig, and stepped inside. Why was everything up here so convoluted?

Marcos was hunched in a chair beside Nora's gurney, worry etched across his face. He sat back, running a weary hand across his close-cropped hair. He looked exhausted.

"Kara. You're all right?"

"I'm okay. How's she?"

"No change from when I brought her in."

The room was barren, marks on the floor where they'd dragged a desk out. Chippy beige plaster covered the walls, and the olive linoleum was worn through in places. At least she was near a window, not that the view of a brick wall was spectacular. Beside the gurney on a rolling cart, a pink carnation poked from a glass of water, Nora's chart next to it.

Kara wiped her eyes and picked it up, leafing through it. Her brow furrowed. Nothing physically wrong. "What happened?"

"Otto did something while we were fixed. Nora went limp after. I can't…I can't feel her."

Kara's stomach dropped, dread rising up to choke her. Flynn's concern echoed back. She took a breath. "I'm just going to take a look." Probably. Flynn wouldn't mind if she did that. He'd had her examine at Bea, surely her mother was a priority.

Lies, lies, lies. She'd be locked in the flat if Flynn knew what she was about to do.

Kara didn't care.

She pulled talent, her fingertips grazing Nora's temples.

The inside of her mother's mind was a mess. It looked like it'd been hit with a battering ram—cognizance and memories scattered to the far reaches of Nora's consciousness…picked through bits wafting on streams of sentience, disjointed…

Kara stumbled back. She made for the trashcan, her stomach rebelling.

Marcos was at her side, holding her up. "That bad?"

She nodded. Her mother had been psychically raped, splayed out, and left a vegetable.

"Can you bind it?"

"No." Kara's hand trembled across her mouth.

But she might be able to unmake it.

CAL LEANED AGAINST THE WALL, eyes glued to his least favorite grandson. He snorted. Least favorite. Leo barely qualified for that, but ascribing traitorous, lying sack of shit to someone he shared blood with rankled, however accurate.

It also looked like a self-limiting problem. Way Flynn was seething around his cigar at him, on the off-chance Leo wasn't as close to death's door as Miriam seemed to think, he'd get a free ride the rest of the way. How she'd gotten a bead on the boy down here…

Woman fretted at his bedside, spoon-feeding him broth and crooning at him. She'd propped him up with pillows, and he slumped against them, dark circles beneath his eyes, skin waxy and sallow. She dabbed the corner of his lips with her ever-present towel, and Flynn glowered.

Miriam sniffed. "Two of you look like gargoyles standing beside the door like that. Don't know why you feel it's necessary to gawk. Can't you see how sick he is? He should be in the infirmary, not shut up in the servants' quarters like a commoner!"

"House Matter, Miriam," Cal said, lighting a cigarette. Spark in

Leo's eye at that gave the lie to his invalid status. God, he was a snake. "We need to speak with him."

"House Matter? What could possibly—" She waved at the smoke in the air, glaring. "Well, I'm not leaving his side. Anything you have to say to my Leo, you can say in front of me."

"Don't know that's a good idea—"

"It's a great idea." Flynn pushed off the wall and stalked across the stark room to rest his hands on the footboard, looming over them both. "She should know what a backstabbing, two-faced fuck-piece he is, so she stops hiding him under her skirts."

Cal's lips pursed. Well, there was something to be said for that...

"Language!"

"How 'bout we start with him working with Titus, and sending a fucking squad of 'keepers after us? Shit, I know you hate me, but Graham's your fucking brother!"

Miriam's jaw dropped, her hand rising to her lips.

"It's not what you think." Leo scowled, unrepentant.

"You sure?" Flynn laughed. "Cause I think you instigated that reel to drive me south, then got yourself and Julia into some deep shit you're still swimming in. You should do everyone a favor and fucking drown instead of dragging us down with you."

Leo went gray, sagging against his pillows. Miriam whimpered, but Cal didn't have much sympathy for her. She'd had the chance to leave, and it wasn't like this was out of the blue. The petty thefts, lies...boy had shown his colors early, and she'd never done a damned thing but dote on him and make excuses. Christ, they all had.

"Okay, it is what you think, but I never meant it to go that far. The whole thing... You knew and you didn't fucking care. I thought if she could see you..." Leo barked out a weak laugh, his eyes hard. "Worked better than I ever dreamed."

Flynn growled, his knuckles sparking on the footboard, ready to draw blood. Cal wholeheartedly understood the inclination, but they needed to keep him taking.

"When did you run into Otto?"

Leo glanced over at him, annoyed. "A couple months prior to the reel. Smearing Flynn was his idea, but I'm not sorry. Julia deserved to know what a piece of shit he is. Everybody did."

Flynn pushed off the footboard and put his back to Leo, hand on his hips, fuming. Flames flickered up his forearms. That couldn't be good.

A smile flitted over the little shit's lips, and Cal wanted to put his fist through it. "Ever cross your mind what that would mean for House Scot?"

"Graham—"

"Would be another mouthpiece for the Prydees." Cal's eyes flicked to Miriam. She'd pulled out her rosary, worrying it. Goddamn that House. Jon's temperament aside, making Lot head had been in large part to keep their hooks out of his affairs. They must've viewed the entire scandal as divine providence. "Think you've heard enough, Miriam, and I'll remind you, this is a House Matter—House *Scot*."

Her mouth clamped into a frown, but she nodded, and shifted out.

"So what about the kid?" Flynn asked, eyes on the ceiling. "He yours?"

Leo didn't answer.

That'd be a yes. Cal tossed his butt into the bowl of broth Miriam had left, and started rolling another cigarette. "So Titus is holding him hostage for your good behavior. You still bonded to her?"

"No." His voice caught. "She doesn't even remember who I am, and the kid doesn't care."

Flynn's knuckles cracked, the room uncomfortably hot. "Then you knew exactly what you were doing when you tried to turn Kara and me in. What they do to bonded couples, the kids. What they'd do to Graham, all those Talents you handed over… Jesus fucking Christ."

"Why would I give a shit about some runaway Binder and the asshole that fucked up my life?"

Flynn spun and they glared at each other. "And everybody else?"

"Price of doing business." Leo held out his wrists, a nullifying shackle strapped around one. "I'm ready. Hang me for treason, King Scot."

"Nah." Flynn laughed. "You're not getting off that easy. What were you doing down there with that cell of Breakers?"

"I—had to check in." Sweat broke out across his brow and he went pale.

"Bullshit." Cal's halos flared, cloaking himself and Flynn. "We're not gonna get any more out of him, and you need to calm down. Whatever he was doing, a reaction like that means we're pushing against a directive. Otto sent him back here for a reason, and until Nora can look inside his head…shield the room. I don't want any more surprise visitors. House Matter or not, I expect the Prydees are gonna do their damndest to make this as painful as possible."

Flynn grunted, only half listening as he made for the door. Leo scowled as it opened, arms crossed over his sunken chest. Flynn's halos flared once they got into the hall, setting the shield. Not a damned thing was getting in or out of that. He slumped against the wall, looking preoccupied. "What about the kid?"

"I'm guessing he's at the Triam, but until Nora can verify going through the gate scrubbed Leo of bots, I'm not risking giving Titus the heads up that I know about it. He'll use the boy as leverage if he thinks there's any possibility House Scot gives a shit." And Lord help him, but he did.

"Your contact know anything about it?"

"No, but he's tendered the offer, for all the good it'll do. I'm close to finalizing the sale of the Source to our holding company. Could be some clues there, but I wouldn't hold your breath. Between the damage Titus's troops left and the looting, won't be much left by the time we get there."

Flynn ran a hand over his jaw, sans flames. "They formally oust him yet?"

"Paperwork for you assuming chair and the liquidation of his shares is in limbo. My suspicion is the board's waiting to see how this shakes out before they declare one way or another. Titus may be a guilty of crimes against humanity, but right now humanity's looking up here at what you're capable of, and wondering if that's such a bad thing. That damned holo of you in the tunnels dropped. What the hell were you thinking?"

Boy shrugged. "Does it matter?"

"You know you're just proving them right." And it was scary as hell. Way he'd carved those men up—

"They were all along."

Cal pinched the last drag off his cigarette, feeling the boy's eyes on him. "Regardless, we wipe each other out, rest of the world figures it's a win-win. How's Kara?"

"Not good, or where she should be." Flynn frowned, halos pulsing. "She's at the commons infirmary. Christ, Cal, she knows I don't want her going anywhere alone—"

The color drained from his face, and he was gone.

Cal dropped his smoldering butt to the floor and scuffed it out with a toe, wondering how much this was gonna cost him.

NORA DRIFTED.

Opalescent tendrils of psyche feathering out like ink dripped into the Lethe. Writhing in dark currents, they sank, heavy, blooming outwards, into oblivion…lost…

Then found.

Sucked back, rising, sepia swirls of talent drawing her together. Shards of memories integrating, sensations and emotions softening their edges with the cohesion of consciousness—

She had shattered. Been shattered.

Otto.

Her mind—Nora pulled talent, bathing the ragged edges in a golden glow, aiding in her reconstruction, the sepia retreating, drawing her to the surface in its wake—

Her eyes fluttered open. How long? Where—?

Dingy room, IV stand. Chair beside a railed bed.

The infirmary. A man—men—arguing. The air thick, a woman between them—

Kara.

"Stop it! I'm fine!" She staggered against the side of the gurney.

"The hell you are! What were you thinking?" Laughlin. Pulling his hair, jaw tight.

Nora worked her tongue in her mouth—so dry. "H-how long…?"

Marcos was at her side. "Sixteen hours."

Too long, and she was in the commons. Serra had been busy—

"If I hadn't unmade the damage, she would've been a vegetable!"

"And if you keep this up, you'll be dead!" Laughlin shot back.

"I'm going to be dead anyway, at least I can save her!"

He ghosted white.

God, hearing that from Kara's lips—Nora's vision misted, a sob bitten back. Marcos sat, pulling her close and rocking her in an awful silence.

"What d'you mean?"

"Source Breakers don't survive pregnancy, Flynn. Rogan said—" She flinched back at the rage contorting his face.

"You did this because of that asshole filling your head with shit? You're a Binder, a Breaker, a goddamned Unmaker, the fuck you're gonna die! I brought you back from the bloodlust, and I'll be damned before I believe that goddamned prick or anyone else. Christ, Kara, there's never been a Talent like you, how the fuck can anyone apply a blanket statement like that? How can you believe them?"

"I—You don't feel what I feel—"

"The hell I don't! You have any idea how much talent I'm pushing you? I know exactly how you feel, and shit like this makes it worse!" He raked at his hair, halos sparking.

Kara looked like she'd been slapped. "Why didn't you say anything—"

"Why would I? You don't want to talk about it."

"*I* don't want to talk about it?" She laughed. "You never talk about anything! Not your past, your mother—"

He jabbed a finger at her. "Don't bring her into this. I know what you're doing."

"What am I doing?"

"Being fucking reckless! I swear to Christ, if I gotta lock you in a goddamned—" His jaw clenched, talent flickering up his arms from his fists. He raised them to his temples and they snuffed out, force rippling from him, shaking plaster from the walls—the window cracked, and Flynn glanced over at Nora's gasp. God, the heat coming off him with the hatred in his eyes—he stepped close to Kara, a growl rumbling in his chest. "I won't lose you, or them. Especially not over this fucking bitch, or that prick!"

Kara slapped him. "She's my mother, and Rogan almost died because you're too stubborn to ask for help! You can't control your talent—Why do you think he brought me down there, Flynn? He knew I was going to lose it, and wanted to make sure you could bring me back!"

Nora put a hand to her lips. The rage on Laughlin's face… Kara's drained of color. The temperature in the room ticked up a good twenty degrees.

"Is that right?"

"No—I mean, yes, but it's not—"

"I'm gonna kill that motherfucker—Stay here!" His halos pulsed, and he was gone. The floor where he had stood smoldered, the air rippling with heat.

Kara slumped against the wall, shaking. "What have I—the Trials, where are they being held?"

Marcos's jaw tightened, tension between them thrumming. "You were told to stay here."

Kara's face went stoney. "Where. Is. Rogan?"

The staccato ice in her voice—Nora shivered. "Tell her."

Marcos looked between them. "He's been sparring at the Pony, but Lord Scot said—"

The door slammed behind Kara. Nora threw back the blankets, and swung her legs over the side of the bed, the room spinning. Marcos was at her elbow. She pulled talent, steadying herself. It was time for her to spar as well and there wasn't time for this. She pushed the hair from her face with a laugh. God, she was as foolhardy as her daughter.

"Not going to try to talk me out of it?"

"I'm assuming it's Binder Business." Marcos frowned, helping her to her feet.

Nora's face was grim. It was at that.

CHAPTER TWENTY

*"…A Breaker's talent is both a divine gift and a curse. In the dark days
following the Surge, we saw far too many of our brethren succumb, unable to
control their power, dragging others into the darkness with the strength of
their 'lust. The other lines rallied against us in our madness, hunting us like
animals until the Alpha Prime stepped forth, might making right. At his
hands, a great culling ensued. Any that would not submit to the hierarchy
and walk the Way were put down, and so it stands today, lest we risk a return
to that time of chaos…"*

– Lord Grimmight, Breaker Menot,
Glynfyls

"ARE YE FUCKIN' kidding me?" Fitz ran a hand over his jaw,
standing betwixt the tall metal shelves of a storage room in the
commons infirmary. Weren't much of anything on 'em, and the price of
Gran's laudanum were gonna beggar him. "S'what I paid Pithy t'heal
the harpy."

" 'Fraid not, friend. With all the doings and goings on, stuff's at a
premium," Trick said holding the little bottle up to the light and
squinting at it. "Could cut it with glimmer…"

"Christ, ain't nobody needs t'see that," Fitz muttered, digging into his pocket. Made him sick just thinking about his gran all hopped up, feeling frisky.

Trick chuckled. "Can't say as I blame ye. Though, I hear tell she were a piece back in the day."

"Ya, back when the Pinch were a thing of beauty." Fitz peeled off a scant few units from what Crandall had given him. Trick snickered, trading him the thicker stack for the bottle. "Pithy around?"

"Should be up front. As always, pleasure doing business with ye." He tipped his tam and shifted out.

Fitz sighed at the little bottle in his hand. Winnings from the Pony had gone to Pithy, and most everything from Crandall to this. How the fuck were he gonna pay for somewhat other than hash and Jet's ma to watch Gran? He shoved the bottle in his pocket and kicked open the door, meandering toward Pithy's office. Needed t'hustle. Mayhap pick up a shift or two down at the docks. His mouth puckered, not relishing the prospect or having t'bring his chit for Joey to sign off on. Rat bastard would short him again for sure.

Door to Pithy's office were cracked and he knocked. Umari opened it the rest of the way. She narrowed her eyes at him. "Trick ain't here."

"Eh…nah. Here t'see Pithy about me gran."

Her face softened, and she stepped aside to let him into the room. The door closed after her, leaving him with the Binder sitting behind his scarred oak desk. Were covered in papers and books left open. More lay around the floor, pages bristling with sticky notes and scribbles. Rest of the room were file cabinets and a couch that looked a sight more comfortable than the one Fitz had slept on.

"How long do she have?" Weren't no point in belaboring it.

Pithy's fingers danced. *"There's no telling. She wouldn't let me examine her. Blacklung takes some fast, others linger."*

"Ain't an answer. She ain't eating and is coughing up blood. Piss smells off."

"Sounds fairly advanced then, but with adequate nutrition, men have been known to live with the condition for a decades—"

"Men maybe, this is me gran."

"True." He tapped his lips. *"Figure on a century easy, the woman's too mean to die."*

Fitz grunted, he weren't wrong there. "And that shite ye gave her?"

"It's not a necessary medication, but it will dull the pain. She go through it already?"

"Just about."

Man frowned. *"My instruction were for her to take a drop or two to sleep. That bottle should've lasted her the month. I'd suggest you monitor her usage."*

Great, just what he wanted t'hear. "Somewhat else I can do for her?"

"Aside from dragging her out of that hovel? I'm afraid not."

Fitz nodded. That weren't happening while she were still breathing. He thanked the Binder and left, staring at his boots crossing the floor. Why the hell did she have to be so damned stubborn—

"Fitz!"

His head jerked up, Lord Scot's angel were coming at him in a state. "Eh...ya?"

"I need you to shift me to the Painted Pony."

What? Were she serious? She gripped his sleeve.

"Now, please. Flynn's gone down to find Rogan. He wants to kill him, and it's all my fault!" Her eyes welled up, looking at him like he were her only hope...

"Shite, ya, okay, but ye gotta stay close. Ain't no place for a lady." And with Adelaide working, it weren't no place for him, neither. *Cajetan, if yer still listening, I'd appreciate it if she were busy with a bloke...*

Fitz pulled talent, shifting them.

Place were packed with Breakers. The angel's arm looped through his, pressing up against him way too familiar like. Fitz swallowed, mouth dry, and started to move through the crowd toward the warehouse. More than one set of eyes gave him and the lady the once over. She pressed closer. He ducked his head and kept moving, face afire as they passed the stage. Not that he didn't appreciate the show, but the lady didn't need t'be seeing—

Shite. One of 'em were Adelaide. She stared after them, fit t'be tied.

The angel's steps slowed, looking over her shoulder. "She the one that punched you?"

His throat bobbed. "Eh...ya."

"She's coming."

Fitz's pulse sped. They'd almost reached the warehouse. Doors was closed, man taking cover held out a hand.

"Breakers and skirts is free. Thirty-five if ye want in."

He did, but didn't have it. Shite…

The angel popped up on her tiptoes and kissed his cheek. "Thank you. I'll be fine." She dropped his arm, and pushed through the doors, wading through the kneeling throng inside. Fitz raised a hand to his cheek, a stupid smile splitting his face. Weren't gonna wash that off.

The man at the door snorted. "Yer one lucky son of a bitch."

Fitz turned to him, laughing.

And into Adelaide.

ROGAN LANDED A JAB, sending another Breaker sprawling. Christ, this was getting fucking tedious. He turned his back on him, not bothering to see if he was going to get up. Didn't have the patience for it, and wasn't worth his time. None of them were.

A flashbulb went off, and he scowled, blinking. The warehouse around the ring was packed with Breakers waiting to place. Other lines were sprinkled throughout the stands making bets. The press was just making a royal pain in the ass of themselves. Would've preferred to do this shit at the conclave, but it didn't have a bar.

He prowled to the side of the ring. Mangleshield was waiting for him, *The Way* in hand. Great. A manual to go with his pee-wee boxing league. Rogan grabbed his bottle from the ring's margin and glared at the man through the chain-link.

"I'm not in the mood for a sermon."

"Not here to give one." Mangleshield held up the tattered tome and grinned. "I was hoping you could sign my copy. It's something of a collector's edition, and I'm a big fan."

"Sure, I'll make it out to the third biggest prick I know."

He laughed. "I'll take that as a compliment."

Rogan snorted, tipping back the bottle. He would. "What do you want?"

"You've been a busy man past couple of days, thought I'd check in—"

"Haven't spoken to him, if that's what you're asking."

"I wasn't," Mangleshield said, looking over Rogan's shoulder. "But I think you're about to get the chance…"

Rogan turned, ducking as a fist crashed into the chain-link where his head had just been.

"The hell, kid?"

"Where the fuck do you get off telling Kara she's gonna die?" Flynn glared at him, the air thickening into oily ripples.

Christ, what the kid was putting out was dank. Too bad he didn't know how to focus it. Rogan ran a finger under his nose and spat. The crowd outside the ring wavered, falling to their knees. Pussies.

"That what she told you?"

"It was the goddamned gist of it."

"Wasn't what I said." He tipped the bottle up, and Flynn went to smack it out of his hand. Rogan jerked it back with a growl. "Don't fuck with my rum."

"Don't fuck with my wife."

"Little late for that." He laughed, a grin splitting his face. "Who do you think broke her in?"

KARA PUSHED through the kneeling crowd to the side of the cage, her fingers digging into the chain-link. Her throat was in her mouth, air thick with 'lust. Rogan and Flynn stood on the other side, nose-to-nose. The rumble of their voices too low to make out, but from their expressions, someone was going to get hurt. Ugh, this was all her fault…

Phyllis sidled up to her, halos flaring. "Well, you've certainly claimed him, now haven't you?" Kara turned crimson, wishing the woman would go away. "And he's marked you back, in spades, no less."

"If you say so."

Phyllis looked at her askance. "I wasn't aware you were able to pull Breaker talent."

She glanced at the woman. "Not well."

"Well enough. You're lucky. Without it, he wouldn't have been able to bring you back."

Kara kept her eyes on the two in the ring.

Phyllis didn't take the hint. "I don't know the details about what happened last night, but I've been there too. If you ever need to talk to someone, I'm more than happy to listen. Being a Breaker…there's a lot to it. We should take tea together, soon."

Kara wiped a tear from her cheek. "Thank you."

Rogan's laugh boomed out, and he nodded in her direction, saying something.

Flynn's head snapped up, his temper jumping as his eyes landed on her. He stalked over and laced his fingers over hers through the chain-link, his halos a tempest. The rust had come to the forefront and was being swallowed by scarlet undertones. Her mouth went dry. She'd never seen him so angry.

"It true? You fucked him?"

The blood drained from her face.

Flynn laughed, pushing away. "He's dead."

FLYNN PHAZED his jacket and shirt, rolling his shoulders and cracking his knuckles. Talent sizzled around his fists, flecking up his forearms, past his elbows. That motherfucker had put his goddamned hands on Kara, then sat at his fucking table—

Rogan flashed those pearly whites of his and laughed. "You challenging me?"

"No. I'm gonna fucking kill you."

Asshole took another swig off his bottle and set it down. "Sure. Give it a go."

Flynn threw a punch, cracking the son of a bitch's teeth together. Rogan grunted and his fist slammed into Flynn's gut, a wave of terror hammering him with it. He doubled over, bathed in sweat. God the stench—last time he'd felt like this—

...He cowered, pressed up under the gable's eaves, ground far below him. Boot falls heavy in the attic, coming closer.

"I know you're up here you little shit..." Whisper of a belt sliding free, and the jingle of the buckle. Warm wetness trickles down his leg, and he bites at his knuckles, not again—

Never again.

Vomit stung the back of Flynn's throat. His teeth ground together, a growl rumbling through his chest, all that ugly he kept under lock and key coiled with the writhing blackness. It suffused him, drawing him upright, knuckles popping. The darkness surged, and he slung it out with his fist, a roiling cloud of noxious hurt.

The uppercut took Rogan in the jaw, and he and flew back, slamming against the chain-link, onto the floor. The enclosure rattled, metal clanging loud in the silence—

The Breaker gave a sharp laugh and flipped to his feet. He shook his head blinking. "Shit, they weren't kidding. If you knew what the fuck you were doing, you might actually be dangerous."

<hr>

KARA PANTED AGAINST THE CAGE, the rest of the room prostrate from the density of warring 'lust. Her pulse pounded with what she was feeling from Flynn—

Rogan laughed, and it redoubled. Her knees threatened to buckle. Why was he baiting him? Beside her, Phyllis moaned, hand on her head as she struggled to her feet, gripping the chain-link for support.

In the ring, Flynn's chest heaved, closing in on Rogan again. Ugh, the 'lust crackling through their bond—Kara closed her eyes, whimpering, the crack of flesh on flesh in her ears—she flinched at the hand settling on her back.

"It can't touch you unless you let it. You know your enemy now, Kara. Find zero."

Find zero. Kara laughed, biting her lip. For all the good it had done —Phyllis raised up her chin, locking gazes. "That place of calm, expand it outward. Build your platform and rise above. Though the waves may lick at its footings, none shall touch you…" The woman's voice lilted, the notes of the waltz falling in behind them. Instead of floating, Kara let them buoy her up above the darkness—and it was a thousand feet below her. Phyllis was right, it couldn't touch her here…

"How? Why was it so easy now, so—"

Phyllis's brow quirked. "He had you trying to sink into zero didn't he?"

"What? Um…yes?"

She rolled her eyes. "Men. You'd think he'd know by now women belong on a pedestal. Having us sinking into it is the equivalent of telling us to go drown ourselves."

Kara laughed. And all this time she'd thought she was defective.

FITZ RAN a shaky hand over his mouth. "Eh…ye look real fine, Adelaide. Blue suits ye." What little there were of it. She crossed her arms under her breasts, popping them up to an advantage and glaring at him. Man at the door weren't the only one appreciative.

"The hell ye say. How long ye been cozying up t'the Lady Scot?"

"What?" Fitz pulled at his patch. "Nah…it ain't like that. Shanghaied me from the infirmary. Were getting somewhat for me gran."

Her eyes went soft, hands dropping to fiddle with the ties on her nightie. "S'that where ye been?" She stepped close and his hands were on her hips. Fabric slid nice.

"Eh…ya. Woman keeping her up and quit."

"Don't blame her, for all the money ye been pissing away on the hag." Adelaide pushed his hair behind his ear. "Heard tell what ye done. Sarah ain't come out of her rooms since. Ye mad at me?"

"Nah." His fingers teased the edge of her panties. Damn, she were a right fine looking whore. "How much ye charging?"

Smile flickered over her lips as she played with his shirt buttons. "Fifty for the works, but I get off in another hour. Ye gonna be home?"

"Dunno. Ye gonna be wearing this?"

"Could be."

"Then I could probably be there."

She kissed him, tweaking the ring through his nipple as she pulled away. Fitz licked his lips, watching her sway through the crowd. Man at the door shook his head.

"One lucky son of a bitch…"

———

TITUS LOOKED up at Brix poking his ugly head into his cabin. "Yes?"

"Live stream from Glynfyls. You're gonna want to see this."

Titus flicked through his channels, pulling it up. The feed was jumpy, rebroadcast from somewhere in the Deep South. Scot and the old Breaker were doing their best to kill each other inside the cage where Riegel had met his end. Titus's eyes narrowed. The place was packed with Breakers, their halos casting the room a sea of red.

"What am I looking at?"

"A challenge," Brix murmured, the man's halos glowing like the crowd's. The camera angle changed and he swore.

Titus concurred, pain stabbing behind his eyes.

The Jester girl stood at the side of the ring. She looked more wan than the last time he'd seen her, but there was no doubting it was her, nor that she was sane.

"I thought you said she'd succumbed?"

Brix looked profoundly troubled. "She did. I don't understand…" He pushed off the wall, staggering from the room.

"I didn't dismiss you." The man froze, his spine stiff. "Why should you care whether she's there or not?"

Brix turned, running a hand over his mouth. "If she came back…"

What a laughable suggestion. The Breaker met Titus's eyes. "You're serious."

"We saw her succumb."

Titus tapped his lip, trying to give credence to his suggestion. Perhaps her Binder genes… "If that were the case, which I highly doubt, you can be assured her duality was the cause of it."

Brix grunted, rubbing his scalp. "The men...this is gonna cause issues."

"Then I suggest you solve them. We march within the hour."

KARA WATCHED the two men circle, trading blows. Flynn's frustration at being unable to put Rogan down ate at their bond. He was playing with him and Flynn knew it. So did Phyllis and she was drinking it in, far too appreciatively for Kara's taste. Not that she could blame her, the light playing over Flynn's slick skin, muscles shifting— Phyllis's breath caught as he turned his back to them. Kara glanced at her.

"Yes?" the woman asked softly, not taking her eyes from the fight.

"You tell me, unless it's Breaker Business."

Rogan got through Flynn's right side and landed a mean cross. His head cracked back, and his brow split, bleeding in earnest. He drove a fist into the man's ribs. Someone had opened the doors and a frigid breeze blew into the room, breaking up the stagnant funk. Breakers got to their feet, more crowding in from the other room.

"First blood to Rogan. I'm not surprised the way Laughlin leaves that right side open. He needs to stop holding back. I say you're a party to Breaker Business now, wouldn't you?"

Kara's mouth went dry. *Binder, Breaker, Unmaker...*

Phyllis smirked, watching the fight. The similarity of the men's builds and the way they moved was uncanny. "When the last Overlord refused to use his power, our line was all but decimated. A few injured males escaped the harvest, but most were killed. Only the very old and very young were left to despair our line would end. House Carmody made a foretelling." She touched the top of her spine, and a soft murmur passed through the crowd, their halos igniting to bathe the room crimson. Kara shivered.

"He bears the mark."

The mark? There was a crunch and Flynn bellowed. He fell back, blinking, his nose a broken smear. "Fuck!"

Rogan laughed and said something, spitting gore to the side. He raised his fists back up, bleeding from an ear and a cut under his eye, his face swollen and bruised. The murmur had died, the crowd eerily quiet. Flynn went at him again.

"Good. Now we'll see what he can do," Phyllis murmured, watching the two intently.

FLYNN WIPED an arm through the blood dripping into his eye. He ducked Rogan's fist and threw another punch, winded. Motherfucker wouldn't go down—

Fuck this. He'd fry the asshole.

He pulled, talent crackling around his fists, the ground smoldering beneath them and bursting into flames—

Snuffed.

Rogan snorted, snot bubbling red. "You really gonna trying to best me with my own extra? Take notes, kid."

Wait—his extra?

The Breaker's halos flared, and a wall of flame sprang up around them, whipping into a tornado. Flynn stumbled back, in the center of a firestorm. The cement beneath him blackened and glowed amber, the inferno sucking the air from his lungs—he threw up a shield, phazing it. A ring of flickering carbon surrounded him. The air shimmered with heat and stank of burnt stone.

Rogan tsked. "Using any talent other than Breaking during the Trials is considered cheating. You wanna try that again?"

Trials—Flynn's stomach dropped.

Goddamn his fucking temper. Asshole had taken it and run, baiting him into this shit, and now he was playing with him for the crowd. Realization killed his 'lust. A manic laugh burbled past Flynn's split lips. God, he was a fucking idiot. He glanced out at the sea of red halos surrounding them, unclenching his fists, his hands dropping to his knees. He crouched, panting, then fell back onto the floor..

"Fuck the Trials, and you." He spat to the side.

"You ready to find out who that is?"

Flynn grimaced, head hanging. Didn't really giving a shit, but he suspected the man was gonna tell him anyway. Rogan retrieved his bottle and joined him on the ground, just as winded.

"Shane was my daughter. What the hell she ever saw in Cal…" He tipped the bottle back, draining a goodly portion of it and wincing. He rocked his jaw. "Christ, you've got a hook."

Flynn glared at him from beneath his bunched brows, this asshole was his great whatever the fuck it was?

Rogan snorted. "Yeah, trust me, I feel the same way. Look, all those Breakers out there are expecting the hierarchy to be settled by this shit show."

"Nothing's been settled."

"No, but it's about to be. You need to take First."

KID LAUGHED AND SPRAWLED BACK, putting a hand to his ribs like it hurt. Good. Rogan's felt cracked in at least three places. Shit, when was the last time he'd had a bout like that—

James. He tried to push thought away, and it didn't want to leave. Him, Quint, Liam, and Shane. All his kids had had the same potential.

And all of them were dead.

"There's not a fucking chance I'm taking First," Flynn said, staring up at the ceiling. "Besides, you could've buried me—"

"Only because you don't know what the hell you're doing. I've got experience, but you've got more in the tank." Shit, that wasn't easy to admit, but it was true, and he knew damned well what would happen if he didn't man up. Rogan finished off the bottle and slung it to the side. He couldn't watch—let—that happen again. No matter how much he missed his goddamned beach. "I'll make a deal with you. I'll step up until you've got a handle on shit, but you've got to agree to let me be your Menot."

"You gonna quote me that bullshit book?"

Rogan snorted. "I'll leave the doctrine to Mangleshield. Talent, 'lust…you've got to get a grip on things before it eats you and everything you love." Not to mention all the shit he didn't.

Kid pushed up on his elbows and scrubbed at his hair, eyes going to Kara. He sighed, head hanging, smart enough to know when he'd been beat, and man enough to own up to it. "Yeah, fine. But I swear to Christ, if you touch her—"

"How much of an asshole do you think I am?" Rogan laughed at the look Flynn shot him, and clambered to his feet. Fuck, the last time someone had kicked him in the ass this hard…

Rogan's jaw tensed. This time would be different. He turned to Flynn and offered him his hand.

KARA'S BREATH CAUGHT, watching the two men in the center of the ring, their voices rumbling low. The amount of damage they'd dealt each other was impressive. How they were laughing… What had Rogan said to make the fight go out of Flynn like that? His begrudging acceptance colored their bond, threaded with relief. She couldn't understand it. Around them, the room collectively held its breath, the air thick with tension instead of 'lust.

"What is everyone waiting for?"

"They've come to a draw," Phyllis murmured. "In lieu of a clear victor, a compromise must be met."

"Compromise?"

"On rung."

"But Flynn's not—"

Rogan got to his feet and held out a hand to Flynn. After a moment, he clasped it, and stood beside the Breaker. Rogan addressed the crowd. "Hear my words! A compromise has been met, and the hierarchy reestablished. By might, I am Alpha Prime and claim First! I name Laughlin Scot, Breaker, Firestorm by blood, my heir, and Beta, until such a time as he's prepared to take up what's rightfully his."

The room broke into excited whispers and, at Rogan's side, Flynn ghosted white beneath the gore, his irritated shock lancing through their bond. Kara leaned close to Phyllis. She'd gone as pale as Flynn.

"What did Rogan just do?"

"He reestablished his House and named Laughlin his successor."

How could Flynn be heir to two Houses? Phyllis put a hand on her arm, stilling the question before she could ask. An old man in a long gray robe walked out into the center of the ring. He pounded a staff on the ground thrice and the conversations that had sprung up died.

"I speak the Way."

"We listen." Phyllis and the rest of the room touched between their brows.

"Blood has called to blood! The council's edict satisfied." A broad grin smoothed over his face. "Welcome, Laughlin Firestorm nee Scot. We've been waiting for you."

CHAPTER TWENTY-ONE

"...Regardless of outcome, certain powers will refuse to remain idle, and despite Albanach's assurances that he can control Scot, it would behoove us to make alternate arrangements. Although the loss of Talents is a foregone conclusion, we need to take steps to secure the iridium mine in the North to maintain our global dominance..."

– Encrypted Private Transmission, Corporation Server

TITUS REVIEWED the vanguard forming up for the first line-of-sight jumps into the Northern Territories. The wind picked up, cutting through his coat. Gah, it was miserable. He tugged the fur-lined collar closer to his neck, the foul weather exacerbating his throbbing temples.

At the edge of camp, the corpses of just over five hundred of his finest warriors were being unceremoniously dumped into a mass grave. Brix hadn't understated the fallout from the Jester girl's appearance, and it had been more far reaching than Titus could have imagined.

Silver lining: his dwindling supply of suppressant no longer needed to be rationed quite so carefully. Many of those put down had required a double dose. Waste not want not. Titus's lips quirked. Perhaps he should consider butchering some of those corpses. Protein was such a vital part of a Breaker's diet...

Brix approached, hunching his shoulders against the wind. He'd insisted on putting the majority of the men down himself. Some ridiculous bastion of Breaker honor. Titus pressed a hand to his aching brow, heartily tired of their inbred idiosyncrasies. It had cost him far too many men today, and over what? A bunch of spent bitches.

He turned in disgust, making for the transport. Brix fell into step with him. "It's done?"

"No. That footage of the fight—"

Titus slapped open the hatch. "I have a difficult time believing you've all been intimidated by it."

The behemoth shot him a dirty look, ducking to clear the doorway. "The men aren't buying that duality shit. She succumbed and came back. Every man who's lost a bond is an incident waiting to happen. If there's a chance we could've saved them…" He looked away.

Titus pulled off his gloves, head throbbing at the swelling auras around the lights leading to his cabin. These damned migraines… Damned Breakers. Brix was designed to be a killing machine, not some love sick puppy. This obsession with their females was untenable. He poured himself a drink, and sat at his desk, reaching for his pills.

"You're talking about half my troops, yourself included." He threw back a handful, chewing.

"I still have Tonya's bond, she went into stasis just before we left, but there will be blood shed over this, Titus. It's your choice who's."

His eyebrow quirked, micro-beads bursting between his molars. "Are you threatening me, BrE2?"

"We'll win your little war, but after, no more culling as standard procedure. We want to try and bring them out."

Titus washed down the acrid tang with a swallow of bourbon, pulling up the grainy holo of the last attempt, over a century ago. Moments after birth, it showed techs frantic to get the offspring and themselves out of the birthing room. The female was half the size of the male, yet managed to pin him, tearing his throat out with her teeth in under a minute flat. Uncontrollable, a bullet subsequently sprayed her brains across the room's mirrored plex. Titus raised an eyebrow at Brix.

The Breaker squared his jaw. "It's a good way to die."

It was a waste, but perhaps he needed to set an example. This little ultimatum had certainly earned Brix the opportunity to provide one. Titus templed his fingers before his lips, ignoring the pain lancing through his temples.

"And yet, the only way they live is at my sufferance. The Triam's air systems are scheduled to go offline in ten days. I suggest you deliver me Glynfyls, and the Scots, precipitously. Do so and I'll recall the order." He sipped his bourbon. "As far as bringing them out of it, I'll allow you to be the first to try."

Brix grunted, with zero surprise over the disclosure. "Agreed."

"Then enough delay, issue the order to deploy."

He pulled up a holo, the man leaving to see it done. Titus reviewed the last missives from his remaining agents in Glynfyls. Any further correspondence would have to be smuggled out, and tagged with a beacon transmitting to a predetermined frequency. He ran a finger across his lips, eyes lingering on the report.

That old Breaker, Rogan Firestorm, had taken control of the line, and the shield wall was functional. Impervious to talent or ballistics… but no mention of biologicals. A smile flickered over Titus's lips. Nothing like a good plague to get the ball rolling. He had several to choose from. One of the more virulent ones should suffice, perhaps targeting Finder DNA…

Pain shot through his head and he gasped, slumping over his desk. His hand shook, emptying the last of the pills from the bottle into his open maw. He panted, brow cradled in the nest of his arms and stomach roiling.

In thirty-six hours his army would be on the plateau. Another day to crack the city.

God help him if Otto wasn't inside.

THEY SHIFTED BACK to their rooms at the flat. Kara chewed her thumb, watching Flynn pace. He held his shirt against his ribs with a grimace, eyes at the ceiling.

"You want to talk? Let's talk," he growled.

"About what?" She threw up her hands at his glare. "Rogan? It happened once, a little over two months before I left the Source. Cal found out, they had a huge fight, and then they both abandoned me there. I didn't—I didn't think I was going to see either of them again."

Flynn stopped in the center of the room, looking at the ceiling again. "You love him?"

"Rogan? I—yes, but—it's not—it wasn't, *isn't* like that."

He pinched the bridge of his nose, eyes already starting to blacken, and his knuckles a bloody mess. "Then what's it like?"

"He's just always been there for me. It was stupid. I…I don't remember a lot of it, not clearly anyway. I'd just failed out of that coercion program. I must've gone down to the gym… It was like my happy place, okay? We got stinking drunk, and it just kind of happened."

Flynn closed his eyes, emotions rioting through their bond. "You gonna leave me?"

"What? No, I love him, but he's not—he's not you." She stepped close and ran her thumb over his battered cheek. His arms were around her, swollen lips pressed to the top of her head.

"You should. He'll keep you safe, the babies. The shit I've done… when this is over, they're gonna put me down. The way they all look at me…" He laughed. "And they're right. I'm a monster."

"No!" Kara blinked back tears. "Stop it. You're not, and I'm—" Telling him she wasn't going anywhere died on her tongue. She couldn't lie to him. He reached down to splay his hand over the small rise of her abdomen.

"You really believe it, don't you? That you're gonna die."

The look in his eyes…she couldn't hold his gaze.

"I…there's no balance to this, Flynn. It feels wrong. I swing from one extreme to the next, talent, no talent, exhaustion to being so pent up with so much energy I'm twitching, and my bloodlust…" She bit her thumb. They both knew what that was like. Even after Phyllis had shown her how to rise above it, she could still hear it whispering the black seduction of what it wanted. "I'm scared, and it's only going to get worse, I know it, and—"

"I'm scared, too." He sighed, pulling her close. "I feel more of it than you think, Kara. What this has been doing to you, I know it's wrong. Our bond—if you go, it's gonna take me with you, and I won't fight it. There's nothing for me without you."

"What if the babies make it?"

Flynn frowned. "I dunno." He raised a hand, talent scintillating around his fingers before he snuffed them in his fist. "If I lose it like I did when they took you...I dunno. Bad things are gonna happen."

"What about everyone else?"

He snorted. "The Assembly, shit, everyone on the hill wants to put me down. Sooner or later a bullet's gonna find me."

"What? No, they wouldn't—"

His face softened at her expression, and he let out a frustrated growl. "I'm not—look, Cal thinks Leo knows where the Triam is. Titus's females are there and all his breeding records. If we can get access to them, Jon, your mom, we'll figure it out, Kara."

An awful hope bloomed in her. "Do you really think so?"

"Yeah, and I swear to Christ, I'll move heaven and earth to get my hands on anything that's gonna make this right."

She smiled through her tears at his conviction. "Then if I'm not going anywhere, neither are you. You're not a monster, Flynn. I'll unmake every last one of them before they lift a finger against you, starting with that jerk, Morris."

"I'll let you do that even if they don't come after me." Flynn laughed, pulling her closer to him. "I'm sorry I lost my temper."

"What did Rogan say to you out there?"

He sniffed, wincing. "Heal this shit first."

Her lips quirked as she pulled talent, the damage fading. A neat white line bisected his right eyebrow, stark against his dark hair. He took a deep breath, stretching out his shoulders.

"Thanks. Asshole said he's my great-grandfather."

"What?"

He shrugged. "It's convoluted, and I don't care who he is, I still don't like him, but... Christ. Respect's the wrong word, it's—he irritates the fuck out of me, but it's different now. I can't explain it. Long story short, he's gonna teach me how to control this shit, my talent, 'lust... I dunno what the hell all that crap with the hierarchy or being his Beta means, but I suspect the prick's gonna fill me in." He gritted his teeth. "I fucking hate that he's had his hands on you."

"If I can deal with half the women in this stupid city having been in your bed, you can deal with Rogan."

"None of them are living under my roof," he muttered.

She laughed and kissed him, her arms twining around his neck. "This one is."

He gazed down at her, thumb skating over her cheek. "You're right, and I swear to Christ, Kara, nothing is gonna change that."

Something would, but as his lips claimed hers, she didn't argue. That awful hope had taken root, and in his arms it was impossible not to see the garden it could become.

***

CAL STOOD on the shielded roof of the flat, surrounded by bees. His talent the only thing standing between them and the Plaz contamination that'd sent every other creature in Glynfyls scurrying elsewhere before it couldn't scurry at all. Temperature was just warm enough for them to make cleansing flights. He closed his eyes, and for a moment, he was back in his family's apiary. Shit was simpler then, though he sure as hell hadn't known or appreciated it.

Hindsight was a bitch.

The access door opened, ending the illusion, and familiar footsteps crunched on the gravel.

"Let me guess, I'm an asshole."

Rogan flopped down on one of the benches with a bottle from the private stock. Man was beat to shit, and looked pleased as punch about it. "No more than usual."

"We celebrating?"

The Breaker sat beside him, leaning back against the wall. "Nope. Drowning our sorrows." He flipped open his knife to pull the cork, then tipped the bottle back. "Damn that's smooth. I told the kid."

Cal snagged the scotch. Should be considering how old it was. "All of it?" He snorted at the look the Breaker shot him.

"No, but he's officially a Firestorm. I made him my heir."

Cal choked on his mouthful. Well, that was gonna kick up a whirl of shit, but he supposed it couldn't be helped. Might actually help protect the boy when all was said and done. The legalese coming across his desk wasn't anything he could buy his way out of. Cal pulled out his pouch of tobacco. "You take the line?"

"Yeah, didn't have a choice. Roll me one of those." Rogan took another swig. "Titus crossed the border. We've got a day and change. Deep South still sitting tight?"

"For now, but I don't know how long we can count on the Corporation to keep them at bay. They're all a bunch of damned jackals, and Flynn's got them nervous. Soon as one of them gets ballsy enough to cross me, the rest'll pile on. We gonna be ready?" He handed him a smoke and started rolling another.

Rogan laughed, lighting up. "Nope." His lips popped smoke on the 'p.' "Never are."

"Ain't that the truth." Cal sat back, exhaling. "History repeats itself."

"Until it doesn't."

Cal took another pull off the bottle. And if Flynn didn't get his shit in gear, it wouldn't.

"…A man shouldering the crescent moon rises, red tide in his wake. Waters clash about his feet, becoming a single swell. He turns to the leviathan, exposed —

Darkness.

I despair as I record this, and pray I have only lost the vision, and that the last is not true-sight…"

— Excerpt from the dream journals of House Carmody

BRIX STORMED down to the makeshift barracks in the belly of Titus's transport. A sub cowered in a doorway as he passed, and Brix lunged, growling at the man. His high-pitched squeal didn't elevate the Breaker's piss-poor mood. Of course Titus rigged the Triam. They'd all expected it. Wasn't the fucking problem. He slammed his hand across the access panel for the hold, cracking the plaz. Should be that red-headed bastard's skull.

Men were gathered around that fucking holo of Scot's female. Brix crossed to his bunk, raking a hand across his oiled scalp, eyes glued to it despite himself. That she'd succumbed there was no doubt. The 'lust-glazed animal staring into Br221p's eyes as she ended him was proof positive. The holo paused on her face, then another was brought up from an hour ago, the chaos behind her eyes gone.

Brix dropped to sit on the hard mattress, rubbing the back of his neck. How the fuck was that possible? Once the 'lust had you, you didn't come back. Shit, how many times in the field, they'd tried—he'd tried—

"What'd he say?"

Eshmiel. He would ask in front of everybody. Brix grimaced. Screw it. They might as well know. He looked up and the squad stared back, less Uriah, rocking in the corner. Man was gonna be a problem. "As long as we get this shit done, he's fine with it, but I was right. We got ten days before the Triam's power gets pulled."

"See right there?" One of the men pointed to the holo. "She spoke. That other one answers her." They all turned back to the holo, mesmerized.

"Not possible…"

"Wait, back it up—"

A low keening came from Uriah, and the men's attention snapped to him as one, edging away from the acrid metallic funk he was putting off.

"She could've come back!" He stood, the tendons in his neck bulging, spittle roping from his lips. "Lin could've—"

His head cracked to the side, crimson-gray spatter fanning across the wall, body thumping to the floor. Brix trained his gun across the rest of them.

"Anyone else?"

He waited for the bloodlust to dissipate, silence stretching before he lowered his piece.

"Fuck, Brix, if they can come back…"

"Wise it." He glared at Eshmiel. "Don't even fucking think about it. We go up there and do what we gotta do for the rest of them." They'd failed the others, let them be murdered—fuck, he needed to take his own goddamned advice.

"And Beritram?" The man motioned to the nullified cell at the end of the hold, door bowed out between the titanium bars latticing it, barely containing the monster behind them. "Titus cut his meds."

Brix ignored dread prickling his nape and holstered his sidearm. "Don't think about that either."

OVERLORD

THE PRICE OF TALENT: BOOK FOUR

FLYNN'S BEDROOM door slammed open and the lights flicked on.

"Get up."

The hell? He blinked, lifting his aching head to glare at Rogan. Man looked even more beat to shit now that the bruising from their fight had set in. One side of his jaw was twice the size it should be, and he didn't look any happier to be standing there than Flynn was to see him.

"Fuck off," he growled, his arms tightening around Kara. She murmured in her sleep, a "V" between her brows as she snuggled against his chest.

Rogan laughed. "Wish I could, kid, but Titus's troops are crossing the border, the city's burning down again, cattle are running riot through the streets—" He swiped up a pair of pants from the floor and chucked them at Flynn. "—and we're on fire brigade."

Goddamn it.

"Are you serious?" he hissed, catching them as he pushed up to sit.

Kara huffed and curled into a little ball, out cold despite the asshole's bullshit. Flynn frowned, but wasn't surprised. She hadn't slept at all the night after succumbing, and he damned well knew the toll of unmaking the damage Otto had done to her bitch mother was more than Kara was letting on.

Rogan's gaze dropped to her bared shoulder and slid down her back to the blankets pooling around her hips. His tongue flicked over his lip. "Think I'd be in here otherwise?"

Flynn growled, pulling the covers over her. If that motherfucker even thought about—goddamn it. Man had just handed Flynn his own ass in front of the entire Breaker line. If Rogan, the Alpha fucking Prime, wanted to challenge for her, he'd win, and they both knew it.

Didn't put Flynn in a particularly cooperative mood.

He slung his legs over the side of the mattress, talent crackling around his fingers. He snuffed them in his fists and pulled on his pants. Fabric was still sticky with gore. What time was it? His eyes found the clock as he zipped up. A little after two in the morning. Didn't this fucking city sleep? "When did Titus cross the border?"

"Vanguard is about three hours in, and it looks like they plan on pushing straight through," Rogan said as he reached down to scritch behind Hiss's ears. Stupid cat let him. "They called quorum. I was on my way to wake your ass up for that when the fire broke out. Shit's officially hit the fan."

"Fine. Let's go." Flynn grabbed a shirt and kicked into his boots, still glowering at Rogan. Asshole shot another look at Kara before he flashed that goddamned grin and backed from the room. Flynn killed the lights and just stopped himself from slamming the door. God, he hated that prick.

"What the hell are they rioting about now?" he asked, smacking the button for the lift.

Rogan shrugged and stepped in. Flynn followed. "They're throwing one hell of a party on the lower rungs, but this ain't that, far as I can tell. Heard somebody say a cow kicked over a lantern, and it's Chicago all over again."

"Chicago?"

The Breaker rolled his eyes at Flynn's blank look. "You know, big fire, O'Leary's—never mind. All you need to worry about is it putting it out." He pushed past him as the lift door opened and stalked toward the gate.

Flynn's temper spiked and his talent sparked with it. "Me? How am I supposed to—" He stopped to scuff out a patch of smoldering carpet. Christ, that was getting old.

"Right there all the time, isn't it?"

Flynn scowled. "Yeah. Weren't you gonna do something about that?" Talent flared around his fingers again, and he swore.

Rogan sighed, glancing at the gate. "Right. How do you control your Shade ability?"

Was he an idiot? "Control my—I don't. It's not like—I gotta pull it to use it. They call it cloaking for a reason. It's like gathering— whatever, it doesn't matter. I asked about this Breaker shit."

"Everything matters. Nothing's important."

"Did you just quote Nietzsche?"

Breaker cocked an eyebrow. "Did you just call me out for quoting Nietzsche?"

"Christ, you're a dick."

"You should talk. Look, in case you haven't figured it out, Breaker talent isn't static. It's tied to your emotions, just like bloodlust. The fact that you're as moody as a teenaged girl doesn't help."

Flynn glared at the man, his teeth gritting together at another flare of talent. "So, what do you suggest?"

"You know anything about physics?" Flynn's eyes narrowed, and Rogan sighed. "Look, I'm not any more thrilled about this arrangement than you are, so let's do it and have done. Easiest way for me to explain it is to equate Breaker talent to Ohm's law—"

"Ionic flow. Got it. Energy is dissipated as heat. Then what?"

Rogan's brow raised. "Then you reach equilibrium by dissipating it, maintaining the state by breathing the potential out, and letting talent cycle through you," the Breaker said. "You don't let it build until you need it."

"How the hell do I do that?"

Rogan made a come hither motion. "Watch and learn."

They stepped through the gate and into hell. Flynn wiped his brow, his skin abruptly too tight. Smoke seared down his throat and hung thick in the air, stinging his eyes and occluding the morass of standing water and hard baked sludge coating the street. The haze softened the edges of the blaze as a line of Fixers fought to keep it in stasis, while every Fetch able to shift an oxygen molecule battled to snuff the flames. Their crimson blue flicker and the silver and bronze glow of talent warred, filling the streets with an unearthly glow. Within the thin shell of talent, booms shook the ground. A rain of smoldering debris peppered the street, and a fucking cow ran by.

Rogan held out a hand to him, and Flynn scowled. "Thanks, Gramps, but I promise I'm big enough not to get lost."

"Asshole. I want you to feel how I channel the fire's potential."

"I gotta hold your hand to do it?"

"I can put my foot up your ass if you'd prefer."

Flynn eyed the man's outstretched hand. Something big exploded, accompanied by a whomp of flame

"Take your time. Not like there's any reason to hurry."

Flynn glared at him and slapped his palm across Rogan's. The Breaker's halos flared and talent welled, crackling between them. Instead of something blowing up, it was a steady draw. The raging flames shuddered in response, dying back, and the ground beneath them hummed with a weird vibration. What the hell?

"Feel that?"

"Yeah, what're you doing?"

Whatever it was, wasn't easy. Sweat poured from the Breaker, and it wasn't from the ungodly temperature. His halos bathed everything within a fifty-foot radius a gruesome scarlet. "Acting as a ground," he said through gritted teeth.

"Like it's electricity?"

"Yeah. Same principle, and you keep shorting." He snorted at Flynn's scowl. "Instead of letting the energy flow to heat, I'm converting the fire's potential and acting as a conduit, redirecting it out and away. Try reaching for it. If you can call it, you can snuff it, and I could use the help. There's some kind of accelerant in there—" The ground shook violently with another series of explosions and hot concrete rained down around them.

Fuck that. Flynn threw up a shield. He pushed it out and away, reinforcing the Fixer's line. They slumped against one another as he took up the burden, the power of the battering flames sending him back a step. Christ. Yeah, there sure as hell was some kind of accelerant in there. Shit was burning like it was jet fuel. He wiped a hand across his brow, dizzy with the heat.

"Wrong talent, asshole," Rogan gritted out.

Flynn scowled at him, trying to focus. Reach for the fire…how the fuck was he supposed to…he eased his shield and the sense of it hit him square in the chest. Flynn grunted, stumbling back again.

"Yeah, no shit. Now let it flow through you and ground it out."

Flynn took a shaky breath; the intensity of that potential Rogan had been talking about was crushing. How the fuck was he handling all that? Man should be a blackened smear—

"Anytime now, kid," Rogan grimaced.

Shit. Flynn's jaw tensed, trying to take a hold—he eased his shield again and the flames surged forward. He slammed it back up and the fire's potential bypassed him, arcing from his grip. Christ, he couldn't—

"Kara still make that little noise when she comes?"

Flynn's shield disintegrated as the blaze's potential flooded into him with his rage. It built, his hair standing on end. He was gonna kill—

"Ground it!"

That motherfucker. Flynn bellowed, channeling it into the ground along with what Rogan was converting. The street buckled and the surrounding buildings listed. The two men fell to their knees, the inferno sucking down like someone had pulled its string, guttering.

Rogan collapsed to sit, swiping a hand over his brow. "Not bad—"

Flynn's fist took him in the jaw, knocking him back. "Anything about that ever comes out of your mouth again, I'll fucking kill you."

"No promises." Asshole chuckled, wiping the corner of his mouth as he sat up. "And don't expect it to go any better than your last attempt…but you're welcome to keep trying."

God, he hated him. Flynn's brows furrowed, taking in the smoking ruins. At the far end of the block, Markham spoke to a group of Fetches. He patted one of them on the shoulder, and they staggered off, too exhausted to shift away.

Christ, Flynn knew how they felt. His insides were hollow with what'd just gone through him. His glower deepened as his eyes flicked to Rogan. Shithead had baited him, again, and he'd played right into his hands, again. Flynn stared at his palms, curiosity getting the better of him.

"When you call it, where does the fire come from? Doesn't the potential need a catalyst?"

"Look at you all brainy when you're not taking potshots," Rogan muttered, rocking his mangled jaw. "That's a little more complicated, and I'm spent. It'll wait."

Flynn's brows bunched, glaring at the man who'd claimed to be his great-grandfather. Attitude was on point, but any physical resemblance…to him, to Lot. Complexion was all wrong, but maybe something around the eyes…

The man flashed his teeth. "Yes?"

Christ, that was it. That goddamned grin. Flynn looked away. Markham was headed in their direction, albeit at a snail's pace. "You the one that figured out how it works? The whole electricity thing?"

"A Breaker's talent? No. Not controlling it, at least. I was pretty hell-bent on everything but. When I was ready to listen, most of the hard work had been done."

Flynn flicked a bit of rubble away. Asphalt had caved in around them like a giant fist'd smashed into the street. "Did you want it?"

Rogan's face went stoney. "When the Surge blasted us back to the Dark Ages, people lost their shit, turned on each other. Nobody understood it. Thought the world was coming to an end, God was punishing us…first to espouse the Sons' ideology were Talents. Turned into a goddamned cult of suicide bombers. You could hear them imploding. See them flare up at night, taking out everything around them until the Corporation showed up with their promise of a cure. So, no. None of us wanted it, but it's what we got. Didn't that asshole teach you anything?"

Flynn chewed his lip. "Cal wasn't around all that much." Not even when he was.

"What about Lot?"

A surge of temper sent talent flickering around Flynn's fingers. "What about him?"

"Never mind." Rogan swore under his breath. "You're clamping down and getting all pent up again. Breathe it through you."

Flynn let out a slow exhale. Damn, he wanted a cigar. Thinking about his father…his Shade talent coming in… Christ, that'd been a miserable fucking experience, but at least the only person that'd gotten hurt had been him. Accident or not, he'd killed people when Kara had been abducted. Guilt tamped down his anger, self-loathing rising up to snuff what was left of it. He needed to get a handle on this before he lost his shit again and took out any more of the city. Another incident like that, and the Pinch would be prime real estate.

Rogan's mouth screwed up like he wanted to ask something and knew he wasn't gonna like the answer. Goddamn it.

"Look, the less Lot and I see of each other, the better," Flynn said, beating him to it. "Ascending to Head was supposed to be the end of it. Come up here, assume the fucking position, and spend the rest of my life voting on granite curbing." Shit, that almost sounded good. He kicked away some debris, the warmth of the ruined pavement cozy in comparison to the arctic air battering down the radiant heat.

"Funny. You don't strike me as a white picket fence, two kids and a dog kind of guy."

A gust of wind sent a squall thick with ash at them. Flynn put a hand up, keeping it from his eyes and spat the grit from his mouth. He'd take the fence and kids in a heartbeat right about now. The dog could go fuck itself, but the rest of it sounded like a dream come true. "Kara would've been happy. Safe."

Rogan cocked an eyebrow. "Would she?"

A defeated numbness stole over Flynn. Probably not on either count. She wasn't like anyone he'd ever met. Didn't want the same things. Christ, what did she want? It pissed him off that figuring it out was taking a backseat to everything else, and there wasn't a fucking thing he could do to change that.

He grimaced as he met Rogan's eye. "Probably not. I just— It feels like I'm being steamrolled towards something, and no matter what I —" Flynn flushed. What the hell had possessed him to drop that nugget? He mussed ash from his hair, a sense of defeat weighing him down. The remaining flickers of talent around his fingers drained away. Damn. This shit really was tied to his emotions.

"That's it. Low and slow. Breathe it out. You get worked up, ground what pulses through you." Rogan leaned back on his elbows. "The universe usually pushes you for a reason. Why fight it?"

"Because I don't trust it."

"No, you don't trust yourself." Flynn scowled, and the asshole's grin was back. "You should. That was good work just now, but it would've been better if you'd get over that goddamned reluctance and stop second-guessing yourself. You're Breaker, kid. Acting on instinct is what we do. Leave the overthinking to the Binders."

Markham huffed over, and Rogan stood. Flynn rose with him. The only thing his instincts were screaming at him to do was to bury the prick.

Except he'd tried that and failed miserably. Motherfucker. "What's next?"

"Combat nap. Phyllis has already filed the paperwork to officially step down. Between assuming First and everything else making up this shit show, I'm pretty sure I'm gonna have to drink breakfast if I want to get through the rest of the day." Rogan frowned, scratching his stubble. "Should probably shave."

Flynn rolled his eyes and he got to his feet. "No, I meant talent-wise."

"Try to not blow anything up until the Source gets here. If there's an after..." Rogan shrugged. "We'll work on your control. Start with little shit. Light some candles, break frozen peas." A smile ghosted over his lips, then he pushed past Flynn with a growl. "Get a handle on your equilibrium first."

Man stalked to the gate and was gone. What the hell had that been about?

Want More?

GET YOUR COPY AT: books2read.com/Overlord-Vol4

ACKNOWLEDGMENTS

I'll start out by thanking all of the usual suspects. You guys are amazing, and by now you know who you are. That said, I'll move on to the people who have most recently bailed my ass out of one fire or another.

Jena, I could not have logistically managed any of this without you making sure everything in the background runs smoothly. You're more incredible than a dress with pockets, and I appreciate you so frickin' much.

Lori, thank you for balancing my bullshit with yours and trading rants over text.

Julie & JD, you two ground me.

And Grace…where the hell did you even come from?

All of you ladies help keep me sane and I am so lucky to have you in my life. My writing is definitely better for it.

Which I should probably get back to. See y'all in the next installment…

BOOKS BY AK NEVERMORE

THE DAE DIARIES - URBAN FANTASY WITH SPICE

- *One Night in Bliss* — FREE TO READ
- *Flame & Shadow*
- *Air & Darkness*
- *Playing with Fire* — FREE TO READ (October 2024)

THE PRICE OF TALENT - SPICY DYSTOPIAN SCI FI ROMANCE

- *Breeder* — FREE TO READ
- *Breaker*
- *Destroyer* — FREE TO READ
- *Binder*
- *Conspirator* — FREE TO READ (October 2024)
- *Split*
- *Overlord* — (January 2024)
- Exile — (March 2025)

THE MAW OF MAYHEM - PARANORMAL MC EROTICA

- *Bites of Mayhem* — FREE TO READ
- *The Maw of Mayhem* — FREE TO READ
- *Grimdarke*
- *Darker*
- *Kit-Kat*
- *Katherine*
- *Deuce* — (Forthcoming)

ABOUT THE AUTHOR

AK Nevermore writes science fiction and urban fantasy. She enjoys operating heavy machinery, freebases coffee, and gives up sarcasm for Lent every year.

A Jane-of-all-trades, she's a certified chef, restores antiques, and dabbles in beekeeping when she's not reading voraciously or running down the dream in her beat-up camo Chucks.

Unable to ignore the voices in her head, and unwilling to become medicated, she writes full time. Her books explore dark worlds, perversely irreverent and profound, and always entertaining.

Want more Nevermore?
Sign up for her newsletter and never miss a release!

aknevermore.com

Cover design by Beholden Books

Hardcover ISBN: 978-1-964466-06-4

Paperback ISBN: 978-1-964466-05-7

Digital ISBN: 978-1-964466-04-0